A MORE PERFECT UNION

A MORE PERFECT UNION

by

Steven Burgauer

iUniverse, Inc.
New York   Bloomington

A MORE PERFECT UNION

iUniverse books may be ordered through booksellers or by contacting:

iUniverse
1663 Liberty Drive
Bloomington, IN 47403
www.iuniverse.com
1-800-Authors (1-800-288-4677)

Because of the dynamic nature of the Internet, any Web addresses or links contained in this book may have changed since publication and may no longer be valid. The views expressed in this work are solely those of the author and do not necessarily reflect the views of the publisher, and the publisher hereby disclaims any responsibility for them.

ISBN: 978-1-4401-3018-2 (pbk)
ISBN: 978-1-4401-3019-9 (ebk)

Printed in the United States of America

iUniverse rev. date: 3/13/2009

To those who understand that freedom had to be won at the tip of a bayonet.

ACKNOWLEDGEMENTS

▼

Writing a book is never easy, and I struggle with every word. But some of the hardest tasks fall to those who agree to read my manuscript in its various versions. These talented individuals have to run a hospice, manage an emergency room, and staff a funeral home all at the same time.

For this book, emergency care initially came from my first-responders, readers who had to deal with the patient in its roughest form: my daughter Kate Rose Burgauer, my mother Margaret, and the most important triage nurse of all, my wife Debra, who had to listen to the patient howl and whine like a stuck pig.

But once the patient managed to survive triage, it then had to graduate, first, to the operating table, then, to managed care. In all, seven specialists had a greater or lesser hand in bringing the patient safely through, and I want to thank them all for their intense labors: Loren Logsdon, Sarah Miller, Brian Tonti, Steve Howery, Jim Duffy, Bill Knight, and John Huff.

Thank you. This would not have been possible without your help.

CHAPTER ONE

▼

The sniper was in position, in his nest, well before the big game got underway. He was camouflaged from view by a chameleon ghillie suit. The barrel of his rifle was sheathed in an identical chameleon barrel wrap. The material on both the ghillie and the wrap was adaptive and light-sensitive. It adjusted to the tapestry of its surroundings, became neutral to thermal. It made the nest virtually indistinguishable from the background. No one would see him lying there on the rooftop taking aim, not even the surveillance drones that regularly circled overhead.

This man was a cold-hearted killer, a washout from the U.S. military, Omega Special Forces to be exact. He had no confusion about bonding with his targets or holding back on his adrenaline. Once everyone in the stadium was on their feet standing — and while the National Anthem was still being played — he was going to murder as many spectators as he could before he ran out of ammunition. *This time, there would be no holding back.*

The sniper's name was Branislav Karpinski. Friends called him the "Carp." But then again, enemies were few. — And not because the man was so well liked; because they didn't last long. The story was still told of an occasion when a chap he knew called him Bran Flake, trying to make light of his first name. That man had suffered a brutal end. When his body was found a week later, he was so badly beaten around the face, not even his wife was able to make a positive I.D.

Branislav Karpinski was an immigrant from Central Europe. He had a head of dark wiry hair, plus a mouthful of straight white teeth. Sadly, those teeth rarely smiled; for Branislav Karpinski was not a happy fellow. And yet, on those rare occasions, when he saw a funny cartoon, he would laugh so hard, tears would roll down his cheeks.

The man was only vaguely interested in people, though he was always amused by life's little surprises. Branislav was religious to a degree, liked what he'd heard in Puritan City from the Reverend Roland Whitmore. He was also the most unforgiving and ruthless killer to ever walk God's green Earth.

Branislav reached into his bag, now. This wasn't the first time. He had done it every hour like clockwork since first settling into position in his nest.

The bag was filled with fine sand, very lightweight. Branislav extended his arm, let a handful slip through his fingers, watched it settle to the ground. The particles drifted slightly to the left with the breeze. He looked at a distant flag hanging nearly motionless, ran the numbers through his head, compared the results to the dial on his shooter's watch. The rule-of-thumb formula for wind velocity was straightforward enough:

Hold paper, dust, or grass at arm's length and allow it to drop. Point to where it lands. Divide the angle between the extended arm and the body by four to get wind velocity in miles per hour. To get the answer in kloms, divide the angle by two point five.

Then, to manually adjust the rifle's sight for wind shear, take the range to target in hundreds of yards, multiply it by the wind velocity in miles per hour, and divide the product by fifteen. This is the number of clicks left or right needed to adjust the setting on the sights. An equivalent formula existed for metric ranges and velocities.

For those weak in mathematics, a shooter's watch could take out some of the guesswork. But, on this particular occasion, precision shooting wasn't the objective. Today, Branislav didn't care who he hit. Unlike a traditional hostage situation, where there were hostages whose lives had to be spared, collateral damage was not an issue here. In those other situations, a sniper didn't want to accidentally hit one of the hostages. What he wanted to do was kill only one person in the group — the terrorist — and do it at long range, without harming anyone else. That made his job extremely difficult.

But on this particular day the sniper didn't care who he hit. It just didn't matter. All he wanted to do was kill as many spectators as he could, and do it in as short a time as possible.

To do the job, Branislav used a solid, hard-jacketed, military-issue round. The "Unlucky Thirteen," as it was called in the trade, was known for its accuracy, stability, and penetration. Legend had it the big shell got its name on account of its approximate weight in grams. It was a big mother of a bullet, and only an M35 sniper rifle could deliver it reliably on target.

Branislav's nest was an air-conditioning unit atop a multi-storied building four blocks from the stadium. He had scouted it on multiple occasions. The vantage was good, escape easy and quick. Not that it mattered. Even if Colonel Barnes wanted him to return to base camp unscathed, Branislav Karpinski didn't particularly care if he got away clean.

The sniper had made his way to his rooftop nest in the wee hours of this morning, while darkness still hung over the land. After settling in, he made some initial measurements with his laser rangefinder. Hardcore old-timers might take sightings and calculate angles on nearby objects, then use the trig tables in their sniper data book. But this sniper liked his high-tech toys, especially his shooter's watch.

He looked down at it now on his wrist and gently peeled back the dark, vinyl cover to reveal its illuminated face. A shooter's watch was more like a wrist-capable minicomputer than an actual timepiece. It was a tactical watch engineered to perform a specific set of aiming calculations for the long-range shooter. It accepted a series of critical inputs, then displayed on the watch face the appropriate number of clicks to make on any model riflescope to properly adjust for wind and elevation. The input variables were many. Bullet weight. Muzzle velocity. Height above bore. Calibre. Barometric pressure. Air temperature. Wind speed and direction. Angle of inclination. Distance to target.

Branislav found comfort, in the dark, in his adaptive ghillie suit. Though only millimeters thick, the suit made him feel warm, as if he were home, in the loving arms of a woman.

The darkness closed in around him, now. He drifted off to sleep. But it was "field sleep," not natural sleep, an inbetween state familiar to any combat soldier.

When a man is in field on a mission, perhaps days on end, he cannot stay awake around the clock. But a trained man can trust in his concealment to "field sleep" at night. He can sleep, yet still keep part of his mind on alert. He is asleep but also awake. His mind is resting and his eyes are closed. Yet, if anything moves nearby or if something makes a sound that registers as being dangerous, he is instantly and completely awake.

Field sleep is not the only behavioral skill an accomplished sniper must master. He must also learn how to consciously slow his heart rate. This enables him to literally shoot between heartbeats, a critical skill once you realize that the thump of a single heartbeat can throw a shot off by as much as a meter at long-range. It is all part of his biofeedback training — being able to selectively warm a trigger finger or foot that has gotten cold, being able to lie perfectly still for hours, being able to let the body rest while keeping the mind active. *Fatigue kills snipers, not other snipers.*

As for other bodily functions, a man does what he has to do. Liquids go in a bottle, solids in a plastic bag. Both go with the sniper when he leaves his nest.

As for nourishment, a man eats when he's hungry — usually trail mix — and drinks constantly. Dehydration leads to fatigue, and fatigue kills snipers.

.

.

Branislav jerked suddenly awake. A robin was tending to her young nearby. They were chirping loudly. The sun was coming up.

Kick-off was scheduled for 11 a.m. That meant the stadium would be abuzz with activity by 8 a.m. First the robo-vendors, then the janitorial people, the press, then the fans. Concession stands usually opened by 9:30 a.m., the first drunks getting rowdy by 10 a.m.

Branislav had breakfast, a chocolate bar, a handful of walnut bits, two pieces of dried fruit. He took a swig of water to wash it all down.

He brought out his scope and laser rangefinder, readjusted his sights for a range of eight hundred and twenty meters, the distance to Section BB in the upper stands.

A shadow passed overhead, a surveillance drone. In these United States, there were precious few open-air stadiums. The few that did still exist were patrolled by drones, both overhead and in the stands.

But Branislav wasn't worried. His camouflaged suit would keep him hidden from prying robotic eyes.

Karpinski waited for the drone to pass, then once again slid his hand into the bag. Once again out came a handful of fine sand. He extended his arm, let the sand slip through his fingers. This would be the last time. Then a final, tiny adjustment to his sights.

Branislav lowered the handle of the bolt fully. This action locked a round securely in the chamber. The heavy, tripod-mounted gun could be single-loaded or clip-loaded, nineteen rounds to a clip. He had eight clips within easy reach of his gun. Each was filled with a full complement of Unlucky Thirteens, all machined to be lethal, all machined to be virtually identical.

Branislav took a sip of water, let his finger find its place on the trigger. He adopted a breathing rhythm that would cause the least amount of movement to his sights. He adjusted for the first shot by sliding his right knee back and away from his heart.

In contrast to the last seven hours of inactivity, things now moved with uncanny speed. People were wound up, excited for the big game, waving, jostling for seats, balancing food in their arms, chili dogs, popcorn, beer.

The announcer quieted the crowd. People came to attention, hands over their hearts. The singer began to belt out the National Anthem. The sniper held his sights on the upper lip of a big, pot-bellied fan with an orange and black tee shirt.

Thwoomp!

The rifle spat out its venom with barely a cough. Branislav rocked back with the gentle recoil.

A killing shot drops a man so fast, it seems the earth just swallows him up.

The only hint that a large man had been standing there an instant before was a faint pink halo of bloody tissue and bone suspended briefly in the morning air. The pink mist dissolved almost as fast as it formed.

Thwoomp! Thwoomp! Thwoomp!

Three more bloody mists. Three more dead bodies. The dead fans collapsed in the stands even before the sounds of the shots reached the rest of the crowd.

Thwoomp! Thwoomp! Thwoomp! Thwoomp! Thwoomp!

Now some people in the crowd began to scream. A few tried to run, elbows flaring. Most didn't know what to do. One or two stooped over the crumpled bodies, horror on their faces. A few of the more sensible ones hurled themselves to the ground, frantically urging the rest to dive for cover.

Thwoomp! Thwoomp! Thwoomp!

The music stopped. Airborne drones began to take notice, started to triangulate his position. Panic began to grip the stands. A crushing stampede got underway. No one had yet figured out from which direction the shots were coming.

But the Unlucky Thirteens kept on coming. The sniper wasn't done yet. Not by a long measure.

Three more minutes and nearly eighty more rounds were still to be fired before the murderous rampage was over.

CHAPTER TWO

▼

In Orbit, High Above Mars

"I tell you, Red — I wouldn't want to be one of those boys working a tug out on the edge. What a lonely job, pushing comets around all day long."

The speaker was a powerful man, built like the Marine he once had been. His name was Butch Hogan. Like Red Parsons, the man working beside him, Butch wore a rugged, brown spacesuit bearing the insignia of EMD Enterprises. The suit was made of tough, rigid material and was fully pressurized inside. The sound of rushing air always filled their ears when they were floating free, working in space. Because the suit was stiff, it took effort to move, even to open or close their hands.

"You and me brother: we're no comet-pushers."

The two were EVA, repairing the servo on a damaged electromagnetic mass driver. Under their spacesuits, each man wore a tech-shirt with built-in comm and personal locator.

"I mean, there's no women out in the Oort Belt." Butch leaned in as he spoke. Red Parsons, his co-worker, opened his kit, lined up the tools Butch would need, in the order he would need them.

Butch Hogan moved slowly and with deliberation. Even an experienced spacejockey could make a wrong move in zero-g. He could set a huge calamity in motion and not even realize it until it was too late to correct his mistake. Then the whole thing becomes a theatre of the absurd, as the spacejockey watches himself fail miserably in slow motion.

"Not like that slice of heaven you had the other night, Butch. Anyway, I think they call it a cloud, the Oort Cloud."

The inside of a spacesuit isn't smooth. In fact, it's quite rough. Lots of internal stiffness. Bearings, joints, seams. After a couple hours battling inside a suit like that, a man is nothing but a mountain range of bumps and bruises.

"No, I mean no women at all."

Butch Hogan stared through the visor of his spacesuit at his co-worker. The first thing a man learns about working in space is to conserve his hand strength.

"Not even bio-bims like they got in Hedon City?"

"Nothing. Nada. Nilch."

In a weightless environment a man doesn't use his legs much. He moves himself around with his arms. A newbie constantly grabs onto things. It's instinctive. But it's also wrong. Working a thousand kloms up, on the really high steel, requires a man to break down and re-learn just about every physical act he once did back on Earth without a second thought. At first, his tendency is to grab tightly onto things to support his body weight, like he would back home. But, in space, he learns to grasp things more lightly, maybe with only one or two fingers.

"No women? Now that would be hard. I don't get myself off a couple times a week, I start climbing the walls."

Red had a way of putting things that sometimes made Butch feel uncomfortable.

"So what do the guys do for relief out there?" Red asked.

"Mech-love, I guess."

"Ugh. Machines. Frigging hell! What man wants to make love to a frigging machine?" Red shook his head.

"I think it makes love to you, not the other way around."

"Either way. I'll stick to natch snatch, if it's all the same to you."

"Here, hand me that adjustable wrench, or we'll both be reassigned to a tug in the Oort Belt. Excuse me — Cloud."

"Get it straight, stud. It's the Kuiper Belt, part of the Oort Cloud."

"Are you going to hand me that bloody wrench or not?"

"Just take it slower this time. Don't juice the torque. That wrench locked up on you last time, nearly sent your ass looping off into outer space."

Butch nodded, rested his hand. Space gloves were inherently stiff. Even fifteen minutes of work could be painful and wearying. While he rested, he spoke:

"It's like so many things we do up here, Red. But try convincing the boys back home. Everything's counterintuitive. Try brushing your teeth in zero-g,

I tell them. Or taking a shower. Or turning a door latch. No sooner does a man grab hold of the latch than he finds himself spinning in the opposite direction."

"Quit belly-aching, it's not your first day on the job. You know the drill. When you use a wrench, you have to grip it tightly the first turn, then loosen your grip for the remaining turns." Red glared at Butch through his visor, twisted his wrist as if he were tightening a bolt.

"Yeah, okay, a wrench is not like a power tool."

Red laughed. "If the business end of a power drill is spinning clockwise, the tool wants to spin you the other way, counterclockwise. A man learns to adapt. Just make damn sure the tool isn't pushing against the weak side of your hand. Otherwise, you'll exhaust yourself in no time at all. It takes a while for the newbies to learn, but you of all people . . . "

Butch kept working at the bolts, six in all. They were stuck fast. "No way are these puppies coming loose without some encouragement. Hand me that Pigtail."

"Ah, the Pigtail. My favorite. An overgrown cordless drill on steroids. The Pistol Grip Tool."

"Just hand it to me, will you? A Pigtail saves the arms."

"And the brain. The bloody thing counts the number of turns needed to secure or loosen a bolt. Keeps those of us who are light in the head from over-tightening the heads."

Butch took the tool, slowly fitted the grip to the bolt. Since ordinary steel turned brittle in the intense cold of space, all their tools were made of a beryllium copper alloy. Between the two of them, they carried a veritable tool chest, either on their belts or in a front or backpack — a manual ratchet capable of a hundred foot-pounds of torque, a half-dozen adjustable wrenches, the Pigtail, a crowbar, two vise grips, a pair of cutters, plus a deadblow hammer with a pocket of shot in the head to absorb the recoil.

As the bolts came loose, Red caught them and dropped them one by one into a catch bag. Up here in space, at orbital speeds, anything not strapped down, anything floating around loose, could become an unguided missile that might strike with devastating results.

Experienced spacejockeys, like these two, knew their jobs were dangerous. It came with the territory. It could also be unnerving. That monkey we evolved from doesn't want to fall out of his tree.

The funny thing is, whether we like it or not, our brain quickly decides which way is up and which way is down. It is an amazing feat, especially when you consider how it makes absolutely no difference whatsoever when a man is weightless. Still, half the spacejockeys that work for EMD Enterprises vomit their first time out. And they hurt, too. Severe back pain is not uncommon.

The spine stretches in the absence of gravity. Plus, bathrooms are like being stuck in a really bad hotel with facilities you don't want to use or even go near.

Butch loosened the last bolt, popped the protection plate off the panel. He craned his neck, took a gander inside. "Can't see a damn thing."

Red positioned a light so they could both see better. He gasped. The motherboard and microworks were blackened and melted. Something had caused a serious short.

"Frigging hell, Butch. Ever seen innards messed up like that before? I guess those factory boys are slacking off. They sure don't make these EMDs like they used to."

"The servos on the new generation electromagnetic mass drivers have always been a little hinky. And a man doesn't want to go perfing the skin. He'll go up like a Roman candle and his carcass'll go shooting 'cross the Kirkwood gap like a torpedo."

"That's why they're paying us the big bucks, isn't it? 'Cause there's risk at every turn. I love the rush, I really do."

"No, Red, you love the money. Feeds all your bad habits."

"I do like pussy, brother. Never seen any as fine as what you had the other night, though."

"The woman was a looker, wasn't she? And she smelled awfully nice. Can't quite get her out of my head. Thing is, she's something of an Enviro. You know — hug the trees, save the dolphins, outlaw terraforming, that kinda thing."

"Well that'll never work. You're a throwback, Butch. A complete Neanderthal. You like guns. You like uprooting trees on your papa's ranch and bulldozing new logging roads for the Wyoming lumberjacks. Hell, you only work for the biggest goddamn terraforming company this side of the Belt."

"EMD is a helluva good company to work for, I'll grant you that much. But I do like the woman, tree-hugger or not."

"Aw, Butch, don't go getting soft on me. My daddy always said: It's okay to bed 'em; just don't try to wed 'em."

"And you're calling me the throwback? Hand me that wire cutter, will you? We have to pull out this old unit and pop in that new one."

"You gonna see her again?" Red pulled the wire cutters off the Velcro pouch on his belt and handed them across to his partner.

"She's headed back home on the next ship, same as us." Butch began to snip wires.

Red held the light. "I thought it was just gonna be the two of us — you and me bobbing for babes."

"I do like bobbing. But let's face it — Some apples are juicier than others."

"Frigging hell, you are soft on that bird, aren't you? What a complete zibb you have become."

"Can you blame me?"

"What's the skirt's name anyway?"

"Kaleena Flanagan." Butch handed the wire cutters back to Red and yanked out the damaged unit.

"Flanagan? Like the Senator?"

"Spelled the same. Though I don't think she's any relation."

"You know one Irish, you know 'em all. They're all tree-huggers, if you ask me." Red took the damaged unit from Butch and tossed it in his catch bag.

"Yeah, maybe. I don't know that much about her yet. I do know she works for the Commission."

"Like that's gonna work. A spacejockey and a sappy Enviro. Oil and water, if you ask me."

"No one asked you."

"You *are* soft on the woman. Dear God, save us all. Girls everywhere will rue the day Butch Hogan took himself off the market." Red unpacked the replacement unit and handed it to his partner.

"Heh, at least I'm sincere when I shop. All you do is play the field and return the merchandise damaged and soiled."

"Soiled? If God above didn't want us men to play the field, he never would have planted it with such fine looking stems and bulbs. Anyway, women love me."

"More of your daddy's philosophy?"

Red shot his buddy a mischievous grin. But Butch wasn't done with him yet.

"Aw, yes. Red Parsons of No-Wheres-Ville, Colorado — a legend in his own mind."

"I was born in No-Wheres-Ville. But I grew up in Pueblo."

"Yeah, like that makes a difference."

Butch took the new unit and started sparking wires. It was the spacejockey's version of soldering back home, only without the solder. The hardest part of the job was nearly complete.

CHAPTER THREE

▼

A hundred million kloms of wide-open space hung beneath their legs as the two men worked to replace the busted servo.

These two men — Butch Hogan and Red Parsons — occupied the lowest rung on a very tall corporate ladder. This is not to say their jobs were unimportant, for they certainly were not. And yet, these two men were but cogs in a giant machine, an integral part of an audacious project.

The firm they worked for — EMD Enterprises — was actually but one part of a much larger conglomerate, a company known to the world as Transcomet Industries. Aside from the asteroid-harvesting venture, Transcomet's other lines of business included capturing comets in the Oort Cloud and crashing them into the Venusian atmosphere. The idea was to cool the planet down for eventual colonization. This was an extremely long-term investment in the future, but the payoffs were considered to be enormous. On Venus, the manufacturing possibilities were endless, with no Enviros underfoot to interfere.

Transcomet Industries was by far the world's dominant player in the global space industry. It was a public company traded on every major stock exchange. But, like every large organization, it attracted formidable enemies. Even now, powerful forces were allied against the giant outfit. No threat to the company was too small for the Board of Directors to ignore. Indeed, the Board took great pains to defend the firm's near-monopoly position over all things space. This included, among other things, making generous use of the Board's extensive political connections, senators, governors, even the President of the United States.

Steven Burgauer

But out here, seventy-five million kloms from Earth, more pedestrian matters held sway. Out here, the workers on that lowest rung of the corporate ladder were hard at work on the highest of all steels. For these people, the job always remained the same: Capture an asteroid in the Belt; secure an EMD onto the asteroid's main axis; drive the hurtling rock back through the solar system to high-earth-orbit, where it could be profitably mined. The central hub of the entire operation was here, on Mars, where the motor factory was located. This place was also home to one of the many links in the EMD tracking-chain.

Right now, on the ground, below these two men, down on that factory floor, some of those powerful, allied forces were gathered. While Butch and Red worked in orbit far overhead, members of the Terraforming Commission were being feted by executives of EMD Enterprises. Today was the last chance they would have to make their case to members of the Commission before that august group headed back home to make its final report to Congress and to the rest of the nation. A lot was riding on this meeting, and tensions were running high on both sides.

The Mars Station had not been built with large groups in mind, and there was only one room on the planet large enough to handle such a crowd, the company dining hall inside the factory itself. The room was plain, but it was filled to capacity, now, with Commission members and other bright lights. Near the doorway was a large device. It looked rather like a jet turbine, but much larger and with multiple nozzles and coils. On a table beside it stood a large placard. It read "Prototype Electromagnetic Mass Driver."

The speaker wasn't much to look at, a small, pencil-necked man with a narrow necktie and ill-fitting suit. He took a glass of water from the table, cleared his throat to speak. Overhead, on the ceiling of the plant, tiny bots constantly checked the seams for deadly air leaks.

"Gentlemen. Ladies. Thank you for making the long journey. As you all probably know by now, maneuvering a spinning rock through the asteroid Belt is an immensely complicated business. The mathematics of real-time multi-body motion are daunting. Just one nonlinear equation after another. Most computers are simply not up to the task."

"Good God, man. You think we came halfway across the solar system just to hear you complain about your computers?"

The speaker was a slim, good-looking woman with fiery, red hair and a demeanor to match. Her name was Kaleena Flanagan and she wore the sort of perfume a man was unlikely to forget. Kaleena was daughter to a prominent United States Senator and an adjunct to the Commission. She continued:

"Given the size of your budget, you would think your organization would have the best computers money could buy."

"That's true, Missy. We have lots of expensive computers, and even more high-priced programmers. And, no, I'm not here to complain. But, given the number of unknowns, it is all but impossible for us to chart a precise trajectory for any given harvested asteroid, at least not in advance, and certainly not through the maze of moons, planets, and random bits of rock and space-junk that comprise our solar system."

"I'll kindly thank you to call me by my given name. Unless you want to see some real fireworks around here, you will refrain from calling me Missy, Mister Whatever-The-Hell-Your-Name-Is."

That brought on a few snickers from around the room.

"Krotchmeier. Frederick Krotchmeier. I apologize for not properly introducing myself. But here's the thing about those fancy computers. With one main-sequence star at the solar system's center, plus nearly a dozen planets, hundreds of thousands of asteroids, and upwards of fifty moons, every single one of them constantly in motion, every single one of them constantly interacting with one another — and with the incoming asteroid — there are just too many variables to handle, no matter how big a computer a man has."

Kaleena Flanagan glared at the fellow. "Mr. Krotchmeier, every single person sitting in this room has come weeks out of their way for just one purpose — to try and properly judge the safety of everything your company is doing out here. Do you actually believe that you are going to ease our collective minds by telling us no computer you own is up to the job?"

"Lady Flanagan, please allow me to tell you what we're actually up against out here. Estimates place the total number of asteroids in the main Belt at upwards of one million. They range in size from as little as a speck, up to as much as eight hundred kloms across. All evidence points to a common origin for these countless, irregularly-shaped chunks of rock. The thinking is this: Long ago, when the solar system was first forming, one or more of the early planetoids were torn apart under the influence of Jupiter's tidal forces. Today's asteroids are remnants of that long-ago explosion. Like all the rocky planets — including our own — the asteroids are laden with valuable ore. This is what our company is after."

"We all know what you're after," Kaleena chided. "More tax dollars, less regulation, total immunity from legal liability should something go wrong."

"Kaleena, why don't you let the man speak?" This was a new voice, the voice of Elijah Montrose, Ph.D., economist and advisor to the Commission. Everyone respected him greatly.

"Thank you, Dr. Montrose," Krotchmeier said.

"Don't thank me. But do cut to the chase already, young man."

"Yes, of course. Now where was I? Oh, yes. Nearest the sun and accounting for roughly fifteen percent of the Belt's population are the S-type or siliceous asteroids. These bodies consist of an olivine shell surrounding a core of nickel-iron alloy. Interesting, but hard to mine.

"Inhabiting the Belt's outer reaches and making up three-quarters of the Belt's population, are the C-type asteroids, the carbonaceous or carbon-rich asteroids. Easy to mine, but not particularly valuable.

"The really valuable stuff is in the middle, the M-type or metallic asteroids. These big chunks of nickel and iron emerged eons ago from repeated collisions among the S-type bodies. There aren't many of them out there — barely ten percent of the total — and they are separated from the other two rings by a large Kirkwood gap."

The thin, pencil-necked man stopped, clicked on a vid machine, brought a chart up on the big, overhead screen.

"Here's where the complex mathematics kick in. Daniel Kirkwood, an American mathematician. He was the first scientist to link unoccupied orbits in the main Belt to Jupiter's gravity and orbital frequency."

Krotchmeier pointed to a complex graphic on the screen. "Our Mr. Kirkwood made the following argument: Any asteroid circling the sun at a rate that was a simple fraction of Jupiter's orbital period of twelve Earth-years — say, an asteroid with a four-year orbit (3:1 resonance), or one with a six-year orbit (2:1 resonance) — would get a gravitational boost every time it lapped the gas giant. After repeated boosts, it would eventually be kicked out of that particular orbit. This happened millions of times over, some asteroids being slowed, others being hurried along. Over long stretches of time, these repeated pulls and tugs eventually swept eight different orbits clean, empty tracts now known to us as Kirkwood gaps."

"Yes, yes, the Kirkwood gaps. That's what you want us to put in our final report? — Kirkwood gaps?"

"I'm simply trying to put the risks in perspective for you. The physical risks of working out in the Belt, among all those moving bodies, are many. Countless things can go wrong, many of them beyond our control. Even if Congress is reluctant, we need legal protections against lawsuit."

Elijah Montrose spoke up. "Here's where you lose me, Krotchmeier. Given what you're doing out here, the financial payoffs ought to be enormous. Every economist will agree: a profitable company should be made to cover its own financial risks. Otherwise, there is a moral hazard. The company will begin to accept unnecessary risks, which they will eventually dump on the rest of us. We in the trade refer to this act as free-riding. According to your prospectus, a single M-type asteroid a mere klom in diameter houses a treasure-trove of nickel and iron, plus lesser amounts of manganese and bauxite. The infrastructure is already in place. That asteroid of yours will arrive in high-earth-orbit as one neat and tidy package. It will be easily susceptible to mining techniques perfected during the lunar gold rush. Where's the risk?"

"Dr. Montrose, your comments are insightful, as always. It goes without saying that this operation is a unique combination of enormous payoff coupled with relative economies of scale. That is what first fired the imagination of the financial muscle behind EMD Enterprises. But let's not forget: incredible sums of money have been put at risk here. The financial muscle behind this project includes some of the world's savvier business minds. People like Keith Roberts, Chairman of the Board of Transcomet, and Spencer Trask, now Chairman of the U.S. Federal Reserve."

"No one wants to make waves," Elijah said trying to remain neutral.

"Speak for yourself," Kaleena interjected. "On a good day, an asteroid that size could fetch something on the order of five trillion dollar-equivalent credits on the international market."

"Don't tell me you're trying to hold my company personally responsible for the state of prices at home?" Krotchmeier replied testily.

"Isn't that what a monopoly does? — manipulate prices?"

"Honestly! Ore prices are high with good reason. Those prices are testament to the severity of raw ore shortages that have become legend in the past few decades."

"And why is that?"

"You know very well why. On Earth, inexpensive and easily accessible veins were mined out long ago. The Moon has been mostly a bust. The mineral deposits there were thin and mined out early on. Plus, even at one-sixth earth-gravity, raising metal ingots to orbit from the Moon's surface means contending with a seriously deep gravity well. Recycling materials bound up in other products is prohibitively expensive. Plus, the amounts recovered are trivial. Even the comparatively complex matter of swinging an asteroid out of the Belt and into Earth orbit is cheaper than any of the alternatives. Asteroid-harvesting is the only course of action that makes economic sense."

"Let's get back to the risks, shall we?" one of the other Commission members observed. "Getting that big hunk of rock three hundred million kloms across the solar system entails countless risks, doesn't it?"

"Moderating those risks is high on our list of priorities. Slinging an asteroid around the solar system begins with a sophisticated piece of equipment called an electromagnetic mass driver, or EMD for short."

Krotchmeier stopped, then pointed to the large device on the factory room floor near the doorway. "A properly calibrated EMD uses the asteroid itself as fuel. By ejecting tiny bits of rock forward — into the asteroid's orbital path and thus counter to its present direction of travel — the big rock slows down. A slower-moving rock begins to fall. It falls in toward the sun. Which means it also falls in towards the Earth."

"My very point!" Kaleena exclaimed, jumping to her feet. "As soon as that big rock begins to drop out of its orbit, the danger to Earth starts to rise. The closer it gets to Earth, the worse the risk becomes." She slowly settled back into her seat.

"It has to be a controlled fall, of course. Otherwise, as you said, the results could be calamitous. We all know this. But assuming the fall can be properly guided, the ore-laden asteroid, once slowed, can be safely delivered to those same smelters in high-earth-orbit that once served the moon-mining enterprises. While this method of propulsion consumes about fifteen percent of the asteroid's mass in transit, it doesn't use it all. Sufficient raw material remains to cover expenses and still turn a tidy profit for those Wall Street financiers who have been kind enough to bankroll this asteroid-harvesting venture."

"Capitalism is about kindness, then?"

"No need for sarcasm."

Kaleena was insistent. "I think there is every need for sarcasm here. You aren't answering our questions. Each and every one of us still wants to hear more about the safety measures you have put in place, the tracking stations and such." Kaleena knew her father wanted reassurance. Senator Flanagan was one of the chief proponents who favored outlawing terraforming and putting a halt to the asteroid trade.

"And hear about it you will. Capturing an asteroid isn't like roping a steer; though I dare say, it does have some of the same bravado."

At this point, Krotchmeier squeezed out an effeminate laugh. It took a moment for him to realize that his laugh was out of place. He continued:

"To rope a mineral-laden M-type asteroid and nudge it closer to Earth requires motors unlike any the world has ever seen. These mass drivers are of such complexity and such dimension that an entirely new breed of factory — this factory — had to be hammered out of the Martian bedrock.

"Each EMD manufactured here at the Motor Works is more or less identical, at least from a hardware point of view. Nozzles, jets, combustion chambers, antenna-units, servos, that kind of stuff.

"The differences lay in their programming." Krotchmeier ticked them off: "The coordinates in 3-space of the target asteroid. Its velocity and spin. Its mass and average density. The negative acceleration-coefficients necessary to maneuver such a mass Earthward. The physical location of the Earth itself, both at the time of the asteroid's capture and at the expected time of rendezvous. The expected timeframe for reversing the particle flow from the mass driver, so as to slow the asteroid's fall and avoid a horrendous collision with Earth . . . "

By now, Elijah Montrose had become bored with Krotchmeier's presentation and begun to tune it out. He reached across the aisle, tapped Kaleena on the shoulder.

"What is it?" she growled, still trying to listen.

"Did you ever see two finer kids?" He handed her his e-pad. Displayed on the screen was a digi-pix he'd downloaded off the e-net this morning. "Wife just sent it up to me," he whispered.

"Lovely, Doc," she said, handing it back to him. "Now would you please be quiet? I need to hear what this man has to say. My father wants answers, you know?"

Still admiring the digi-pix of his children, Elijah interrupted her again. "That's them. My kids. Standing next to the Liberty Bell. Aren't they just darling?"

"Can't we talk about this on the ship-ride home?"

"Sure. I just miss them. That's all. And Barbara too. You have to understand that."

Krotchmeier was still talking. He was pointing now to that giant contraption near the doorway of the mess hall.

" . . . Nowadays, in this very factory, workers assemble gigantic EMDs like this one, which make the whole thing possible. The EMD is hitched first to a railgun, then catapulted to escape velocity. These massive, fully automated motors literally fly themselves out to the Belt, navigate a minefield of S-type asteroids — plus a large Kirkwood gap — then automatically attach themselves to a preselected target-asteroid using twenty tungsten-steel-hardened pitons equipped with explosive tips. Finally, without need for further human intervention, they start the rocky mass on its month-long journey back towards the inner solar system and Earth."

He continued. "The whole process, from start to finish, is Newtonian physics at its most basic. That business about opposite and equal reactions. Think of those tiny bits of rock as retro-thrust. Like I said: the EMD utilizes the asteroid itself as fuel and spits those bits of rock into the asteroid's orbital path. This retro-thrust slows the asteroid's orbital velocity. It also helps guide the remaining portion of the planetoid forward along its looping trajectory towards Earth. Once the asteroid is within reach of any of a dozen earth-orbiting smelters, Space-Traffic Control will use the giant motor to brake the asteroid's fall and insert the valuable chunk of rock into geosync orbit. From there it can be easily and safely mined — just as Dr. Montrose said — and the finished ingots dropped to the surface by inertial skyhook or used as ballast for the Space Elevator."

Now Kaleena interrupted. "And yet, despite the apparent simplicity of your plan, there is still one subject you absolutely refuse to address."

"Oh, and what subject is that?"

"The cataclysm that would unfold if an EMD-guided asteroid were to suddenly spin out of control. The results could be disastrous!"

"Yes, yes," someone else heartily agreed. "That errand slab of rock of yours might spin harmlessly off into space. Then again, it might lurch awkwardly into orbit about the Earth, much as our own moon did eons ago. Even then, without a direct hit, the consequences could be dire — Crushing tidal forces that destroy coastal cities. A devastating wobble in the Earth's axis that disrupts weather patterns. A horrendous collision with the Moon itself."

Now Kaleena jumped back in. "Or, calamity of calamities, the beast might slam into the Home Planet. A direct hit would be planet-killing, on the order of all the dinosaurs dead!"

"Please! Please! Let's all be reasonable, shall we? What you describe is an outcome no one wants, least of all the investors at Transcomet."

"So what are you going to do about it?"

"Any number of redundancies have been built into the system — EMD-tracking stations both aloft and on the ground; sophisticated onboard computers; remote-controlled explosive charges designed to alter the asteroid's flight path; standby tugs with trained crews for active intervention. The list goes on."

Krotchmeier continued. "As the asteroid draws closer to Earth, midcourse corrections will be frequent and expected. Space-traffic controllers down on the surface and in any of several EMD-tracking stations closely monitor the progress of each incoming asteroid. Should one wander even slightly off its optimal flight corridor, a radio signal will be sent aloft, directing the onboard servo to tilt the mass driver so as to redirect the particle flow and alter the asteroid's trajectory."

"And what if a servo is damaged?" Elijah asked. "What then?"

"Servos don't get damaged. They're manufactured only to the highest standards."

"By the lowest bidder, I suppose."

Krotchmeier didn't answer. He'd already read the preliminary report from the two men whose legs hung suspended in space a thousand kloms above their heads. Servos *did* break, and Krotchmeier was lying to these people sitting before him about the risks.

But then again, it wasn't as if his bosses had given him much choice in the matter.

CHAPTER FOUR

▼

Senator Alexander Hoagland stood at his window in the Senate Office Building and stared glumly out onto the National Mall. It was alive with people, many thousands of them.

These were angry people, a seething mob. Reaction to the slaughter at the stadium had been intense and immediate. Gun-haters from across the country had descended on Washington like flies to the kill.

The demonstrators were not alone on the Mall. Eyeing the protestors uneasily were scores of riot police dressed in full battle gear. Backing them up were security bots of various configuration, some armed with projectile weapons, others with pulse guns. From his perch at the window, Hoagland could see bots everywhere, in the crowd as well as along the sidelines.

Protecting the organs of government was a complex task, one that had to balance the rights of a free people to peaceably assemble against the bureaucracy's need to maintain order and run a large country. The D.C. Dome was particularly tricky in this regard. It was huge, one of the larger domes in the nation, stretching across the entire tidal basin, from beyond the Potomac to encompass the entire metroplex of the District of Columbia plus the surrounding suburbs.

Senator Hoagland's gaze trended upward, now, toward the faraway glass roof of the Dome. He could see hordes of tiny dots moving about up there. These were surveillance drones, and they patrolled endlessly overhead. On the ground and overhead were countless vidcams, some stationary, some mobile, as well as security bots of every sort. On order of President Benjamin, the bots were out in force today. In Hoagland's view this was a tragic mistake, for it had all the hallmarks of a giant confrontation.

What began as a rally against guns had, in the space of a few hours, evolved into something more serious. Members of this disparate mob found themselves united in the hatred of a great many things, not simply guns. The placards they carried ran the gamut. Anti-gun. Anti-science. Anti-terraforming. Anti-everything that made America great. Hoagland shuddered to think how these many disparate forces might suddenly coalesce into something more dangerous that could tear apart the country he loved so dearly.

Senator Alexander Hoagland saw the placards from his window. So, too, did Senator Patrick Flanagan, from his window one floor up. The two men were mortal enemies. They stood on opposite sides of the aisle in almost everything that mattered. Now they both read the placards they could see, and tried to digest their meaning.

PROFITS ARE EVIL

SCIENCE IS DEATH

CONFISCATE THE GUNS

GUNS MURDER THE FUTURE

MAKE LOVE, NOT ASTEROID DUST

EVOLUTION IS EXTINCT

Upon reading them, Senator Patrick Flanagan swallowed a guilty smile. From his window on the upper floor of the Senate Office Building, he had seen the rabble gather. These were people Flanagan felt allied with, people who held the same narrow views he himself held. Senator Flanagan thought the Second Amendment was silly, an anachronism held over from an earlier, much cruder age. Civilized people didn't need guns, not any more than they needed technological advance or genetic engineering or even a capitalistic reward system. *Wasn't change in and of itself evil?*

Flanagan wasn't a Luddite, not quite. But now, after the mass murder at the stadium, he finally saw his chance, his chance to advance stringent Gun Control legislation to the floor of the Senate.

And yet the man suffered no illusions. Even with all the excitement;

even with revulsion gripping the nation; this was not going to be easy. No Senator could manage this feat alone, and certainly not one with as few allies as Patrick Flanagan. No, to get his pet legislation through the Congress, he would need help, help from across the political aisle. From one man in particular — Senator Alexander Hoagland.

Flanagan stepped back from the window, now, adjusted his cravat. He was a tall man, tall but not terribly distinguished. He swung on his coat, palmed a copy of his weapon-control legislation, started down the corridor. The office of Senator Alexander Hoagland, senior senator from the great State of Texas, was down one floor, at the opposite end of the building.

Senator Flanagan felt good about his chances. He took his time descending the single flight of stairs, then walking the length of the corridor. His slouching figure seemed to lack Senatorial dignity. Though he often tried, he really had never been able to dress the part.

Protective guardbots lined the hallway. Flanagan felt tempted to address them as he passed but decided against it. He knew the machines had no soul, that they didn't care one way or the other whether he spoke to them. *So why waste the time?*

Flanagan nodded at Hoagland's secretary as he entered the vestibule. Hoagland was at his window, watching the demonstrators. Flanagan crossed the vestibule, knocked at his door.

"Come."

Senator Flanagan pushed open the door. "Can I disturb you, Alexander? We need to talk."

Hoagland stepped back from the window. Anyone could see he was not a happy man. His close friends called him "Xander." But Senator Flanagan wasn't a friend. He chose to remain formal, address Alexander by his given name. That set the tone right away — not that Hoagland minded.

Alexander Hoagland stared hard at the other man, unsure what to say. The Justice Department had Patrick Flanagan under constant surveillance, this at the behest of Hoagland's sub-committee. There had been rumors of extensive and illegal influence peddling between Senator Flanagan and Transcomet Industries, allegations that deserved investigation. Flanagan didn't know, yet, that his life had been put under a microscope, or that Alexander Hoagland was the one with his eye upon the lens.

"I suppose you're enjoying this," Hoagland finally said. "These protestors are handing you exactly the sound bite you've been looking for."

"No man should have the right to take another man's life," Flanagan said. The Senator was tall, lean, and freckled, with reddish hair and hazel eyes. And yet his dress was casual, approaching sloppy.

"Not ever? How downright noble of you." Hoagland's words fairly seethed with sarcasm.

"You know how I feel about this, Alexander. Only the Lord himself can decide such things. The taking of another man's life is a power too great for any one man."

"That sounds more like your son talking than you."

"Joseph is closer to God than I am; that is true. But that doesn't change a thing. The taking of another man's life is a power too great for any one man."

"But certainly even you must grant that there are exceptions. What about capital punishment, the kind meted out by a jury? That takes the unanimous decision of twelve citizens, not just one."

"That may be fine for a gun-slinging State like your own. But whether it's twelve or twelve hundred, civilized people don't commit murder, not as a matter of public policy anyway."

"No? What about a soldier in battle? Or a police officer in the line of duty?"

Flanagan was becoming flustered. He fancied himself a mere child of nature, a simple, unaffected man; yet one surrounded by good books and classic architecture. He fancied himself all these things, rather than what he really was: an aristocratic snob, a perverted hedonist, and a clever, ambitious politician. He wasn't about to give ground now.

"Here's the thing, Alexander. God might approve of a man killing another man to defend his homeland. But an offensive war is an abomination. And a police officer doesn't have to shoot to kill — there are other ways."

"So what are you saying? — that law enforcement can maim and cripple so long as they do not kill?"

"For the police, stun guns or pulse bullets will usually do the trick. But even in law enforcement, no man should have the right to take another man's life."

Senator Hoagland stared in disbelief at the other man. He loathed Patrick Flanagan, held him in utter contempt. Flanagan wore the annoying look and mannerisms of an academic. Over-educated, self-important, holier-than-thou. Strong on theory, weak on commonsense, full of conjecture. A bit too much wave in that hair of his to suit a practical man like Alexander Hoagland.

"I believe that God put the firewood here, but that every man must gather and light it himself."

"Alexander, I'm not going to stand here and tell you I have even the foggiest idea what that means." Flanagan shook his head, as if in pity. Anyone could see that Hoagland was a cowboy, a throwback to an earlier time, where people were free to roam the open prairie. Flanagan hated that about the other man.

"Sooner or later we must all settle with the world and make payment for what we have taken."

"A little early in the day to be drinking, don't you think, Alexander?"

"You know very well I don't touch the stuff, Kemo Sabe. Sober as the day I was born."

"What then?"

"This mob troubles me," Hoagland said, returning to the window. A picture of his wife Laura sat on his desk. Another of his son, now deceased, hung on the wall.

"You have a problem with demonstrators? Is that your philosophy? — the Second Amendment's okay, but the First makes you uncomfortable?"

"Don't put words in my mouth. I don't have a problem with the First Amendment. But these people are idiots, and the riot police make me nervous. Just look at those signs. They make no sense to me. — SCIENCE IS DEATH? — GUNS MURDER THE FUTURE? — MAKE LOVE, NOT ASTEROID DUST? — What's wrong with these people?"

"Just ordinary Americans exercising their right to free speech and peaceful assembly." Flanagan sat down, made himself comfortable. He sat in a lounging manner, leaning on one hip, with one shoulder elevated above the other.

"You're as blind as they are, Patrick. You say no man should have the right to take another man's life? That's horseshit. What about home invasion? Shouldn't a man be able to use deadly force to defend his family, his home, his castle?"

"Alexander, all I know is this — guns should be banned, now and forever, pure and simple. It's Original Intent. The Founders never meant for the common people to possess handguns. The Founders were referring to an armed State militia in the Bill of Rights, a sort of National Guard. The firearms can be kept in an armory. No one need take them home with them."

"You're dead wrong about Original Intent. The Founders would have been unequivocal about the need for a citizens' militia. They meant for everyone to be armed. These people lived on the frontier. They needed guns to defend themselves, for God's sake. They hunted animals for food, to eat. The Founders understood this. Their intent was clear. Everyone should have a weapon, and their weapon should be at arm's reach, not locked up in some warehouse somewhere."

"You're a Neanderthal. Almost no one thinks like that anymore."

"Maybe no one in Connecticut. But out West, plenty of people still do. Plus, the Supreme Court has ruled in favor of guns on more than one occasion."

"Your constituents deserve you."

"My constituents respect me."

"Every Senator thinks that, Alexander. But whether they respect you or not, I still believe guns ought to be outlawed."

"There is an awful lot we don't see eye to eye on, Patrick. The history of gun control is simple. Registration of handguns was the first step on the long road to confiscation. But there have been others. — Mandatory gunlocks. Ammo fingerprinting. Serial numbers. Compulsory testing. Background checks. The whole, dreadful, anti-gun, lemmings march of the past two hundred years."

"It's been a long and winding road, to be sure. But now it seems we are finally nearing the end."

"Patrick, the argument here isn't about who has the right to take a life, the argument here is about liberty and how best to preserve it. A nation's greatest enemies aren't always foreign invaders. Just as frequently, they are internal subverters, destroyers from within. And that includes governments that coerce their own citizens."

"You're paranoid. People are inherently good, just like my daughter says."

"I would agree; people *are* inherently good. But they are also naked opportunists. Crime rates always fall in jurisdictions where guns are legal. Statistics bear that out. In those places where guns have been banned, crime rates invariably rise."

"If we show people the right way, the Lord's way, then people will no longer need weapons to protect themselves."

"Don't tell me you're now shilling for the Reverend Roland Whitmore? If people don't need weapons, then why the hell does the federal government need them? Let the central government lead by example. The FBI, the National Guard, the local constables, even the security bots — make every last one of them surrender their weapons first. Then — and only then — will I think about surrendering mine. But until that day actually comes, the Second Amendment should not be tampered with."

"Oh, tamper I will — and plenty. I don't want any more stadium massacres. Next week I plan on introducing a bill. I call it the Flanagan Gun Control Act."

"Named it after yourself, did you? Once again, how downright noble of you, Patrick."

"Name recognition resonates with the voters."

"And with your enemies. Such personalization puts a bull's eye on your head."

"Is that a threat?"

"Not at all. You know very well I fight my battles in the halls of the legislature or in the editorial pages, not in the streets with guns. But sure as I'm standing here, you must know there are others out there with more violent tendencies."

"My bots provide adequate security."

"As do mine. But if you're going to put your name on this legislation, I would keep my wits about me."

"Good advice always."

Flanagan stepped forward now, handed Hoagland the booklet he had carried down with him from his office. It was the size of a medium-length paperback.

Hoagland took it grudgingly, turned it over in his hand. Again he caught sight of his son's picture on the wall. If Xander had any shortcomings, it was that he had been a limited father. His wife Laura and he were deeply involved in each other's lives, in Alexander's life. Their son, their only child, got little attention. The boy had accepted that. His father was a great man, a controversial man, and his mother cared only about her husband. But their marriage was a small house, with but a single room, and the boy wasn't allowed to set foot inside it. He had grown up and gone elsewhere to breath, eventually to the Army, where he was killed in action.

Senator Patrick Flanagan eased himself towards the door. He had accomplished what he set out to do, stir up his opponent. Mission complete. He said:

"I can see you have a lot on your mind today, Alexander. So, if it's all the same to you, I'll be going now. In the meantime, I will leave this draft with you. It's an advance copy of the legislation I plan on introducing next week on the floor of the Senate. Please keep it. Read it at your leisure. Share it with your staff. You can download e-copies from my Senate website. You'll want to be up to speed when hearings open."

Flanagan turned to leave. All in all, he felt pretty good.

"Honestly, Patrick — this isn't a bill, it's a book."

"Then just read the Executive Summary. There are only five provisions."

"Just five? How downright concise of you." Senator Hoagland hefted the legislation in his hands.

"Practice your sarcasm on someone else for a change, will you?"

"But it fits you so well."

"Have it your way."

Flanagan stepped out of Hoagland's office and began to make his way slowly back to his own.

Alexander Hoagland went back to the window. Natural light was streaming in from outside. He tilted the paper into the light and began to read:

==

THE FLANAGAN GUN CONTROL ACT

EXECUTIVE SUMMARY

1) All firearms, whether or not previously registered under state or local law, must be surrendered to the proper authorities within sixty days of the passage of this Act. Violators will be subject to a minimum sentence of five years in a federal penitentiary for each separate count of non-surrender, without possibility of parole.

2) The sale, shipment, manufacture, distribution, or importation of firearms — and of ammunition for said firearms — is strictly prohibited. Violators will be subject to a minimum sentence of ten years in a federal penitentiary for each separate count of sale, shipment, manufacture, distribution, or importation, without possibility of parole.

3) Regardless of intent, discharging a firearm anywhere in the continental United States — or in any of its territories — is strictly prohibited. This includes discharges related to hunting, target or other skill practice, in defense of home or self or others, or in the commission of a crime. Violators will be subject to a minimum sentence of fifteen years in a federal penitentiary for each separate discharge, without possibility of parole.

4) A legal search may be conducted without benefit of a search warrant, whenever a firearm is believed to have been used in the commission of a crime, including any of the foregoing crimes.

5) Certain governmental employees, as well as all Level One security bots, are exempt from provisions 1 and 3 of this Title, including police officers, members of the judiciary, and members of the military, including the National Guard, but only when not operating on U.S. soil.

For purposes of this Title, the term "firearm" shall include any projectile-dispensing weapon, whether designed for children or for adults, plus any energy-discharging device. The term "ammunition" shall include but not be limited to bullets, darts, arrows, pellets, or other projectile similar in shape to any of the foregoing which may inflict harm should it strike a person or thing.

==

Senator Alexander Hoagland finished reading what Patrick Flanagan had given him, shook his head and put aside the legislation. He thought about some of America's great leaders, how they might handle such a threat as Flanagan posed to a fundamental American freedom. Then he remembered the book his wife had given him for his last birthday. It was filled with quotes from previous presidents.

Hoagland picked up the book, turned to a page he had previously read. It was a notable quote from Calvin Coolidge. The man was speaking on the occasion of the one-hundred-and-fiftieth anniversary of the Declaration of Independence, in Philadelphia:

There is a finality about the Declaration that is exceedingly restful. It is often asserted that the world has made a great deal of progress since 1776, that we have had new thoughts and new experiences which have given us a great advance over the people of that earlier day, and that we may therefore safely discard their conclusions for something more modern. But that reasoning cannot be applied to this great charter.

If all men are created equal, that is final. If they are endowed with inalienable rights, that too is final. If governments derive their just powers from the consent of the governed, that is final. No advance, no progress can be made beyond these propositions. If anyone wishes to deny their truth or their soundness, the only direction in which he can proceed historically is not forward, but backward toward a time when there was no equality, no rights of the individual, no rule of the people.

Those who proceed in that direction cannot lay claim to progress. They are reactionary. Their ideas are not more modern than those of the Revolutionary Fathers, but more ancient.

Senator Hoagland put aside the book, again considered Flanagan's legislation. If this was the future, he wanted no part of it.

Outside, on the Mall, the voices grew louder. The roving guardbots were getting nervous, hands on their weapons. People were alternatively cheering, then booing, placards waving. The rabble was about to lose all semblance of order.

Every man must gather and light his own firewood, Alexander Hoagland thought.

But these people were playing with matches. If not contained, the fire would surely burn out of control!

CHAPTER FIVE

▼

No man alive was more pious than the Reverend Roland Whitmore. — Or more hypocritical. Or more lecherous. Or more deceitful. If this is what God intended in a preacher, then maybe we have the Big Guy all wrong. In which case, God sits not on a throne but on a barstool, not in Heaven, but in the middle of a sewer. He whores by night, gets inebriated by day, takes mind-altering drugs inbetween. This God didn't create the world in seven days, he decimated it. He had a bastard son, along with a flock of unrepentant children.

But then again, maybe the Reverend Roland Whitmore is not what God intended in a preacher.

Contrast the Reverend Roland Whitmore with a man like Alexander Hoagland. Here was an honest man like few others. Some observers accused Xander of being lazy or naïve. Others said he was tiresome, perhaps even stupid.

But such talk was all politics and innuendo. Alexander Hoagland had many detractors — as all politicians do — but no matter how much his opponents disagreed with him, no one ever accused the man of being low or unkind or dishonest or untrustworthy.

Alexander Hoagland was a decent man. He was skeptical of great power centers, the kind that could push small people around, the kind that might abuse people or take advantage of them, perhaps incarcerate them without benefit of a trial. He was especially skeptical of liberals, the kind who might swaddle every last one of us in a one-size-fits-all, leak-proof diaper, then trade away what remains of our freedoms for a vague promise of more security.

Alexander Hoagland was an unlikely politician. He came to politics from the world of finance. As a broker on Wall Street, his life was marked by challenge met by effort which yielded reward. But in those days, as in these days still, Wall Street was a hard place for an honest man to work. Thievery of one sort or another seemed to lurk behind every oaken door, and a young Alexander Hoagland went from surprised to perplexed to indignant to angry. This was his great education, the time in his life when he ascended from naïve and trusting to knowing and tough.

But he also met good people on Wall Street, people like Spencer Trask (now at the Federal Reserve) and Thadamore Mills (now Governor of Texas). These were people who believed in honesty and transparency in business and honesty in government.

Xander was not malicious, and he tried hard not to lie. When faced with great pressure, he did not bend. With his investment clients, he was always clear and candid. Everyone knew where Alexander Hoagland stood, even those who did not understand why. When weaker men simply gave in or gave up or walked away, Xander remained on the field, ready to defend his principles.

The perplexing thing about these two men — the Reverend Roland Whitmore and United States Senator Alexander Hoagland — both so different, so inherently antagonistic — was that they were both trusted advisors to the very same important man — Texas Governor Thadamore Mills. Individually and collectively, Thadamore Mills owed each of them an enormous debt of gratitude.

Associates since their college days, Senator Hoagland used every considerable resource at his command to back Thadamore's run for the State House — and he was successful. Texas was arguably the most important State in the Union, the most populous, the one with the largest industrial base, the one with the most electoral votes. Xander helped Thadamore gain working control of the influential National Governors Association, an august body that lobbied the President and the Congress to shape legislation important to the States.

The Reverend Roland Whitmore was a tireless worker in his own right. Sitting astride his pulpit in Puritan City, the Reverend helped deliver the Christian vote, without which Thadamore Mills could never have won. He also helped keep that disparate group in line, a thankless job by any measure. These people, who called themselves Christians, were prone to adopting nonsensical agendas for no apparent reason, then galvanizing every possible resource to get their way. This might include anything from a nationwide boycott to a march on the capital to a sit-in on the National Mall. Their causes might be anything from preventing a brain-dead patient from having her life-support turned off, to putting a stop to the execution of a serial killer as a sort of misguided statement on the preciousness of life.

And then there was Thadamore Mills himself. Mills was a bit of an odd duck. Great-great-great-great-grandson of Wilbur Mills, Arkansas congressman made infamous for having been caught in a drunken incident with a D.C. stripper of some repute. Heir to a Dallas oil and banking family. Related by marriage to the Bushes of Crawford, Texas, a family that included four presidents, three governors, and a dozen diplomats.

The Reverend Roland Whitmore was Thadamore's spiritual advisor. This apocryphal firebrand Texas minister slept with the Governor's wife, molested their children, beat their dog. Yet, in spite of the man's indiscretions, Roland could do no wrong, not in the Governor's eyes anyway. The only one Thadamore consulted more was his Ouija board.

Actually, that is not entirely true. The Governor was partial to this one particular wiccan who lived in eastern Tennessee, an alluring vixen named Elixir Coventry. "Licks," as she liked to be called: a woman who lived according to the Wiccan Rede — *An it harm none, do what ye will.*

Licks had a head of gorgeous blond hair, always done up in tight, corn-row-style braids, as was the fashion with the AfriAms, but long, down to the middle of her back. The woman was athletic — obsessively so. An athletic Athena. Extremely fit. A totally intoxicating package from head to toe. Nothing delighted Elixir more than cavorting around her house and yard completely naked — except, of course, for those bright yellow tennis shoes of hers, which she never took off, even at night. She visited the Governor frequently but was happiest at home among the hills of eastern Tennessee.

Even in the middle of his most hectic days, Thadamore Mills found it impossible to fight back the image of that woman working on him down between his legs. Licks was always quite the sight. Her breasts were large, her nipples always hard and erect. She liked to fuck. But she especially liked to wrap her mouth around a man's zibb. She regularly fellated Roland, the Governor, two Justices of the Supreme Court, one general on the Joint Chief's, and countless others. Her nickname said it all. Licks.

But now came one of those moments when Thadamore Mills would have to put aside thoughts of his favorite woman, one of those moments when a decision had to be made. It had been a week since Senator Patrick Flanagan of Connecticut introduced his anti-gun legislation on the floor of the Senate. Though no one gave it much chance at first, after the riot on the National Mall and the cracking of several skulls by a cordon of security bots, there was suddenly a real possibility now that the bill might pass. This had a lot of people seriously worried. Thus the meeting today.

Governor Thadamore Mills huddled with his two top advisors, Senator

Xander Hoagland and the Reverend Roland Whitmore. They were at the Governor's mansion north of Austin, perhaps an hour's drive away from Puritan City by gcar. It was a wonderful spot, on a high desert plateau, overlooking a large manmade lake.

"The people of Texas will absolutely not stand for this shit," Whitmore said, pacing the room. "Be strong on this one, Thad, and come election time you'll win again by a landslide. From there, it's just a short step to the Presidency."

"Let's not get the cart before the horse. We have to first beat back this thing, either in the House or the Senate or, God forbid, at President Benjamin's desk."

Hoagland nodded. "The President will listen to you, Thad. He'll listen to the National Governors Association. If you tell President Benjamin in no uncertain terms that he must veto this crap, I guarantee you he will. But you have to physically go there, to the White House. You have to tell the man in person."

Roland Whitmore grumbled. "Personally, I'd rather see this thing die in the House, so that it never actually reaches the President's desk. But, there may be an upside to this disaster."

"Do tell."

"Despite all the bad news, I believe the longer this thing plays out in the public arena, the more potential there is to garner valuable publicity. That ultimately might work in our favor."

"My people are pulling out all the stops on the floor of the House," Hoagland said. "But this thing's like a tsunami. We may not be able to put a stop to it in the House."

Governor Mills shook his head. "How could it ever have come to this? Our country was built on guns. We conquered the frontier that way, put an end to Spanish and British rule that way. Texas would likely secede before it gave in to a universal gun ban."

"And it probably wouldn't be the only State to do so. A good part of the West — excluding possibly California — plus much of the South. Places like Kentucky and Tennessee want no part of gun control."

"Gun control is mainly an issue in the big industrial states, the ones with lots of unions and even more mlorons," Hoagland said. "Illinois, Ohio, Michigan, places like that. Lots of electoral votes but precious little commonsense."

"It's funny you should mention Tennessee. That's where Elixir Coventry and her wiccans hold court, up there in the mountains east of Nashville. Those girls run some sort of utopian colony up in those mountains. Coventry calls it Davy Crockett country. Says the landscape is as wild as the Indian tribes that once fought tooth and nail to keep out white settlers. Her people are pro-gun, which is good. But they're also fervently opposed to terraforming, an issue that may come back to haunt us yet."

"Yes, Thad, that's what we really need — a wiccan to spearhead the movement to defeat Flanagan's gun bill." There was sarcasm in Alexander Hoagland's voice.

Whitmore frowned. "Who the hell is Davy Crockett?"

"A frontiersman of some note," Xander replied.

"I'll take your word for it," Whitmore said. "But don't kid yourself, not even a little. There are more wiccans in this country than you can possibly imagine. Plus, Licks is pretty well known in the Tidal Basin. She's been with just about every important man in the District."

"Yeah, yeah, sure — I've heard all the rumors. Don't go stirring the pot with that one, or the liberals will be banning blowjobs before the ink is dry on their Gun Control legislation."

"Liberals or mlorons?"

"Now who's being the moron? A mloron *is* a liberal. That's where the word comes from, my good man. Liberal moron — mloron."

"Flanagan may outlaw blowjobs, but the man will never vote to outlaw buggery."

"You saying the man pitches for the other team?" Mills questioned.

"Is that so far-fetched? His wife divorced him. He's estranged from his only son, a junkie priest holed up in Hedon City somewhere. His daughter left home about the time she hit puberty. Now she's on Mars engaged in some sort of fact-finding tour for the old man. I ask you: What kind of father lets his daughter take on a risk like that?"

Thadamore looked at the Reverend with disbelief.

"Honestly. I'm not making this up."

"Could we please just get back to the subject at hand?" Hoagland said, beginning to lose patience. "The Bill of Rights is in trouble here, and you two are talking blowjobs. In the first place, Governor, I've told you on more than one occasion that you shouldn't be hanging around with that wiccan. Her sort can only hurt you politically. But more to the point: we have to convince President Benjamin to veto this legislation before anyone actually makes a move to secede from the Union. He has to do it for the good of the country."

"I think Xander is right," Roland agreed.

Hoagland continued. "Back in my Wall Street days, I learned a few things about successful negotiating. There are rules, some formal, some less so. A man needs to know how to play tough and be tough. How to feint. When to stall for more time. How to wait out the opposition. How to hold 'em, when to fold 'em. I learned all these things the hard way. If it's not personal, it's business. And if it's not business, it's politics."

"When is it ever not politics?"

Alexander Hoagland's face was stern. "The lessons of history are clear. More often than not, freedom has been taken from the people, not in armed conflict by outside invaders, but in the silent and relentless encroachment of those currently in power. Let's face it: almost from the dawn of the Republic, those in D.C. have been trying to reduce our States into little more than administrative units of the federal government."

"I think they may have succeeded already," Mills said.

"And yet, the Founders had a much different idea at the outset. They regarded the central government's role as more limited — providing national security, protecting our democratic freedoms, restricting the government's ability to intrude into our lives."

"Nice words, Alexander. But the reality is different, isn't it?"

"The Founders never envisioned a vast bureaucratic agency in Washington, not one with tentacles reaching out to every corner of the land. These people, this bureaucracy, they damn near control everything. They tell our farmers what to plant. They tell our teachers what to teach. They tell our industries what to build and our people what to eat. Now they want to tell our citizens how to defend themselves? I don't think so."

"So what do you propose we do?"

"Reach out to the President — and be quick about it."

CHAPTER SIX

▼

Despite the technological difficulties, the serious business of tracking an electromagnetic mass driver through the solar system was in the hands of quite ordinary people. Their work was repetitive; it was boring; and it was almost always uneventful. Guards walking the wall at night face the same challenge — performing an extraordinarily important job that is almost never exciting.

But, on those rare occasions when it is exciting, the circumstances are usually dire and immediate and require absolute concentration with no room for error. Like the men who must launch an intercontinental ballistic missile on a moment's notice or those who must shut down a nuclear reactor before it goes supercritical, the men who track EMDs must be alert for that single moment of action in a sea of complacency.

Their workplace was a mammoth room atop a giant tower. Inside that room were countless computer screens amid dozens of tiny cubicles. On first glance, the arrangement had all the trappings of an ordinary control tower at any of a dozen suborbports around the globe. But a more careful study would reveal two important differences.

This tower was much taller than an ordinary control tower — over a hundred meters taller than the one which stood outside Hilo — and that tower serviced all the air traffic over the Pacific, not to mention monitoring the comings and goings of the Space Elevator.

But great height wasn't the only thing unusual about this control tower. Several things were unusual by their very absence. Alongside this control tower, there was no suborbport. No runways. No passenger terminal. No hotels. No tube into the city. Nothing. Just a parking lot filled with motorbikes and gcars.

In fact, this control tower housed the space-traffic controllers who kept an eye on incoming asteroids. Each time an electromagnetic mass driver was railgunned into space from the motor factory on Mars, where it had been assembled, the EMD was given a tracking number by ground control. Then, along each step of its journey earthward, detailed entries were made in a sophisticated logbook as to its progress — x, y, z coordinates at time of launch from Mars; time of first contact with its target-asteroid in the Belt; initialization of retro-thrust; moment when the combined assembly made its closest inbound pass with Mars; time when each of the seven planned midcourse corrections took place; time when it began its deceleration; moment when it swung into earth-stable orbit; things like that. Lists and checklists. Procedures and rules. Managers and underlings. Computers and monitors. All designed for no other purpose than to keep the Home Planet safe from the unthinkable.

It was in the wee hours, now, of a Thursday morning. A fourth-class assistant, new to the job, sat before a flickering screen. His eyes were bloodshot, from hours of concentrating. This was the second straight night he had seen the same strange anomaly on EMD 14, and he wasn't quite sure whether or not to raise an alarm.

Did he dare mention the anomaly to Master Cromwell, his shift supervisor? Or should he remain silent?

If the young, fourth-class assistant was mistaken about the anomaly, Master Cromwell might well send him packing. Jobs were scarce, and this one paid well, had room for advancement. In six months' time, he might be promoted to Assistant Third-Class. Then he and the wife might be able to afford that new couch she had her eyes on, the one with brown leather on the armrests.

On the other hand, if he failed to point out the anomaly, and it turned out to be something major, that could be grounds for dismissal as well. *What should he do?*

Trembling, the young man brushed back a lock of hair, rose from his chair and trotted to the door of his boss's office. Timidly, he knocked.

"Excuse me, sir? I was wondering if perhaps I might disturb you for a moment? If it wouldn't be too much to ask, I would very much like you to come over to my cubicle and take a look at my screen."

Supervisor Cromwell had just opened the pages of his *Daily* and sunk into the deep folds of his Comfy Chair. Nothing irritated the man more than being bothered in the middle of reading the sports page, especially when he was trying to line up bets for the weekend.

"What is it, Doffsinger?" the shift supervisor boomed, obviously put out by the interruption. At the sound, other heads turned in the main room.

A bot skittered across the floor bearing data spools for Lieutenant Colonel William Norris in the next building.

Assistant Fourth-Class Leif Doffsinger tried to be as conciliatory as possible. "Sir, I do apologize for interrupting you. Perhaps when you have finished with that section of the *Daily*. Then, if you wouldn't mind coming over to my cubby and taking a look at something. I would sure appreciate it. But only when you have a free moment."

"It's too late for that already!" Cromwell thundered, slamming down the *Daily* and rolling to his feet. "You have already broken my train of thought with your damnable insolence. This better be good, Doffsinger. Just exactly what is so damn important that it couldn't wait 'til I was finished reading?" Newspapers were an anachronism in an electronic world but common among the less-well educated.

The big man lumbered across the room to the cubicle of Assistant Fourth-Class Leif Doffsinger. Cromwell was a large man, big and fat. His belly jiggled with each and every step. Leif had run ahead of him and now sat trembling before his screen.

"If it pleases you, Master Cromwell, please take a look at these 3-D holographs."

Doffsinger fumbled with the knobs until the image came into sharp focus. There were hundreds of blips on the screen, some large, some small. One was illuminated in bright red, all the rest in pale yellow. Like beads on a tiny string, each blip was perforated by a gently curving line — an ellipse — which carved out its path through 3-space. Two arcing lines emanated out in front of the red blip — one red, the other green. The red one was flashing.

Master Cromwell stared blankly at the holo-screen. He studied the 3-D image from several angles. "What is it that I'm looking at here?" he asked finally.

Doffsinger bit his tongue. Life was strange that way. Supervisors the world-over suffered from the same shortcoming. They were not trained to perform the jobs the people they supervised were capable of. It was obvious to this fourth-class assistant that his boss didn't have a clue what he was looking at — or the dangers that blur of curves revealed.

But rather than just owning up to his ignorance, the big oaf huffed. "I see nothing here. Are you hopped up on blue-devils, boy?"

The color ran from Leif Doffsinger's face. To be accused by a superior of taking a controlled substance while on the job meant almost certain dismissal. Suddenly, the young man was afraid.

"I beg to differ with you, sir. I am not now — nor have I ever been — on drugs of any kind. Perhaps you are unfamiliar with this particular screen. It is a newer one — release six point four, I believe."

By couching it in these terms, Fourth-Class Assistant Leif Doffsinger could avoid directly accusing his boss of being the fat, lazy slob he actually knew him to be.

"Sir, if I may. This newer machine plots an asteroid's projected path against its actual path. We use it to . . . "

"I know what the friggin' thing is used for!" Cromwell exploded. "To program midcourse corrections! And I can see that your 'roid is off course. Just fix the damn thing at the next interrupt point. Is that so frigging hard?"

"Not at all, sir. But there may be a problem. Three days ago we signaled EMD 14 to make a major Z-axis turn. It shouldn't be off course this far this fast."

"You musta screwed up the turn," Cromwell snapped.

"With all due respect, I used the figures you gave me."

"Then you keypunched them in wrong."

"No, sir. Checked that."

"Okay, then run a relay loop. See if the onboard antenna acknowledges the test signal."

"Already did that, sir, and . . . "

"You ran a relay loop without my permission?"

Cromwell's angry voice reverberated throughout the control room. Every head in the place turned to see what was afoot. If a newbie got fired, that might improve their own, rather meager prospects.

"Due respect, sir, but I don't need your permission to run a relay loop."

"You need my permission to go to the bathroom."

Doffsinger calmly reached for the Operator's Handbook in the bottom right-hand drawer of his desk. He had marked a certain page with a red plastic paperclip. He began to read:

"Regulation fourteen eighty-two slash fifty-three. In the event of . . . "

Cromwell slapped the book from Doffsinger's hand. It slid across the linoleum floor, came to rest near the wall. "Okay, already!" he stormed. "We both agree you did the right thing. Forget what I said — I'm not going to write you up. But tell me what the hell happened when you sent that test pattern message to the EMD."

"Nothing. Nilch. Nada. Not a damn thing. There was no response."

"And the backup antenna?"

"Sir, backups only became standard beginning with unit fifteen. This is EMD 14."

"So we have a free bird?"

"It would seem so."

"Lord, have mercy."

CHAPTER SEVEN

▼

Gritty.

That is about the only word to describe the life of a bimbooker in Hedon City. Gritty.

For a woman of the streets — an AfriAm woman like Muffy Brown — nothing in Hedon City was ever clean. Not the streets, not the air, not the gaming halls, not the restaurants, certainly not the johns. These men, they came to the City to be serviced. They came from everywhere, from all across the country, especially the Bible Belt. They came to be fucked or sucked or just simply jerked off. The more a woman would do, the better she would get paid — and looks were rarely at issue.

For the women that serviced these men — women like Muffy Brown — disease was always a consideration, had been since the day the first female parted her hairy legs in the grasses of the savanna to entice a man to feed her starving children.

But it wasn't just the disease. Some of these men smelled, hadn't showered since God knows when. They would blow into town, fresh from their white-bread world, go on a seventy-two-hour binge, then prowl the streets 'til they found a girl willing to let them jam their smelly, uncircumcised zibb up her snatch or in her mouth. It wasn't pretty. But then nothing about Hedon City ever was.

And, if that weren't enough, there were those men who were violent, which was pretty much all of them. Muffy could never understand it. The mystery wasn't in why a man would pay for sex; that part was easy. He may think himself ugly, perhaps inadequate, maybe afraid of commitment, pressed for time, terribly lonely — there were many possibilities. *But where was all that rage coming from?* What would possess a man to reach in his pocket to pay a woman for sex then mess all that up with a fist to the jaw or a punch in the face? It didn't make any sense. But then nothing in Hedon City ever made sense.

Actually, that wasn't entirely true. Certain things about the place made sense once you understood what Hedon City really was: a no-holds-barred sin city born of tax-starved municipal budgets and moralistic grandstanding. It was a byproduct of corrupt politicians and shortsighted compromise. Rather than try and ban strip clubs one by one in a hundred different jurisdictions, why not restrict them all to a single, economically depressed spot on the outskirts of a major metro area? The same goes for every other sin of the body, soul or mind. Sex, booze, porn, drugs — all for sale in a single megalopolis parked at the foot of Lake Michigan.

Mired in this sewer called Hedon City was Muffy Brown, an AfriAm prostitute working the gritty streets. Muffy was a runaway. Black-skinned. Short, kinky black hair. Sparkling white teeth. Wide hips. Thick thighs. IV tracks on her arms.

As a husky teenager, Muffy had been violently raped. The man beat her, slashed her abdomen with a knife, tore her vagina with a stick, damaged her anus. Biometric surgery repaired her body, but the nightmares never ended. Now, wherever she went, she carried with her a pulse blaster to protect herself.

People cope with anger in different ways. Booze, drugs, gambling, pain. To help Muffy cope with the anger of her attack, she soon developed a nasty addiction to blue-devils. In Hedon City her supplier was a junkie priest, a quirky, little man by the name of Father Joseph Flanagan. Rumor had it, he was the estranged son of a U.S. Senator with the same last name.

Muffy saw Father Joseph now, at the next street corner. He was swaying gently with the breeze, his collar hanging askew. She hurried to his side.

"Well, if it isn't my girl, Muffy Brown. Come to fill that little glass vial of yours with blue-devils?" The man reeked of alcohol and sweat.

"Father. I'm buying if you're supplying."

"Addiction! All those happy neurotransmitters bouncing awkwardly 'round the brain. Does a body good, you know, that dopamine stuff. Helps make a body complete."

"Next week's sermon?"

"Never underestimate the needs of the flock, child. People like to be preached at. Some insist upon it. Just another form of addiction, if you ask me."

"So, tell me, Father. How does a man of the cloth become a drug dealer anyway?"

Flanagan became incensed. "You, a bitch of the streets? You mean to stand in judgment of me? A Catholic priest?"

"Some priest you are. From where I stand it looks as if they took the 'h' clean out of hypocrite and stuck it right smack in the middle of Catholic. Not all street people are stupid, you know."

Muffy scratched her butt, straightened her skirt, tried not to slouch. The last stop in the bathroom had been sans toilet paper and she was still damp.

"And just how smart can a blue-devil addict really be?" Father Joseph chuckled imperceptibly as another customer approached.

"Drugs are my way of coping, you know that."

"What does a nigger whore like you have to cope with?"

"No need to get snotty about it. Back in the day, before you dealt drugs, you heard confession. You know very well my pain. My father was strict, too strict for a free spirit like me. I ran away from home at a young age. My first week on the streets, I was beaten and raped."

"They don't let me hear confession no more. Truth is, I never met a black woman who didn't deserve to be beaten." He turned to sell a bag of goodies to another junkie. Money quickly changed hands.

"Your father teach you to be a bigot? — Or did you learn that one on your own in the priesthood?"

"Leave my father out of this."

"The Senator actually queer, like they say in the coffins?"

Flanagan punched her in the face. "I warned you, woman!"

Muffy Brown touched her fingers to her cheek, where he struck her. She came away with a drop of blood. "You queer like your father? My mama says all Catholic priests are. Pedophiles or fags. — Or both."

Flanagan punched her again, harder than before. Blood dripped from her mouth.

"You best not do that again," she said.

"What's a whore junkie like you gonna do about it?"

"I was just a kid when I was beaten and raped. Now I carry protection."

"Condom?"

"Smith & Wesson." She drew the pulse blaster from her purse. It had a silver grip.

"You threatening me?"

"Touch me again and I'll kill you."

"No one murders the son of a U.S. Senator and gets away with it."

"Estranged son, don't you mean? Fag son of a fag Senator."

Father Joseph Flanagan's eyes shone red. He reached for the woman with both hands, as if he meant to throttle her.

Muffy stepped out of his reach, gun arm extended. "I warned you."

He laughed and lunged again.

She pulled the contact twice, at pointblank range. Father Joseph staggered backward and fell to the concrete in a widening pool of dark blood. The junkies that had gathered nearby to watch the fracas now scattered into the streets and alleys.

Muffy took Flanagan's stash from his coat pocket, his money from another. It was mostly government-issue scrip. Then she started across town to the coffin dormitory, where she often slept at night. Muffy Brown didn't know the history of the city she called home, and might have been surprised if she had.

In the new century, what began as a few docks jutting out into the foot of Lake Michigan near the site of the once-proud steel mills of Gary, Indiana, had over time become a major metropolis, though of a sort not seen since the days of Sodom and Gomorrah.

A few docks. A handful of gambling boats. An assortment of offshore hotels. Then more hotels, bigger hotels, an airport. Then more hotels, narrow streets, robo-cabs, coffin dormitories. In no time at all, Hedon City was a mega-dock covering several thousand square kloms of land and open water. It reached up the shores of Lake Michigan as far north as the Chica River on the west and the Indiana-Michigan state border on the east. As a political subdivision it was neither part of Illinois nor Indiana nor Michigan. Enabling legislation between the three states established Hedon City as a quasi-independent anything-goes red-light district. Sort of like the Vatican, only with Satan in charge.

Early successes with gambling boats set the stage. Right on their heels came the brothels, the drug halls, the holo-bars. Then the virtual sex suites and live-ammo parlors. All parked safely offshore, yet within easy reach of the major metroplexes — Chica, Minnepaul, Sane Lou. The curiosity seekers came in from every direction.

In its heyday, Hedon City still retained the character of a wild, colonial station. In those early days the City was a fast-living place with fancy gcars and glamorous places. In the clubs, the standard question was, "Are you married or do you live in Hedon City?" The men were hard drinking and rough, the women beautiful and loose. The pattern of life was no more predictable than the wild boar hunts that ranged over the rugged countryside in the nearby animal preserves each weekend.

The three border-states split the tax revenues, which were substantial. Civil order was maintained by a mercenary police force, though there wasn't a lot for them to do. Crime rates were comparatively low, especially in the arenas that mattered most to people — murder, rape, burglary. The so-called "moral" crimes of the mainland — prostitution, drug-use, gambling — were exempt from prosecution offshore. Only paper scrip was permitted within the walls of Hedon City. It could be purchased at all ports of entry after payment of the requisite exchange tax. Likewise, to assure anonymity of the sometimes upper-crust clientele, identicards had to be checked at the borders in special failsafe lockers.

Rooms in the better hotels were not cheap, although a bio-bimbo often came with the price of a room. Muffy wasn't like those women; she was a hundred percent natch snatch. But these girls had been genetically modified for pleasure. Tall, strong, insatiable. Extra body parts, too. An extra vagina on the lower abdomen, non-reproductive, but otherwise fully functional. For handling two men at once.

A lot of men didn't go in for such things, of course. But some men did. Others preferred octoroons, white prostitutes who were one-eighth AfriAm — very popular with the Christian Fundamentalists. Sometimes they'd come by the busload from Puritan City.

Then there were the mommasitas, Hispanic transsexuals with a taste for bondage and pain.

Lowest on the totem pole were the street girls like Muffy Brown. Girls like her managed from trick to trick and meal to meal. They also managed from night to night. That's where she was headed now, to a coffin dormitory where she could sleep until morning, a place called The Last Resort.

•

•

The Last Resort was in the original red-light district of Hedon City, a confusing congested realm where winding and sometimes unpaved streets converged with dark shadows at the water's edge. It was easy for suburbanites to forget what a hellhole a big city could be — stifling pollution, insane crowding, forbidding crime.

But, for someone like Muffy Brown, who lived there, Hedon City had its attractions. A bimbooker could murder in cold blood a junkie priest like Father Joseph Flanagan and perhaps get away with it.

Muffy's kinky black hair was gritty, her face pocked and dirty. Nothing that couldn't be solved with a little soap and a basin of hot water, she thought. Luckily, she now had some scrip and a stash of drugs she could trade for certain amenities.

Muffy approached the splintered doors of The Last Resort. It was as it always was, dirty and rundown, a genuine eyesore. She paused on the steps leading up to the front door to catch her breath. A foul-smelling man and two colleagues emerged from a cramped, subterranean bar next-door. The drunken man was a revolting specimen of humanity. Rancid breath, greasy hair, a beer gut that hung down over his belt. She could smell the booze from where she stood, five meters away.

The drunken man teetered back and forth, halfway up the concrete stairway. Then he suddenly groaned and threw up his last meal on his pants and shoes. Muffy stepped around the man, marched through the front door.

The air inside the narrow hotel lobby was stale and surprisingly muggy. There were bugs everywhere. Muffy felt a bead of sweat work its way out of her unshaven armpit. She felt it roll slowly past her breast and down her side. Another accumulated in the crotch of her panties. Overhead, a feeble excuse for a ceiling fan struggled to push the thick air aside. It was making little headway.

Two white men sat off in a corner, their bloodshot eyes focused on a visicast screen. Muffy turned to see what they were watching. It was an explicit pornovideo featuring a female AfriAm straddling a middle-aged male Euro. The star of the screen had once been a street girl like Muffy, one of her soul sisters, now promoted to making porn.

The two men looked up at Muffy with a longing gaze. To them she was little more than a supple set of hips and a pair of large tits. Muffy turned away. Ahead of her was the registration desk.

The night manager emerged from behind a curtain. He looked her over. There was a hint of recognition. "You bin here before?" he asked through a mouth full of teeth in bad need of orthodontia.

"Yeah, I been here before. But I never seen your skinny white ass before."

Now came an explosion of laughter from the two deadheads watching the pornovideo. The manager sucked his blackened teeth for a few seconds, glanced at the other clerk sideways. "Sorry, full for the night."

Muffy was dog tired, in no mood for bullshit. She had to have some sleep. "Actually, I like skinny white ass. Be a doll and rent me a box already."

The clerk thought it over, nodded and smiled. Beyond the lobby was an old stadium, used perhaps in the old days for indoor football or similar sport. Inside were hundreds of tiny fabricated units, each roughly one meter wide, one meter tall, and two-plus meters deep. They were piled four-high throughout the room, like Pullman berths in a giant morgue.

But Muffy thought of the units as coffins. To her, this was a place to die, a place where people came to die, a coffin dormitory. The stacks of coffins were arranged in long, ghastly rows around the perimeter of the morgue, with each coffin pointed feet-first towards the center of the room.

The skinny white manager asked for forty credits, which Muffy paid from Father Flanagan's money. He also asked for her shoes, which she reluctantly surrendered. It was a security measure, to discourage people from leaving in the morning without first stopping to pay their bill.

Then he handed her a ragged towel, strapped a locker key to her wrist with a Velcro band, and pointed her to a unisex locker room.

Muffy made her way down the hall and to an empty stall. She went immediately to the washbasin to scrub her hands, face and hair. Within the past hour she'd shot a man. Before that she'd fucked two, blown three more. Now she felt dirty.

Barefoot, she tiptoed into the lavatory, clutch in hand. The ceramic floor was cold and wet. She placed her handbag on the edge of the sink, within easy reach. With so many unfamiliar faces around, she wasn't about to let that pulse blaster out of her sight.

Muffy brushed her teeth, washed her face. She looked at the key velcroed to her wrist. There was a number etched on it. It told her which locker she was assigned to. It also told her which sleep-capsule was hers.

But before settling down for the night, Muffy first needed a fix and something to eat. She popped a couple blue-devils from her vial like Pez and quickly swallowed them. Then she moved beyond the locker room, back toward the front desk. The night manager with the bad teeth peeked out at her from behind a curtain.

At close quarters was a commons area where the lowlifes she encountered earlier outside on the stairs were now bivouacked at a table watching the second half of the same pornovideo that had been running in the lobby. Muffy watched it for a minute, let the blue-devils take effect. Her soul sister — the large Negroid woman — was performing fellatio on some man with stupendous proportions.

Muffy felt wet between the legs. She retraced her steps backward, toward the door, bumping into a lounge chair and nearly falling to the floor. The blue-devils were kicking in. She was unsteady on her feet.

The cretins laughed at her antics. One of them offered her a helping hand in exchange for a hand job.

Suddenly, Muffy was afraid. Paranoia was the stepchild of blue-devil addiction.

Muffy felt hemmed in, encircled by chairs and walls and scores of vending machines. These machines dispensed everything imaginable, from contraceptives to pep drinks to seaweed, dried squid, Deludes, even dog-penis aphrodisiacs. No food, though. Muffy's stomach was empty. She was sure she was going to retch any moment now.

Muffy covered her mouth with her hands, made for the door. The taste of phlegm was on her tongue. The pair of ruffians laughed again, this time cruelly. She stumbled towards the nearest stairwell.

Muffy descended one flight, hand still clutched over her mouth. The next level down was the restaurant floor. The eatery wasn't much, but it did serve noodles. Normally, they were cold and limp.

The restaurant's decor was something out of a bad vid. A large carpeted dining area, fake fireplace, six small round tables. On each table were free nicotine sticks. They were stuffed, business end up, in a dark beer glass. There were also dispensers for cocaine-soaked toothpicks. She took one, stuck it in her mouth. Placed between the teeth, touching the gums, the pick made for a quick high.

A large visicast set was suspended from the ceiling on steel tethers. It was broadcasting the same sick pornovideo Muffy had now twice caught a glimpse of this evening. For a small extra charge a customer could rent a full-body sensor-wrap, so he could feel on his skin what he was seeing on the screen.

The tables were arranged in a semicircle around the screen, so that everyone could see. The patrons — one woman, five men — were laughing, joshing each other, smoking weed and slurping limp noodles. They had rented two full-body sensors between them and were passing them around as they got high. The men eyed Muffy like a piece of meat as she entered the restaurant, one man in particular. He was a big, burly fellow who hadn't shaved in a week. His breath reeked of tortan and tobacco.

The restaurant menu was written in a sort of Pidgin English common to the streets. She ordered *ramen*, a noodle dish, for five credits. The waiter, a servant bot, recorded her wristband number on the ticket. She would have to pay for the meal in the morning, when she went to collect her shoes and check out.

The bot scurried away, like a rat coveting a big piece of cheese. Muffy looked around. At the next table over, a lout fell asleep. His forehead descended slowly into the plastic soup bowl sitting empty before him. Two tables further on, two other men were hooting their approval as the big black woman on the screen fixed her gelatinous hips down on the pelvis of partner number three this hour. Across the room, one of the men who had eyed her so closely when she first came in, licked his lips with a tongue made red by a wine-fused pep drink. He looked Muffy over again. She had seen that demented look before, out on the streets. It was a dangerous look. She shivered and turned away before he could finish his appraisal.

Muffy finished her noodles. Now, with something in her stomach, her nausea passed. Yet, she suddenly felt tired, as if she hadn't slept in days. Muffy needed some rest. She left the restaurant, went back to the lobby level, withdrew in the direction of the coffins and her sleep-capsule.

The hotel's stacks of sleep-capsules were located within an angular labyrinth. The capsules themselves were square — when viewed face-on — and made of plastic. The room was eerily reminiscent of a big-city morgue, though it was actually an old stadium. Each capsule was blandly colored and covered on one end with a poorly fitting plastic shade that was spring-loaded and could be raised or lowered with a gentle tug. Muffy glanced again at the number on her wristband and compared it with the numbers on the four-high stacks of capsules. She was assigned to Row 188, Level 3.

For a woman the size of Muffy Brown it was no easy matter to enter an upper capsule. First she had to climb six steps up a narrow ladder that was bolted to the left side of the stack of capsules. Then she had to twist sideways to sit on the ledge of opening number three. Finally, she had to lean back and launch herself headfirst and horizontally into the opening of the square, coffin-like capsule. Obviously, the drunker or more stoned the patron, the more difficult the task.

The smell inside the smooth plastic capsule was appalling — a vicious mixture of chlorine vapors descending from the hot tubs upstairs, dirty dishwater rising from the kitchen below, plus urine, feces, and vomit from God knows where, probably one of the other capsules.

A one-inch-thick futon lay on the floor of the tiny capsule, cushioning her bottom ever so slightly. After scooting backward inside the capsule and readjusting the futon beneath her legs, Muffy now leaned forward to pull down the translucent shade which covered the opening.

But it was a shade in name only. In fact, it barely covered the opening. It certainly did not lock shut in any meaningful way, clipping loosely over an eyehook instead. Plus, it did nothing whatsoever to shut out the presence of a dozen or more live bodies that weighed on her from every side. Like a low-tech pup tent, the capsule walls blotted out nothing except the view. For an unattended woman, even one in her profession, it was unnerving. Muffy took out her blaster and positioned it within easy reach of her hand.

At the foot of the capsule lay a white bed sheet and a ratty beige blanket. The two were folded together accordion-style, like unperfed sheets of computer paper. At the opposite end of the capsule, the end farthest from the opening, there was a tiny visicast screen. That, plus a music pod, reading lamp, mirror, and digiclock.

The source of sound for the visicast module and the music pod was the same, a tiny speaker positioned right next to her ear. This way, the sound wouldn't annoy any of her neighbors — except that it did.

Muffy turned on the picture and adjusted the volume. Among the many offerings was the same pornovideo being shown throughout the entire establishment. Muffy turned it off and turned on the music pod instead. She fiddled with the knobs but all she got for her trouble was static. She turned the pod off as well and got ready for sleep. She spread the bed sheet out over the futon and laid down. A sigh of exhaustion issued from her lips.

From the outset it was apparent sleep would not come easily. She wanted to go home, back to Chica, back to her father. Her father Lexus was a good man. He had been stern yet never mistreated her, not even once. But she had run away anyway, too proud to forgive or forget, too ashamed of her behavior to apologize afterwards.

But tonight, in the coffins, her sleep was interrupted by more pedestrian things. The blanket was too short to cover both her chest and toes at the same time. When she did pull it up to warm her neck, her feet caught a breeze from the aisle just outside.

But it got worse. All around her was snoring, some of it gasping for breath, like untreated sleep apnea. Though she had slept here in the coffins many times before, tonight the vibrations rattled her nerves. It felt as if the fellow on her left were shoveling a pint of phlegm back and forth inside his nasal cavity. On the exhale, the mucous would flap out to the edge of his nostrils before he caught it and breathed the sticky mass back in again, nearly swallowing it whole, but not quite. The noise he made was not so much deafening as it was sickening.

From nearby capsules came other sounds. A cellophane wrapper being torn then wadded. A helping of squid being chewed for a very long time by someone who didn't close his mouth. Teeth being brushed by someone who had returned from the washroom with the toothbrush still stuck in his cheek. Heavy staccato breathing as someone close by masturbated himself to sleep. One noise after another. Together, these noises generated an uninterrupted dull growl that kept her continuously on edge.

Muffy felt the press of bodies around her. Five human beings within one radial meter. Each stranger projected a force, a force that pressed against *her* force, *her* personal space, *her* privacy, trying to invade it, extinguish it, violate it. She had been violated enough in her life. Now she felt uncomfortable, hemmed in. A pool of sweat formed in the pocket behind her knees, another in the small of her back. The partially digested noodles in her gut began to do barrel rolls.

The person below her, the one who had been masturbating himself to sleep, shifted violently, slamming his body against the side of his capsule, shaking hers. Something that could only have been his face smacked against the thin, plastic wall like a slab of uncooked meat. She felt him drag his beefy arm along the coffin's smooth wall. His watchband, maybe his wedding ring, scraped the interior wall of his capsule, jarring her to attention.

Two rows over, a new capsule tenant struggled to draw closed the shade at the foot of his capsule. Hooking the latch at the bottom of the shade was not a complicated procedure; Muffy had mastered it stoned. But this guy, well, he was fumble-fingered. Each failed attempt sent the spring-loaded shade chattering upwards like a machine gun. It took him eight tries and plenty of swearing before he could get the job done.

From another capsule came the sound of dry retching. From another, a cough. From another, a sneeze. Then a loud, wet fart. Another sneeze and a burp. Muffy hated these men around her, these sick broken specimens of humanity. Yet their incessant noisemaking is what ultimately saved her life.

Muffy's first hint of trouble came when she sensed a presence out on the steps of the ladder that ran vertically past the entrance to her sleep-capsule. *She hadn't heard a nearby shade being unhooked and opened — yet someone was there!*

Muffy quickly took inventory of the noises around her. The retching, the coughing, the phlegm processing — all still there. Muffy was certain all the neighboring capsules were still occupied. That could mean only one thing — *someone new was coming up the ladder, someone who did not belong.* Their destination was a berth that was already in use — her berth!

Suddenly terrified, Muffy grabbed for her pulse blaster. She held it flat against her tummy, below her breasts. Her breathing was shallow.

The intruder fumbled with the hook on her shade. He was trying to unclasp it quietly, but was clumsily botching the job.

"Who's there?" she said, her voice barely a whisper.

Her answer came in the form of an angry grunt. The intruder, seeing no further need for silence, tore the shade from its moorings and commenced his assault.

At first the man tried to climb in the capsule on top of her, thinking perhaps that there was enough room inside to rape her where she lay.

But Muffy wasn't about to submit easily. With a vicious snap of the leg, she kicked the man in the face as hard as she could. There was a sickening crack then a gush of blood from his broken nose.

The man fell backwards to the floor, his hands gripping his face. But he lay there only an instant. Then the adrenaline kicked in.

The man came at her, now, with blood and fury in his eyes. In that instant, she recognized him, the night manager, the man with the skinny white ass. He clamped his muscular hands around her ankles and tugged.

Muffy put up a terrific fight, all the while screaming like a banshee. But, without anything solid to brace herself against, there was no way to stop him from pulling her feet-first out of the sleep-capsule.

The man tightened his grip, tugged at her writhing body with all his might. Then, with one final jerk, she flew out of the smooth plastic capsule, futon, blaster, blanket and all. She crashed to the concrete floor, landed on her back. The force of the impact knocked the wind out of her lungs. She fought for air.

"You like skinny white ass?" he sneered. "Now you gonna get some."

Then, before she knew it, he was on her, spreading her legs apart with his knees and tearing at her clothes.

Muffy fought like a wildcat, gasping for air, clawing at his face with her fingernails, screaming at the top of her lungs for help.

But, no one came to her aid. For anyone who cared, this was amusing, a live show broadcast for their entertainment.

The night manager ripped off her panties. Then, stroking himself twice with his bloody hand, he began to move in on her, his manhood extended like a cannon toward her genitals.

Muffy scooted backwards as far as she could. But her head banged up against the bottom rung of the ladder.

Then her hand was on the blaster. She pulled it up in front of her, aimed it at his chest. He was only inches away, at pointblank range.

Muffy pressed the contact with her finger. There was a flash of light, and then the air was filled with a warm pink mist.

The man's wound was devastating. Blood streamed like a fountain from the massive hole in his chest. — But the threat was no more.

What remained of the decimated carcass fell against her body like a side of beef. Muffy was exhausted and out of breath, and the deadweight crushed her chest.

The man's weight surprised her. She never expected a small man like that to feel so heavy.

Now the stench of seared flesh filled her nostrils. Revolted by the smell, adrenaline began pumping through her system like a juggernaut. Muffy had a moment of superhuman strength, tossed the dead man off her like he was nothing.

From the nearest capsule came an explosion of laughter. For some reason the occupant peering out at her from behind the shade of his sleep-capsule found her predicament amusing.

Muffy leveled her pulse blaster in his direction and squeezed off a round. The blast of energy shattered the capsule into a thousand pieces, collapsing the four-high stack of cubicles and spilling the mostly naked occupants to the floor. Angry shouts and raised fists ensued.

Muffy snatched up her belongings from around her and bolted for the lobby and the front door beyond. The look on her face was drawn, the face of extreme exhaustion. She knew she had to get out of there, stay low for a while, until things blew over. Maybe her aunt's place in N'Orleans.

If Muffy remembered that her street shoes were still in the custody of the front desk, it didn't slow her departure in the least. Nor did the fact that her half-naked body was splattered with blood and covered only in torn shreds of cloth. Muffy paused just long enough to retch at the top of the stairs. And then she was in the street, barefoot and running.

Not even her closest friend would have recognized her. Muffy's chest was soaked in the blood of her attacker. A trickle of pee ran down the inside of her leg. Her hair and face were a mess. The woman hadn't slept in twenty hours. Whatever little she'd eaten, she'd now thrown up. Her head was pounding. And now, under the influence of those blue-devil pills she'd swallowed, her legs were like pillars of concrete.

Pushing her muscles to the limit, Muffy crossed the street at a trot. The sun was at a low angle, just above the horizon. It was early morning. When she rounded the corner, she suddenly found herself bathed by a blinding flash of sunlight.

Muffy threw up her hands to shield her eyes. But it was a mistake. If not for that raised arm, she might have seen the delivery gtruck. It struck her broadside when it darted from the blind alley.

There was a crunch of skin and bones as the fender shoved her half-naked body roughly aside like so much street litter. Then, a crinkle of metal and glass as hard rubber tires flattened her blaster against the pavement. Finally, a cry of anguish followed by a moan as consciousness faded away.

Then all was quiet on the wet morning streets of Hedon City.

CHAPTER EIGHT

▼

"FIVE MINUTES TO DROP! FIVE MINUTES TO DROP!"

The announcement came across their cranial implants. Omega Forces had long ago dispensed with external comm equipment; it only got in the way.

Branislav Karpinski's heart was beating faster. Ever since that violent incident as a young man, Branislav Karpinski had wanted to escape, escape from responsibility for what he had done, escape from a world that didn't understand his kind. It's all Branislav thought about. He wanted to escape, get off the grid, and do so as quickly as possible.

At that early age, no escape seemed quicker or more complete than signing on with the military. They trained you, housed you, fed you, gave you something to be proud of. Then they shipped your butt off to some hotspot somewhere to fight bad guys. *What could be better than that?*

"THREE MINUTES TO DROP! THREE MINUTES!"

There were nine airchops in the formation, eight jumpers per airchop. Now, with the three-minute warning, the men moved to the opened doors. Each man positioned himself in the doorway, seated, facing out, feet hanging outside the airchop, above the skid bar. Rushing air blew past their faces. It was dry and cold desert air. The airchops were moving fast, low against the hills of scrub brush in northeastern Mexico.

Branislav had washed out of Omega Forces. Something about his psychological profile. But he found a new home with Colonel Pappy Barnes. Pappy, a former Marine, now retired, headed a rogue militia that worked the hill country of Texas. At the outset, Pappy's force was little more than a vigilante group, patrolling the border with Mexico, lynching illegals when they could, always on the prowl, always willing to go where the police or regular army would not. They were funded by an odd assortment of ranchers, oil men, and labor unions.

Tonight, his men were engaged in an Assault & Destroy mission, an A&D. A renegade branch of the Mexican Army had set up a sizeable outpost in a northern river valley to protect illegals attempting to cross the border into the United States. American armed forces were reluctant to engage the Mexican Army, but Pappy Barnes certainly was not. The very idea of backing down from a fight was an affront to American dignity. His assignment to his men today was to penetrate behind enemy lines inside Mexico, take out an ammo dump, destroy the outpost, assassinate the rebel leader.

In order to quickly get in as close as possible to the rebel camp — and to avoid a long, treacherous foot-march through the semi-arid, pockmarked desert — the Colonel's plan was to have his men arrive in darkness by airchop, rappel to the ground, and gather at the rally point overlooking the river ahead of the attack. The sky was black, an absolute must for this sort of assignment.

Branislav was animated. Rappelling could be fun. Only they didn't do it for fun. Not if there was some other way. In fact, rappelling was a last resort. Soldiers only rappelled from hovering airchops when they were compelled to, when vegetation or ground configuration or other factors made landing an aircraft impossible. Now they were barely five kloms out from the drop zone and everyone's hearts were pumping like mad. Adrenaline could do that to a man, even an experienced one.

"ONE MINUTE!"

The rappellers had been safety-checked and hooked up to the line since before becoming airborne. While in flight, they had had their brake hand in position, gloves on, with no slack running between their brake hand and the Donut Ring. A "log" of coiled rappelling rope sat beside each man on the flat deck inside the airchop.

Branislav looked down, now, at the line running through his brake hand. The Donut Ring was an important part of a man's rappelling kit. Four U-bolt clamps, seven static line-snap fasteners, three meters of half-inch steel cable, a foot-long keeper chain, and one floating rappel safety ring.

In machine-gun fashion, now, came the commands:

"CHECK EQUIPMENT!"

With expert eyes, Branislav inspected his Donut Ring, then tugged on his rope to be sure it was secure. Each rappeller did the same. He checked his rappel seat and his rappel ring to be sure the rope had been inserted properly. If everything was in order, the rappel rope would be looped through the rappel ring. The snap link, with gate down, would be attached to both the rappel ring and Swiss seat. Both hands would be gloved. Black leather gloves, reinforced in the palm, were standard fare.

Branislav looked up. Everything checked out. Everything was as it should be. Now each rappeller reported in by the numbers, one after the other:

"CHECK!"

Branislav placed his right hand — his "brake" hand — on the rope. He had done it many times before, often enough for it to have become instinctual. When the moment came, each rappeller would descend his rope at a speed dictated by the amount of pressure exerted by his brake hand on the rope. Reckless rappellers would descend very fast; soldiers rarely did.

"IN THE DOOR!"

If not already, each rappeller now assumed the Ready Position. That meant he was seated in the door, feet hanging out towards the skid. When the "GO" command was finally given, the sequence of exit from the airchop would be Left Front and Right Rear, followed by Left Rear and Right Front. The object was to keep the men from hurting one another as they descended. A man on a mission rappelled with bulky equipment — radio, jumek, force gun, explosives, rucksack attached with chest harness. Branislav knew the drill. Safety was always an issue. *No need to turn hard-ass into dumb-ass unless absolutely necessary.* Pappy Barnes' words.

"ON THE STRUT!"

Branislav pivoted on the skid, steadied himself using his left hand — his "guide" hand — plus the anchor end of the rope. He assumed an upright position in the wind, facing toward the inside of the airchop. Down the line, on the skid of each airchop, each rappeller did the same.

Now, both rappeller and safety officer made a final check of ropes, snap links, and rappel rings. At least forty meters of double-nylon rappelling rope lay coiled on a log in front of each man. The log kept the rope from becoming tangled or bunched up, something that could get a man killed.

"DROP ROPES!"

This was the call to action. The airchops were now hovering directly over the drop zone. Each rappeller used his guide hand to push the rope log over the side and out of the airchop. The guide hand was always the left hand. It was used strictly for balance and guidance.

"CHECK ROPES!" There was urgency, now, in the commander's voice.

Moving quickly, Branislav checked his dropped rope to be sure it was touching the ground and wasn't tangled or knotted in any way. This was an uncertain business in the dark, hovering over a windswept parcel of hilly, semi-arid desert. All depth perception could be lost in the shadows.

"POSITION!"

Now each of the rappellers assumed the "L" position on the airchop skid awaiting the command to "GO." In this position, a man would stand with legs parallel to the ground. The upper portion of his body would be bent slightly forward at the waist. His brake hand would be on the running end of the rope and positioned in the small of his back. His left hand would be gripping the standing end of the rope well above the rappel ring. Branislav didn't need to look around to know hearts were beating faster with anticipation.

"GO! GO! GO!"

The Master Sergeant reinforced his verbal command by actively pointing with extended arm and forefinger to the waiting men according to the sequence of exit — Left Front, Right Rear, Left Rear, Right Front.

Branislav Karpinski flexed his knees, straightened his legs vigorously, then loosened his brake hand long enough to drop three meters below the hovering craft. There he stopped an instant, before again letting the rope slide through his gloved palm.

To keep the ropes from overheating during descent, an experienced rappeller would apply his brake hand every three to four meters on the way down. One thing he would not do is slip out of his "L." A good man would maintain that position all the way to the ground.

At the bottom, as each man reached the ground, he quickly backed out of his ropes and just as rapidly stowed his gear. Then he promptly left the drop zone and made for the rally point, force gun in hand. There, each man would link up with his pre-assigned team members for the assault. Karpinski's team was composed entirely of snipers. They had to take out the guards and any soldiers fleeing the scene during the attack.

•

•

What nearly killed Branislav Karpinski that night wasn't enemy gunfire, but actual fire, wildfire, the sort with flames. The blaze began about two hours after the operation got underway.

The rebel camp they had targeted was set up along the region's only river. They knew this in advance from the recon vid. A dense forest filled the widest part of the river valley. They knew this as well. Off to one side was a small lake, and bordering it, a wide swamp. Higher up, vegetation was sparse. But, because of the season, the vegetation was dry, like tinder. When the attack on the ammo dump led to an explosion, a seething wildfire resulted. In the confusion, Branislav got separated from the other men on his team.

Imagine, now, that you are him, Branislav Karpinski. You have been lying in the tall grass for sixty minutes, first picking off guards at a great distance, then waiting. You hear the Enhanced C4 explode, then there are a series of smaller explosions. Next, a fireball lights up the valley and the heavens above. You rock back on your knees as the night becomes light as day. Now you see the rebel camp on fire, and, in the dry conditions, the fire is soon spreading rapidly, coming your way, driven by the wind. Soon you are facing a raging wall of flame. It is approaching you at high speed. The seething wall is a sheet of chemical energy, an inhuman beast, snarling, crackling, exploding before your very eyes.

Whatever animals can escape the inferno do so, brushing past you at top speed as if you weren't even there. Insects, birds, wild dogs, it doesn't matter. In their panic to escape, they don't even notice you as they rush past, not even the predators. *Who has time to stop for a meal, when death is upon the land?*

Then, before the sound even arrives at your ear, comes the heat and the light. You think a flame is yellow. But it is not. The wall of heat hits you, plus light across the spectrum: reds, blues, yellows and greens.

Riding the outbound shockwave are smells. The air begins to taste strange, the stench of ions fried electric by the rapid conversion of organic matter into energy. The smell of acrid ozone fills your nostrils. Angry electrons and acrid smells. Like dry lightning on a hot Kansas summer night.

Now comes the sound. Once a fire reaches a certain temperature, logs no longer burn, they explode. And they do so with a thunderous roar. Unguided missiles whiz past your ears at frightening speeds. If a man could slow the logs down and examine them carefully as they sailed past, he would see that only the outer layers of wood have been flashburned; the interior of the log is unmarked by flame.

But the log will burn soon enough, as the forest is rapidly decimated, reduced in a matter of hours to carbon and heat what took Nature a generation to grow.

Trees topple and the ground buckles. Moisture in the upper layers of soil is boiled to gas, and as it does, a wall of steam shoots from the earth like a geyser, scalding your flesh before it can even be licked by flame. You have to run, and run hard, just to stay ahead of it. Only a deep and wide pool of water will save your life, and maybe not even that.

At first, after the explosion at the ammo dump, Branislav didn't panic; none of the men in his patrol did. They had no reason to.

But then the fire grew larger and he suddenly realized they had no easy way to put it out. Their arsenal of survival gear included no fire buckets, no carbon-dioxide extinguishers, no hand-pump fire hoses. *Who comes prepared to fight a forest fire as part of an A&D mission? Who even thinks of such things in the middle of a desert at night?*

The wind got stronger as Branislav waited in the grasses. His patrol was supposed to flush out any survivors from the explosion. But no one was running this way. Things were burning. Grasses mainly, maybe a few small trees.

The wind was growing stronger, now, and the flames were dancing up the closest tree trunks. Branislav quickly gathered his belongings, slung his rucksack over his shoulders, started to back away from the advancing flames. The other men scattered.

A big fire can propagate by one of three mechanisms — by crawling, by jumping, or by crowning.

A "crawling" fire spreads on the ground via low-level vegetation, principally bushes, grasses, and other ground cover.

A "jumping" fire is one where burning leaves and branches are carried by the wind and deposited elsewhere, soon to start more distant fires. Propagating this way, a fire can literally jump over a natural barrier like a road or river, even a manmade firebreak.

A "crown" fire is a forest fire that has gotten off the ground and reached into the treetops. It burns thirty meters up, jumping quickly from treetop to treetop.

Once a fire has crowned, it can spread with tremendous speed, leaping from tree to tree and creating its own ferocious windstorm. It is completely within the realm of possibility for such winds to rival a hurricane in strength. They are easily capable of snapping a thirty-inch diameter tree trunk like a pretzel and hurling burning embers and branches as much as 15 kloms away into unburned forest.

For the inhabitants living underneath the forest canopy — be they human or animal — a crown fire is nothing to be taken lightly. The flames can spread far more quickly than any two- or four-legged creature can possibly run, particularly when the flames are pushed ahead by a strong wind, as they were now.

Plus, when a large stand of wood is rapidly oxidized, a vast amount of pent-up chemical energy is just sitting there waiting to be released. What took the sun a generation to build up by the slow calculus of photosynthesis will be freed by burning in a matter of moments. A large wildfire can generate the energy-equivalent of an atomic bomb every two minutes. And, like a nuclear blast, the physics can be awesome to behold.

A fire this size can exhibit extreme behavior — prolific crowning, intense fire whirls, and a strong convection column. In fact, the updraft associated with a large wildfire is so powerful, it will draw in air from the surrounding area, creating what is known in the business as a firestorm.

The leading edge of a wildfire is shaped by the wind, pure physics in motion, elliptical or pear-shaped, with the major axis pointed in the same direction as the prevailing winds.

But the physics are not strictly academic. Knowing a fire's intrinsic shape can suggest an escape strategy, albeit a desperate one:

The optimum escape path from a wildfire is at right angles to the direction of the prevailing winds, i.e. moving north or south when the wind is blowing from the east or west.

Which is what Branislav did now, run at a ninety-degree angle from the direction of the wind. He ran as hard as he could, and he kept on running until he intersected with a large pond. This pool of water saved his life.

Instinctively, Branislav knew which way to run. He had studied the topos before the mission, committed the terrain nearly to memory. He simply had no choice but to know the lay of the land if his team was to be successful hunting down enemy soldiers fleeing the scene.

The fire came, now, in great-sheeted flames from hell, a flaming wall of horror that swept along the shores of his little lake. The sky became red with balls of flame. Dense clouds of burning embers pushed relentlessly forward, riding the raging wind.

Suddenly there was a whirlwind of blazing, towering flames that rose high above the treetops. Branislav knew if he breathed in the superheated air he would die instantly.

Branislav peeled off his rucksack, emptied the contents in the sand at the edge of the lake, inverted the empty pack over his head and dropped down into the water, holding tight to the shoulder straps to keep it firmly in place. He swam as hard as he could for the middle.

The pack was watertight, and Branislav knew the small bubble of air he had captured inside it would act like a diving bell for a deep-sea diver. The trapped air would give him five to ten minutes of oxygen, enough perhaps for the firestorm to roar past. Either that or he would be brought to a boil, like a big chicken in a giant crock-pot.

Branislav could feel the heat as the fire closed on his position. The canvas of the rucksack was beginning to get warm, the water starting to churn. Fire was a death he did not relish. Better a bullet to the head or a knife to the belly.

•

•

It took fifteen minutes for the leading edge of the fire to rush past. By then he was out of air — and he thought — out of time. He peeked above the water, took a cautious breath and coughed.

Branislav dragged himself wet, cold, and overheated from the water. His face was badly burned on one side, as well as one hand. His buddies were nowhere in sight.

Branislav collapsed at the water's edge on the scorched earth. Everything was hot. Gingerly, he collected his essentials from the lake bottom. At the last second before he went under, he had had the presence of mind to dump the contents of his rucksack beneath him in the water — his jumek, his waterproof matches, his survival kit. Now he collected them, plus his gun, and stuffed them all back into his rucksack, along with whatever else he had dropped and could find. Survival, not killing the enemy, was on his mind.

The forest around him was a moonscape. Trunks of trees half-burned. Earth denuded of all ground cover. Smoking logs, burning bushes, smoldering bark. Unless they'd been in that lake like he was, no one could have survived the inferno.

The ground was too hot to walk on, so he retreated, stood knee-deep in the water for half a day. He had a bandana — which he kept continuously wet — over his nose and mouth. His eyes stung from the fumes, his throat hurt. *If only it would rain and wash some of this crap out of the air*, he thought.

But at least he still had his jumek, his jungle medical kit. Branislav knew his face was badly burned. Infection couldn't be far behind.

A soldier's jumek was normally stored in a waterproof satchel. And it was a good thing too, given what had happened. Plus, a jumek was far more complete than an ordinary home medical kit. A partial list of its contents would include such things as morphine, sulfa, a supply of gauze bandages and surgical tape, a syringe, laser scalpel, water purification tabs, assorted topical ointments and suppositories, including a microbicide antiseptic like Betadine, plus a two-week supply of Acceleron, and at least one bio-algorithm, for regrowing severely damaged tissue.

Still standing in the water, Branislav cut a strip from the sheet of bio-algorithm, smeared on a thick coating of Acceleron from the tube, and pressed it to his face. He winced. *It stung like hell!*

It was a mangled job, that face repair, done in the field under less-than-sterile conditions and without a mirror. But it would have to do.

In the next moment his head started to buzz and Branislav thought he might pass out. That's when he realized his comm implant was still functioning and that someone was trying to raise him on the military channel.

Now Branislav's spirits soared. *He was about to be rescued from this nightmare.* A line fed down from the airchop circling overhead and he reached for it.

Thank the Stars for Colonel Pappy Barnes!

CHAPTER NINE

▼

The solar sailship *S.S. Mars Voyager* unfurled its giant, titanium-ribbed sail and turned into the sun.

This was neither a quick nor a quiet process. The immense sail was stored in two footlocker-like compartments, one on either side of the massive ship. The compartment doors rode on a series of huge hydraulic pistons that also drew out the guide wires on which the sail's titanium ribs were suspended.

When completely unfurled and set at the proper angle to the sun, the thin filaments that lined the body of the sail would catch the solar wind and fill, just like a canvas sail would back home when stretching tight against the wind. Think of a big-masted sailing ship before the age of steam or coal or diesel. Fully extended, the solar sail was slightly egg-shaped, a giant ellipse nearly a full klom from tip to tail, with the big ship at its center.

The technology that made this all possible was rudimentary. Untold gigawatts of static electricity would build up each minute on the sail's surface as it billowed, and the ship would begin to lurch forward. Velocity was slow at first, but acceleration was nearly constant. Unfortunately, there was a constant crackling, practically a roar, as every few seconds the charge was bled off with a loud pop and a flash of white light. — But the ship itself would keep right on accelerating.

The noise and flashes of light took a bit of getting used to. But the passengers had plenty of time, six weeks in all. That's how long it took to tack back and forth across the solar wind to get everyone home to Earth from Mars. The outbound trip took half as long.

Butch Hogan looked down, now, watched Mars slip away beneath his feet. Though superficially alike, the Earth and Mars couldn't be more different. Mars was dry, with very little rain, although terraforming was beginning to change that. Its gravity was much weaker, barely a third of Earth's own. A visitor from Earth noticed the difference right off, from the very first step. No casual saunter here. Taking a step on Mars was more like swinging a pendulum. People tended to walk about sixty percent faster on the Red Planet than at home — and burn up about half as many calories doing so. A man had to watch his pizza intake; it was easy to get fat on Mars. Women were prone to forgetting. They all ate like horses, swelled up like balloons and looked hideous. Except one. She was onboard the *S.S. Mars Voyager* as well. He just hadn't gotten around to talking to her yet.

Down below, in the thin Martian atmosphere, temperatures fluctuated widely and rapidly, as did air pressure. Winds could be wild. Gusts up to a hundred kloms per hour were not uncommon. But they lacked destructive power, as the force they exerted was low, and they didn't cause the kinds of damage similar winds would on Earth.

In the morning, a man might see fog or frost or wispy blue clouds. Depending on which direction he looked — and at what time of day — the sky would likely have a different color. At noon, if you looked towards the horizon, dust scattering made the sky look red. The rising and setting sun was blue. Elsewhere, the sky was butterscotch. At all times, foot-traffic was treacherous. The principal reason was the ground never looked the same.

Butch looked at Mars, now in profile, as the big ship pulled slowly away. The sun shone on it, throwing weird shadows. Mars was boringly flat. Even Olympus Mons, the largest mountain in the solar system, though steep in places, had an average grade of only a few percent. Only on the rim of Valles Marineris did the topography get interesting. There, it was a bit like Canyonlands, in Utah, a place where Butch had often hiked with his father.

One other notable difference. Unlike the Home Planet, Mars lacked an ionosphere. Radios were useless except for point-to-point communications, never more than seven kloms apart, the distance to the horizon. The limiting factor was the planet's small size. Without a fortune in relay satellites or else tens of thousands of microwave towers, the planet could never be settled in a big way, a real drawback.

But from way up here — they were already five thousand kloms out and moving fast — none of it made any difference. Up here, in the sailship, so far away, it was all static electricity, crackle and pop and flashes of white light.

Butch couldn't be happier. After a long stint on Mars, he was finally on his way home, along with his good friend, Red Parsons. They were close, the two of them. They worked together, played together, chased tail together. But what really made Butch happy was that *she* was here too, onboard the

Mars Voyager. He had been with her only that once and hadn't been able to think of anything else since.

Butch began to say something to his friend. But he was interrupted by a sudden loud humming. Though the interior of the ship was heavily insulated, the buzz of the solar sails could at times be deafening. The noise often made talking difficult. It would remain that way for a short while then stop. A buildup of static electricity that had to be sloughed off.

The two men shrugged shoulders, slapped palms, and said "Later." Red decided to grab a nap before dinner. Butch excused himself, walked to the small aft lounge. There were windows back there, fairly large ones, where a person could safely look out at space.

The windows were darkly tinted now, on one side of the ship, to protect a passenger's eyes from the unfiltered sun. One thing stood out clearly, though — a trans-comet speeding its way through space from the outer reaches of the solar system to its eventual rendezvous with Venus. Wrapped in its thick plastic liner, the trans-comet was all shiny, far out of proportion to its size. As always, Man was fiddling with his environment, altering it, molding it, remaking it to his liking, just as He had been doing since that morning long ago, when He first climbed down out of the trees and stumbled out onto the African savanna.

But, for every man who wanted to change the environment to better meet Man's needs, there was another who thought it wiser to leave it alone, even if it meant suffering a lower standard of living or having a shortened lifespan. *As if the Garden of Eden were an actual place, and every bite of the apple since then had somehow distanced us from that idyllic time.*

Butch went to the bar, sat down, ordered a beer. Unlike some bars earth-side, no bot or other hardwired marvel of technology stood behind this counter. Here, service was doled out by a real, live bartender.

Besides the bartender, an older man was already sitting there at the counter, nursing a drink. The man was distinguished looking, like a college professor. Here, in the center of the ship, the crackling of the solar sails was barely audible. A man could have a conversation.

"What's your poison, old-timer?" Butch asked, sucking the head off his beer.

"Such endearing arrogance. And from such a young man too."

"Tell me, old-timer. Just how far up your ass can you get that thumb of yours anyway?"

"Do you always make friends so easily?"

"Only with korinthenkackers," Butch said, downing his beer and ordering another.

"Ah, the arrogant lout seeks to impress," the older man said, studying the contents of his glass. "Dare I ask what that foul-sounding word means?"

"Korinthenkacker. Translated from the German. It literally means 'raisin-crapper'. An anally retentive person. One who is overly concerned with trivial details. A word my father taught me one day when we were out hunting quail."

"Which is what you're now calling me? A raisin-crapper? I say again, young man — Do you always make friends so easily?"

"I work the high steel, tightening bolts, welding seams, that kind of thing. Making friends isn't really a job requirement, staying alive is."

Butch threw back the beer, ordered a third. "What do you do to make the mortgage, old-timer?"

"Can't say as I much care for the 'old-timer' label, young fella. But if you must know, I'm an economist. I make the mortgage back in Philadelphia, working for the Terraforming Commission."

"God save us, not the Flat Earth Society."

"That would be Kaleena Flanagan, not me."

"That sweet-smelling woman with you?"

"Kaleena's not my bunkmate, if that's what you mean. I already have a wife. But that sweet-smelling woman — to use your words — is an adjunct to the Commission. And she is influential. EMD Enterprises has plenty of detractors back home. It has plenty of allies back there as well, people who depend on that giant company to make *their* mortgages. The trans-comet trade has stirred up quite a hornet's nest in Congress. Some people want it shut down. That includes our Senator Flanagan. Now there's a man who you might classify as the original Flat-Earther. Sent his own daughter to poke around the Martian Motor Works, he did. Be his eyes and ears on the ground, as it were. Of course, Kaleena meets the definition of your standard tree-hugger type."

"But the woman is a real looker, isn't she?"

"Out of your league, chum."

"Is she actually the Senator's daughter? My impression of her was somehow different."

"They all look different when you have them horizontal, chum. But like I said: she's out of your league. Now tell me more about this high-steel job of yours."

"It's the highest of steel. Orbital steel. Me and my buddy, Red — he's also onboard — we repair EMDs aloft, in space, fifty or more kloms up."

"Working in space. Now that impresses me. And I'm not easily impressed. Didn't catch your name, young fellow."

"Butch. Butch Hogan. And yours?"

"Elijah Montrose, Ph.D."

"Glad to make your acquaintance, Eli. But I thought they kept all the economists locked up in the basement of the library? Why send one all the way the hell out here?"

"Let's see if I have this right. First I'm an old-timer. Then I'm a raisin-crapper. Now I'm some library geek that goes by the name of Eli? How do you expect to win me over if you insist on running me down?"

Butch softened. "Okay, let me apologize. Maybe I got off on the wrong foot and can start over. Hi, I'm Butch Hogan, God of the High Steel. What's your poison, professor?"

"A glass of red wine would suit me just fine, thank you." They shook hands. Butch ordered his new friend a flask of merlot.

"So tell me, Doc. Why the hell would they send an economist all the way out here?"

"To fix a broken window."

"Come again?"

Elijah Montrose was about to explain, when Kaleena Flanagan walked into the room. Butch's eyes immediately lit up.

"Not you again," she growled.

Up she strolled, this tall, leggy woman in full bloom. Butch must have audibly sighed his approval when she came into view, because she gave him a dirty look. Gorgeous women are like that. They know they're gorgeous. They prefer men who don't fall all over themselves to get attention. But Butch couldn't help himself.

"Seriously, Kaleena. You can't just stand there and tell me we didn't have fun together the other night."

"Any fun we may have had together that night was purely accidental, the alcohol talking."

"Nah, it was more than that. A righteous man deserves the truth."

"Says who?"

"A righteous man deserves the truth. He also deserves one mortal life, long and sweet, complete with carnal love, irresponsible youth, disappointing adulthood, and healthy old age. How would you like to spend that life with me?" Butch smiled his most adoring smile.

Kaleena rolled her eyes and turned away.

"Looks like you two want to be alone." This, from Elijah Montrose. "Told you she was out of your league," he whispered as he got up and moved a few barstools down to give them some space.

"Doc, no need to relocate on my account," Kaleena said. "I have no designs on this man." She moved to the opposite end of the bar.

Butch followed her with his eyes. He couldn't help but notice the girl's fine-looking bottom. It was round in all the right places. He thought to comment but decided against it.

Kaleena turned and caught him staring at her. No dirty look this time. "We need to find you a steady woman, Butch," she said. "Someone other than me. I know for a fact, there are a number of unattached females onboard. Perhaps one will suit your needs."

Butch drifted down to join her, put his hand on the bar near hers. "You make shopping for a woman sound like a trip to the clothing rack in a department store. Take one in the dressing room, try it on for size. If the bloody thing doesn't fit, return it for a full refund."

"Well, yes, it is a little bit like that."

"You can't possibly be serious. Does that include you?"

"I'm currently unattached, if that's what you mean."

"Believe me, I'd shop no further if all the merchandise looked like you."

"I come at a pretty steep price."

"Money's no object with me."

"No? What makes you so special?"

"I'm filthy with the stuff."

"Really?"

"It comes with exercising great care in the selection of one's parents."

"Now you're pulling my leg."

"Indeed I am. And the damn thing came right off in my hand."

"So you're poor?"

"That's not entirely accurate either. I stand to inherit a five-hundred-acre ranch someday. Plus, I have a job. It pays rather well."

"True happiness is neither places nor things."

"Spoken like a true trust-fund baby. Why didn't you tell me you were the daughter of a United States Senator?"

"Would it have made any difference? Any fool knows true happiness is not money; it is the supremacy and achievements of the mind."

"Is that why they call you Kaleena? — because you're some sort of Hare Krishna Buddhist monk?"

"No, my brother's the one in the religion business. But he would say the same — As we use mind, we grow more mind."

"I think I need another beer."

"Don't be a drill bit. The Creator Himself is a Universal Mind. We know Him by His works. The Heavens, which are also His works, declare His glory. The Firmament showeth His industry."

"What the hell kind of religion is that? — And what does your brother have to do with it?"

"My brother Joseph is a Father."

"Of the Catholic persuasion?"

Kaleena flashed her best Irish smile. "The discovery of steam turned the Earth into a factory. It sent trains at fearful speed down iron tracks. It sent ships to plow the deep. The Man who harnessed lightning made it as docile as a lamb. That same Man, the one who can now flash messages to the far ends of the galaxy in no time at all, He has become all-knowing, like his Father. By wire, by cable, by comm, by radio — there is no place, now, where Man's voice cannot be heard."

"I don't know if another beer's going to be enough. You're beginning to scare me."

"I don't mean to be scary, Butch — or sacrilegious. But I'm not sure I like everything that technology has wrought. The more Man uses the intelligence and life breathed into him at Creation, the more he destroys the very God that made him."

"Honestly, girl. We've never known more, had more, or been further . . . "

" . . . or had more starving people, or more slaves, or more political prisoners . . . "

" . . . or better health care, or more leisure time, or longer life spans . . . "

" . . . or dirtier water, or fewer acres of unspoiled wilderness, or more endangered species . . . "

"Is it progress you hate, Kaleena, or just free enterprise?"

Her face reddened. "How can I make you understand?"

"I've upset you, and for that I apologize." He touched her hand, gazed deeply into her eyes.

She appreciated the attention. "Now I see what must have turned me on to you the first time we met."

"My good looks?"

"There is that. Plus those wonderful, boyish eyes."

"Comes from constantly being out-of-doors. Back in the world, I fairly live outdoors. When I was a kid, growing up in Wyoming, I was a Boy Scout. Went to summer camp, hunted weekends with my dad, spent plenty of time sleeping under the stars."

"I like the part about sleeping under the stars. But you get no points from me for being a hunter. I'm not a big fan of guns."

"Maybe it is you who doesn't understand. We could make a life up there, you and me, in the wilds of Wyoming somewhere, away from the hustle. The Hogan Ranch is in the shadow of the Laramie Mountains, south of Casper."

"Yeah, maybe. I do love the out-of-doors. Though you'll have to leave the firearms at home if you want to be with me."

"Nothing like making an easy decision tough."

"I know you may find this hard to believe, but when I was a kid, I was a tomboy."

"A spoon-fed girl like you?"

"The spoon only came later."

"Actually, the way I see it, a tomboy's the best kind of girl a guy could ever have."

"How's that, tough guy?"

"A girl like that can wrestle a man to the ground, yet still know what to do with him once she's got him pinned."

"The Laramie Mountains, eh?"

"Yeah, in the Medicine Bow National Forest."

"Sounds nice."

"That sounds suspiciously close to a 'yes' to me."

"Perhaps it is. I like the way you think, Butch Hogan."

"In that case, my shopping days are over. I've found the merchandise I was searching for."

"Don't be too hasty, Pilgrim. This merchandise can't be returned once the packaging's been removed. Plus, there's no warranty. You break it, it's yours. What you see is what you get."

"I like what I see — and I'll take what I can get."

"You'll have to do better than that, if you want to strike a deal with this girl."

"A test run, then. Say, six months. Give me six months to close the deal. Otherwise, you can return the merchandise for a full refund, no questions asked."

"Six months is too long. I give you the length of the trip home, plus one month earth-side, to make the sale. After that, I'm gone."

"I can live with that. Anyway, I work best under pressure."

"I guess we've struck a deal then. Now as to price. You'll have to negotiate that with my father."

"A bride-price is a little old-fashioned, don't you think?"

"What I think is that you have the cart before the horse. On some things, the Senator is very old-fashioned."

"From what I've seen of your father in the news, I should think the Senator would be a pushover, where his daughter was concerned."

"Don't count your chickens, Pilgrim. Once my father sets his sights on something, there'll be no backing down."

CHAPTER TEN

▼

It had been a quiet night in Hedon City. There were only three new dead bodies in the Hedon City morgue when Senator Patrick Flanagan got the call from the District Coroner to come claim his son's remains.

One of the dead was a busty black woman whose body had been crushed and mangled in a gtruck accident; the second, a skinny white man, who had died of a massive gunshot wound, no doubt from a force gun at close range; the third, another white man, emaciated like the first, also dead from a pulse blaster, but dressed in vestments, tattered and soiled. All three were clearly drug addicts, one with a serious blue-devil addiction. Two of the three had been easily identified by their subcutaneous implants, tiny microchips every citizen carried, which stored all of a person's essential biometric data — blood profile, identicard number, interbank sequence, gene-map. The third, the one dressed as a priest, had had his implant surgically removed within the last year.

Father Joseph Flanagan's death hadn't come as a complete surprise to the Senator — his son had been committing suicide the slow, painful way for years. The surprise was in the manner of death, a gunshot wound to the chest. It was like a sign from God, a picture-perfect opportunity for the Senator to put a personal face on his Gun Control legislation and thus advance his political agenda.

Senator Flanagan thought carefully about what he must do — and how he must do it. The Senator was not a fancy dresser. It was said that only Senator Flanagan could turn frumpy clothing into a political statement. But this occasion was different. It called for him to look the part. He put on his best dark suit and, before boarding a suborb for Hedon City, had his chief of staff call a news conference on the steps of the Capitol. Invitations went out to President Noah Benjamin's entire administration, plus most of the Congress. The Senator rehearsed his lines as he dressed. Now he stood before them all with vidcams rolling and security bots trawling the crowd for trouble.

Senator Patrick Flanagan cleared his throat. He brushed back a tear, wiped his eyes. In the audience, Senator Alexander Hoagland watched the man perform. It made him sick.

"Fellow citizens. Today I am forced to perform a most distasteful task. Today I must travel halfway across this great land of ours to visit a coroner in Hedon City. Once there I must go down to the city morgue and make a positive identification of my dead son.

"Now, as painful as this is for me, this simply is not news. Every day in this country a parent somewhere must do the same horrible thing.

"But let me tell you what is news. My son wasn't a threat to society. In fact, my son was a priest, a man of the cloth. He ministered to the poor and the forgotten. But, like so many others, he was also a man who was gunned down in the streets of his hometown like a common criminal. Like so many other American families, my family has become victim to the scourge of the past two centuries, the very scourge I have been trying to eradicate my entire adult life, the cancer that has been gnawing at the soul of this great nation — guns in the hands of the irresponsible."

Flanagan choked back a tear, certainly for effect. "Do you see now what I mean, America? Guns have become the scourge of the land. You know my feelings about this, America. For me, this is no longer a theoretical discussion about the Second Amendment. Nor is this merely a question of whether or not the Second Amendment ought to be repealed. No, after what has happened, this is now about the death of my one and only son."

The reporters started to bark out questions. But Patrick Flanagan waved them off. "I'm sorry, but I'll not be taking questions today. That's all."

When the vidcams went cold and the microphones moved away, Senator Alexander "Xander" Hoagland approached Flanagan on the Capitol steps. Hoagland detested the other man. He hated everything Flanagan stood for. In public, Flanagan had a folksy air. His demeanor charmed people. It was the perfect costume for a crafty man intent upon fooling the citizens into thinking that he spoke for the common people, when in fact he claimed an elite pedigree on both sides of his family.

Yet, despite his dislike for the other man, Xander did feel genuinely sorry for him. Losing a son wasn't easy, not at any age. Xander had lost a son himself, to war ten years ago.

"May I accompany you?" Hoagland asked earnestly as the steps of the Capitol cleared.

"Excuse me?"

"May I please come with you?"

"To the coroner's office in Hedon City?" Flanagan growled.

"What you have to do today isn't easy. Please allow me to accompany you."

"You're not trying to run some kind of game on me, now are you Hoagland? Trying to steal some of my thunder?"

"No game, Patrick. But when I lost my son, all I can remember thinking is how I could have used some moral support. I wouldn't have made it without Laura. You don't even have that."

"I don't want your sympathy, Alexander. But we can talk shop on the flight over there, if you want. Most days it's about a fifteen-minute hop from D.C. to Hedon City. But we do have to hurry. My driver says the suborb is fueled and ready to launch."

Flanagan had a limo waiting and the two men got in, along with their security bots and flesh bodyguards. The driver, a dark-skinned AfriAm, whisked them away, turning onto Congressional Parkway, a private roadway reserved solely for a short list of high-ranking government officials. The roadway had been built at extraordinary expense in the name of national security. But the real reason was so that a select few — namely busy lawmakers and their chief campaign contributors — wouldn't get caught in traffic and be late for an important meeting.

Xander had voted against building this roadway, and the waste of money still got his goad. *This sort of extravagance marks the beginning of the end for democracy,* he thought as they drove. *When government hands out privilege to government.*

"And how do you like my ride?" Flanagan asked, raising his hand in an arrogant fashion.

A limousine liberal, Xander Hoagland thought grimly. *Someone who has absolutely no idea where money comes from or how the less fortunate struggle to get by.*

"This is your ride?" Hoagland harrumphed. "Maybe you have it confused. All the privileges you enjoy are paid for with the People's money."

"Don't hold it against me if you're a sap. Don't make it my fault if you choose to naively save the taxpayers' money by driving something more sensible. Honestly, Alexander. If you're upset with me now, wait 'til you see my suborb. I spared no expense."

"You mean the taxpayers spared no expense."

"Yes, whatever."

Hoagland shook his head. Xander had made his money the hard way, one dollar at a time. He was proud of that. Chance favors the prepared mind. When you come from people who have inherited, the work ethic is diminished. When you come from people who have achieved in life, you tend to absorb the habit of achievement.

"I don't hold it against you, Patrick. I just question your motives."

They were just now approaching the river and the outer edge of the Dome. All of the District of Columbia, parts of Virginia and Maryland, virtually the entire tidal basin was under one glass roof, the D.C. Dome. The suborbport was beyond the Potomac in Maryland.

"I have the most noble of motives. The people know that. But the people don't know what is best for them. Someone has to decide, someone of higher moral stature, someone of greater intellectual accomplishment."

"And that someone is you?" Hoagland was incredulous.

"Indeed it is. And you as well."

"Don't include me in your sick parlor game. I have a different vision, a different idea of government, an older idea."

"Neolithic, I would suppose."

"Make fun if you like. It's an old idea, I admit. But it's still the newest, most unique idea in all the long history of Man."

"I suppose you're talking about democracy."

The gcar slowed. The driver showed his identicard and the limousine passed out of the Dome and into the commercial district.

"Yes, Patrick, the idea that government is beholden to the people. This is the central issue in every election. Do we believe in our capacity for self-government, or do we abandon the American Revolution?"

"You make the whole thing sound like Rome and the death of the Republic."

"Isn't it? The conceit that an intellectual elite in a distant capital can plan the people's lives better than the people themselves can plan them. This *is* the death of the Republic."

"You question my sincerity, my humanitarian motives?"

"Not at all. But these elites — people like yourself — would gladly trade our hard-fought freedoms for ever-greater security. Where does it end?"

"Seriously, Alexander. In a world of bloodthirsty terrorists and determined State enemies, the people simply have to accept the obvious. To remain safe, they must be willing to surrender some of their privacy, some of their liberties."

"The people need not surrender anything. I think it was C.S. Lewis who said it best: 'The greatest evil is not done now in those sordid dens of crime that Dickens loved to paint. It is not even done now in the concentration camps or labor camps or gulags. In those places we all see its final result, and understand it. Nowadays the greatest evil is conceived and ordered — and moved and seconded and carried and logged in the minutes — by quiet men with white collars and clean fingernails and smooth-shaven cheeks, by men in clean, carpeted, warm and well-lit offices, men who do not need to raise their voices to have their instructions carried out'."

Flanagan was about to mount a rebuttal when his driver said, "Senator, we are here. At the suborbport."

"Thank you, Jones. Drop us at the ramp, will you?"

"Very good, sir."

•

•

Minutes later, they were airborne, the two of them, with their security detail, headed fifteen hundred kloms to the northwest, where Hedon City lay at the foot of Lake Michigan. Senator Flanagan's personal suborb was every bit as luxurious as he had intimated. Nonetheless, they felt the sting of two-g's of acceleration as they rose steeply over the D.C. Dome and into the morning sky.

Hoagland apologized as soon as they broke through the clouds. "I'm sorry we fought. That was not my intention. I know you have a hard day ahead of you. The morgue and all that."

"The morgue's the best place for him."

"You can't possibly mean that."

"Oh, but I do. Now, may we please change the subject?"

"If you wish." Hoagland took a moment. "I read what you gave me."

Lost in thought, Flanagan was slow to reply. "What did I give you?"

"A copy of your Gun Control bill."

"Oh, that. I truly didn't think you would get past the first page."

"I barely got past the first paragraph. It literally made me sick to my stomach. Honestly, Patrick. Something like fifteen percent of the population owns a firearm. You really want to make all these good people felons simply because they refuse to surrender their weapons? All you'll get for your trouble is armed insurrection."

"Fifteen percent of the population still smoked tobacco when we outlawed smoking. No one objected to that."

"At the time, it was a highly questionable move, to be sure, just as outlawing alcohol was back in the twentieth century. But neither of those pursuits were guaranteed by the Constitution."

"We have had this discussion before, Alexander. It's a nonstarter."

"But your Gun Control bill calls for legalizing warrant-less searches."

"Only in the narrow instance where a firearm is believed to have been used in the commission of a crime."

"But that excuse could become routine. Is this your idea of surrendering more of our hard-fought freedoms in order to secure our safety? You can't unring a bell."

The sky briefly darkened and the g-forces lessened. The suborb was approaching the apogee of its flight and would soon start down.

"Tough times call for tough measures," Flanagan answered.

"Another sound bite?"

"Say what you will, Alexander, but the time is ripe for this legislation."

"The Second Amendment protects us all."

"Except, of course, those who happen to get shot. Or those who happen to die at the hands of a gun-toting criminal. Or an angry husband. Or a jilted lover. Or a crazed maniac. The Second Amendment certainly didn't protect my son."

"That's what prisons are for."

"Is my son's killer in prison?"

"No, not yet. But then it's only been a couple of days."

"How about the sociopath who slaughtered those people at the stadium? That was weeks ago."

"He'll be brought to justice. The police have leads. The Bureau has an entire task force on it. Give them time."

"There'd be no need for the police — or the Bureau — if we made the people surrender their weapons and took the frigging guns off the streets."

"Then the criminals would have all the weapons and the people needing protection would be defenseless."

"Like my son." Flanagan got quiet. There was a moment of weightlessness as the ship came over the top of its flight path and they began their descent into Hedon City.

"Sometimes it happens to even the most well-intentioned parent. Unfortunately, Patrick, this is what professional ambition sometimes does to a man. It takes him into the world and away from his family. He spends his weekends at the office arguing over child-friendly welfare legislation, while his kids are at home pushing rocks with a stick in the driveway thinking: *When is Dad coming home?* It happens to the best of us."

"I never had any time for the boy, it's true. Joseph was drawn to the Church because those people paid attention to him."

"Tending to the flock is an honorable business."

"No, Alexander, it really isn't. The boy had unnatural urges. That's why he turned to drugs."

"You can hardly blame yourself for that."

"Oh, but I do. I may have unnatural urges as well."

"About being homosexual?"

"You know about that?"

"Yes, I do." There was suddenly newfound confidence in Hoagland's tone.

"Even in this day and age, that is highly inflammatory information."

"But only because you've vehemently denied it all these years."

"Just exactly what do you propose to do with this information?"

"Perhaps I can threaten to make it public. Perhaps I can leverage that threat to keep you from pursuing this cursed Gun Control bill of yours."

"The faggot's soft on the Constitution. Is that what you have in mind?"

"Yes, something like that."

"Well then go ahead and make the nasty information public. I won't back down. I don't like threats, and you have no evidence."

"Actually, I do. We have you on tape."

"You're taping this conversation? How dare you!"

"I think you said it best. — Desperate times call for desperate measures. Plus, I have vid."

"What vid?"

"Well actually, we have several vid streams. At your home, in that nice limo of yours, here aboard this fancy suborb, even inside your love shack in Hedon City. One vid is particularly revealing, a vid of you with a male prostitute. First in some sleaze-bag, charge-by-the-hour joint in Hedon City, then again later in a private apartment, which it turns out is owned by you."

"How?"

"That estranged son of yours. I guess the boy needed money. Father Joseph set you up — but good. The building manager had the room wired. We've got you in your own love shack doing it with your boyfriend. Sound and vid. A real drill bit, if you ask me, a big black guy, an AfriAm. We have his statement, signed, sealed, and delivered."

"It'll never stand up to scrutiny, Alexander. You had no warrant. You had no right."

"Ironic. Your defense is to claim a warrant-less search? Tell that to all the law-abiding citizens you want to make into felons just because they own a gun."

"I could be ruined."

"The thought had crossed my mind."

"What do you want from me, you bloodsucker?"

"I told you. Put a stop to this Gun Bill."

"I can't do that."

"I could just as easily call a press conference of my own for after we land. Think of it, Patrick. I would be live with Annabel Clark of the American News Network inside that hotel room, inside *your* hotel room. The network would run some vid of the liaison that took place inside your apartment. Then a cut to your last public denial claiming not to be a homosexual. It could be juicy, real juicy."

Flanagan was quiet for a moment. The suborb was on final approach, and the ground was rushing up to meet them. Finally, he spoke:

"I'm calling your bluff, Hoagland. I think the electorate is more forgiving than you give them credit for. There have been other gay legislators. Go ahead, do your worst. I am not backing down."

"They might not forgive murder."

"Murder? That's ridiculous!"

"You certainly had motive."

"To kill my own son? I didn't even know what he had done to betray me until you told me, just moments ago."

"Innuendo and implication. Let the public draw their own conclusions. But no matter what you do, one fact is indisputable. You were here, in Hedon City, with your boyfriend, the night before last, the same night your son was murdered."

"Like I said, Alexander. Go ahead and do your worst. I have a son to bury and a daughter to notify that her only brother is dead. Kaleena is still five weeks out from Earth, onboard the *Mars Voyager*, trying to get me some answers on this latest venture of that giant octopus, EMD Enterprises. Maybe the public would be interested in what she has to say. Your old Wall Street buddy, Spencer Trask, now head of the Federal Reserve, is a major investor in Transcomet Industries. Two can play at this game, you know."

"I know that very well. How do you think we came to surveill you in the first place, and to do so in so many different locations?"

"We? Who else is involved in this nonsense besides you?"

"At the behest of my sub-committee, the Justice Department has been looking into your financial affairs."

"You brought Justice into this? What gives you the right?"

"Before you go squealing like a stuck pig to the press claiming that your civil rights have been violated, let's be clear. The legal eagles at Justice executed valid search warrants for every plug placed on your comm lines, plus every inch of vid shot, in every location. All strictly by the book, Patrick. The warrants were duly issued by a proper judge with valid authority."

"You saying I'm being investigated? — On what grounds?"

"I suppose there is no harm in telling you now. The investigation is nearly complete anyway. Should any indictments be forthcoming, that's really not my decision. That's up to the boys at the Justice Department."

"What am I being accused of?"

"For a long time now, there have been persistent rumors of influence peddling. Illegal payola. That kind of thing."

"You take me down, I'll take down your boy Trask too. You really want the head of the Federal Reserve dragged through this muck? It should work wonders for investor confidence in our banking system."

"The problem with brinkmanship is that one never knows until afterward when he has gone too far."

"Then I suggest you not stand too close to the edge on this one."

Alexander Hoagland turned thoughtful. "I suppose I might be persuaded not to disclose the fact that you were here in Hedon City the night your son was killed. For the moment anyway."

"In which case, I suppose I might be persuaded not to out your friend Spencer Trask."

"And maybe Justice can be persuaded to sit on those indictments a while longer, at least until after the election."

"So you see? We have managed to step safely back from the brink."

"For now."

CHAPTER ELEVEN

▼

Butch washed down the last of his lunch, pushed back from the table and strolled down the wide main corridor to the Commons.

The *S.S. Mars Voyager* was a large ship, the size of a major resort back home. It had to be. There was no other way to keep one hundred and eighty-two people from going stir-crazy in the six weeks it took to get from the Red Planet home. People needed diversions. They had to be entertained, made to feel at ease. Amenities included multiple visicast theatres, exercise rooms, several eating facilities, a swimming pool, putting green, that kind of thing. Each passenger had ample private space — a large bedroom with private bath and emote wall, plus dining area, sitting area with Comfy Chair, and workspace with e-net access. There was a park, complete with ducks and paddlewheel boats. The *Voyager*'s constant acceleration produced about one-g of pseudogravity, enough to keep water in the pond and everyone's lunch in their stomach.

Even with the diversions, it didn't take long for people to begin getting on each other's nerves. In no time at all, every subject discussed had a grinding, jagged edge to it. Religion, politics, sports. It didn't matter. People were long on opinion and short on patience. Every topic was explosive, to be discussed only at great personal risk.

The weather? — There was no weather, just blinding darkness with the occasional flash of blue light.

Fashion? — Forget it. People stopped caring early on how anyone else dressed, least of all themselves.

Food? — Bland, like wallpaper paste, with little specks of meat thrown in.

Entertainment? — Anyone who had been on Mars a while had already viewed the entire library of vids, or at least the ones that interested them. What remained was pathetic junk, and no new vids had been added to the library since the last ship from Earth set down three months ago.

Spiders on the wall? — Everyone had begun to see them. Whether or not they were actually there was an open question. *But the hairy things scared the hell out of Butch at night when he couldn't sleep.*

Fear of confinement did not mix well with spaceflight. Indeed, the voyager who journeyed into space dare not have phobias of any kind, not claustrophobia, not agoraphobia, no unnatural fears whatsoever. Oh, there was medicine people could take — sedatives and the like — but being doped up for six weeks could lead to a lifelong addiction all its own.

Still, people had fears. Any ship could become a coffin, no matter how sophisticated. A spacejockey knew this instinctively. But a man had to bury that thought deep down when he was aloft. Better to focus instead on the little things — his next meal, his next exercise period, saving his shower minutes for when he really needed them.

Now about those showers. At one time or another in his career, Butch had traveled aboard just about every sort of iron bucket Space Command had in its fleet, from the tiniest tug to the largest transport. In all but the largest ships, where space was not at such a premium, the showers left much to be desired. A tiny cubicle, a handheld hose with a pathetic nozzle, a metal drain in the floor, a plastic tent cocooned around your body. The water pressure was a joke, the soap would never lather, the spent water would hardly run off a man's body. The cubicle was so cramped, a man couldn't pick up a dropped bar of soap to save his life.

And how many hands did the engineers think a person had anyway? One to hold the hose, another to hold the bar of soap, a third to wash himself with, a fourth to keep the plastic tent from collapsing around his body? Made a man want to forget the whole damn thing, go native, and spray on a bit more deodorant in the morning.

But it was far worse in microgravity, everything was. When a ship was coasting along in zero-g, all sorts of space anomalies began to pile up. Warmer air and gases refused to rise, colder liquids and water wouldn't sink, candles refused to stay lit. Flames that were normally oval-shaped back on Earth were now suddenly hemispherical.

In a zero-g environment, everything was off-key. Without gravity, there was no convection. When a person slept, a thin layer of nearly-body-temperature air would form around them — and it would stay put. In zero-g, warm air wasn't any lighter than the cold air around it. Thus, it wouldn't rise and drift away. Instead, it would collect at its source. Unless a man ran the air conditioning all night long, he would sweat like a pig.

But the anomalies didn't end there. Zero-g wreaked havoc on the human form, playing a host of nasty, body-deforming tricks on it. The human body is mostly water. It depends on gravity to maintain its shape and to function properly. Without gravity, faces bloat, tits shrink, hips expand. Bladders won't empty. Neither will colons. Constipation becomes a problem. So does keeping food down. Menstrual cycles are in a class all their own, and must be suppressed.

And then there is the anomaly no one is brave enough to talk about. Every single morning the men wake up with amazing, rock-hard erections, erections so hard they can sometimes be painful. Now mind you, this isn't your ordinary morning wood; this is morning lumber, morning Ponderosa-pine-style lumber. It's just one more gift courtesy of zero-g, as excess fluid collects in the penis, just as it does in the face and other parts of the body.

But, with or without gravity, living at close quarters aboard a spaceship took its toll. Spend enough time cooped up in a small space with enough people and fights will erupt, even between close friends, especially between lovers. They were three days out from Mars, when the wheels first fell off the wagon.

On that fateful day Butch made the mistake of talking religion. The news had come down in the daily vidcast that the Pope had died and that the cardinals were gathering in Rome to pick a successor. Butch wasn't the sort who attended church regularly and, in fact, held organized religion in rather low esteem. He seemed to have forgotten Kaleena was a Catholic, when he made a crack about the gathering of the cardinals. Then again, maybe he just wanted to pick a fight.

"Why bother?" he said, treading in dangerous water.

"What do you mean, why bother?" she snapped sharply.

"Nothing new under the sun, not where that bunch of pointed hats is concerned."

"The cardinal system helps keep out the radical elements."

"Thus leaving a dead religion completely devoid of new ideas."

"More like a venerable institution, one that has been a moral compass for nearly 2500 years."

"Moral compass? — Don't make me laugh. That moral compass you value so highly ran whorehouses back in the Middle Ages, harbored pedophiles and fags in every age, became the world's largest owner of shopping malls and shipping lines in modern times, and generally turned its back on the very poor it professed to protect. Hypocrites. The entire lot of them. Hypocrites."

"Is that a chip I see on your shoulder or just bird poop?"

"No chip, just anger. Hypocrisy wigs me out."

"And to think I was falling for you."

"And I for you."

"Well, this could be a deal-breaker. So you had better start explaining yourself."

"Okay, I will. Let's say I send you to a stockbroker for investment advice . . ."

"What the hell does investment advice have to do with being Catholic?"

"Do you want me to explain it to you or not?"

Kaleena harrumphed and began to pout.

"Okay, then shut up and listen. I send you to a stockbroker for investment advice. At your first meeting, the man tells you he never invests, never buys a mutual fund, avoids government bonds like the plague, in fact thinks that capitalism itself is a little weird. Just how comfortable would you feel entrusting your hard-earned money to this man?"

"Not very."

"But, as a Catholic, you are willing to take advice — family advice, no less, moral advice, sexual advice — from a man who has sworn off sex, sworn off marriage, sworn off children, and forsaken the accumulation of property and wealth? Something doesn't seem right here, sister."

"I see where you are going with this."

"Do you? Do you really? The plain truth is that in this world there is an exceptionally narrow void between savagery and idealism."

"Could you be just a little more jaded?"

"Perhaps not. But just look at what idealism has given us — communism, Christianity, and frequent use of the guillotine. Savagery has given us equally fine results — gulags, more Christianity, plus the firing squad."

"How is it that Christianity made both your hate-lists?"

"Savagery and idealism. The twin evils of mankind. Each one reeks of prejudice and intolerance. Everything we hold dear manages to exist only in that narrow void between the two extremes."

"But isn't religion an important part of what we hold dear?"

"Religion, yes. Christianity, no. Near as I can tell, every last one of them is either a pagan or a hypocrite — or both. And the papists, well they're the worst."

"I'm Catholic. That makes me a papist."

"If you want to call yourself that. But think of all the harm these people have done, all the pain they have inflicted on the world — the Crusades, the Holocaust, white slavery, ethnic cleansing, the Inquisition. No matter which way you turn, it's always the same. Savage and naïve; crude and idealistic."

"This has gone on long enough."

"Yeah, nearly 2500 years."

"No, I mean this discussion has gone on long enough."

"But do you at least see now what I've been trying to say?"

"All I see now is the two of us sleeping in separate beds tonight."

"Kaleena . . . "

But she was already walking away.

CHAPTER TWELVE

▼

By ship's clock it was now midday.

For the six-week-long trip home from Mars, the ship and crew stayed on a 24-hour day, with fifteen daylight hours, nine darkness hours, plus a brief dusk and dawn each day. Studies had shown that stress levels were reduced when there were more light hours than dark and when a regular daily rhythm was maintained.

About this time each day — midday — most people had lunch then milled around the Commons a few hours to gab before taking a late-afternoon nap. The blue-ribbon delegation to Mars was a sizeable group, government types from the Terraforming Commission, plus stiff necks from EMD Enterprises, a few journalists and a handful of academic types. That last group included Elijah Montrose, Ph.D. For days, now, representatives of each group had been trying to arrive at some consensus regarding the safety issues Frederick Krotchmeier refused to address in his presentation that day back on the floor of the factory dining hall.

Butch entered the Commons, spied Elijah Montrose sitting in front of an e-terminal. People spent hours in front of these machines, playing games, sending messages, running sims, searching for information. In their rooms, they mainly watched porn. There was an extensive library of it onboard.

"How's it hanging, Doc?"

Elijah looked up from the machine. "Always on the jazz, aren't you?" There was a complex, multi-stage spreadsheet on the screen.

"I got sidetracked yesterday with Kaleena."

"A girl like Kaleena will sidetrack a guy like you every time."

"Ain't that the truth."

"And don't you forget it."

Elijah saved his work. With the new 3-D screens, graphical presentations of complex data sets were much easier to visualize and digest compared to earlier, flat-screen methods.

As the machine hibernated, his screensaver popped up, a digi-pix of his wife and children. Elijah missed them all badly.

"Before I got sidetracked, you were saying something about being sent to Mars to repair a broken window. What was that all about anyway? There are precious few windows on Mars, and certainly no broken ones."

For a second the older man looked confused. Then he remembered. "Ah, yes, the Broken Window Fallacy. Strange that you should remember that."

"Something about the way you said it sparked my interest. In the year and a half since I landed on that rock, I never once heard of anyone breaking a window. Why would they send an economist all the way to Mars to repair something that wasn't broken?"

"The Broken Window Fallacy is a metaphor. My interests are purely academic, I assure you. I am conducting a study of *choice* and *maximization*."

"You do research, Doc? Is that what I saw on your computer screen?"

"Yes, I have to participate in several symposiums when I get back to Philadelphia. Right now my team at Carnegie-Mellon is working on buying-habit surveys. We're in the process of developing a qualitative scale that economists can use to judge whether or not a given consumer is actually a maximizer when they make a choice."

"I only had one semester of econ a thousand years ago in, like, the twelfth grade. I didn't really pay much attention. But isn't the assumption of every consumer being a maximizer a bedrock belief in your line of work?"

"It most certainly is — and that's precisely the point. But is it actually true? Do people actually maximize? To find out, we have people rate themselves on certain statements. True or false? — *When I watch a vid stream, I constantly channel surf, scanning through all the available visicasts, even while attempting to watch a single program.* Subjects rate themselves from 1 to 10 on fifteen statements of that sort, from Completely Agree to Completely Disagree. Then, depending on their score, we rate the subjects one of four ways: as a maximizer, an extreme maximizer, a satisficer, or an extreme satisficer."

"I guess I never really thought much about it. Isn't everyone a maximizer in one way or another?"

"Barely a third. Which kicks away one of the three legs holding up traditional economics. More choices make you happy, right? Wrong. More choices make you tense. They make you nervous, even irritable. Should I have picked the yellow one or the red one? Did I get the best deal or not? After a certain point, more choices only serve to make us *un*happy."

"That's certainly the opposite of what I was taught. Plus, it runs contrary to commonsense."

"Much of economics is like that — counterintuitive. And that includes the Broken Window Fallacy."

"I wondered when you were going to get around to explaining that."

"The Broken Window Fallacy is the central fallacy underlying all socialist thinking. Whenever a government program is justified by the number of jobs it promises to create — rather than its merits — remember the Broken Window Fallacy. The plot goes something like this: Some teenagers, being the sub-human primates that they are, toss a brick through the window of a local delicatessen. A crowd gathers and laments: *Oh, what a shame.* But before you know it, some idiot comes along and suggests a silver lining to the whole sordid affair. The deli owner makes a lot of money, he says. Now he'll have to spend some of that fat bankroll to have his window repaired. This is a good thing, he says. This will add to the income of the community, beginning with the window repairman. After fixing the window, the repairman will spend his newfound income on other goods, which will add to another vendor's income, and so on around the block. The chain of new spending will multiply and it will generate higher income and employment throughout the community."

"Doc, what kind of weed they let you smoke there in Philadelphia? That's just about the dumbest thing I ever heard. Please don't sit there with a straight face and tell me that if these teenagers later go on a rampage and break a whole lot of windows, that all that damage will produce an economic boom. — Because that's just plain crazy."

"Now you're beginning to grasp the essence of the Fallacy. Most people fall for it. But guys like us say — *Heh, wait a damn minute.* If the deli owner hadn't spent his money fixing that broken window, he might have blown his wad on that new suit he was saving up for. Had he done that instead, then the tailor would have had that new income to spend, and so on down the line. The broken window didn't create any new net spending; it simply diverted spending from somewhere else. Whether it's caused by a hurricane or a tornado or an idiot teenager with a brick in his hand, the broken window does not create new activity, just different activity. People see the activity that takes place and draw conclusions based on that activity. What they don't see is the activity that *would* have taken place. Thus, the wrong conclusions are drawn."

"I see that all the time. People are constantly drawing the wrong conclusions about things. Remember all that business years ago about global warming? The sky never did fall."

"The problem runs deeper. The Broken Window Fallacy is perpetrated in many insidious ways. If you substitute taxes for the broken window in that story, you get the idea. A jobs program has to be paid for. Raise a guy's taxes to pay for it and his other spending declines. A government cannot create jobs by raising taxes. Economic growth does not spring from job creation, it springs from job *destruction*."

"Now you've lost me. I'm a bit of a drill bit, I'll admit. But I thought the goal of government was to maintain full employment."

"Hogwash. It once took 90 percent of the population to grow our food. Now it takes under two percent, and the numbers keep right on dropping year after year. Pardon me, Mr. Drill Bit, but are any of us worse off because of the job losses in agriculture?"

"Of course not."

"Right again. The might-have-been farmers are now something else: college professors or e-techs or EMD repairmen. If all you want to do is create jobs, trade in the bulldozers for shovels. If that doesn't create enough jobs, replace the shovels with spoons. Still not enough? Try chopsticks. How 'bout tweezers?"

"Now you're being a pain in the ass."

"I know that. But there will always be more work to do than people to do it. But let's not be democrats about it and destroy all the machinery. Let's not become protectionist and try to grow bananas in the tundra north of Calgary. Why the hell must people do dangerous jobs by hand when machines can do them so much safer and quicker? Job destruction is part of progress, part of raising our standard of living."

"I do a dangerous job. Do you want to see me get laid off?"

"It has nothing to do with what I want. If a man can be replaced cheaply enough, he should be."

"Does that go for Ph.D.'s as well?"

"No, of course not. We're irreplaceable."

Butch laughed.

"The point is: No one in the history of the world ever washed a rented gcar. And why is that? Because at the end of the day it is someone else's capital that is at risk in a rental gcar, not your own. Preserving a gcar's value only becomes important when it actually belongs to you."

"I get that."

"The same logic holds true for other pursuits. Farmers who don't own their land don't worry about depleting the soil. Companies that don't own the forests they log don't worry about sustainable harvesting. Nor do fishermen who don't own the fishes. Over-hunting, over-grazing, clear cutting — these are all symptoms of a deeper economic problem."

"Symptoms? You make it sound like a disease."

"It is a disease. In those settings where free-riders are at liberty to indulge themselves at the expense of their fellow citizens, resource depletion becomes a way of life. But there are alternatives. In those settings where prices are free to fluctuate and where all economic goods are in the hands of profit-maximizers, free-riders will be shut out. People will wash their own gcars, fishermen will protect their spawning grounds, and loggers will re-seed their forests."

"But how does this relate to what you were saying earlier? I still don't buy what you were trying to say about choice. How can more of it possibly be bad?"

"Look at it this way. While some choice is obviously better than no choice at all, more choice is not always better than less. It is another one of those paradoxes we discover all the time in economics. As a society grows wealthier and people become more able to do as they please, many actually find themselves less happy than before."

"I sense that that is the case, but I really don't understand why."

"We call it the Paradox of Choice. On our survey, those people who come up as extreme maximizers always aim to make the best possible choice. That's why they're so unhappy."

"All right, I'm hooked. Try out another one of those survey questions on me."

Elijah turned to his machine, brought it out of hibernation, keyed in a file name. "Try this one on for size — *I am a big fan of lists, especially those that rank things important to me — the year's ten best vids, the ten best new vocalists, the season's best athletes, the best e-books for the beach, that kind of thing.*"

"I get the idea. But not everyone is a high-octane korinthenkacker like that."

"Thank God for small favors; although our research suggests that about one-third of the population is. And about one-third of those are *extreme* maximizers. This ten percent or so of the population expends enormous effort in pursuit of perfection — reading labels, checking out consumer mags, testing new products and then often returning them. They also spend more time than most people comparing their purchasing decisions with others."

"But, Doc, no one can check out every option, not even a hardcore raisin-crapper like yourself. That would make a man crazy."

"Not crazy — unhappy. That's why, for these sorts of people, making a decision becomes increasingly daunting as the number of choices rise. Then comes the real nightmare. Having now arrived at a decision what to buy, these sorts are continually nagged by the alternatives they *didn't* have time to investigate. But talk about making yourself nuts. Should a time constraint intervene and force an extreme maximizer to prematurely end his search and make a decision, his apprehension about what might have been will take over in a big way."

"Hence the unhappiness."

Elijah nodded. "Economics is all about opportunity costs. One of the costs of making a choice is losing whatever opportunities a different choice would have afforded. Studies have shown conclusively that losses — in whatever guise — have a much greater psychological impact on people than similarly-sized gains. Losses make us hurt more than gains make us feel good."

"Say that again."

"Losses make us hurt more than gains make us feel good."

Butch nodded knowingly, as if he understood. "That explains why people refuse to part with a losing stock."

"Or a lousy spouse."

"To sell a loser is to admit a mistake — and that hurts."

"Exactly my point. The opportunity costs associated with making a decision include the time and effort that go into deciding. These are fixed costs we must pay upfront, and they have to be amortized over the life of the decision. The more we invest in making a decision, the more satisfaction we expect to realize from our investment of time and energy. If a decision provides substantial satisfaction over a long period of time after being made, the costs of making it recedes into insignificance. But, if the decision provides pleasure for only a short time, those costs loom large. For extreme maximizers, their satisfaction with a purchase is always short-lived, so they're always unhappy."

"Wouldn't the correct response to unhappiness be to quit wasting so friggin' much time and energy trying to make up their minds?"

"I do like the way you think, Butch. But an extreme maximizer can't help himself."

"Can't help himself? That's pathetic. My teacher always said economics was the Dismal Science."

"He didn't say it for that reason. Early economists, like Thomas Malthus, predicted that population growth would outstrip food production, leading to widespread famine."

"But he was wrong, wasn't he?"

"Malthus didn't take into account technology — on either side of the equation. Technology ramped up food production. It also curtailed baby output. Global population leveled off decades ago. Nowadays, relatively few people go hungry, and almost no one on account of insufficient supplies."

Doc turned thoughtful. He was just about to launch into a lecture on Game Theory, when Kaleena came into the room. She was white-faced.

"Goodness, girl, what's wrong?" he said.

"I just heard from my father."

"Everything okay at home?"

"My brother was murdered. Gunned down on a street corner in Hedon City."

"How awful." Butch reached out to her. They hadn't made up since their fight yesterday.

"The funeral is tomorrow. My father has arranged for the network to stream me vid, so I can attend the funeral in a long-distance sort of way."

"Do you want me to be there with you?" Butch asked.

"You would do that for me?"

"We both will," Doc replied.

CHAPTER THIRTEEN

▼

Fourth-class assistant Leif Doffsinger was now in the Base Commander's outer office, sweating profusely. It was summer in this part of the world, and the air conditioning wasn't up to the task. Supervisor Cromwell had gone in the Commander's office first and only just now exited, white-faced. In a moment it would be Leif's turn. While he waited, he made some further notes on his e-pad.

For Leif, the last few days had been a whirlwind. His discovery of the errand EMD ran up the chain of command to Director Keith Roberts, Chairman of Transcomet Industries, and back down again. The final okay came in the form of a communique from Zuzana Nordstrom, Mr. Roberts' executive assistant.

Once the word came down, Leif was relieved of his regular duties at Space-Traffic Control so he could spend all his time on this problem.

But, before Leif knew it, he was a nervous wreck. He began having anxiety attacks, getting in everyone's way, walking the halls of the control tower in a complete daze. His petite, carefree wife took to calling him a "meanderthal." Martha was more educated than he was and loved wordplay. This little gem of hers was a merger of "meander" and "Neanderthal" — meanderthal — an aimless, slow-moving ape-man who mindlessly got in everyone else's way, at home, on the sidewalk, in the mall, all because he was preoccupied with his own problems. But having his wife make fun of him didn't improve Leif's mood one little bit.

Leif Doffsinger had never met the Base Commander before. He was understandably nervous. Lieutenant Colonel William Norris had a reputation for being an angry son-of-a-bitch. Norris was too well qualified to be a mere major, but not well enough connected to get his stars as a full-fledged general. In fact, lieutenant colonel was what the Army called a "shit-house rank." Each day brought nothing but shit from above and crap from below. To make matters worse, Norris' post was quasi-civilian. It was a post from which he could not expect to be transferred or promoted. While the military had jurisdiction over all manmade objects moving through space — including all satellites, EMDs, trans-comets, and spaceships — EMD Enterprises was a strictly private company, one with close ties to the administration of President Noah Benjamin.

Who, then, could blame the Lieutenant Colonel when he didn't seem especially happy to have this particular problem dumped on his desk?

"Come this way, please." A protocol robot led Doffsinger down the corridor to Norris' office. Except for a picture of the President, the corridor walls were completely bare.

Leif was uneasy around robots. Oh, they could be made to look human enough. That wasn't the problem.

Leif knew that someone somewhere had at one time devised laws of robotics, laws designed to govern their behavior, and that somewhere someone else had dutifully imbedded those laws into their programming.

But he knew equally well that every computer program ever written was infused with bugs and that programmers themselves were not above intentionally planting bugs, some for the sheer pleasure of watching software fail, others because they were sick pranksters.

Did we really want to trust our safety to such machines? Leif thought not.

The protocol bot looked at him, now, with dark cold eyes, opened the door to Lieutenant Colonel William Norris' office, showed him in.

Lieutenant Colonel William Norris was stern-faced and curt. With a grunt, he nodded for Doffsinger to be seated.

Doffsinger let himself sink slowly down into the chair. Behind the Lieutenant Colonel, on the sideboard, was a live-feed vid. A stunning woman sat behind her desk, nodded to him as he settled in. Despite her good looks, she was obviously all business. Norris introduced her.

"This is Zuzana Nordstrom. She is with the civilian authorities. Ms. Nordstrom will be listening in on our conversation. She may even have a few words to add. But you can be sure: my authority on this project comes from the highest levels."

Doffsinger nodded his understanding, though truth be told, he was quite confused. *What civilian authorities? And what did some woman sitting in a room a thousand kloms from here have to do with this matter?*

Norris cleared his throat and began. "Supervisor Cromwell informs me that we may have a problem. But the man's a blithering idiot, if you ask me. I want to hear it directly from you. So does Ms. Nordstrom."

"Sir, it's our belief . . . "

"Cut the crap, boy. The way I hear it, you were the one who discovered this anomaly, weren't you? There's no 'our' about this, is there?"

Leif sat up straighter, his pride growing. "It's true. I did do the original work on this. I'm quite certain EMD 14 did not respond to ground control's latest midcourse correction."

"And why would that be, son?"

"I couldn't say for certain, sir."

"Speculate."

"If you insist." Doffsinger sat forward in his chair. "The most likely scenario would be that a small, companion-asteroid, swept along by its mother . . . "

"Its *mother*?" Norris roared. "Have you gone completely mad?"

"Well, sir, that's what we call them up in the tower. Two asteroids, one big, one small, moving along in tandem. The big one's the mother, the little one's the daughter. When they're in a group, they move like a family of ducks on a pond."

"I see," Norris said, though he really didn't. "And this companion-asteroid of yours, what did it do? Smash into its mother, destroy the antenna?"

"I'd rate that as a strong possibility. That's the working theory anyway."

Suddenly the vid screen came alive and Zuzana Nordstrom spoke. "If I may interrupt. We're trying to reprogram the Solar Observer satellite to get some close-up pictures of the EMD."

"Good, that'll help clarify things," Doffsinger said. "There's also a strong possibility that a chunk of rock flew off the main body of the asteroid and wrecked either the antenna or the servo. Same outcome either way. Asteroids aren't solid like larger bodies — pieces are flying loose all the time. That's why the Space-Traffic Board demanded EMD Enterprises start putting redundant antenna-units onboard the newer mass-drivers coming off the line. To deal with this very scenario."

Nordstrom took umbrage with that statement. "We weren't cutting corners, if that's what you mean, young man."

"I didn't mean to imply that you were, ma'am."

"You best watch your tone with me, boy. I don't think you know who you're dealing with."

"If I have offended you, ma'am, I apologize deeply. Maybe I was mistaken, but I thought we were all on the same side here."

"We need to leave personalities aside a moment and get to the bottom of this," Lieutenant Colonel Norris said. "Could this failure have been the result of sabotage?" he asked, spinning around in his chair to shoot Zuzana Nordstrom an accusing stare. They had discussed this possibility before Doffsinger entered the room. She had made him aware of swirling rumors implicating terrorists, who were organizing to shut down the Motor Works. They had spoken with Frederick Krotchmeier in the interim; reviewed his security procedures.

"Sabotage?" Leif answered. "I don't see how."

"What if, way back in the factory, an explosive charge had been planted on the frame of the mass-driver, right alongside the antenna housing?"

"Well, that would do it okay. But what would be the motive? Why would anyone want to do such a thing?"

"The world is full of crazies. There are those who want to put a halt to terraforming."

"I've never been to Mars before. Surely their security must be tighter than all that."

"Apparently not tight enough." Norris sighed, thinking of Krotchmeier's weak answers. He looked at Zuzana Nordstrom on the vid feed. She was busy making notes on her e-pad. "So tell me, young . . . I'm sorry but I've forgotten your name."

"Doffsinger, sir. Leif Doffsinger."

"So tell me, young Doffsinger, how do we get the bloody thing back on track?"

"I don't think we can. Not without an antenna anyway."

Lieutenant Colonel Norris felt his collar tighten. "So where will the bloody thing go if we can't control it?"

Doffsinger answered as forthrightly as he could. "We don't know for sure yet. There are too many variables. But it'll be close."

"Close? Close to what?"

"Close to us. Close to Earth."

"How close?"

Assistant Fourth-Class Leif Doffsinger lowered his eyes.

"Good God, man! Do you know what you are saying?"

"I think I do," Doffsinger replied with levelheaded precision. "I have been running some numbers on my e-pad. According to the log, the asteroid headed our way is approximately 1400 meters across on its narrowest axis, 2500 on its widest. And it's traveling very, very fast. I've done some rough calculations. The kinetic energy of an object is equal to one-half m times v squared, where m is the mass of the object and v is the bugger's velocity. If we use joules as a measuring rod — a joule, by the way, is the work done when a force of one Newton moves an object a distance of one meter in the direction of the force, then . . . "

"Bloody hell, I get the idea! Planet killer. Death of the dinosaurs. Nuclear winter. Am I close?"

"Close enough."

"How long until you have a clean fix on this thing? We need to know the asteroid's actual glide path ASAP."

"I guess that's up to Ms. Nordstrom, isn't it? I need those pictures from the Solar Observer satellite. I need them digitized and converted to a 3-D holograph. Once I have those files, I should be able to make the calculations. But it'll take me most of the night."

"No way are you going to stay up all night-long waiting on those holos. You already look like bloody hell. I need you on your A-game for this, Doffsinger. If you do a good job, it will make me look like a hero, set me up for a promotion. So you and that e-pad of yours had better get a few hours shut-eye first. Then back to work in the morning."

"Sir?"

"If this thing *is* on a collision course with Earth, what are our options? What steps can be taken to prevent a devastating collision?"

"I've given that some thought," Doffsinger said. "I understand from the ship's manifest that we may have two highly qualified men onboard a transport home, the solar sailship *Mars Voyager.*"

"I know the ship's captain personally." Zuzana Nordstrom interrupted. "And those two men work for us."

"That may come in handy. The ship is filled with VIPs, government types from the Terraforming Commission. That includes a Senator's daughter, by the way. Those people will scream bloody murder at the delay."

"Let 'em scream. What do you have in mind?"

"The *Voyager* is scheduled to pass within a few hundred thousand kloms of that EMD. We could re-route the ship. Those men could take the ship's dinghy, go out to the asteroid, fix the broken antenna-unit."

Zuzana Nordstrom got red-faced. "You want to maneuver a billion-dollar sailship within dinghy range of a tumbling, out of control asteroid? I don't know if I could lend my approval to that scheme."

"Still cutting corners, ma'am?" Leif Doffsinger said, without reservation.

"You like your job, son?" she shot back angrily.

Doffsinger stood his ground. "Which would you rather risk? — a billion-dollar sailship or an entire planet? I doubt seriously if anyone's going to get rich on a dead planet."

"Point made," she replied testily. "But isn't this a pretty risky operation?"

"Extraordinarily risky. But there may be no other way."

"And what if it's not the antenna-unit that's wrecked but the entire mass-driver?"

"Then there'll be no fixing it."

"I understand. General Norris is right. You should go get some sleep. We'll talk again in the morning."

"Due respect, ma'am. It's Lieutenant Colonel."

"It's like you said, Colonel. Doffsinger does a good job on this, you're looking at a commendation followed by a quick promotion. Are we all on the same page now?"

Both men nodded their heads.

CHAPTER FOURTEEN

▼

Elixir Coventry undid the buttons of her white cotton blouse, dropped her bra to the floor and let her breasts hang free.

This was one good-looking woman, and she admired her reflection in the glass of her wall-sized mirror.

Her breasts were taut and high as always, her nipples thick and hard. Being young and fit was important to this woman. Getting old was for someone else. Her time, if it came at all, was far in the future.

Now she undid the clasp at her waist, dropped her skirt to the floor. Her underwear was shear and the dark triangle of feminine hair was visible through the fabric.

She placed her hands on her hips, tightened the muscles of her buttocks and abdomen. Elixir was firm in the right places, soft everywhere else. No bodybuilding for this woman, just hard physical labor, chopping wood in the forests around her Tennessee home, planting flowers, mopping floors, washing walls. It wasn't that she couldn't afford help, for her father had left her well-off. It was that she equated hard work with femininity. This is where Elixir felt the modern woman had gone wrong. By seeking equal opportunity in the workplace, today's woman had abandoned the home. Washing dishes and scrubbing floors was beneath the modern woman. *Could refusing to service their husbands be far behind?*

Elixir Coventry was all about sex. More delicious than food, she would say. More fulfilling than a career.

The tight-fitting panties were next to go. Now she stood naked before her mirror dressed only in her bright yellow tennis shoes. They hardly ever came off. The reason was simple. Even naked Elixir could go outside, find her favorite spot to masturbate and not cut her feet. In the mountains here, east of Nashville, the ground was rough and hard. No place for bare feet.

Eastern Tennessee. Elixir called it Davy Crockett country. Crockett was that rarity among nineteenth-century American legends — a frontiersman whose exploits matched his legend and were in large part real. Here was a man, a self-made individualist, who hunted, fought Indians, blazed trails, served in Congress, and died a martyr at the Alamo. Those attitudes still echoed off the mountains that surrounded her home on all sides. They made her proud.

Elixir's hair was long and blond, done up in tight braids, what some called corn-rows. That was fine for public events. But when she wanted to get naked — really naked — she would undo those braids, as she was doing now. To get the full release, the heart-pounding orgasm she was after, all the constraints had to go, physical as well as spiritual. She would start at the emote wall, then sometimes move outside into the garden. There was a big, flat rock about twenty meters beyond her porch, where she could recline on a small body pad and get herself off.

From the mirror she moved, now, to the emote wall. This was a curious invention. It was governed by a learning program. With repeated use the wall would come to "know" its owner, what music they liked, what colors they preferred, what smells they found most appealing, what images they liked displayed on the wall, and where. A pedophile might want pictures of little boys; a masochist, images of pain. Licks liked pornography, hard pounding scenes of women with men, sensual moaning, blue colors, the smell of wind or rain.

Now, as the naked Elixir approached the emote wall, the wall sensed her presence, began to search its database for the things that turned her on. She stood before it, watching, feeling the warmth grow between her legs. This was sex taken to a higher level — pleasant music, enchanting smells, bewitching images — all programmed to make its owner happy.

Elixir went to her medicine cabinet, found the small mechanical device that in an earlier age would have been called a vibrator. This it was — and much, much more. The business end of the Autoclit featured a small, rotating head that she could brush or press against her privates. Rapidly moving microfilaments would give her a buzz like no man ever could.

But the Autoclit was more than just a simple mechanical device. It employed sonic waves to heighten the experience, plus biologic agents that accentuated the engorgement of her female parts. The sonic waves were timed to match the tempo of her contractions.

Licks sat in the nearby Comfy Chair to begin her therapy. The Chair softened as it recognized its master and spread and flattened to the position that afforded her the most access. She began to softly moan as she gently touched the apparatus to its intended spot.

The emote wall sensed her sounds and the visual imagery changed. It was more raw now — female mouths, male parts, women stroking themselves, softer lighting.

The vibrator changed shape in her hand, conforming to her carnal needs, spraying a delicate mist of testosterone and other hormones where they would do the most good. Elixir was losing control.

Now, in a great rush Elixir arched her back and let it happen. She let go of the Autoclit and gripped the rounded arms of the Comfy Chair with both hands. The mechanical device could operate on its own, without her directing its movements. It was an e-tool, a smart tool. It knew what she wanted, for it had learned from being used so many times before. It knew how to pleasure her better than she knew herself.

Then finally it was done. She screamed, but then caught herself. Wave after wave of tumultuous pleasure pounded through her pelvis until she could take no more.

Then slowly, everything powered down. The emote wall darkened, the vibrator shut itself off, the Comfy Chair cradled her, a blanket rolled out of one side and covered her. Elixir fell asleep, a look of remarkable, everlasting contentment on her face.

·

·

An hour later Elixir woke up. A light on her comm indicated that there had been a call. The Comfy Chair would have communicated with the comm. Both devices knew better than to disturb her during a session in front of the emote wall, or immediately afterward.

Elixir showered, washed her privates with the lavage tube, and dressed. She went online, glanced at her mail, scrolled through the *American Rights Journal*. There was another good article by Morgan DuPont. Morgan was a champion of the Second Amendment, and Licks was concerned about Senator Flanagan's proposal to ban guns of every sort.

Now she went to her comm, replayed the message. Texas Governor Thadamore Mills had called. In two days' time he would be flying his personal suborb — the *Lone Star* — from Houston to D.C. to meet with President Benjamin. How would she like to come join him for the flight, perhaps become the first wiccan to ever qualify as a double member of the Sixty-Mile-High Club? Sex over the top was, well, over the top.

Her first thought was "Wow, what fun!" A chance to do something she'd never done before. *But two men at once?* Didn't that cross a line?

It was a thin line, to be sure, but a line nonetheless. Licks was no whore, and she didn't like the idea of being used — and certainly not for someone else's pleasure!

But two men at once? — In a suborb soaring ninety kloms above the surface? What could be grander?

It might cross a line, but it also might be a rush. To become a double member of the Club meant servicing two men at the same time as the suborb came over the top of its apogee, at that brief moment of zero-g. Only a limited number of positions would work, and only if all straps and harnesses were already in place.

But who was the second man? The first was obviously Thadamore Mills, Governor of Texas. It had been his invitation, after all. The man wasn't much to look at, of course. But Thadamore could be creative, and the man did have money. So maybe that part wasn't so bad.

But who was the second man? Probably the Reverend Roland Whitmore. He was not only the spiritual founder of Puritan City, he was also titular head of the Sect of the Most Sacred. Except for perhaps Alexander Hoagland (and Hoagland would never go in for such things), few men were closer to Thadamore Mills than the good Reverend. Which was a shame; for when it came to sexual experimentation, the Reverend Roland Whitmore had the imagination of a fence post. "On your knees, woman!" was about the only position that beady little mind of his could conjure up.

The man had to be taught some manners, she thought as she speed-dialed Thadamore's personal line. To get to Houston in time to make the flight, she would have to take the afternoon Bullet from Nashville via Memphis.

Though some might think Elixir crude or immoral, that really wasn't the case. Elixir actually had a rather complicated personal philosophy.

She would say that morality wasn't universal, that it couldn't come from religion. The reason was simple. Since no single religion was universally practiced all of the time by all of the people everywhere, it must vary with circumstance, from place to place and from person to person.

If religion wasn't universal, then how could morality possibly be? Indeed, a great many people were clearly moral without ever believing in a higher power.

Plus, no matter what some people claimed, morality had very little to do with the so-called sins of the body — alcohol consumption, drug use, fornication. It wasn't a sin to have sex with a man, no matter how much the silly bastards twisted the truth.

Elixir's free-wheeling philosophy is what initially drew her to the practice of Wicca. What began long ago as a fringe cult — one that mainstream Christians found decidedly pagan if not downright Dionysian — had matured over time into a more organized belief system. At its core was a tenet, the Wiccan Rede — *An it harm none, do what ye will.*

"An" was an archaic contraction of the word "and." In this context it meant "if" — *If what you do harms no one, then do as you please.* Thus, the rule set the boundaries for a way of life. Not quite the Golden Rule, but something very close.

Wicca was not without its stable of pantheistic gods. But it was more than just an archaic belief system. It had its complex rituals, as well as its liberal code of morality.

Newer practitioners of Wicca were known to the outside world primarily for their emphasis on community service — *So long as you help others, you are free to do as you please.*

This motto or creed helped define the way in which Elixir lived her life. She was active in several volunteer organizations, though her one true love was the Wiccan Nurse's Association. The WNA assisted at hospitals and medical centers and often worked in conjunction with the North American Red Cross in relief efforts to help people displaced by flood or tornado or other natural disaster.

But despite the Wiccans many good works, the free-spirited sexual overtones of their rituals and ideas often brought little more than derision, sometimes outright persecution. Thus, they tended to live apart, in more rural areas or mountain hideaways, sometimes in isolated groups of eight or ten.

If Elixir's moral code could be boiled down to a few commandments, they might run something like this:

(1) Do not kill with malice.
(2) Do not cause pain.
(3) Do not deprive of freedom.
(4) Do not deprive of pleasure.
(5) Do not cheat or deceive.
(6) Keep the promises you make.

But even these rules weren't hard and fast absolutes. A person might kill in self-defense or lie to save an innocent life. But there should be no hypocrisy about it. A person should break a rule only if he would be willing to allow everyone else to break the same rule under the same circumstances.

Even if Licks did not believe in killing, she did firmly believe in guns. A gun was for protection, the one thing that might keep a body alive if someone were threatening you with violent harm. She owned two guns herself. Any talk of destroying or short-circuiting the Second Amendment ran counter to her moral code.

And while Elixir saw no moral issue attached to drug use or alcohol consumption, she would never pollute her own body with either. Nevertheless, she was staunchly opposed to governmental interference in what were essentially private acts.

For much the same reason, Elixir was in favor of protecting the environment and adamantly opposed to terraforming. Destroying the environment was tantamount to killing with malice, terraforming a kind of deception.

Pollution caused pain. Censorship deprived of pleasure. High taxes deprived of freedom. Capital punishment was state-sanctioned killing. Speed limits restricted pleasure.

Her morality defined her politics.

Her politics framed her morality.

CHAPTER FIFTEEN

▼

The ship's dinghy was designed to be a lifeboat in the event of emergency or else used as a passenger transport when the *Mars Voyager* was docked at the orbiting Space Station.

Now, though, it had been pressed into service for a different enterprise, to ferry Butch Hogan and Red Parsons, lately of Mars, across the gap that lay between the parked *Voyager* and the misfit asteroid barreling uncontrollably through space and badly in need of a replacement antenna-unit.

Neither Butch nor Red were qualified pilots, so tonight a new man was at the controls, Woody Dunlop, former military, now attached to EMD Enterprises, a subsidiary of Transcomet Industries. In his time Woody had piloted nearly every sort of powered craft known to man — aircraft (both fixed-wing and rotary), spacecraft (both passive and fueled), plus a half-dozen types of ocean-going vessels. Next to Woody in the cockpit sat Gus "Gulliver" Travels, his longtime nav officer.

Locating the hurtling chunk of rock in space had actually been the easy part. The search began with an emergency order from the corporate headquarters of Transcomet. Then a secure voucher from Space-Traffic Control. Then a closed-circuit vid meeting with newly promoted Assistant Supervisor Leif Doffsinger and two other parties; Zuzana Nordstrom of Transcomet Industries and General William Norris of Space Command. Doffsinger simulcast the EMD's current x, y, z coordinates and heading from his 3-D holo-screen — as well as its projected position each hour for the next 100 hours. He also transmitted detailed close-up pictures of the damaged area as taken by the Solar Observer satellite. The need was so urgent, Space Command had re-positioned the satellite for this very purpose.

But reaching that location in 3-space was a daunting task. A sailship didn't turn on a dime. In fact, nothing quite matched the challenge of tacking across the solar wind like a big, old schooner from the nineteenth century on a windy day. Plus, the rendezvous point was itself constantly in motion. Computers both on the ground and onboard the *S.S. Mars Voyager* were working overtime to plot the optimum track so the ship could overtake the asteroid at the earliest opportunity. This was a complicated maneuver, which included furling the sails at the correct moment and altering the ship's trajectory so their paths crossed at the exact point in 3-space.

But even now, having accomplished all that, what was to come next was rather more difficult. While at the helm of the dinghy, Woody had to match the asteroid's rotational attitude, the "rotatt," as Gulliver blandly put it.

Though the asteroid was falling inward towards the center of the solar system along a smooth if highly elliptical path, the rest of its motion was anything but smooth. Instead of flying nose-first through space like a ballistic missile might, the big rock was in a multi-axis spin, tumbling end-over-end and from side to side like a poorly thrown football, only worse.

In order to level out the asteroid's spin and permit Space-Traffic Control to reestablish communications with the EMD, a replacement antenna-unit had to be hooked up next to the existing electromagnetic mass driver. This was no easy task. It meant someone or something had to approach to within two hundred meters or so of the planetoid, cross the remaining distance "on foot," as it were, then perform the actual installation atop a spinning gerbil. That someone was actually two men, Butch Hogan and his buddy Red Parsons. The two spacejockeys not only had the requisite skill, they were the only qualified people near enough to the asteroid to get there in time.

To achieve the necessary rotational synchronization of the dinghy with the asteroid's crazy rotatt, Woody used a special tool, the ship's laser-guided docking array. The LGDA sat on the outside of the ship's hull. It was an important navigational tool, originally designed to be used by a pilot when maneuvering around the outside of the Space Station, to ensure safe docking under every conceivable condition. When coupled with the onboard nav-computer, the LGDA repeatedly adjusted the angular thrusters until the dinghy assumed the identical rotatt of whatever surface it was trying to dock against.

And yet, even with the benefit of this highly-advanced piece of navigational hardware, maneuvering through space in such close proximity to a wildly spinning asteroid was a gut-wrenching experience of the first order for everyone concerned. Consider a small sailing ship anchored in choppy seas. You are trapped alone on deck, strapped to a chair. But not just any chair. It is fitted with coasters at the bottom of each leg, so that the chair rolls quickly and easily in every direction. You have been forced to down several liters of dark ale. Now, with each roll of the ship, you wheel uncontrollably to and fro across the wave-splashed deck. Overhead, an airchop slowly circles. It is hauling beneath it a weighted rope. The rope is swinging back and forth in front of your eyes. Try to imagine it, if you can, and you will quickly realize why it won't be long before nausea crowds out every other sensation.

The asteroid the four of them were now fast approaching was in a similar triple-axis roll. That meant it was tumbling not only end-over-end but also spinning clockwise on its long axis and counterclockwise along its short axis. The laser-guided thrusters onboard the dinghy were operating as they should, methodically working to match the ship's rotatt to the big rock's rotatt. Nevertheless, the adjustment process was halting and jerky. It took time to make the corrections, and it proceeded in fits and starts.

Like that rolling chair on the deck of that bobbing ship, this was not a pleasant undertaking. Without a fixed reference point to focus their bloodshot eyes on, watching the slow dance of asteroid and dingy unfold through the bulkhead window was a sure recipe for scrambling one's guts. Plus, it didn't help much *not* to watch, because once the brain caught a glimpse of what was going on outside, the stomach quickly followed suit. Of the four, only Woody the pilot didn't throw up, and that was probably because he had his hand on the tiller.

Finally, after twenty long minutes of jockeying for position, the relative motion slowed to a stop. The rock was large, much larger than the little dinghy. When the four looked out the porthole, the asteroid completely filled their field of vision. Their telemetry told them it was an oddly shaped monstrosity, with one side backlit by the sun and the rest a mysterious place of unseen shadows, black and gray. The hideous thing seemed so close, now, they could just reach out and touch it.

The mass-driver itself was big, over a hundred meters long, attached directly to the bedrock. The electromagnetic inducer coils were the guts of the motor. The rest was just so many gears and magnets, relays and logic circuits.

The hard part still lay ahead of them, a spacewalk from the dinghy over to the asteroid, followed by a tricky antenna-unit extraction and repair.

They were in the prep room now. Butch held the replacement antenna-unit in his hand. It seemed rather small and unpretentious, especially considering how vitally important it was to controlling something the size of an asteroid. Luckily, antenna-units were pretty much standard throughout the fleet and the sailship stocked spares. When Gulliver signed out the unit from the storeroom and handed it to Butch to hold, the entire assembly was still sealed in a durable poly bag. Butch felt its weight as he dropped it into Red's knapsack.

Safety considerations demanded they risk only one of them out on the line at a time. The two had drawn straws and Red was elected to shinny out and make the repairs. Right now Red was securing the last of his tools onto his external toolbelt. These included the standard adjustable wrenches, manual ratchet, vise grip, cutters, deadblow hammer. Plus, an electro-solder gun, pair of pneumatic pliers, a Pigtail, spool of 5th-generation beryllium copper duct tape, plus a riveter and Bolt Gun. The Bolt Gun was the same kind of high-powered gun alpine climbers used to secure a climbing bolt to solid rock when making an ascent up the side of a mountain.

"I guess it's time," Red said, pulling the last of his shoulder straps snug. He already had on his tech-shirt and enviro-wristband.

Turning now to Woody, the big man double-checked the biometric readouts on his wristband with the levels Woody was tracking on his onboard monitor. Oxygen, heart rate, pressure — all greenline.

"Are you sure about this?" Butch asked, still feeling a little woozy from the rotatt synchronization. The Tranquil patch hadn't yet settled his stomach.

"Man, look at you. You're in no condition. Besides, we drew straws. It was fair and square. Anyway, why should you be the one who captures all the glory? Girls love a hero. Why not me?"

"Screw Krotchmeier and screw the rules — we should both be out there. First thing they taught us in flight school: Never Spacewalk Alone. I don't like this hotshot woman from Transcomet telling us how to do our jobs. We're the spacejockeys; she rides a frigging desk."

"She also signs our paychecks."

"It's cutting corners, if you ask me."

Red shrugged his shoulders, shook his head. He fastened his helmet shut, listened for the reassuring rush of fresh air, then edged out of the prep room towards the airlock. The suit was stiff, and he shuffled forward awkwardly.

Butch and Red traded jibes as he trundled along, chatting with one another on the remote until they were both absolutely certain everything checked out and was in working order. No "maybes" when a spacewalk was involved.

"Open the hatch," Red instructed, clipping himself to the safety tether. Several hundred meters of line lay neatly coiled on the deck behind him. If Red got into a jam out there, Butch could engage the winch and haul him back inside in nothing flat.

Butch pressurized the airlock, and Red stepped in. As the outer door swung free, Red floated out into empty space. But then, of course, it wasn't actually empty. Directly in front of him, some two hundred meters away, was an enormous snarling piece of rock, a rock that carried with it a frightful amount of kinetic energy, some 40 trillion joules, according to that same deskjockey, Leif Doffsinger, down in the Control center on Earth. The exact number wasn't important. Even a mloron could see that this rock was of planet-killer proportions.

Red looked at the asteroid, now, with amused eyes. It seemed so tranquil, even idyllic, not dangerous at all.

But the serenity was an illusion. The enormous boulder was spinning madly, careening ever closer to Earth. Even so, since the asteroid's motion, relative to Red's own, was presently zero, the big rock seemed to just hang there quietly, patiently waiting for him to make the first move.

Red Parsons swallowed his fear and began. His plan of attack was simple and straightforward. He would use the Alpine Bolt Gun to secure a tether in the rock close to the repair site. Then, employing the same sort of mechanical-ascender spacejockeys regularly used to clamber around the outside of the Space Station, he would cross the approximately two-hundred-meter gap that separated the dinghy from the asteroid. Next, he would rivet the new antenna-unit into place, strip and wrap a few wires with advanced duct tape, and presto, EMD 14 would be back online.

Attached to the bolt Red would be firing was a loop. And snaked through that loop was a cable. This was the cable Red would be "hanging" from when all the connections were secure.

Aiming and firing the bolt had to be executed with a degree of precision. If he aimed too high, the bolt would go flying off into space at high velocity, cable attached — and him with it. If he aimed too low, the bolt would punch a hole clean through the side of the electromagnetic mass driver. While the mass-driver was unlikely to blow up like a can of petrol might, the electromagnet would not take too kindly to being punctured and might never operate again.

Thus, it was with a clear understanding of what he was up against, when Red gripped the Bolt Gun in his right hand, steadied himself, and directed his full attention to getting the bolt on target.

But, so intent was Red on doing this correctly, he forgot one very important thing — *the Bolt Gun packed a kick like a mule !*

As soon as Red pulled the trigger, he knew he was in trouble. The Bolt Gun had been designed with mountain climbers in mind, not spacemen. Indeed, it fired a diamond-tipped bolt with such force, the bolt was capable of penetrating nearly any type of rock. Out on the mountain, where there was plenty of air friction — as well as gravity and restraining ropes — the recoil from firing a bolt into a rock face was of small consequence. Oh, there was the occasional bruised shoulder or broken finger, but certainly nothing to compare with the devastating consequences of firing the thing in frictionless, zero-g space.

It all happened so fast, Red never knew what hit him. In the span of a microsecond, everything was a blur.

One moment he was floating in space a meter or so away from the dinghy, the next he was in excruciating pain.

This was Red's second big mistake of the evening, being so close to the hull of the ship when he pulled that trigger. The recoil from the Bolt Gun immediately hurled him into a vicious clockwise spin. His right hand, which is to say his gun hand, was kicked backward so violently by the force, there was nothing he could do to prevent it from slamming against the ship's hull with tragic results.

At the collision of flesh against metal, there was an awful cracking sound, which could be heard even inside the dinghy. The suit Red wore was tough, but not tough enough to save his wrist and right hand. Both were shattered by the impact.

Red screamed out in pain. Then, in a moment driven by reflex, he instinctively pulled his mangled appendage in closer to his body.

This action had unintended consequences as well, for it added even more inertia to his already quickening spin, much as a professional ice-skater might, to liven up her performance. After three or four dizzying revolutions, Red blacked out.

Inside the ship, Woody Dunlop was the first to realize that something had gone terribly wrong. All the readouts on his bio-monitor briefly spiked then flatlined. Though Woody didn't know it yet, along with Red's broken wrist and hand, the accident had smashed his enviro-wristband.

"Oh, my God, something's gone wrong!" Woody yelped, seeing the needles sink and bottom out. "Bloody hell, what is going on out there?"

Butch jumped to the porthole, hand on the comm. "I can't see him. For God's sake, Red! Answer me. Where the Devil are you?"

There was no reply.

"We need to haul him in!" Butch shouted. Then, without waiting for confirmation, he hit the POWER button on the winch.

The cable engaged.

But it returned at a depressingly slow rate of speed.

"Why the hell is this thing taking so damn long?" Butch screamed.

"Cool down, mug," Gulliver said. "If the cable's coiled too fast, it can become brittle and break. Then where would we be? Plus, if you coil it too fast, the cable can suffer a massive static-electricity buildup, like on the

Voyager's solar sails. The charge must be bled off slowly or else all our onboard electronics will short-out and fail. I'm sorry, but slow is the only way."

Butch shook his head in disgust. More than two minutes passed, an eternity. If Red's air supply had been interrupted, he was long dead. Without any biometric data, they wouldn't know for sure until they got the man back in the airlock and popped his helmet and mask.

Red was in the airlock, now, a crumpled, still form. Butch hit the lever to close the outer door and re-pressurize the hatch. Another minute lost. Still no movement out of Red.

Finally, the air pressure inside the airlock was normalized and Butch unsealed the inner door.

The three of them grabbed hold of Red's spacesuit, yanked him bodily out of the airlock, and tossed him onto the prep room floor. Butch peeled off his friend's helmet and mask. Red promptly puked.

"Roll 'em over. Keep his airway clear."

Woody and Gulliver worked frantically to loosen the bolts on Red's suit. Red moaned then winced as they tried to remove his glove. The air in the cabin smelled funny, as it always did after a spacewalk. Pungent. Like seared meat. Like the smell of an acetylene torch on steel.

"His hand's swollen. The glove won't come off."

"Try the other side."

That glove came off easily.

"Alright, put the handle of those pneumatic pliers between his teeth."

Woody looked at Butch as if he didn't understand.

"You know, like the bit of a horse. So he won't bite off his tongue, when we peel off that other glove."

Now Woody understood. He placed the handle of the pliers gently between Red's front teeth.

"His hand is swollen. He probably broke it. I'll bet that frigging Bolt Gun is what did him in."

After several tries, they managed to extract Red's broken wrist and hand from the glove. Now the rest of the suit unbolted easily. The pliers fell out of Red's mouth, clanked to the floor.

Red's hand was red and swollen. Gulliver applied a chem-ice wrap to slow the swelling. Red slipped in and out of consciousness.

"He needs a doctor," Gulliver said. "There's a medic onboard the *Voyager*. Maybe we ought to go back."

Butch shook his head. "We don't have time to go back. You heard what Doffsinger and that lady said. This is time-critical. We need to finish this job as soon as possible. If Red had his wits about him, he would agree."

"No, Gulliver's right," Woody said. "This is too dangerous. We're pulling out."

"Don't be a chickenshit. Before we even talk about pulling out, let's first see if Red's aim was any good. If he secured that bolt, I can easily finish this thing, no problem."

"The man's right," Gulliver said to Woody. "We're already all the way the hell out here. Beating that rotatt won't be any easier the second time around."

"Okay, take a look at it through the binocs. Set it to maximum mag."

The two men switched jobs. Woody continued to apply the chem-ice to Red's hand, while Gulliver set up the scope and brought it to bear on the asteroid.

"I think he hit it square on," Gulliver said after a moment. "See for yourself."

First Woody, then Butch looked through the viewfinder. All three men agreed: Red's aim had been superb. The bolt was secure, precisely where it ought to be.

"It's settled then. I'm going out," Butch said. He turned to retrieve his spacesuit from the locker in the prep room.

CHAPTER SIXTEEN

▼

Butch wasn't the natural-born-hero type. Oh, he talked a good game, and he was about as fearless as they came. But the man was still human, and adrenaline could still do strange things to a man's mind.

For some inexplicable reason Kaleena was suddenly in his head. That long, wonderful hair, that tight little laugh, that pouty look when she was trying to get her way. She was still there, in his head, when he clutched the handgrip at the doorway of the airlock, and again when he reached for the crossbar on the mech-asc and stepped out into space.

Butch tried to slow his breathing. The bar he now hung from was attached to the mechanical-ascender, which itself was suspended from the cable strung between the small ship and the big rock. The cable was anchored to the rock by the bolt Red had shot from his Bolt Gun before the accident.

Butch counted to three, drew a breath to flush the adrenaline from his system. Then he switched on the mech-asc and held tight to the crossbar. Ever so slowly it began to ferry him away from the tiny ship. The arrangement was sort of like a zip line, only at very low speed.

Butch glanced about. It was peaceful out here, he thought. Peaceful and quiet. Quiet and cold. Like during the winter at home. After a snowstorm. Beneath a blanket of fresh snow. All sounds muffled. Even laughter.

Butch hadn't gotten far, perhaps fifteen meters, when it happened.

It began much like a summer rainstorm out on the western prairie. First one drop, then a second, then a third, then a torrent. Only, this was no rainstorm, not of the liquid water variety anyway. No, this was a rainstorm of particles, large and small, a virtual hailstorm of pebbles and rocks!

Asteroids were much like ducks on a pond, little baby chicks trailing behind their mother, something newly-minted Assistant Supervisor Leif Doffsinger had once tried to explain to then Lieutenant Colonel William Norris. Only now, propelled by the asteroid's centripetal force, loose bits of rock were flying everywhere, some as large as three-quarters of a meter long and weighing up to . . .

Thunk!

When the boulder struck Butch's helmet just behind the ear, it gave off a low, hollow sound, like a cinderblock being dropped into deep water from a boat dock, or the shoe of a horse striking the wooden slats of a covered bridge. *Thunk!*

Instinct ruled response — and no response was more instinctual than a blow to the head. Here was a reflex action honed to perfection by a thousand generations of hominid evolution:

Clasp fingers around base of skull. Press arms flat against temples. Ward off further blows to head.

All this Butch did instinctively, without giving it a second thought.

In nearly every conceivable situation, this built-in, automatic response to a threat made perfect sense. Except this one. Now, when Butch swept his hands back to protect his head from further impacts, he released his grip on the handlebars of the mechanical-ascender. This was a mistake he wouldn't soon forget.

The blizzard of particles thickened and Butch was caught in the wash. No longer connected to the mech-asc, he was swept along by the current, like a rafter thrown from his craft in a fast-moving river. The glittering whitewater carried him downstream, away from the dinghy. If not for the safety tether, he would almost certainly have been dragged out to sea and been lost forever.

In the moments before the accident, Woody had been paying out the safety rope to Butch in regular lengths. Now, suddenly, it streamed out of his hand like mad.

Woody slammed on the friction brake with his foot. It was the only sure way to stop the rope from paying out any further.

Gulliver jumped in to help. Together, they started to draw the rope back in. But even with the two of them working in tandem, there was no way to haul Butch back in quickly.

"You okay?" Woody asked breathlessly over the remote as they worked.

"Actually, I'm fine."

Though badly shaken, Butch didn't seem any worse for the wear. For the first time since he started, he flipped on the lumina-beam that projected from the top of his helmet. In the darkness it threw faint light.

Woody's face was grim. He had wanted to put a stop to this back when

Red got hurt. Now they were running out of time. Soon the asteroid would accelerate beyond the point of no return.

"Can you finish this goddamn thing or not?"

"Yeah, can you finish this goddamn thing or not?"

"That you, Red?"

"Yeah, it's me, you mug. It'll be a while, though, 'til I can pick my nose again with this busted hand. But otherwise, no complaints."

"Listen, you two. I can finish this. Pull me back in close enough to reach that cable. I can make it from there."

"Okay, but damn-it-to-hell, this time feed the bloody tether through the loop on the mech-asc," Red instructed, still nursing his busted wrist. "That way it'll stay with you no matter how much you muck it up."

"Now there's confidence for you."

"And another thing. — Don't forget to lock yourself down at the other end before you start popping rivets. We don't want a repeat of my dumb-ass move, now do we?"

"Roger that," Butch said, focusing on his next move. Like an obedient puppy, the mechanical-ascender was still sitting out there on the line, waiting for him to climb back aboard. It had stopped moving the instant he let go of it. Now he had to find a way of getting back out to it.

Butch grabbed hold of the cable, kicked off the hull of the dinghy with his feet. He covered the fifteen or so meters out to the mech-asc, hand-over-hand, hanging like a trapeze artist from the line. Nearly weightless, it was a piece of cake.

When he again reached the crossbar of the mechanical-ascender, he ran the safety line through the loop as Red instructed. Then he switched the machine back on and continued his journey. One hundred and eighty-five meters of open space remained.

Butch ran the steps through his mind. Ride the mechanical-ascender across the cable. Use the Pigtail or the pry bar to loosen the old antenna-unit. Rivet the new antenna box into place, one rivet in each corner. Hook red wire to red, white to white, green to green, black to black. Wrap and seal loose ends with beryllium duct tape. Hurry back to the ship.

These were the technical details, and Butch knew them well enough. But, like learning to ride a bicycle, little of a practical nature can be garnered from reading a book about it. You have to fly over the handlebars and skin your knees at least once to master the art.

Much the same process was at work here. There were technical details, and then there was reality. Replace the terror of flying over the handlebars with the terror of hanging in open space 200 million kloms above nothing at all, and you get the idea.

Or, how about the dread of touching the wrong wire with your space pliers? Or of heating up the EMD beyond the melting point, then being liquefied into a sticky blob of human flesh?

Then there were the purely mortal fears. Like the fear of being held personally responsible for destroying an entire world if he was a drill bit and mucked things up.

His breath came in great gulps now.

All Butch could hear was the sound of metal scraping against metal as the mechanical-ascender ground its way across the remaining distance from ship to rock. A cable, a double-wheeled pulley, and a locking device were all that separated this usually fearless young man from oblivion.

Butch could feel the veins in his temple pop out. He could feel his heart pounding within his chest. His breath coming faster. — And faster.

All of a sudden, Butch didn't seem to be getting enough air! Something had gone terribly wrong !

Woody screamed at Butch through the comm. "You fool, you're hyperventilating! Slow down your goddamn breathing or else you'll pass out!"

Woody had been closely monitoring Butch's vitals on the screen inside the ship. Now Red joined in. "Get your head out of the Oort Cloud, you drill bit, and start paying attention!"

That voice sounded familiar, so Butch stopped to listen.

"I mean it, Butch! Slow down your breathing! You're gonna pass out any second now!"

The words made sense and Butch reacted. He scolded himself for his stupidity. *Some hero you turned out to be*, he thought grimly.

His breath came slower now. The big rock filled his field of view. Here, somewhere in the void between planets three and four, the future of mankind would be decided. There was no tomorrow, only today, right now in fact.

The nearer Butch drew to the egg-shaped asteroid, the heavier he became. It wasn't that the asteroid was massive enough to produce measurable gravity, only that he was gaining centripetal force the closer he got to his quarry. Rather than being located near the spinning planetoid's center of gravity, the unit that needed replacing was out along one axis, where the spin rate was higher. He could feel the pseudo-gravity building up on him the closer he got.

Where before, he was weightless and giddy, now he was heavy and lethargic. Where before, the contents of his stomach were floating uneasily in a soup, ready to gurgle up at any moment, now everything had sunk like a rock to the pit of his abdomen. His arms, once light, now felt heavy. Even the weight of his suit began to drag him down.

Sensing danger, Butch slowed his approach. The g-forces were tugging at him now with some conviction. His legs began to drift up and out to his left, away from the center of gravity of the spinning rock. Except for the lumina-beam shining from the top of his helmet, everything else was dark.

Butch tightened his grip on the crossbar of the mech-asc. The closer he drew to the big rock, the harder he was being pushed away from it. The gears were straining under the burden.

Only ten meters to go.

Butch was close enough, now, to clearly see what had happened. A big piece of space dust had torn away the entire antenna housing. It was a blackened mess. Had something bigger hit, the mass-driver itself might have been ruptured, making this whole exercise useless.

Butch clawed his way the last few meters against the crushing centripetal force. Finally, with almost no strength left in his arms, he reached out with one hand and clipped himself directly to Red's diamond-tipped bolt. *Now it was time to get down to business.*

The rivet gun was in his hand. The spool of beryllium copper duct tape was in his outer pocket. The knapsack was off his back, now, and in his other hand. He tore away the poly bag protecting the new antenna-unit and tethered it to the Velcro strip running down the length of his right leg. He let go of the rucksack. It floated away from him, propelled by the same g-forces that were playing havoc with his body. The bag drifted off in the same general direction his legs were pointed. For the next several minutes anyway, that direction was "down." The poly bag followed close behind.

Butch moved quickly but safely. There was no need to pry off the old unit, as it was already gone. But he did have to secure the new one.

Butch braced himself. In went one rivet. Then a second. But just as he was about to punch in the third, calamity struck. — Butch was suddenly blinded by the most intense light in the solar system.

Butch reeled backwards. Up to this point he had been working in the shadow of the asteroid, on the side opposite the sun.

But now, all of a sudden, he had ridden the beast through a revolution and been spun into the light. *The timing couldn't have been worse !*

As Butch's gloved hands flew to his face to shield his eyes, the rivet gun fell from his grip. The glass on his visor darkened almost immediately, though for an instant he couldn't see.

Butch reached blindly for his rivet gun. But already it was too late. The tool had been swallowed up by the darkness.

"Damn!" he swore, alarming everyone in the cabin.

"What the hell happened now?" came the anxious reply over the mike.

"I lost the rivet gun."

"What do you mean, you lost it? Who the hell loses a rivet gun at a time like this?"

"It wasn't on today's to-do list, if that's what you mean."

"Can you get the bloody thing back?" Woody was getting worked up. "We don't have another one, you know. Is there any way to attach the bloody thing without rivets?"

"Don't have a cat, Woody. I popped in two rivets before the sun blinded me and I dropped the frigging gun. Upper left and lower right. Even with only two rivets popped in, the unit ought to hold. And about that cat — you might have warned me I was about to spin into the sun."

Woody fumed. "You saying this is my fault? How dare you! What say I ring your bloody neck when you get back in here? And here all along I thought you were an experienced spacejockey. I never realized I'd first have to wipe your ass for you."

"Wipe my ass? I'd like to see you put on a suit, come out here and do this."

Red interrupted. "What's it gonna be, boys? — Pissing for distance or for accuracy? Two rivets ought to hold her. But damn-it-to-hell, Butch, you simply have got to quit arguing and save your breath. You've only got about eighteen more minutes of air. Can you put this thing to bed in that amount of time or not?"

Butch answered "Yes." But he wasn't so sure. There was still the small matter of reconnecting the loose wires.

Truth be known, Butch Hogan really wasn't that big on God or religion. But all things considered, he really didn't think a silent prayer could hurt his chances at this point. So he prayed: *Dear God, I beseech you. Please let these wires be magnetized.*

All the wires onboard the Station were. On the Station, each color wire was charged with a slightly different polarity. That way, they would adhere only to another wire of identical color. Any other way, the job might prove impossible. Space gloves were bulky. They made their wearer clumsy, especially when manipulating tiny instruments or devices.

Butch reached for the spool of electrical tape in his pocket. He pushed back the insulation on the first wire and found his prayers answered. The wires *were* magnetized!

Butch moved quickly now. Red to red. White to white. Green to green. Black to black. He wrapped each connection securely with the beryllium tape, then unlocked himself from the bolt and started back.

At first, Butch was thrown outward by the same centripetal force he had gained coming over from the dinghy. He actively countered that. He slowed his descent down the cable using the manual brake on the mech-asc.

Slowly, weightlessness returned. His legs hung free once more. His breathing slowed. His stomach grew unsettled. The dinghy filled his field of vision. *It was over!*

Red helped pull his buddy back into the airlock. They re-pressurized the chamber and Butch collapsed onto the floor, exhausted. Woody helped him pull off his helmet, while Gulliver cut the cable loose and edged the dinghy away from the big rock. Just as soon as they were a safe distance away they would radio Space-Traffic Control that it was time to warm up the electromagnets and get EMD 14 back online.

Butch quickly fell asleep. The rich oxygen mix and all that adrenaline burning through his system. Saving the world had been sort of a heady experience; yet, it paled next to the task that lay immediately ahead — figuring out where he stood with the woman he loved.

CHAPTER SEVENTEEN

▼

President Noah Benjamin.

His great-great-grandfather on his mother's side was the archetypal West Virginia coal miner, complete with pickaxe, coveralls, dirty hands, and a lumina projecting from his helmet. The old man worked deep underground in one of the few remaining pit mines of his time. His son Mordechai — Noah's great-grandfather — was a bookkeeper for that same company in that same West Virginia coal town. Noah's grandfather, Abraham, was that town's mayor. Noah's father, that State's senator. Noah himself, President of the United States. That's how it was in America, even for a Jew. Work hard, stay the course, climb the socioeconomic ladder.

Noah's grandfather, the mayor, purchased a large tract of land in the wooded mountains outside of town, where he built a grand house. There, he and his wife Rose raised four strong children, all boys, all ambitious. The oldest, Noah's father, while well on the road to becoming a U.S. Senator, enlarged the house and expanded the landholdings significantly. It came to be called "Blue Ridge Manor." Now, with Noah well into his first term as President, the palatial estate had evolved into the so-called Mountain White House, complete with hospital, airchop pad, and wellness center. Here was a place where Noah Benjamin could retreat to, a place where he could escape the confines of the D.C. Dome, not to mention the watchful eyes of the world. This secluded, park-like setting was also the perfect locale to meet and greet foreign dignitaries and large campaign contributors.

Noah stood, now, on the balcony of his second-floor bedroom. His wife Ruth stood beside him. She was a quiet, usually patient woman. Noah was expectant, knowing what the day would bring. From here he could see the motorcade as it came up the valley.

The line of limousines wound their way up the curvy mountain roads. The foothills of the Appalachian Mountains, pushed up eons ago by geologic forces and later softened by wind and water erosion, were now fertile, green and wooded. Winters were hard, summers long. In the spring the creeks ran high. In the fall the forests were a blaze of color.

High fences surrounded the entire property, put up and manned round-the-clock at taxpayer expense. Overhead, surveillance drones circled. Hidden in the woods were security bots, both fixed and roving. Security at the fence-line was tight.

But inside those fences, life was quiet and peaceful. The President liked to ride horses and housed a large stable of fine Tennessee Walkers. He liked to watch vids and had a large, indoor theatre with the latest accoutrements: active Comfy Chairs, emote wall, surround-sound, the whole nine yards.

When Noah wasn't engaged in official business, as he was today, he might spend as much as twenty consecutive hours viewing his favorite vids. Some, he'd watch over and over again. Like that old Western, the one with the football player turned Omega Special Forces hero turned actor turned politician. Noah Benjamin fancied himself a gunslinger of sorts, though the last member of his family to actually handle a gun was his great-grandfather Mordechai.

Noah watched from his balcony. The line of dark limousines drew closer, kicking up dust as they came. This would be Noah's backers from Transcomet Industries, part of the conglomerate that included EMD Enterprises. Without their money, Noah might never have been elected President. Without their money, he had little chance of being re-elected. But today, the men in those limousines were here to collect on that debt. There would be certain niceties first, of course. But the inevitable was, well, inevitable.

The President's first surprise of the morning came when he saw Senator Patrick Flanagan exit the lead gcar with his security detail. Noah looked first at his wife, then at his Chief of Staff for confirmation. The Chief shook his head. There had been no advance word that Flanagan would be part of the entourage that included Keith Roberts and the rest of the Transcomet Board.

Noah Benjamin got red in the face. The man did not like surprises, and certainly not on his own turf. If Flanagan was now suddenly in cahoots with Keith Roberts and the rest of the Board, that meant he planned to run against Noah in the upcoming election — and with their blessing. Hardly an auspicious start.

On the other hand, Senator Flanagan was a staunch opponent of terraforming, hardly a position Transcomet could endorse. Noah couldn't help but wonder what kind of mixed-up agenda could possibly draw two such disparate souls together at a time like this. — And why?

Senator Flanagan waited for Keith Roberts, the Board Chairman, to catch up. The two walked together a moment, shared a laugh. Then Roberts took the lead. Half a step behind him was his very capable assistant, though for the life of him, Noah couldn't remember the good-looking woman's name. The President waited a moment to calm himself before going downstairs to greet the new arrivals. Ruth stayed upstairs alone. She had an intense dislike for Keith Roberts, and it was hard for her to hide her feelings.

The troupe came up the front porch steps, passed through security. Inside the fence, security was more perfunctory than real. The outer gate was where the real pat-down occurred — vehicles, belongings, personnel. Now, at the front door, it was just so much ritualistic protocol.

"Mr. President, so good to see you again. Thank you so much for hosting our little parley."

Noah winced. Keith Roberts, the Board Chairman, always liked to sprinkle his speech with foreign-sounding words. If anyone asked, he might explain that parley was from the French verb *parler*, meaning discussion or talk.

"Keith, you know as well as anyone that the pleasure is all mine," Noah replied.

"And well it should be."

"And who is that I see with you?"

"Mr. President, you know perfectly well who that is. Patrick Flanagan, senior Senator from the great State of Connecticut."

"Tell me the man was hitchhiking, Keith. Tell me that, in a moment of weakness, you stopped the motorcade to pick the man up by the side of the road. Tell me a pathetic tale. Otherwise, I can't see why the bastard is even standing here in my front room." Noah Benjamin looked at the Board Chairman with hard eyes. "Or is Patrick here for a reason?"

"You never were one to mince words, were you, compadre?"

Noah knew this one. Compadre. It meant friend or godfather, something along those lines.

By now the rest of the Board had cleared security and reached the front door. Noah's aides were busy showing them in. Beyond the front hall was a large room, with plenty of seating around a large, oak table. Hot and cold food was laid out on a side table. A wet bar stood in the corner, manned by the best on Noah's sizeable domestic staff.

"You know my Executive Assistant, Zuzana Nordstrom, don't you?"

Keith Roberts introduced a stunning woman. She was well-built, but dressed very conservatively. "Zuzana is — What do your people say? — a *berrieh*. That's Yiddish. But then you probably knew that, eh Noah? It is a complimentary term for a woman with lots of talent. One with a reputation for getting things done. That's my Zuzana."

"How do you do?" Noah was polite. He reached out his hand to shake hers. "I know we've met before, Ms. Nordstrom. And I sincerely apologize for not remembering your name."

"No apology necessary, Mr. President. But please call me Zuzana. In your line of work, you meet lots of people. You can't be expected to remember everyone's name."

"Our President is no *dowfart*, if that's what you mean."

"Dare I ask?"

"*Dowfart*. It's a Scottish word. Though back then, some pronounced it *duffart*. A stupid, dull fellow. Same root that gave us such dandies as doofus and dullard and duffer. A great word, if you ask me."

About then Senator Patrick Flanagan strolled up strutting like a proud, game hen. He had a cocky look slapped across his big, Irish face. The sort Noah's great-great-grandfather would have summarily smacked off. Noah remained stiff if polite.

"I'll bet you never planned on seeing me here today," Flanagan said.

Roberts interfered before Noah could answer. "Senator, you know what they say in New Guinea? — *biga peula*. Fighting words. Certain unspoken truths better left unsaid. Let's not be antagonistic."

"I descend from a different culture," Noah snapped back, his anger rising. "My people know full well that leaving a thing unsaid is a sure recipe for misunderstanding. In my culture we solve problems by talking them out."

"Do your people wear grass skirts and hail from the Big Island?" Keith Roberts' tone was meant to rankle, and it finally triggered a hostile response.

"You know very well where my people hail from — and it certainly isn't the Hawaii Free State!"

"No, of course not. But in the Free State, the locals have a word for what you describe — *opono* — solving a problem by talking it out."

"Well then, let's talk the mother out. — What in blazes is Flanagan doing here? This is my house. This is my meeting. This was supposed to be a gathering of *my* financial backers. I invited all these good people here to thank them for what they have done for me in the past — and to ask them for their support in my reelection bid."

"*Mokita* — that's the word for it. A truth everybody knows but nobody is willing to say. Also from New Guinea. Senator Flanagan has shone a bright light into our eyes, made converts of us all. We have likewise made a convert of him."

Noah Benjamin was flabbergasted. "Don't tell me Transcomet is going to get behind this mloron? Have you even read this shabby man's gun-banning law? He would make every last one of you a felon. By God, Keith, you of all people. Ever since I've known you, you have always stood firm on protecting the Second Amendment."

"I'll admit, Flanagan's law may need some tweaking. But our change of heart did not come without compensations. Our new amigo, Patrick Flanagan, is finally willing to come aboard the terraforming bandwagon. He now sees the inevitability of it all, just as we now see the inevitable repeal of the Second Amendment. We each get something in the trade."

"Tweaking? That's what you call it? Tweaking?"

"That kind of talk is what the New Guineas call *sanza*. A disguised insult. Like — Now that's a baby! — said of an especially ugly one."

"Tell me this isn't happening," Noah sighed, suddenly feeling old and very tired.

Zuzana Nordstrom spoke up. Her voice was soothing. "Mr. President, I can see how this sudden change in policy might be upsetting, how it might be hard for you to accept. But there are financial considerations that must be taken into account here. Our company's business is out there, in space." She pointed. "Space enterprises are not as tangible as lettuce on a plate. The public doesn't always appreciate how something so distant can have such a direct impact on economic conditions right here at home. For us, the trouble has been this: As the anti-terraforming movement has gained traction, it has hurt our stock price. As part of our deal with Senator Flanagan, the man has promised to withdraw his support from the Anti-Terraforming League when the news breaks."

"When what news breaks?" Noah was vexed.

"A key scientist working for the League is about to be indicted for influence peddling."

"Trumped up charges, no doubt."

"That remains to be seen," Roberts said. "But no one likes a scandal, least of all Senator Flanagan. He has agreed that supporting such an organization while it is under an investigatory cloud would not be a politically wise move. If the Senator is successful in quieting the opposition to our terraforming plans, we have promised to get behind his Gun Control Bill in return. I give you fair warning, Mr. President — before this thing is over, the entire Bill of Rights may come under scrutiny."

Noah threw up his hands in disgust, turned to face Roberts' executive assistant. "Your boss is a bloody fool. Did you know that, Zuzana? A bloody fool. American corporations depend on the protection of American laws. Now you people want to gut the Constitution?"

"This is getting us nowhere!" Keith Roberts roared. "*Prayoga!*"

"No pithy explanation?"

"If you must know, it's a Hindu word. Roughly translated, it means ritual masturbation. Which is precisely what we're engaged in now."

"Honestly, Keith."

"Boss, maybe we should give President Benjamin some time to digest all this," Zuzana suggested, holding out hope of a compromise.

"Time to digest? Give the man an antacid for all I care, but swallow this pill he will. It's *gajes*, Mr. President, *gajes*. An occupational hazard. That's what the Spaniards say. Literally, the wages to be paid. Zuzana already told you there are financial considerations to be taken into account here. If the price of our company's stock doesn't stop going down soon, we will be forced to cut back on our political contributions to you and your party. He who gets our stock price up, gets our money — and that's final!"

President Benjamin was incensed. "So, in the end, this is little more than felony bribery?"

"*Hartducha*, my friend, *hartducha*. That's Polish for 'hard spirit'. To be unflinching. To maintain your dignity, even if oppressed."

"Get the fuck out of my house! All of you! Get the fuck out!"

Keith Roberts shook his head. "You're a fool, Noah. You need us."

"Do I? For what?"

"You'll regret this. I can promise you that. Like it or not, you need us."

"You're whores! All whores! And none worse than you, Flanagan. Your very own daughter is out there in space, doing your bidding, gathering up reasons for you to put a halt to terraforming. Meanwhile, you're down here, undercutting her every move, your own flesh and blood. You should be ashamed of yourself! Now get your butts out of my house! I'll not support a bid to destroy the Bill of Rights."

"Let's go," the Board Director ordered, turning on his heel.

"But, sir," his Executive Assistant argued.

"He'll come around, Zuzana, of that I am sure. The President needs us as much we need him. Otherwise, it's just *bol*. Not bull, mind you — *bol*. Which is Mayan for stupid. Which is what you are, Noah, if you try and fight us on this one."

"Boss, permit me to stay behind and talk to the man," Zuzana offered. "We owe the President that much."

"What did I tell you? — the woman's *berrieh*. Lots of talent. A reputation for getting things done."

"Nordstrom can stay. But I want the rest of you out of here. Now. Leave."

"It's *kulikov*, my friend. That's when someone makes a legal judgment for pragmatic reasons, not because it's the right thing to do. You'll see."

"No, the word is *glorg*," Noah retorted angrily. "I may not know all your fancy frigging words, but I do know that one. It means to work in some dirty business. I see now that that's the only kind of business you know."

"Why, you son of a . . . "

"Boss, leave this to me," Zuzana insisted. "The President and I will talk."

"Make sure that's all you do."

"The man's already lost his straw hat, Boss. Let it be."

The Board, so recently arrived, exited the front room and headed across the lawn to their respective gcars. Overhead, the surveillance drones watched and recorded their every move.

Noah looked strangely at Zuzana as the motorcade pulled away. "Straw hat?"

"To lose your straw hat means to lose your virginity. Keith understood what I meant. He's always using fancy words. I was telling him you weren't a virgin in the ways of the world. But first things first — you and I need to talk."

"What is there left to talk about? It seems as if everything has been decided."

"Not everything. In fact, practically nothing. Please, let's sit and talk this thing out."

President Benjamin agreed and they moved into the next room. He signaled his butler to bring them drinks and a light snack. Then a new voice made itself known. It was Ruth, the President's wife.

"Has that horrible man left?"

"Yes, love, he has. Down the road and out of here. But I'll still be a minute. Please meet Zuzana Nordstrom, Keith's assistant."

"Executive Assistant," Zuzana corrected, reaching out her hand to the First Lady. "So nice to meet you Mrs. Benjamin."

"Let's not stand on ceremony, shall we? If you work for that horrible man that makes you equally horrible. Finish with my husband and let him be." Ruth turned on her heel and went back upstairs. "And don't let the door hit you on the way out."

Zuzana tried to compose herself.

"My wife calls them as she sees them."

"A good woman to have around."

"Most days anyway. But not every day is good." The President's mind wandered as he thought of the other woman in his life. She did for him what Ruth would not."

"May I continue?"

"By all means." He came back to the here and now.

"Mr. President, I think if you were to come out in favor of Senator

Flanagan's bill, the Board might not feel as strongly about needing to line up behind Flanagan himself."

"How does my coming out in favor of Gun Control help get your stock price up?"

"News of the indictment against one of the League's top scientists will force Flanagan's hand, no matter what Transcomet does. He'll have no choice but to distance himself from the League, which will reduce their political clout immensely. You get to run again; Transcomet gets the anti-terraformers off their backs. Everybody's happy."

"Except, of course, Patrick Flanagan."

"Except, of course, Patrick Flanagan."

Noah Benjamin smiled. He liked that answer. The food and beverage arrived, and they broke off their discussions for a moment to partake of both.

"If everything you say is true, then why the hell didn't Keith just come right out and say so in the first place? I hate this cloak and dagger stuff."

"The man loves to grandstand, you know that. Plus, Flanagan was standing right there next to him. Keith had to be convincing. He needs Flanagan to buy the whole subterfuge: hook, line, and sinker."

"But for me to come out in favor of banning guns? That goes to the very heart of my political base. What you ask. — It is much."

"Well, Mr. President, the ball is most definitely now in your court."

"I think my hand is stronger than you know."

"Mr. President, if you have other cards to play, then by all means, play them."

"Three cards actually. I know certain things I am confident the Board of Transcomet doesn't know I know."

"Would you care to elaborate?"

"Do the words 'EMD 14' hold any meaning for you?"

Zuzana Nordstrom's face lost all color. The President continued:

"Let me check my silver ball. Ah, yes, I can see the headlines now. **Electromagnetic Mass-Driver Goes Berserk**. And below it, another headline, in slightly smaller letters. **Transcomet Puts Entire Planet At Risk To Turn A Profit**."

Zuzana got whiter, started to tremble. President Benjamin continued:

"I'll keep this in plain, simple terms even your idiot boss can understand. No foreign words — all English. The fact that one of your precious M-type asteroids spun out of control for an extended period, and was actually on a collision course with Earth, has so far been withheld from the public. But think about the consequences if that information were to somehow now be leaked? What do you think would happen to the price of your frigging stock then? With or without Flanagan onboard, if this information were to fall into the wrong hands — say Annabel Clark at the American News Network — your business would be *out* of business inside of six months."

"I would say this is a card the Board would rather you did not play."

"See? That's what I call *glorg*."

"Yiddish?"

"If only it were. Old English, actually. One of my grandfather's sayings."

"You said you held three cards."

"And indeed I do. Card number Two is quite simple. The influence peddling charges against that scientist are false. It is Flanagan that is guilty of those charges, not some scientist working for the League. This business with the Anti-Terraforming League is totally bogus."

"You have proof?"

"None that will stand up in court yet. But what we do have is getting firmer every day."

"I see. And card number Three?"

"A very close friend of mine informs me that he has incontrovertible proof your new ally, Patrick Flanagan, is a homosexual."

"I have also heard such rumors."

"This is no rumor. We have incontrovertible proof. So tell me, Zuzana — How do you think that particular flag will look blowing in the wind over Transcomet headquarters? A bim Senator from a liberal State is one thing; a sissy in the White House is quite another."

Zuzana Nordstrom got to her feet, turned to leave. "I'll tell my boss I think you hold the stronger hand. You are a good man, Mr. President — and I mean that sincerely. It's clear to me now that you deserve to sit in the White House four more years."

"Funny how you think a day will end one way and then, just like that, it takes an unexpected turn. It reminds me of another Old English term — *gardyloo*. It's from the French — *gardez l'eau*, literally 'save yourselves from the water'. This is a warning, one that the servants in the higher stories of the house would cry out to those down below when, after dark, they would throw their dirty water onto the streets from the upstairs windows. It's the same phrase that gave the British their name for their toilets — the loo."

"I don't follow."

"Don't let the dirty water splash on you, Zuzana. It doesn't wash out that easily."

"I promise to stand back, stay out of the splash zone."

"A good day to you then, Zuzana. My man will show you out."

CHAPTER EIGHTEEN

▼

The dinghy back in the hold, the *S.S. Mars Voyager* once again unfurled her solar sails and began to move forward. It would take several days of rapid acceleration until the ship could once again attain the great speed it previously had before they broke off to repair the antenna-unit. In all, the side trip would delay their return to Earth by as much as a week.

When the four men walked out of the docking bay and through the bulkhead door, they looked as if they had been on the losing end of a short, nasty war. Red's hand was bandaged and Butch was stumbling badly. Red was met at the door by a nurse and taken to the med lab for surgery. Butch was famished, fatigued, and disoriented. To a man, their clothes smelled of sweat and vomit.

Kaleena took Butch by the hand. Adoration filled her eyes. This man who had elbowed his way into her life, this man who was so simple and yet so proud, had suddenly taken on dimensions larger than anything she could have imagined. Here was a genuine American hero. And, if she played her cards right, he belonged to her, and only her. Once her man was properly rested, Kaleena had every intention of being appropriately appreciative. *Her man had quite literally saved the world!*

Butch didn't have the energy to object. He meekly followed Kaleena back to her quarters, where she ordered food and beverage from passenger services. Each room had a touchpad and e-menu next to the door. Prepackaged sim foods took only minutes to prepare. Delivery was by conveyer belt and dumbwaiter.

Kaleena's fingers fairly flew over the keys of the touchpad. She ordered her man soy steak, space spuds, sim cheesecake, cola, beer, milk. Butch ate quickly then fell fast asleep. She was still at his side when he woke up an hour later.

Butch had barely come to, when she grabbed him and kissed him full on the lips.

"Have I died and gone to heaven?" he moaned.

"How many women get to make love to a real-live hero?"

"I could have sworn that the other day you accused me of being a barbaric hunter, a crude man who toted a crude rifle dating to a throwback era."

"That was the other day. We struck a deal, remember? The length of this trip plus one month earth-side. Now take off your pants and do me proper."

"This I can do. Though I have to warn you. I have been accused of being a barbaric hunter, not only out on the trail, but in bed as well. This is to say nothing of the crooked rifle I carry. It much prefers being cocked before being fired, if you grasp my meaning."

"I'll grasp whatever you want. With both hands if you like. You be the barbarian; I'll be the Amazon. Together, us Visigoths can almost certainly straighten out that crooked tool of yours. Plus, we should see what can be done to clear the chamber of any unspent ammunition."

Butch dropped his pants to the floor. "I can't tell you how much I love a good metaphor. Now be sure to pull back firmly on the hammer before cocking. We don't want to gum up the works."

"Only if you promise to hit the target square and hard."

"Lady, I never miss."

•

•

"Ah, the prodigal spaceman returns. Triumphant, I might add."

Elijah Montrose was in the Commons eating. Two representatives from the Terraforming Commission were at the table with him. The three were engaged in a heated discussion. Elijah saw Butch and Kaleena enter the room, signaled them both to come over and join him.

Kaleena whispered in Butch's ear. "You talk, I'll shop," and she hurried away to meet some girls in the midship mall.

Butch continued to Elijah's table. "Prodigal spaceman? Some hidden meaning I'm too ignorant to grasp?"

"No, I mean that sincerely. We're all proud of you, every single one of us." The other two men nodded their approval, shook his hand.

Butch enjoyed his moment. "Odds always were, we would succeed. But there's always that element of chance in everything us spacejockeys do out there. I probably wouldn't have even suited up and gone out to do the job if Red hadn't gotten hurt first. We drew straws as it was."

Elijah took the opening and eased through it. "Most games involve an element of chance. That, plus a bit of strategy and plenty of skill."

Butch glanced quizzically at the two other men at Elijah's table to see if they understood his meaning. The two suddenly looked as if they were trying to find a reason — any reason — to be somewhere else.

"Something you want to get off your chest, Doc?" Butch asked, as the two excused themselves and left.

"I'm twice your age — show some respect, will you?"

"Only twice?"

"Oh, yes, that's right. I keep forgetting. I'm a fossil, aren't I?"

"I don't think I ever called you a fossil. Old-timer? — yes. Raisin-crapper? — yes. But never fossil."

Elijah laughed. "Okay, sit down, have a drink and something to eat, and pay attention. Because of this asteroid thing, we've got an extra week to kill. You might as well spend that time productively, maybe further your education."

"I dropped out of school years ago. Never went to college."

"College or not, when you get home, every one you meet will consider you a hero. I should imagine job offers will be streaming in from every corner of the planet."

"I have a job, a good one. Besides: the planet's round. No corners, last time I looked."

"Did anyone ever tell you you're an impertinent son of a bitch?"

"I guess my father did a poor job raising me."

"No mother?"

"Oh, I had a mother. But she didn't stick around long. My father can sometimes be a hard man to live with."

"I'm sorry to hear that. But it's high time you shut up and listened. I'm going to try and teach you something I happen to know a great deal about. Game Theory."

Butch got comfortable, tugged at his drink, let Elijah Montrose do his thing:

"Let me give you an example of what I mean. Let's say there are these two friends, both students at the same University and both enrolled in the same chemistry class. Both men have done pretty well on all the quizzes, plus the labs and the midterm, so going into the final they have a solid A. The two are so confident of their grades that the weekend before the final they decide to go to a big party at a neighboring college up the road a few kloms. The party is so good, they sleep all day Sunday and wake up too late to study for their chemistry final scheduled for first thing Monday morning."

"Just what kind of game is this anyway?"

"I thought we agreed you were going to sit down, shut up, and pay attention?" Elijah grumbled, before continuing. "Rather than take the final examination unprepared, the two young men go to their professor with a sob story. The two admit going to a party but say they planned on coming home early, certainly in good time to study for the final. However, on the way home, they had a flat tire. Being poverty-stricken, like most college students, they didn't have a spare and spent most of the night trying to get help. Now they were really too tired to perform up to their capabilities, so could they please have a makeup exam the next day? The professor thought it over a moment and agreed."

"He fell for those two bullshit artists? And here I thought college professors were smarter than all that."

Elijah Montrose only smiled. Then he continued with his story:

"The two boys studied hard all Monday evening and came to class well-prepared Tuesday morning. The professor placed them in separate rooms and handed them each a test. The first question on the first page, worth ten points, was easy. They each wrote a good answer and, greatly relieved, turned the page. It had just one question, worth ninety points."

"One question? That hardly seems fair. I really don't understand your professor, not one little bit."

"You haven't heard the question."

"Okay, give."

"The question was — Which tire?"

"Hah!" Butch exclaimed. "The chem professor is not so dumb after all."

"No, he isn't. But let's study this game analytically. It carries two important strategic lessons common to all such encounters. The first is to recognize that your opponent — in this case, the chem professor — may also be an intelligent game player. The professor may suspect some trickery on the boys' part, and he may employ trickery to catch them. Once the professor heard the boys' excuse, his trick question was the only logical way to unmask the subterfuge. It was the boys themselves who made the mistake, two mistakes actually. First, they lied. Then, having lied, they should have foreseen the professor's question and prepared their answer in advance. Taken together, these thought processes represent a very general principle of good strategy, the idea that a player should always look ahead to future moves in a game and then reason backwards to calculate one's best current move."

"So, what you are talking about here, Doc, is truly a Theory Of Games —

complete with moves, countermoves, opposing players, strategies, the whole shooting match."

"Oh, but we've only just scratched the surface. It may not be possible for an unenlightened student to anticipate his professor's every move. Professors, after all, have at least as much experience seeing through their students' excuses as students have in making them up. And yet, the average student isn't completely stupid. Can you see any way for these two chem students to independently manufacture a mutually consistent lie?"

"You mean about which tire went flat?"

"Yes. The two are taking their tests in separate rooms. They can't communicate. But can they still come up with the same answer to the tire question?"

"I suppose mental telepathy is out?"

Doc narrowed his eyes.

"If each boy selects a tire at random, chances are only 1 in 4 that they will both pick the same tire."

"I agree," Doc said. "But they won't reason at random."

"That's probably true as well. Anyone who has ever driven a gcar knows that the front tire on the passenger side is the one most likely to suffer a flat."

"I guess I never knew that."

"You would if you lived out in the boonies like I do. It happens more than occasionally in the backwoods of Wyoming where the Hogan Ranch is located. A nail or shard of glass is more likely to lie closer to the side of the road then the middle. The front tire will obviously encounter it before the back tire will."

"Okay, Pilgrim, I'll take your word for it. But that still doesn't necessarily make the front right tire the best choice in this sort of guessing game."

"For the life of me, I can't see why not."

"Good logic doesn't always make for the best choice. What matters here is not the logic of a man's choice, but being able to make the same choice as his friend. Each boy has to consider whether his friend will use the same logic as he does. Will they both consider a given choice *equally* obvious? And will that choice be equally obvious to the other? The chain of reasoning goes on and on. The point is not whether a choice is obvious or logical, but whether it is obvious and logical to the other that it is obvious and logical to the first that it is obvious and logical to the other. In Game Theory jargon, what is needed is a convergence of expectations about what should be chosen given the current circumstances."

"You mean like a rule of thumb?"

"Yes, although there is no guarantee that convergence will ever occur. It depends on the game. Sometimes, common experience or chance circumstance controls whether or not players' expectations will converge."

"Like what?"

"Oh, I don't know. Maybe these two characters had a flat tire once before. Maybe it turned out to be a memorable experience that they often laughed about. Or maybe, for some strange reason, students at that college call the passenger's front side of a gcar the University side. Then two students from that University may very well choose it on the chem professor's test without any need for explicit prior understanding. But, in the absence of such clues, convergence may be impossible."

"So level with me, Doc: Why *are* professors so mean?"

"There's no percentage in being a softie. To maintain order, a professor has to acquire a certain reputation for toughness."

"I suppose he does this the usual way, by acting tough a few times."

"Acting tough may run against the man's grain, as it does mine. But in the long run it'll make his life a whole lot easier. Once a professor has a rep for being tough, very few students will actually try out excuses on the man, so he will actually suffer less pain in denying them."

"Not everyone's so well-behaved, Doc. What if a kid keeps testing the man, just to see what will happen? I, myself, was a difficult student."

"Why doesn't that surprise me? But the answer to your question has more to do with brinkmanship. And it applies to a whole lot more than just difficult students. — Labor disputes. War. Failing marriages. — In each case, a player allows the risk to escalate until he can't take it any longer. The one least able to cope loses. Each player sees just how close to the brink of disaster he can push his opponent before one of them flinches."

Elijah continued. "Such games can end in only one of two ways. Either, one of the players reaches the limit of his own tolerance for risk and concedes. Or, before either player has conceded, the meltdown they both fear comes to pass, and the blowup occurs — whether it is a labor strike or a call to arms."

"I follow that. In most games, whether it be chess or football, there is but a single winner and a single loser. One player's gain is the other fellow's loss. War and labor strikes are not like that — they are not zero-sum games — losses exceed gains."

"The more serious the standoff, the more likely the victory is to be Pyrrhic. In these kinds of situations, even the winner loses."

"Like nuclear war."

"In a more typical standoff, any attempts the players make to resolve their conflict — whether it be over territory or profit — will be influenced by the knowledge that if they fail to agree, the outcome will be bad for both of them.

One side's threat of war or calling a work-stoppage is their hardball attempt to frighten the other side into acceding to their demands."

"Like a bluff in poker."

"Only much more dangerous. Successful brinkmanship requires two seemingly inconsistent stances. On the one hand, you must let matters spin far enough out of control that you begin to lose the ability to avoid taking the dire action you have threatened. This is the only way for your threat to remain credible. At the same time, you must retain sufficient control over the situation to keep the risk from becoming too large. Otherwise, your threat becomes too costly."

"I have seen this kind of thing go wrong before. It's like a game of chicken, a delicate balancing act, even for an experienced negotiator."

"Yes, and such games often fail. Sometimes, things boil over at the precise moment the heat is reduced. Plus, if at some point your opponent *does* comply with your demands, you must be able to go into reverse immediately, quickly reducing the pressure and completely removing the perceived threat from the picture. Otherwise, your opponent gains nothing by compliance and the situation will spin quickly out of control."

"You're really into this stuff, aren't you, Doc?" Butch could see the fire in Elijah's eyes.

"People make fun of economics, call it the Dismal Science, say it's boring. It's anything but. Game Theory is extremely revealing. A player's strategy changes with the game. Is the game played once or repeatedly? With the same opponent or with a new opponent each time?"

"Why should that matter?"

"A game played just once is simpler to analyze. You can contemplate a one-shot game without ever having to worry about its repercussions on other games you might play against the same opponent in the future, or against other players who might have heard about the actions you took in the first game. As a consequence, actions taken in a one-shot game are more likely to be extreme."

"By extreme, you mean ruthless."

"Yes, I do. Ruthless. Deceitful. Unscrupulous. You name it. Think gcar repair shop. Who are they more likely to overcharge? — a motorist just passing through town or a regular customer?"

"I see what you're getting at. In a one-shot game — that motorist passing through town — how you treat them really doesn't matter in the long run."

"Stealth. Surprise. Secrecy. These are the key components of any good strategy."

"Now you're beginning to sound like some of my old buddies back when I was in uniform. I was a Marine before I started working the high steel.

Many of my buds were on Interrogation detail under the command of Pappy Barnes. They had to break down terrorists, get them to give up their handlers. Talk about your one-shot games."

"And yet economics tells us there are caveats. If the guy you're interrogating thinks you are going to kill him no matter what he says, he will cease to cooperate. Why should he bother? It's a proven fact that when the future becomes cloudy — and perhaps without value — a player is likely to become uncooperative. In the business world, if times are bad and an entire industry is on the verge of collapse, companies may conclude that the enterprise they worked so hard to build has no future. Then competition is likely to become fierce, and in a way that is destructive."

"The idea is to make your terrorist believe that cooperation will net him a lighter sentence."

"Ongoing games involve exactly the opposite considerations from one-shot games. In an ongoing game you have the opportunity of forging a reputation, while at the same time learning more about your opponent. Depending on the circumstances, you might forge a reputation for being tough or fair or honest, whatever suits your particular game-playing strategy. An aggressive strategy might gain you a momentary advantage. It might also cost you dearly in the long run. It all depends on how the other players react to your play. Even in a game with a fair amount of conflict, there is room for cooperation."

"Like when two enemies become allies of convenience to combat a third, more lethal enemy."

"Good example. Then, near the end of the war, as the future becomes the present, cooperation collapses. With the endgame in sight, each of the two original enemies jockey for position, grabbing up land, stealing supplies, undercutting the other."

"But, Doc, in the interrogation chamber, he who controls the information controls the interview and, ultimately, the outcome."

"You get no argument from me there. Access to information is an integral part of every game. In fact, in just about every game ever played, there is some vital piece of information that one player has but the other players do not. When the players then attempt to infer, conceal, or sometimes even *divulge* this vital piece of information, these tactics become an important part of the game and its strategy."

"That doesn't make any sense. What in the world would cause a player to voluntarily divulge superior information? As a Marine, superior intell was our stock in trade; it meant everything to us. Shouldn't a player always conceal superior information from his opponents?"

"Sometimes yes, sometimes no. Think like a businessman. Let's say you're the CEO of a giant pharma firm. Your scientists have just made a breakthrough discovery. Aside from stroking your ego, there may be legitimate if purely selfish business reasons to trumpet this astounding discovery to the world, especially to your competitors. Your success may scare them off. Perhaps, as a result of your stunning announcement, they may suspend their own searches for similar new drugs, thus ceding the marketplace for these drugs to you."

"Tooting your own horn may also backfire. Once the other pharma companies see how much favorable press you got with your new drug, it may inspire them to redouble their efforts to find a look-alike drug. I don't care what you say, Doc, you'll never convince me that it ever makes sense to reveal superior information to an opponent."

"Well, given your military background, maybe this will make sense to you. In war, each side wants to keep its tactics and troop deployments secret. But in diplomacy, if your intentions are peaceful, then more than anything else you want other countries to know and believe this. The general principle here is asymmetric. A player has no choice but to be selective about the information he releases. He longs to reveal good information, the kind that will draw favorable responses from other players that will tend to work to his advantage. He is just as emphatic about concealing bad or harmful information, the kind that might work to his disadvantage."

"Doc, I know you're a bright guy and all that, but aren't you being just a bit simple-minded? In a strategic game, your opponent may be as smart as you are — just like that chemistry professor you told me about. The question he asked the two boys on the makeup test was brilliant."

"I like the way your mind works, Butch. The truth is, we can never underestimate the propensity of players to exaggerate or lie. A smart player knows this intuitively. He will never accept another player's boast about their prowess or abilities without supporting data or objective proof. In the example of the pharma company with the miracle drug breakthrough, credible proof of their discovery would be to see them breaking ground for a new plant to mass-produce the wonder drug."

"So, the manipulation of information itself becomes a game."

"Most certainly. If one party is holding back on information, the less-informed party will try and create situations that will force the more-informed party to reveal his information."

"Now that you point it out, I see that the manipulation of information is a feature in many games. Interrogation. Propaganda. Labor negotiations. Even courting."

"You making some headway with her?"

"I think Kaleena and I are now on the same page, if that's what you mean. But her father remains an obstacle."

"There's no bigger manipulator of information than a politician. Be careful of that one. The man is not to be trusted."

"Well, I'm not completely stupid."

"Did I say you were? . . . But being smart isn't always enough. Mere clever questions won't work against a strategic liar. The better-informed player will either conceal critical information or reveal misleading information. The less-informed player will either elicit information or filter truth from falsehood. He may also remain ignorant. The general rule is for the less-informed player to watch what the better-informed player does, not what he says."

"Sound advice always. Now, if only your Game Theory could be refined enough to help us men understand our women."

"Ah, speaking of women: here she comes now," Doc said as Kaleena approached, a couple shopping bags in tow. "You love her, don't you?"

"Let's just say, I'm impatient for the two of us to get home, so we can see about carving out a life together."

"In any game — including marriage — the more-impatient player nets far less from the deal than the less-impatient player. Studies have revealed that a player's share of any given pot is inversely proportional to their rate of impatience. Not only that, the best way to signal patience is to *be* patient. Never come back with a counteroffer too quickly."

"It may already be too late for that."

"In which case she has already out-maneuvered you."

"Don't I know it."

CHAPTER NINETEEN

▼

"On your knees, woman!"

The booming voice of the Reverend Roland Whitmore filled the tiny cabin, bounced off its padded walls. There were handholds everywhere, as well as padded tethers for holding zero-g passengers in place. The three were roaring skyward, about four minutes from apogee, aboard the *Lone Star*, Texas Governor Thadamore Mills' beautifully appointed suborb. The trio had lifted off about ten minutes earlier from Hobby Field south of Houston. The Reverend had arrived in town by airchop from Puritan City late the previous night.

They were in the upper atmosphere, now, and still rising. Elixir was naked, except for those bright yellow tennis shoes of hers. So were the two men beside her. Thadamore Mills wasn't much to look at, at least not naked. But he was well endowed, and she enjoyed the thrill when he put it to her. The Reverend Roland Whitmore was a bit more handsome, and in better physical shape.

But when it came to sex, the two men couldn't be more different. Mills was creative, even adventuresome; Roland, one-dimensional and boring. Mills wanted to try it every which way; Roland Whitmore could only get off one way, if he was fellated. Together, the two men were going to help her qualify as the first wiccan to become a double member of the Sixty-Mile-High Club.

Elixir Coventry started on her knees, with Roland Whitmore standing in front of her. But to do both men at once, she would have to change position, get on all fours, with the Reverend prone and Thadamore Mills entering her from behind. Thank goodness there were soft holds built into the padded floor and walls, to keep the three of them in place as the *Lone Star* came over the top and offered them a short burst of zero-g before the descent began.

By now her mouth was fully engaged and her hands were moving rapidly. Licks liked nothing better than to wrap her moist lips around a man, and she was concentrating more, now, on the pure pleasure of having sex with these two fellows, than on the ethics of what she was doing. — But this was about to change.

"We're running out of time," Thadamore moaned. He had stroked himself hard and was busy maintaining that stance without anyone else's help. The only thought on his mind was how much he wanted to be firmly rooted between Elixir's legs before the suborb reached maximum altitude.

"Don't be so damn selfish, Roland! Break it off and drop to the floor. Lie down on your back, find some handholds, and let her do you that way. I want in there before it's too late."

"Okay, okay. But she's doing me, oh, so good . . . "

"Don't be so goddamn selfish! There's no time left to spare. I want in, and I've got no frigging access from this angle."

Something about the man's tone rankled, and no sooner did the two men begin to work on her than she wanted them to stop. Elixir had her pride, and on some level this was plainly wrong.

The thought passed through her mind quickly and then was gone. She knew she was on the wrong side of the divide that separated being loved from being used. And yet, on some level it was pleasurable and she was momentarily powerless to put a stop to what was already in motion.

Suddenly, the tug of gravity began to decline sharply. The ship was approaching apogee. Licks pulled the Reverend from her mouth and coaxed him gently to the floor with one hand. She flipped over onto all fours. Thadamore knelt behind her, one hand on her buttocks, the other reaching for a padded hold.

Elixir reached back for him with one hand and guided him forward. She was wet, and he slipped in easily.

Elixir sighed, lowered her head and pushed back hard against Thadamore's hips. Her long, golden hair, done up in tight braids, swung from side to side as she writhed with delight.

By now Roland was on his back, splayed out on the padded floor. Licks grabbed at his manhood with her hand. She guided it back into her mouth and began to work her magic.

Now the g-forces melted completely away. The three started to float off the floor, still joined at the critical points where it really mattered.

But, as the ship came over the top of its suborbital track, their inertia raised them into mid-air, a cavalcade of arms and legs.

Roland started to reach fruition, but Licks held fast to him like a moray eel. Thadamore slipped out of her, wet and long, and came across her backside in great big globs, spraying semen everywhere.

Now the three of them bounced against the padded ceiling and remained pressed against it as the long descent began.

Licks lost suction and Roland exploded over her face and breasts. Soon enough gravity would sort out the mess.

●

●

The descent through the clouds was rapid but controlled. Elixir pressed her nose to the glass as the Earth rushed up to greet them. No matter how many times she flew high over the planet, she never ceased to be amazed by how large the D.C. Dome truly was, even when viewed from twenty kloms up.

As Elixir watched, the giant dome draw nearer. It glinted in the sun, then seemed to explode out of the ground, a huge geodesic glass house, though on a scale unknown to man until little more than a hundred years ago. All of the District of Columbia, parts of Virginia and Maryland, virtually the entire river valley, shrink-wrapped to keep the cogs of government spinning safely and smoothly.

The suborbport was located beyond the Potomac in Maryland. A gcar from the National Governors Association was waiting for them when they exited the terminal. By then all three were back in their street clothes and looking the part. The driver, a longtime member of Governor Mills' staff, rushed the trio up the elite Congressional Parkway and straight into the heart of the city.

Without a specific invitation, it would be impossible for Elixir to gain entry to the inner sanctums of the White House. Besides, President Benjamin was no fan. So they all agreed she would remain in the visitor's center while the two men went in to see the President himself. Governor Mills was expected in the West Wing within the hour, and the Reverend Roland Whitmore intended to be at his side, as always.

Licks didn't mind the snub, not entirely. She had never been to the White House visitor center before and truly had a passion for the history on display there. Afterwards, she would take the Bullet back to Nashville and then on home in her own gcar. The woman had a lot of thinking to do, although one thing was for certain: Never again would she allow herself to be used like these two men had just used her.

President Benjamin wasn't alone when the two men arrived. His aides were there, of course, and his security detail, but so too was Alexander Hoagland. This came as somewhat of a surprise to Thadamore, as he counted Alexander Hoagland among his closest friends. No mention had been made of the Senator being in attendance.

Governor Mills meant to get straight to the point, but President Benjamin stopped him short. His face said it all.

"Don't tell me you've been with that woman again? How could you?"

"Don't knock it if you haven't tried it, Mr. President. Besides, from what I hear, your wick isn't always dry either."

"It may not always be dry, but at least Anna Clark and I exercise some frigging discretion."

"You're just jealous because the Reverend and I inducted her into the Club on the way over here."

"Club? What Club?" The President looked confused.

Now it was Xander's turn. "Governor! Didn't I tell you to stay the hell away from that woman? Your association with a woman like that will come back to bite you in the ass one of these days."

"Well at least I'm getting some ass, which is more than I can say for you, Xander."

"That's right, let's make this about Laura and me."

Hoagland threw his reading glasses on the table. That's what he did, when he got mad, throw his glasses on the table. Alexander Hoagland had a temper, as so many great men did. Sometimes he would swear, sometimes he would clench his teeth and shake his head. Most times he would throw his glasses. That's when his wife Laura would intervene to calm him down. Only, Laura wasn't in attendance today.

"What Club, damnit?"

"The Sixty-Mile-High Club."

"You fool!" Noah roared.

Governor Mills started to apologize. "Mr. President, I didn't come here today to argue . . . "

"Of course you did. Arguing gives you great joy. Almost as much joy as that damn Ouija board of yours."

"Honestly, sir, could we leave my board out of this? — I didn't come here today to argue with you. I came here to try and convince you not to sign Senator Flanagan's Gun Control Bill, should it make it to your desk. That looks rather more likely now."

Noah Benjamin shook his head. "A lot of pressure is being brought to bear on me on this one. Most of the States in the East and Upper Midwest would like to see this legislation pass. I can't mention names, but major campaign contributors, including several large corporations, want to see this demon become law as well. You know my feelings on this, Xander. — I have always been in favor of Second Amendment rights."

"Then stand your ground."

"What good does it do me to expose myself politically by vetoing it?"

"What good does it do you? — That's the question you're asking?"

"Hell, the Supreme Court is going to throw the damn thing out anyway. Everyone knows that, even that fool Flanagan."

"What if you're wrong? What if they don't rule your way?"

"I'm not wrong."

"Mr. President, even if you are right, the hearings could take months. If you don't veto this bastard law — and I mean now — Texas may very well secede from the Republic. Other States may follow. The people in my home state are hyper-sensitive on the subject."

"Seditious talk, but yes, I have heard it too. Is there no compromise to be had here?"

Xander Hoagland spoke up. "I believe in simple things, things like the Lone Ranger's Creed. Surely you have heard me talk of it. You have to stand strong, Noah. This country has been led by all sorts of presidents. Some were ready; some were not. Some were soft and malleable, like jeweler's gold; others hard, like cold tough steel. Then there were those made of corroded lead. None of them were born able; though some were more able than others. The gold got battered, the steel grew brittle and broke, the corroded lead got stamped into ashes. Noah, the country needs you to be strong, like tungsten steel."

"But even steel screams for mercy when it's forged. It gasps when it's quenched. It creaks when it goes under load. Even steel gets frightened."

"But God forbid it ever let us down. Then the entire building comes tumbling down beneath our feet."

"Nice frigging metaphor," Reverend Whitmore said. "Maybe I can use it in my next sermon before the Sect of the Most Sacred."

"Let it go, Roland," Thadamore snapped.

Noah Benjamin seemed genuinely moved. "I happen to like your metaphor, Alexander. But you must know it's not as simple as all that. Flanagan wants to be President. And he wants to use the stadium massacre, plus the murder of his son as springboards to get him to the White House."

Xander spoke up again. "Thadamore hasn't heard this yet and I apologize, Governor, for not letting you in on this piece of information earlier. But I think I may have a way to checkmate our friend Patrick Flanagan."

"You have something juicy on the bastard?"

"You might say that. Two things, actually. One I'm not at liberty to discuss, because there is still an ongoing investigation. But the other is fair game. I have come into possession of certain pictures. They show the man having sex with a male prostitute in Hedon City, a black male."

Whitmore wore a look of sudden surprise on his face. He turned to Thadamore for confirmation, but Mills could only stammer out a reply:

"You have . . . vid?"

Xander enjoyed his moment. "Yes, sound and picture."

"How in blazes did you come to be in possession of such a priceless vid?"

"Again, I'm not at liberty to say. But that's not the half of it. I also have strong circumstantial evidence that may implicate the man in his own son's murder."

Now it was Noah Benjamin's turn to be surprised. "You didn't tell me that."

"My people are still gathering evidence. So far it's only circumstantial. And, of course, the whole thing still needs to be dressed up for public consumption. But between the pictures and the possibility of murder, the two together should be enough to knock Flanagan clean out of the race."

"That still doesn't mean this Gun Control thing is simply going to dry up and blow away. I honestly don't think a veto can be sustained."

"Mr. President, if I may." This was the Reverend Roland Whitmore, in a conciliatory tone. "If your veto is overridden, so be it — at least you have gone on the record and done your duty. But if you want to hold this country together, you simply have no choice but to show your metal, like Xander says. You have no alternative but to veto the damn thing."

"I understand my duty well enough. But I have another duty — and that is to get myself reelected. To finance my reelection bid, I need the financial backing of that megalomaniac Roberts and the Board of Transcomet Industries. Even now I'm sitting on news that could sink the entire company."

"What news?"

"They lost control of one of their asteroids."

Hoagland slapped his hand over his mouth. The color ran from his face. "God have mercy — the Doomsday Scenario. It's what the intelligence agencies have been worried about since the day asteroid mining was first proposed."

"Doomsday? What the hell are we waiting for? We have to take cover immediately!" Governor Mills exclaimed, anxiously edging towards the door.

"Don't throw a clot, Thad. You can't outrun an asteroid and expect to live. Anyway, I already dispatched a team of spacejockeys to remedy the situation. Despite some very long odds, they were successful. The danger has now passed."

Thadamore Mills was still worked up. "Good God, man, do you mean to tell me you have just saved the world? Mr. President, that only makes you the bravest man on the planet. Spin this thing properly and you'll be an instant national hero. The Flanagan problem will disappear in a flash — and all without a messy scandal."

"Calm down, will you? There will be plenty of time for me to be a national hero later on. Right now, holding this information back from the public may work in my favor."

"How so?" Hoagland asked.

"Keeping this colossal blunder secret may head off a worldwide panic. Plus, it gives me considerable leverage over the Transcomet Board. I don't want them wandering out of the barn and throwing their support to another candidate against me."

"But, Mr. President, your leverage only goes so far. Transcomet can get out from under your thumb any time they please. All the Board has to do is come clean on their own." Alexander Hoagland was nothing if not practical.

"And 'fess up to a mistake that might sink the entire company? I don't think so."

"This sort of brinkmanship is dangerous," Xander advised.

"Of course, it is. But if I bankrupt the company, I bankrupt myself. At the price of keeping a small secret, I guarantee myself almost limitless funding for my reelection bid."

Thadamore Mills didn't care for that answer. "This is no small secret, Mr. President. Can Transcomet Industries even be trusted? And what about that team you sent in to remedy the situation? Can they be trusted to keep this thing quiet? Who did this job anyway?"

"Just some no-name grunts from EMD. They were on their way home from Mars, when we re-routed their ship."

"No way does this thing stay quiet longer than an hour after they have landed back on Earth. Annabel Clark at the American News Network will have this thing before you know it."

"I don't think so. Annabel knows her place. Anyway, the boys at Transcomet will want this kept out of the press. No one will know unless I myself let the cat out of the bag."

"Tell me, Mr. President. Just what the Devil is Transcomet's stand on the Second Amendment anyway? I always thought they were ardently pro-gun."

"Historically, they have been. — But apparently not anymore. Dollars Before Principles. That seems to be their current mantra. I went head to head over this with Keith Roberts' Assistant. These people seem to want the Second Amendment thrown out."

Senator Hoagland was aghast. "You can't be serious."

"The NGA, which I chair, speaks with a single voice on this."

"A single voice? The National Governors Association? That'll be the day," Noah intoned sarcastically.

"No, I mean it. As much as a quarter of the Union is apt to bolt if this thing becomes law."

President Benjamin shook his head. "Like I said, I've heard the talk. But I just don't think that's a realistic threat. Bolting from the Union is just not that easy."

"What are you going to do, dispatch Federal troops to put down an insurrection?" Thadamore asked.

"If I have to."

"Have you forgotten about the Posse Comitatus Act? That's been on the books since Reconstruction. Bringing out Federal troops is not only against the law, it would surely lead to civil war."

"Threats and Promises. Carrots and Sticks. I'll void Posse Comitatus by Executive Order, if I have to. Other presidents have. The idea is to push this thing to the brink without going over. If we play our cards right, war can be averted."

"And if you miscalculate? Not every nuke is in Federal hands, you know. Nearly every military installation of consequence is based in a State likely to secede."

"Army bases maybe, but not naval bases. Several of those are in California — which won't wander from the flock — or along the east coast, where sympathies run very much in favor of banning guns. Plus, commissioned officers have signed an oath. They have sworn on their life to uphold the Constitution and to obey their Commander in Chief. I don't doubt their loyalty, nor should you."

"Have you forgotten the state militias? Down in Texas we have a very large and able one."

"Thad, your boys are quite capable, I'm sure. But they don't have the training or the equipment. They're no match for my Federal troops."

"My God! Thadamore! Mr. President! Would you listen to yourselves?" Xander Hoagland was incensed. "Here you are standing in the White House, arguing strategy and tactics for an unthinkable war! Do either of you really think the United States Air Force is going to drop a nuclear bomb on New York City simply because the squadron headquarters happen to be domiciled in Texas? Or that a naval unit out of Norfolk is going to shell Houston from the Gulf of Mexico? These guys are True Blue. They're Americans first, not New Yorkers or Texans. We have the most to fear from civilian militias, zealots armed with guns, like those crazies roaming the border. Hell, I understand one bunch just bushwhacked a regiment of Mexican soldiers — inside Mexico, no less. But we have even more to fear from this sort of talk. Screw your reelection, Noah — veto this frigging bill."

"I wish I had your courage." Noah Benjamin sighed.

"Courage?" Xander scoffed. "I think it was Abraham Lincoln, who said — 'If it turns out right, no amount of criticism will matter. If it turns out wrong, not even ten angels sitting on my shoulder swearing I was right, will make a difference'."

"No, Alexander. If it turns out wrong, you're gonna have a bim mloron sitting in the White House — and Flanagan's Bill will still become law."

"Mr. President, I am an Objectivist of the old school, a libertarian. And a libertarian rejects the arbitrary power of the State. He refuses to subordinate the rights of the individual to that of the State. He realizes that collectivism, in whatever form, stifles the best of human impulses. You used to be one of those sorts of people. What happened to you?"

Noah started to answer, but found he could not.

Xander continued. "Tell me, Mr. President. Do you know of any man who would freely choose to give up his right to vote? Can you point to even a single one among us who would prefer to read free government propaganda instead of pay his own hard-earned credits for an uncensored independent newsline? Or who would voluntarily surrender their guns to a Police State?"

"Okay, I get it."

"Your grandfather — he got it. Your father — he got it too. But you? You may have gotten it once, Mr. President — but you certainly do not get it any more."

"That's harsh."

"And well it should be. Is there a man among us who would rather practice a State-mandated religion than one of his own? Stand up if you are that man. Or would you rather surrender tolerance and diversity for a rigid cultural orthodoxy? Or how about giving up the right to free association or freedom of expression? Pardon me, Mr. President, but the ultimate struggle between Statism and representative government will not be resolved by bombs and bullets. It will be settled by the bloody combat of will and ideas."

Alexander Hoagland folded his arms across his chest. "That is all I have to say, gentlemen. A good day to you all." And with that, he left the room.

Noah watched his friend go. Everyone thought Xander Hoagland was stupid. Arrogant and stupid. His enemies called him warlike. Even his friends thought him naive, an unsophisticated Boy Scout caught up in a moralistic code he called the Lone Ranger's Creed. An unenlightened blowhard who believed in a mythic America that never existed. Shockingly dumb, some said. A laughable dunce. Once, when accused by two of his critics of being stupid, Xander replied — "Everyone knows the dumbest farmers have the biggest potatoes." He was putting them down, and they didn't even know it.

Everyone thought Alexander Hoagland was stupid. But everyone was wrong. Xander would hear the criticisms, the putdowns, the insults. But he would shrug them off. And he could do so without guilt because he had a philosophy about such things. *When a man believes he is right, when he knows his motives are honest and aboveboard, he doesn't lose sleep over criticism.*

Noah knew it now, knew it in his heart. Alexander Hoagland ought to be President. Not Thadamore Mills, not Patrick Flanagan, not even Noah himself; but Alexander Hoagland. The man was an optimist. He had an innate optimism, a quintessential American belief in technology, an absolute and utter faith in capitalism and in scientific progress. But he was also a realist. Xander believed God was everywhere, always. But he also believed a multitude of devils hid everywhere too. The man was tougher than he was vain. But most of all, he was a patriot. Noah could see that. The people could see that. Even an old lion was still a lion.

CHAPTER TWENTY

▼

Puritan City.

Haven for the most faithful. Headquarters for the Sect of the Most Sacred. Seat of power of the Reverend Roland Whitmore.

This morning, like every morning, the Reverend Roland Whitmore enjoyed his morning stroll across the immaculate grounds. Maybe cherished is a better word. He *cherished* his morning stroll across the immaculate grounds.

Acre upon acre of walkways, clipped shrubbery, manicured lawns, delicate flower beds, all lovingly maintained in perfect order by legions of Novices, young people seeking a better life in a confusing world. Male or female, each Novice took a vow of service and of obedience. They agreed to labor twelve months, without pay and for the greater good, then become "ministers," go out into the communities of the west and southwest, the Plains states and the Midwest, spread the Word, find more devotees. It was good work, God's work.

The Reverend Roland Whitmore stopped, surveyed all that was his. The steel minarets of the Tabernacle, the glittering spires of the Cathedral, the golden domes of the Assembly Hall rotunda. He had so much to be proud of — the grounds, his flock, his promising future. Roland was especially proud of his "Sect of the Most Sacred," a cavalcade of strictly white, strictly virgin, girls that were, for him, a constant source of temptation. Why, just this morning he had to discipline one that had gone briefly astray.

The rules of the "Sect of the Most Sacred" were simple and austere — no books, no theater, no music, no concerts, no cinema, no sports, no gcars, no driving, no alcohol, no drugs.

But that was only the beginning. When out of their room the girls had to be covered from head to foot in a white veil, white blazer, white skirt that reached the floor, white slippers. Under no circumstances were they to have any contact whatsoever with a man of any age. They were not permitted to speak to a man, walk with a man, listen to music with a man, dance with a man, touch a man.

The only exception to the no-man rule were Elders of the Church, and only when a second Elder was present. The only values that mattered were loyalty and submission, first to Christianity, then to the Sect.

This particular girl, the one he had disciplined, made the mistake of arguing with an Elder. Not only had she argued with the man, she did it outside, on the sidewalk, where others might be a witness. The girl had finished trimming a shrub then done a happy little jig, as girls are wont to do. Dancing was prohibited. The Elder had threatened the girl with sanctions, a week in solitary for the infraction. She told him where to stick it.

Roland Whitmore took the girl aside to admonish her. He escorted her to a guesthouse on the opposite end of the main courtyard, a secluded, fenced-in area behind a thick grove of trees. This area was usually off-limits to Novices.

Whitmore loosened his tie, made the girl sit down, lorded over her when he spoke. No other Elder was present, which immediately put the girl on edge.

"Do you realize what the punishment is for talking back to an Elder?"

The girl didn't answer. She looked at her hands, began to tremble.

"The penalty for dancing a jig is a misdemeanor by comparison. Either violation is sufficient to have you sanctioned and dismissed. What do you think your parents will have to say when I tell them what you did?"

The girl began to sob softly. "Please don't tell my parents."

"I don't see as if you have given me any choice."

The Reverend Roland Whitmore touched the girl on the head, brushed back her curls. She recoiled sharply. The tears ended abruptly.

"Don't touch me. Touching clearly violates the rules, your rules."

"You dare quote rules to me? You are but a Novice, and a badly behaved one at that."

"Begging your pardon, Reverend, but here in your precious Puritan City the girls of the Sect are little more than indentured servants."

"Sacrilege."

"Is it? We take no exercise. To walk anywhere unescorted is strictly forbidden. And where would we go if we did walk? Inside the fenceline, there are no hotels, no sports arenas, no theaters, no swimming pools, not even a decent restaurant nearby. The few escapes that do exist in this horrible place are exclusively for the men. For us women, no ice cream parlors, no parks, no shops."

"You knew life here in Puritan City would be austere before you signed on. Joining the Sect of the Most Sacred was a voluntary act on your part. There was no coercion or misdirection on the part of the Church, or any of its Elders."

"Perhaps not back then, not when I joined. But there certainly is now."

"The weakness is yours, young lady, not ours — and you will be punished for it, punished severely."

"Truth is, Reverend, I feel as bored and aimless as a goldfish. Each day I swim slower and slower inside an absolutely smooth glass bowl, with nothing whatsoever to do, gulping for air. But even as a lowly goldfish, I am not safe. Think of the hazards. Someone could poison my water or dump it down the drain, maybe refuse to dropin fish food when I am hungry."

"Such insolence! You belong in solitary! Ten days!"

Chin quivering, the girl stammered. "Please! Don't put me in solitary! Can't you understand? I am so desperate for companionship. I can barely manage my vow of solitude even now. Ten days in solitary would be the end of me. Is there no other way for me to get back in your good graces?"

"Now that you mention it, child, there may be a way."

"Anything. I'll do anything. Just please do not place me in solitary. Please. Tell me. How can I make things right with you?"

"On your knees, woman!"

•

•

Roland zipped up, stepped back out onto the lawn of Puritan City, his city. The morning air was fresh and he felt good. It was oh, so nice to have willing young girls to admonish!

A familiar face appeared, now, on the sidewalk coming his way. Pappy Barnes, retired Marine Corps colonel, plus his Executive Officer, Major Branislav Karpinski, sometimes the "Carp."

Whitmore tried not to stare. But something had happened to Branislav since the last time they met. His face was burnt, like he had had a close brush with a big fire. One of his hands was damaged as well. Only later did Pappy Barnes tell him about the mission to Mexico, the wildfire, and the rescue.

"We need to talk," Pappy Barnes said, looking around to see if anyone might be listening. Roland didn't permit free-roving bots within the confines of Puritan City, but surveillance cams were ubiquitous.

Pappy Barnes was a white man of medium build. But he was a square man, all muscle, like a bulldog, a retired Marine Corps colonel, who saw himself as still being on active duty. His Executive Officer, the man he called his X.O., was more angular, a little taller, perhaps of Central or Eastern European descent, dark wiry hair, wild scary eyes. The Reverend Roland Whitmore felt uneasy around this second man, though he felt more at home with Pappy Barnes. The two of them were mostly of the same mind.

Roland led the two men in the opposite direction from where he had left the girl, to a safe room, a maximum secure room, impenetrable to listening devices, no comm lines running in or out.

"Can we talk freely here?" Branislav asked, looking nervously about. Whatever was pleasant about him receded into his face as he examined the wall hangings and light fixtures for electronic taps. Then he moved on to the baseboards and wet bar.

"Relax, will you?" Roland reproached. "The room is fully shielded. Nothing gets in, nothing gets out."

"Trust me, Reverend, a little paranoia goes a long way." Branislav said, flashing those straight white teeth.

Whitmore wasn't amused. This man scared him. "Let's get down to cases, shall we?"

Pappy Barnes got comfortable, took a drink from the icebox. Pappy was a heavy drinker, many military men were. It was his one weakness. Part of the cross he had to bear as the illegitimate great, great grandson of Pancho Barnes, the hard-drinking, wild woman of Muroc Dry Lake fame, bartender and confidante to America's first astronauts. Pappy took a deep tug on his drink, then spoke:

"You met with the President?" he asked, swirling the ice in his glass.

"Yes, I did. Me, Governor Mills, Senator Hoagland, President Benjamin, and a couple of his support staff. We met. We talked."

"Alexander Hoagland was there?" That detail caught Pappy's attention. He had wanted Hoagland as a bargaining chip for some time.

"I have to admit, at the time his presence surprised me, as well. But it seems as if Xander is on our side. I trust the man. More importantly, Thadamore trusts him."

"But I don't trust that kike Jew president of ours," Karpinski said, completing his examination of the room. "You know very well that Jews can't be trusted."

"Forget about the frigging Jews," Pappy ordered, finishing off his drink and reaching for another. "The Reverend is right. Xander Hoagland is a straight shooter. I may not always agree with the man. But he certainly knows which side he's on."

Roland Whitmore nodded. "Xander's sentiments are clearly pro-veto, anti-Flanagan. He wants no part of this Gun Control Bill. Plus, he's got something on Flanagan; I'm not entirely sure what. He was pretty close-mouthed about the whole thing. An investigation of some kind."

"For Hoagland to have mentioned something unseemly like that, it must be pretty big. Truth is: I never doubted the man's stand on Flanagan's bill. But what I really came here to talk to you about today was funding. An Army runs on money," Pappy said. "Guns, fuel, and money."

"It always comes down to money with you, doesn't it? We've already given your people plenty."

"And we've been using it to great effect. In case you haven't been keeping up with the news, we've been aggressively working both sides of the border for a while now."

"I know precisely what you have been up to. But before we agree to hand over any more funds to you, tell me exactly what we're getting for our money."

"*Our* money?" Pappy balked. "I thought this was Transcomet's money. You told me you were only acting as a middleman, that the Church had no official stake in this affair."

"When I said 'ours', I was speaking figuratively, of course."

"Of course."

"So, answer the question. What has Transcomet Industries gotten for their money thus far?"

"Thus far, their slush fund has bought my boys a fair amount of ordinance. But it's barely the rough beginnings of a backwoods militia. My X.O. has all the numbers. I'm sure he'd be happy to share them with you if you ask nicely. Though I must say: it looks to me as if Transcomet is playing both sides against the middle."

"That's a serious charge. Care to elaborate?"

"I think the problem is fairly straightforward. In their public statements Transcomet Industries seems to be coming out in favor of gun control. Privately, however, they're funding the opposition, namely us. This is the most dangerous of all games to play, and I don't want to get it up the ass when they suddenly decide to cut off our funding."

"Did I ever once say that Transcomet could be trusted?"

"No. But you never said they would be two-faced either."

"I think it's high time I saw those numbers."

Pappy Barnes nodded to his X.O., who took out his e-pad, spooled up the proper file. "If it's numbers you want, it's numbers I got. — ten thousand rounds of armor-piercing shells, five hundred auto-load rifle guns, a thousand Kevlar vests with neck and groin extenders, twenty armored vehicles, twelve airchops, four thousand contact grenades . . . "

"Okay, I get the picture. But I'll need an e-copy on fiche."

"No, Reverend, I don't think you do get it," Pappy said, signaling his X.O. to put away his e-pad. "This tidy little weapons hoard of ours might keep our backwoods militia going for maybe six hours of all-out war. We need more money, much much more money, maybe 1000 times as much."

"Just where is all this money supposed to come from?"

"The sinews of war are money. And money comes from industrial might."

"Or maybe pious followers."

"The Church is finally going to lend its support?" Pappy was intrigued.

"There are conditions attached, but yes, it is indeed possible."

"What conditions?" Branislav Karpinski didn't like it when there were strings.

"Two conditions. I am to be installed as President of the New Republic should Texas decide to secede from the Union."

"And the second condition?"

"Puritan City is to be designated capital of the New Republic."

Pappy Barnes was confused. "I had thought Thadamore Mills would be the New Republic's first President, especially considering the courage it would take to pull his State out of the Union. Texas is a rich, powerful, industrial State."

"Thadamore Mills will need to be assassinated." The Reverend Roland Whitmore was cold and matter of fact in his assessment.

"I can do that." Branislav said with pride.

"I thought you might be willing." Reverend Whitmore was beginning to take a strong dislike of this man.

Pappy disapproved sharply. "For God's sakes, Roland — Thadamore Mills is an ally in this war. Why take the man out?"

"It's the only sensible way to rile up the people, to get them to line up behind one unassailable leader."

"You?" Pappy asked.

"Me."

"Is this about the Second Amendment — or just a brazen power grab?"

"This can be about whatever you want it to be about."

"That's pretty lame, even for you, Reverend. Why should an innocent man have to die just to satisfy your blazing ego?"

"Lame? A man might take offense at that."

"So let the fucker be offended!" Pappy exploded. The liquor was beginning to talk. "Your hippie teenage groupies may be willing to lay down their lives for you, but I certainly am not. I will gladly risk my life for a principle. But I'll not risk it for an unprincipled man like yourself."

"My principles are the same as yours."

"Are they? In this country we do two things extremely well, stereotype and overreact. I've heard every excuse in the book for defending the Second Amendment. That it's about hunting or collecting or target shooting. That's all malarkey. The Second Amendment is about defending freedom against tyrants. Let's not forget the idiot French. Before World War II they had stringent gun-registration laws. When the Nazis came, they had only to consult the registration lists at the local gendarme in order to round up all the weapons in a given district."

"Thanks for the history lesson, Pappy, but . . . "

"Shut the fuck up, you moron! And don't you dare interrupt me again. Like it or not, there are principles involved here. I am opposed to all forms of gun registration. Registration is simply the first step towards confiscation. So, don't stand there and tell me that your principles are the same as mine."

"Registration is not the battle here; we lost that one ages ago."

"That is true. But tyrants come in many guises, some foreign, some homegrown. Registration laws place the individual at the mercy of the State, unable to resist. Soon revolution becomes all but impossible. Freedom wasn't won with a handshake, you know. — Or at the tip of a pen. It was won at the muzzle of a loaded gun. Any attempt to license or restrict the arming of an individual is a violation of their Natural Rights. Inevitably, it is also subversive of their democratic political institutions."

"But Natural Rights also accrue to one's God. We need a moral leader as well as a political one." Roland Whitmore was adamant.

"That still doesn't grant you license to assassinate a lawfully-elected man like Thadamore Mills. Gun registration laws are self-defeating. The politicos have always claimed that the purpose of registration-type laws is to keep weapons out of the hands of criminals. — But they do nothing of the kind. Gangsterism has invariably flourished under such laws, and always will. There isn't a man alive who doesn't accept the fact that criminals are never seriously handicapped by these sorts of rules. The bad guys don't care. The only thing such laws manage to do is disarm peace-loving citizens and place them fully at the mercy of the lawless."

Branislav grunted his approval. But Pappy ignored the man and continued:

"Reverend, don't let anyone tell you different. Nothing's changed since the dawn of time. A weapon in the hand is still the best defense an individual can have against a criminal who is intent on invading his home. Any law banning guns can accomplish only one thing — to disarm the victims. This goes in spades for waiting periods as well as laws that prohibit the carrying of a concealed weapon."

"But a solid majority of the population says that guns should be registered, just like gcars."

"An opinion poll is not going to change my mind. Gcars aren't guns. The Constitution doesn't grant you the right to own and operate a motor vehicle — but it does a gun. Plus, the last time I checked, there wasn't a federally mandated waiting period to buy gcars, or a limit on the number of gcars a citizen may own, or a requirement to lock them up when not in use, or empty them of fuel when they're parked. Analogous requirements are standard fare where guns are concerned. Nor do the Feds monitor gcar sales between private individuals, something they take very seriously when it comes to weapon sales. This, in spite of the fact that, in a given year in this country, tens of thousands of people are killed or maimed in gcar wrecks, far more than die of gunshot wounds. Hell, more people drown in bathtubs each day than die of accidental gunshot wounds. Do we ban bathtubs then? Register them with the State for safety purposes? Limit the number of bathtubs per household? No, of course not!"

"Settle down, Pappy," Branislav urged, his facial scar seeming more red than ever.

"Yeah, don't have a coronary, old friend."

"I will *not* settle down — this is important. People abuse alcohol, they abuse drugs, they abuse their right to operate a motor vehicle — but in none of these instances is the law ever held up for ridicule. Instead, it is the abuser who is punished. The same should hold true for guns, and for the people who misuse them."

"Okay, I'm done fencing with you," Reverend Whitmore exclaimed. "What I want to know is this: Can you support me as President of the New Republic or not? I need to be certain of your answer before I will even consider petitioning the Church to cut you a check for more funds."

"Reverend, so long as you come out solidly in support of the Second Amendment, I see no reason not to support your bid to become the first President of the New Republic." Pappy was sincere. "But I have to question how making Puritan City the capital of the New Republic makes any sense."

"Let me explain. Beneath our feet — in fact beneath practically the entire City — are catacombs. They are filled with concrete-hardened bunkers. Dozens of large storage rooms. I can show them to you after we wrap up things here. I already have thousand of pounds of supplies stored down there. There's plenty of room to store much, much more. Food, water, medicine, whatever you want. Plus, we already have thousands of loyal recruits, young men and women willing to fight for their faith, willing to fight for me, even lay down their lives if necessary."

"Ah, now I see where you're going with this." Pappy smiled.

"It's only about time. But the thing is, I need to understand your overall plan. The President promises to bring in Federal troops if any of the State militias bolt, and the Elders want to know how you intend to respond to this threat."

"The President actually threatened to bring in Federal troops?" Pappy was taken aback.

"He did."

"Well then let me lay it out for you. Our first move would be to take control of the Texas and Gulf Coast oilfields, plus the refineries and pipeline terminals. Deny the man fuel. Then we'll close the lower Missup to traffic. That'll cripple trade all up and down the river. Long about the same time we'll block upriver traffic above Memphis. We can . . . "

"I like the sounds of that. It's a good plan, Pappy. I'd like to see the details, study them, perhaps share them with a select few Church Elders, the ones who will be writing the checks."

Pappy turned to Branislav Karpinski. "Give the man the microfiche we prepared."

"I don't know, Boss. The more people that see this, the more likely the cat gets out of the bag."

Pappy Barnes took the microfiche, handed it to the Reverend Roland Whitmore. "I suggest you not let this fall into the wrong hands. Eyes Only. Kapische?"

"I got it."

"Well, then, I guess that concludes our business for today. Branislav and I really must be getting back."

"I thought I might still show you the underground storage areas before you left."

"No time for that today. We'll meet here again in forty-eight hours."

"I look forward to it."

CHAPTER TWENTY-ONE

▼

"I expected to make the repairs myself," Woody Dunlop said, tightening the clasp on his tech-shirt and pulling a spacesuit from the locker. "After all, the solar sail is my particular area of expertise."

"Honestly, Woody, of all the ridiculous times to make ego an issue," Butch Hogan replied, grabbing a suit for himself and throwing another to Gulliver Travels. Butch's friend, Red Parsons, was still sidelined with a broken hand.

"As long as you know who's in charge on this one," Woody said, tightening the bolts on his leg pieces. They were in the ready room, preparing for a stroll outdoors, a spacewalk.

"Bloody hell," Butch replied. "If it's a medal you're perching for."

"No medal, just respect. You EMD spacejockeys think you own the solar system."

Butch refused to get drawn into an argument, and the three of them continued to suit up with a minimum of chatter. This was a crisis every bit as worrisome as the destruction of the antenna-unit onboard EMD 14. When the time came to reel in the *Voyager*'s solar sails, a few days out from Earth, something jammed, making it impossible to stow the two halves of the giant, titanium-ribbed sail. The consequences were immediate and severe:

On the starboard side of the ship the sail remained half-open; on the port side, it folded up neatly, as it should. The net result was to make the ship unsailable and to give it an unbalanced, cock-eyed spin. The ship immediately began to tumble uncontrollably.

The mechanical failure put all their lives in jeopardy. With the ship pitching wildly, they could neither return home safely nor could they successfully dock with the orbiting Space Station. In a matter of days they would pass inside Earth's orbit, soon to become fifteen dozen charcoal briquettes as they burned up nearer the Sun.

Woody had a pretty good idea where the problem lay and the robotic cam helped confirm his fears. But, to fix the problem meant going outside — and that would be an extraordinarily dangerous endeavor. The solar wind was electrically charged. Every few seconds hundreds of millions of volts of static electricity built up on the sail and then had to be bled off. Clearly, no place for a man. And certainly not for a man weighed down by a satchel filled with metal tools. Everyone agreed: this spacewalk would be extremely dangerous.

Butch and Gulliver, both in spacesuits now, helped Woody down the hole. The inner door of the airlock was closed and the air evacuated.

The space beyond the lock was a vast, star-flecked emptiness. They were presently in the shadow of the great ship, on the side opposite the sun. The Earth was not visible. With the big ship pitching wildly, every direction was "down" — down for a hundred million kloms.

As a matter of course, the two men put a safety line on Woody before he exited. But it still gave Butch that sinking feeling to see Woody's head disappear into that bottomless black hole.

Two very large compartments lined the port and starboard sides of the ship. Imagine two giant footlockers, on opposite sides of the ship, each with an immense beryllium copper metal door that could be opened or closed as the solar sail on that side was furled or unfurled. To draw open the doors or to close them back down again required a series of enormous hydraulic pistons. These pistons also drew out the guide wires for the sails' titanium ribs. It was inside these immense storage compartments that the solar sails were stowed when not in use.

The way Woody had it figured, a piece of the starboard-side sail had snagged on one of the pistons or maybe on one of the guide wires. He couldn't clearly tell which from the robot cam. Either way, the result was the same — it was no longer possible to fold up and store the starboard-side sail. Something similar had happened to a ship ten years ago. When the crew couldn't free the sail, the ship in question smashed headlong into the sun, killing everyone onboard.

In the aftermath of that earlier accident, procedures were developed to free a snagged sail. But to date, no one had actually done a live test on a crippled spaceship. Oh, sims had been run, but never the real thing.

There was a first time for everything, Woody thought grimly as he slipped into space. He would have to cut a small hole in the sail at the point where the sail had snagged the hydraulic piston. Then, theoretically, the rest of the sail could be safely retracted.

The safety line attached to Woody Dunlop paid out steadily for several meters. Then it stopped moving and would move no further. Butch waited several minutes then leaned over and touched his helmet against Gulliver's. The tech-shirts they wore doubled as comm links.

"Hang onto my feet — I'm gonna take a look outside."

Butch hung head down out of the airlock and looked around. Woody was stopped, hanging by both hands, nowhere near the compartment that housed the snagged solar sail.

Butch scrambled back up to where Gulliver stood waiting. "Something's wrong," he said. "I'm going out to see what the problem is."

It was no great trick, Butch discovered, to hang by his hands and swing himself along chimpanzee-style to where Woody sat, stalled. The *S.S. Mars Voyager* was a space-only ship; it never landed. Thus, there was no reason for it to be sleek, not like the ones that had to pass smoothly through a friction-causing atmosphere. She was covered everywhere outside with handholds. They were for the convenience of repairmen when the ship was docked at the Station.

Once Butch reached Woody's location, he found it was possible, by holding onto the same rung Woody clung to, to assist him in swinging his way back in the direction of the airlock. Five minutes later, Gulliver was hauling Woody back up through the hole and Butch was scrambling in after him. It seemed Woody had become disoriented by the ship's erratic rotatt and passed out.

Butch wasted no time. He began at once to unbuckle the toolbelt from around Woody's waist and transfer it to his own. The cutting torch was in a sort of spaceman's backpack, which he now winched tight and swung over one shoulder. Working at top speed, he lowered himself back down the hole and was on his way before Woody had recovered enough to object, if indeed he intended to.

There were handholds every meter or so around the circumference of the ship's hull, hundreds in all. They ran in both directions, up and down, around both hemispheres of the hull. There were footholds too, pads actually made of magnetic-velcro. It meshed with similar material sewn into the soles of his boots, the palms of his gloves, and the material around his knee. Thus, a spacejockey could work kneeling, standing, or squatting. There were safety lines, of course, plus mechanical ascenders. But nothing was a proper substitute for smarts and caution — and Butch had both.

Even though all eternity stood spinning beneath his toes, Butch found it rather easy to swing out to the spot where the solar sail appeared to have gotten jammed against the lid of the storage compartment. The stiffness of his suit impeded him a little, as always. Plus, his gloves were clumsy. But

Butch was accustomed to spacesuits and soon worked around the difficulties. He had to admit, though, that he was still a little winded from having just manhandled Woody back into the airlock.

Butch had with him a laser cutting torch. The idea was to cut the titanium rib loose from the solar sail at the point where the sail had gotten hung up on the hydraulic piston, then go home to another hero's welcome.

Before Butch could even get started, sparks were flying everywhere. The half-open sail was still sweeping up charged particles from the ever-thickening solar wind. Only now, their energy wasn't being drawn off properly. This is probably what stopped Woody in his tracks, probably what gave him pause. Without the technical equivalent of a lightning rod in hand to safely bleed off the vast amounts of static electricity, a man was like a human conductor. No way could Butch get in close enough to use his laser cutting tool.

The *Mars Voyager* continued its erratic spin, and Butch spun with it, first into sunlight, then into darkness. The slow revolutions imparted tangential velocity to anything not strapped or bolted down. That included overconfident spacejockeys.

Butch worked as swiftly as he could. He didn't want to be out beyond the safety of the ship long. Even encased in a double-density spacesuit, the exposure to radiation was at a level comparable to receiving eight chest x-rays a day, too large a dose to waste time hanging around enjoying the scenery.

With sparks flying nervously around him, Butch thought to use the docking umbilical as a sort of lightning rod to safely draw the electrical discharges away from him, making it possible for him to do his work.

Normally, the umbilical was extended when a ship was docked at the orbiting Space Station. The umbilical was a big thing, some three hundred meters long, with a metal spine running its entire length. The thing was omni-directional and could be "driven" remotely, either from inside the ship or from a control box located on the hull near the airlock. Butch went hand over hand in that direction, opened the control box, extracted the joystick.

Now, with joystick in hand, he drove the umbilical out to its full length and laid it crosswise over the still-open sail. As soon as the umbilical's metal ribbing made contact with the sail, the sparks stopped flying. Now, as the charge built up on the surface of the sail, it was shunted out to the end of the umbilical — and away from Butch.

Butch worked quickly. But still the minutes passed. Earth's moon could be seen from this distance, a perfect crescent lit by the more distant sun. Without Earth's intervening atmosphere to look through, the moon was magnificent, the detail eye-popping. *It was too close*, Butch thought. *Time was running out.*

Butch hooked himself to the mech-asc and worked his way out onto the solar sail. The snag wasn't far off, just twenty meters away. Even so, he couldn't easily reach it. It was too far to grab onto from the closest handhold. Even kneeling didn't help. The kneepad was too close to the handhold to allow him to safely use the laser cutting torch.

Butch jerked his safety line to signal Gulliver for more slack. Gulliver paid out several more meters of it, then Butch unshackled the line from around his waist. This was downright dangerous and absolutely in violation of protocol.

Working with one hand, Butch passed the end of the safety line twice through a handhold and knotted it best he could. He left about two meters of slack hanging free. The shackle on the free end, Butch fastened to a second handhold. The result was a loop that functioned like an improvised climber's chair. It would support his weight while he cut away the titanium rib.

The laser shone red and sparks flew as it bit into the metal. The titanium proved surprisingly tough, even for the cutting torch. To free up the hydraulic piston, Butch planned to cut the rib in two places and physically remove the excised section. The first cut went easy, but the second proved problematic. Like a handsaw that binds in tight wood, the cutting torch refused to punch cleanly through the metal.

Butch decided to try and release the stress on the metal rib by prying up the loose end. He put the torch in his left hand, then slipped up and out of his improvised chair. Next, he swung across to the other side of the rib, monkey-style, so he could grip the loose end with his stronger right hand.

That's when it happened. The cutting torch slipped from his hand. It fell free, spinning off into space.

Butch watched it go, out and out, down and down and down. In no time at all, the torch was so small, it faded from sight, lost among the blanket of stars and distant galaxies.

It had been an amateur's mistake, first dropping the tool, then watching it drift away. Butch had been too busy, until now, to look down. But now that he had done it, he knew it had been a mistake.

Keep your eyes on your work. That's what his bosses always said. *Never take your eyes off your work.* Even a beginner knew that.

But here's the thing about a mistake: once a man has made one, he can never take it back. That's what makes it a mistake. And the results were predictable.

Butch suddenly found himself dizzy. He could feel the sweat on his forehead, the nausea in his belly.

Butch shivered, then swore. He needed another cutting torch; the job couldn't be finished without one.

Butch started to make his way back toward Gulliver and the airlock. — But found he could not.

Butch had swung out past the solar sail compartment to reach his present position, using a grip on his safety-line "chair" to give him half a meter's more reach. Now the loop hung quietly, just out of arm's length. There was no possible way for him to reverse the process.

Butch hung by both hands, now, and told himself not to panic. He had to think his way out of this. Even if Butch wasn't tired — and he had to admit that he was, tired and getting a little cold — even if he were fresh, it was an impossible swing for anyone short of an orangutan. Plus, to jump across that distance entailed a special risk, as he had already detached himself from the safety line. If he missed . . . well . . . then he was a goner for sure.

Butch looked down and again immediately regretted it. There was nothing below him but stars, down and forever. Stars, swinging past as the ship spun with him. Blackness. And beyond it, intense killing cold.

Butch tried next to hoist his entire body onto the single narrow rung he clung to, trying to gain purchase with his toes. But it was a futile, strength-wasting effort.

Butch slowed his breathing, quieted his panic. Then he hung limp. It hadn't yet occurred to him to call out for help.

Butch found it was easier if he kept his eyes shut. But after a short while he had to open them again and look. The constellations swung past, once, twice, three times. He made a stab at trying to compute the passing minutes in terms of the number of revolutions the ship made. But his mind was fogged and would not function properly. After a couple more revolutions, he again had to shut his eyes.

Butch tried to make a fist, but his fingers were too stiff and cold. He tried to rest them by switching off and hanging by one hand at a time. He let go with his left hand, felt pins and needles course through it, then beat it against his side. Presently, he spelled his right hand the same way.

After a few more rounds of this, Butch no longer had the strength to reach up to the handhold with his left hand. He was fully extended, now, and couldn't shorten himself enough to get his left hand all the way up to the rung. Not enough power remained in his arm to make that extra pull.

Now the feeling melted from his right hand as well. It was numb and dead. He could see it slip off the rung, but was powerless to stop it.

The sudden release in tension let him know he was falling. It felt good at first, the feeling coming back into his fingers, the muscles relaxing in his arm. Then his mind locked horns with reality.

Like the cutting torch, he was drifting away from the ship!

The ship seemed to pull away. But in actuality, it was Butch who was pulling away.

Suddenly, though, he felt something wrap around his legs like a lasso. It pulled tight and snapped him to a stop. He stopped falling.

Gulliver had become worried about Butch's long absence. He had moved out beyond the airlock with a second safety line and roped him like a steer.

For a second Butch just hung there, dangling on the rope like a fish on the line. Then Gulliver began to reel him in. He reattached Butch to his original tether. That did the trick. Though Butch was weak and disoriented, he gave Gulliver the thumbs-up sign.

Gulliver passed Butch a second cutting torch and Butch moved back across the sail to finish the job. It took only a few minutes, then the short piece of rib fell loose and Butch retracted the umbilical.

Now the solar sail could finally be stowed and the ship slowed for the approach to Earth.

CHAPTER TWENTY-TWO

▼

"Reporting for duty, sir."

The young man saluted. He was still in his street clothes, a freckled young man.

"Happy to have you onboard, son."

Pappy Barnes returned the boy's salute. The Colonel was dressed in the last uniform he wore before retiring from active duty. "We can use every young, able-bodied man this man's army can get. You need to sign in with the sergeant at Table 6." Pappy pointed across the freshly-mown, Puritan City lawn to where several lines had formed, all new enlistees.

The boy, barely sixteen, heeded Pappy's instructions and moved along toward Table 6. Several others followed suit.

The dozen or so tables were out of the sun beneath dining-fly-style awnings set up on the main lawn at the center of Puritan City. Men in uniform manned each table. As each enlistee signed in, he was handed a packet of information and a pair of fatigues, then directed to the Health Center for a quick medical examination.

Thousands of men, young and old, had answered the call and were now making their way through the snaking lines. To house them all, an immense tent city had taken shape down the hill from the Tabernacle. The entire compound was now encircled by a twelve-foot-tall, high-security fence. Security bots patrolled the perimeter. Roland hated it, but the robots were a concession he had to make to the realities of the coming war.

Branislav Karpinski, dressed in Army fatigues, approached the Colonel, saluted and spoke. His burns had begun to heal.

"Sir, the turnout is even better than we hoped. I was afraid all this talk of secession was just so much hot air, that no one would actually volunteer to come out and fight this frigging war."

"You underestimate your average Texan, Bran. People are outraged by what has happened. Whitmore was right — the people down here are ready to fight."

Branislav was perturbed. "Boss, explain something, would you? I can understand how a liberal Congress might buy into this gun-banning horseshit. But why the hell didn't the President veto the fucker? I thought that kike had our backs on this? Didn't I tell you the man couldn't be trusted?"

"Frankly, Major, I'm as confused as you are. Politicians are pigs. But now that the milk has been spilt . . . "

"Someone has to go in and clean up the mess."

"Which is where you and I come in. Now that the Texas legislature has made its decision, the Lone Star State will be going its own way, which is to say out of the Union."

"It's about goddamned time!" Branislav exclaimed, watching as more recruits poured through the gates.

"Texas won't be the only one."

"I don't disagree. Other States will surely follow their lead. Oklahoma, Wyoming, Colorado . . . "

"Yeah, those plus Idaho, Montana, Tennessee. We don't know who all just yet. The big meeting gets underway in about an hour."

"What big meeting?"

"It was hastily arranged. You were with the doctor, having your face looked at."

"You should have told me, Colonel."

"Well, I'm telling you now. The first guests should be arriving any time. The Reverend will be meeting with Thadamore Mills and the Governors of nearly a dozen other States here on the hallowed grounds of Puritan City. Mills has tremendous pull with these people. Don't forget, before all this trouble started, he was head of the National Governors Association."

"The Governors are meeting here? In the City? That can't possibly be safe, Colonel. What steps have been taken to protect these people? What's being done about their security?"

"I honestly don't think security is much of an issue this early in the game. As far as the rest of the world is concerned, this place is still a House of Worship. Until there is a definitive statement out of that meeting, no one would dare bust into the House of the Lord. We're safe here, at least until some sort of public announcement is made."

"Pappy, you of all people should know better than that. A soldier is never safe, not anywhere. Doctor or not, you should have told me about this meeting before now."

"Roland asked me not to."

"*Quid pro quo* for handing that evil man a microfiche with our battle plans on it?"

"It's not like that."

"No? What is it like then? The man's a fool."

"Roland Whitmore is no fool, Major. The man is cagey, and he is smooth."

"Smooth enough to fool you."

"Have you forgotten who you're talking to, Major?"

"Due respect, Sir. But is our Reverend still angling to be President of the New Republic?"

"Roland will get his way. With or without our help, he will get his way. The man will be President of the New Republic, whether we support him or not." Pappy Barnes was sure.

"Yeah, especially if we help him take down his chief rivals."

"You talking about Mills?"

Branislav nodded. "Colonel, you know I'm practically the last one to question orders. And make no mistake about it — I'm proud to have been the one asked to pull the trigger. But I have to admit, I'm greatly troubled by Whitmore's decision to have Thadamore Mills assassinated."

"That makes the both of us."

"Fair enough. But if this little uprising of ours is to have any chance of succeeding, all the state militias will eventually have to be brought under a single command."

"You don't think I know that? Once the Governors come to some sort of consensus, organizing the state militias will be my first priority. Your priorities, my friend, lie along a different path."

"What path?"

"What you have to do is much more important."

"I've got the green light to blow the bridges?"

"I'm giving you the green light."

"About goddamned time!"

Pappy looked around to see if anyone was listening. "I want you to start with the commercial gtruck bridge at Cairo."

"The big one the gtruckers use to get across the Missup between Illinois and Missouri?"

"Yeah. Drop both spans into the river. But keep your eye on the ball, Bran. Don't forget that. Our objective here is to choke off barge traffic above that point."

"What about our other objectives? — Like denying fuel to the Midwest?"

"Captain Petri is taking two teams to secure the Gulf Coast oilfields."

"Petri's not up to the task, you know that. Anyway, it's gonna take a lot more than Captain Petri and two teams of retired Omegas to secure the oilfields. You and I went through all this before, when we first laid out our original battle plans."

"As soon as the Governors arrive at some sort of an agreement, more funds will be released and Petri will be given more men. But until that happens, this is what we have to work with."

"What if they don't come to an agreement?"

"Even more reason for you to get a move on. In addition to the commercial gtruck bridge, you also have to take out bridges at Sane Lou and up the Ohio at Paducah, Evansville, and Louisville. Plus, any number of locks and dams inbetween."

"And don't forget about the maglev rail lines."

"You know the list better than I do. Once word filters back to Puritan City what you've done, the Governors will fall in line, I promise you."

"If they don't, this is going to be the world's shortest war."

"Remember what I said, Major. Eyes on the ball. Your team is going to have its hands full the next few days. How is it going with them anyway?"

"You mean the over-the-hill gang of retired Special Forces guys you sent me?"

"It can't possibly be that bad."

"It's not. These men are actually quite good. But they're no longer active duty. Some of them have been out of it quite a while. We still have a bit of remedial work to do."

"You'll have to do it on the fly. Your team moves out by air within the hour. By 1800 hours your team will be back on the ground at an airfield near the Cairo bridge. Then by gtruck to the strike zone. Your men better have it down cold by then."

"We won't let you down, Colonel."

"I never doubted it. You have always been good to your word."

.

.

The afternoon sun was high in the western sky when the air transport roared down the runway east of Puritan City. It was little more than a one-hour flight to the private airfield located in the bottom lands of Little Egypt in southern Illinois. Legend had it that the muddy confluence of two great rivers, plus the numerous pyramid-shaped burial mounds left behind hundreds of years ago by the Mississippian Indian culture is what led early settlers to name the region's first city Cairo. The designation "Little Egypt" followed shortly thereafter.

But southern Illinois was no desert — not like the actual Egypt — and Cairo, Illinois, no ancient city with a royal past. In this Egypt there were rolling hills, thick woods, tangled underbrush, and plenty of bugs. Unlike its namesake, this metropolis was dirty and broken-down, an aging river city that never enjoyed a rise to prominence. The locals were country folk of limited education, parochial bigots mainly. No one would give Branislav's team a second thought when their aircraft roared in low over the river and put down on the airstrip west of town.

No sooner were they wheels-up than Branislav Karpinski hustled his team into the center of the transport, where the seats were arranged lecture-hall-style, with a blackboard upfront and a big, oak lectern he could stand behind. There was only one window in this section of the plane. The shade was pulled, which cut down on distractions. There was a table off to one side, and on it, blocks of Enhanced C4, plus lengths of steel pipe and a few good-sized cardboard boxes painted to look like concrete blocks. Also, lengths of detonation cord, plus a carton of blasting caps, all within easy reach.

The men, already in their tech-shirts, found their seats, got comfortable. Branislav stood behind the podium, surveyed his audience, twenty-four serious-minded men in their 30s and 40s.

Major Karpinski was proud of these men. Without exception, these men were smart, capable, and well-trained. Though a few were arguably a year or two beyond their prime, none was out of shape, and all were still quite lethal. To a man they were muscular and fit, all swimmers or runners, though only a handful were still fast enough to match their competitive best times when they were at their peak.

But, for Major Branislav Karpinski, their ages were not an issue. In the Major's mind, surrendering a bit of youthful vigor for mature, seasoned thinking was a fair trade. He wanted to mold these men into the best Special Forces unit he could. So, for the last month, both before and after his accident in Mexico, Branislav put his men through the paces, running them through a fast-paced boot camp, sharpening their skills, rebuilding their endurance, getting them up to speed on the latest combat techniques and small-unit tactics.

Today would be their final session. Tonight they would be going into action. Branislav had barely an hour for this final lesson before the transport put down on that rural airstrip in southern Illinois.

"Gentlemen. You have all been to Ranger School. Most of you have had Omega Special Forces training. So none of what I'm about to say should be news to anyone. But if you're like so many of us, active fieldwork ended years ago. Now it's time to get back in the saddle — we go active in about an hour.

"Let me begin by handing out your demolition cards. You've all had one of these d-cards in your hands before. You know what they're about. If you've lost or misplaced your original d-card, consider this one a replacement. It has all the conversion formulas you will need to successfully complete our missions.

"Let's not kid ourselves. It's not that easy to bring down a well-built modern bridge. Not without modern explosives anyway, and not unless they have been expertly placed. Around here we use Enhanced Composition Four. You know the stuff, ordinary C4 plus refined Tovex. This mixture is stable, easy to work with, water resistant, and packs a serious punch. Pound for pound, it is about forty percent more powerful than TNT. The velocity of detonation is some 10,000 meters per second, enough to knock anyone's socks off."

There was a round of subdued chuckles. Branislav stopped, let loose a tight smile, then continued.

"Perhaps the nicest thing about Enhanced C4 is that it can be shaped, molded by our very fingers to fit the job at hand. This is important, since our targets are many and varied."

Branislav cracked his knuckles. His one hand was still scarred from the fire. The bio-algorithm had been badly applied.

"Now that you have your d-cards, I guess the first thing we need to do is review some of the most common shaped charges and their best applications. Let's begin with steel pipe." He briefly picked up a three-foot section of steel pipe from off the table and held it up for everyone to see.

"To cut this sort of high-grade steel, we use a linear shaped charge. You form a groove in the C4 that runs the length of the charge."

Branislav took a two-pound block of C4 from the table, split it lengthwise, then used a pocketknife and straightedge to slice a smooth, V-shaped groove that ran the length of the split block. The fresh C4 was greasy to the touch and glistened dully in the light. He took some of what he'd cut away and absentmindedly balled it up like Silly Putty.

"Here, catch!"

He tossed the ball of C4 to a soldier in the front row, who was startled by the act and dropped it.

"See? Stable and easy to work with." Branislav laughed, then continued with his explanation:

"Once you have completed excising the groove on the length of C4,

position the V-shaped groove along the desired cut-line on the target material."
He demonstrated by aligning the groove along a section of the steel pipe still
sitting on the table.

"The charge should be as long as the desired cut. The width of the charge
should be the same as the thickness of the target, in this case the steel pipe.
The charge can be detonated from either end, but never both."

Branislav shoved a blasting cap into one end of the block of C4, held it
and the pipe up for everyone to see, then set the whole assembly aside. He
took a drink of water from a nearby pitcher and went on.

"Okay. That's the drill for ordinary steel. For high carbon steel, as for
instance with a solid steel shaft, a man needs to use a diamond charge."
Branislav laid out a much larger, solid steel rod. He took another slice off the
block of Enhanced C4.

"In this application, the dimensions of the diamond are what is most
important. The diamond should be as long as the target is round, half its
length wide, and at least two-thirds of an inch thick. The points on the long
axis of the diamond should just touch on the far side of the target pipe."

Major Karpinski took his measure tape, measured the circumference of
the large, cylindrical steel rod. He wrote that number on the blackboard.
Then he divided that number by two and wrote the second number under
the first.

"These two numbers represent the lengths of the two axes of the diamond,
a long axis twice the length of a short axis.

With his straightedge and a piece of chalk, Branislav drew a four-sided
diamond on the blackboard, making the length of the long axis equal to the
first number and the width of the short axis equal to the second number.
Then, on the table, he cut the slab of C4 to the same dimensions and held the
shaped piece up for everyone to see. The table rattled briefly as the transport
banked then leveled out again.

"I did this quickly, as a demonstration. But considerable time and care
is required to properly prepare a diamond charge. In the field you won't have
a blackboard. It's best to transfer the dimensions first to a template, maybe a
piece of cloth or a section of cardboard, then lay the template over an uncut
slab of C4. Trying to work directly on a target is extremely difficult and
should not be attempted except under the most extreme circumstances.

"Once you have cut the diamond charge to size, transfer it to the target
and tape or tie it in place. The long axis of the charge should be wrapped
tightly around the pipe to ensure maximal close contact. Again, the points
must meet on the far side of the rod."

Branislav slapped the greasy plastic explosive onto the thick steel rod,
wrapped it around the rod's circumference and demonstrated how the

diamond points would meet on the far side. He took a length of duct tape and secured the charge in place about the tube.

"Both ends of the short axis must be primed for simultaneous detonation. This can be accomplished electrically or by use of equal lengths of d-cord."

Branislav uncoiled a length of detonation cord, folded it in half and cut it at the fold. He held up the two equal-length pieces, then set the diamond charge aside.

Now Branislav took one of the large cardboard boxes made up to look like a block of solid concrete.

"To shatter concrete targets up to four feet thick we use what is called an ear-muff charge. You have to have one-and-a-half pounds of Enhanced C4 for each foot of concrete thickness you wish to shatter. Once you arrive at the total amount of explosive required, divide the explosive into two exactly equal-sized charges. Place the charges precisely opposite one another on the target, which will usually be a bridge or roadway support."

Branislav took a fresh block of C4 from his stash, cut it neatly in two, then stuck one piece on each side of the "concrete" block.

"Prime the two charges to detonate simultaneously. Be sure to prime each charge in the exact rear center of the block of C4." He indicated the correct spot on each charge with the laser light on his pen.

"Our mission profile includes blowing several bridges. But blowing them won't be enough. We also have to prevent the bridges from being quickly rebuilt. Our focus will be on piers and abutments. These are critical elements when repairing a bridge. So, whenever possible, we will use breaching charges to obliterate these key structures. Since tension members are more difficult to replace than compression members, we have to go for them first. A timing delay placed between charges on opposite sides of the bridge will cause the bridge to twist as it falls. This is good because it hampers salvage. Anything that slows the bastards down when rebuilding is a good thing."

Branislav continued. "And it's not just the bridges we have to take out. Colonel Barnes has given me a whole list of targets, and high on that list are several rail lines. So let me run you through a quick refresher course, in case you've forgotten.

"To effectively derail a train — whether it's a high-speed maglev or a slow-moving coal-burner — it is necessary to remove a certain minimum length of track. At the very least, we have to remove a section of track equal to the length of the locomotive's fixed wheelbase. With a standard sized locomotive we're talking at least a twenty-foot section of track. But, on the plus side, only one rail needs to be cut, not both.

"Far and away the best place to set the charge is on the outside rail of a curve. Where there are multiple train tracks parallel to one another, we need to use that proximity to our advantage. Whenever possible, our goal should be to derail the train so it is sure to obstruct all the parallel tracks, not just the track our train is on. If our goal is to destroy the train along with the track, it is absolutely critical our charges be detonated in front of the locomotive, not beneath it."

Branislav pushed his work materials aside and sat on the table, legs dangling. "Like the spacing of the ties themselves, there is a certain mundane exactitude to the proper positioning of charges to take out a train line. With an overt charge — what we call a 10-2-1 — ten one-pound charges are placed against the inside web of the rail, one on top of every second tie. The 10-2-1 is quickly installed. But it is just as easily detected.

"That's why, if we're not pressed for time, we're more likely to use a covert charge, what we call a 3-5-2. Three, two-pound charges, one placed beneath every fifth tie. Compared to a 10-2-1, this arrangement is much more difficult and time-consuming to install. But it is also exceedingly difficult to detect."

Branislav got back to his feet. Just as he did, the transport began to bank and descend. He opened the shade on the single window in the room and looked out. The wide Missup River lay beneath them, wetlands in the foreground, tilled fields farther on, rich black soil as far as the eye could see, breadbasket to the world.

"Back to your seats, boys. We'll be on the ground any minute now."

CHAPTER TWENTY-THREE

▼

The scene in living rooms across America was the same, indeed across the world, even aboard the *Mars Voyager* as it made its way slowly home.

Wherever on the planet where a visicast could be viewed that night — be it a pool hall in Hedon City or a corporate boardroom in Chica — faces were grim. President Benjamin was addressing the nation from the Oval Office of the New White House on a subject of the utmost importance. He was just now beginning to warm to the subject:

" . . . Without warning or provocation, in the wee hours of this morning, and continuing throughout the day, domestic terrorists of the lowest order have attacked us multiple times on our own soil. These villains have committed dastardly acts, and no one, no matter what their sympathies, should take joy or satisfaction from these actions. These criminals have blown up our bridges. They have sabotaged our rail lines. Destroyed locks and dams on our most important waterways. Brought down power lines. Disrupted commerce. Indeed, these villains have struck at the very heart of America. They have made the working men and women of this great nation of ours their very enemy . . .

" . . . Barge traffic on both the Upper and Lower Missup has been brought to a halt. Essential gtruck traffic east and west is at a standstill. Airports and suborbports have been closed for fear of further reprisals. Goods cannot be moved into or out of markets in the Midwest because of supply disruptions. Oil prices are soaring because the villains have captured certain of our oil terminals south of Houston and east of N'Orleans. The villains have put a blockade on the lower Ohio . . .

" . . . So, my fellow Americans, the question before us is simple: What do these people want, these barbaric criminals who would wreck our economy with their heinous attacks? Are we to believe that these acts of violence are about the Second Amendment, as these domestic terrorists claim? Are we to believe that these villains would break our laws, destroy our property, in order to preserve our Constitution? Are we to believe that these people would wreck our economy to save our country? — I THINK NOT! Terrorism is terrorism, pure and simple. And, if necessary, it will be dealt with harshly . . .

" . . . The National War Council, of which I am Chair, has met in emergency session. A plan of retaliation has been decided upon. Our response to these terrorist acts will be firm yet measured. Even as we speak, elements of the Illinois, Indiana, and Ohio National Guards are crossing into Missouri and Kentucky to retake key river crossings. They will also retake any bridges or highways that have fallen into enemy hands. Elements of the United States Navy will shortly move from Pensacola into the waters of the Gulf of Mexico. They have been instructed to shell enemy positions in and around Houston, Texas. Other elements of the Navy, as well as elements of the Coast Guard, will move up the lower Missup River Barge Canal and along the Gulf Coast to retake the oilfields and refineries and oil terminals so critical to our nation's commerce . . .

" . . . Unfortunately, lives will be lost in this process, and property destroyed. As Commander in Chief, I apologize in advance to the parents whose brave sons and daughters may die in the coming days. The price will be steep. But this is the price we must pay in order to vanquish these terrorists and to preserve the Union. To ensure our success in these weighty matters, I have this day suspended by Executive Order the Posse Comitatus Act, which forbids the use of Federal troops on U.S. soil. The violence may escalate very quickly, and the other side must know we mean business . . .

" . . . We did not ask for this war. But we will not sit quietly by as domestic terrorists disrupt our way of life. However, if these scoundrels want to step back from the brink, I am willing to offer them a way out. If the terrorists do not want all Heaven and Hell to rain down upon their heads, there is still time for them to give themselves up. But the time is short, just three hours from my mark. After that, my orders will become irrevocable and we will hunt the perpetrators down to the last man . . .

" . . . As I am sure you all know, the Congress has passed a bill suspending the right of private citizens to possess firearms. I have signed this Bill. It is now the law of the land. As head of the Executive Branch of government, I am obligated to enforce it. Thus, I have this day ordered our federal militia to begin enforcing this new law and to start rounding up all firearms. I humbly remind the citizens of our peace-loving nation not to turn their backs on their civic duty. That civic duty includes obeying the laws of this great land and complying with all officers of the law who are trying to enforce those laws. People, please surrender your weapons. Please do so voluntarily . . .

" . . . When civilized peoples disagree, there are civilized ways to settle differences. By way of example, the Great State of Minnesota has filed suit in federal court to compel the Supreme Court to rule on the constitutionality of this new Gun Law. I cannot say how the Justices will rule, but this is how our system of checks and balances is supposed to work. Civilized people fight their battles in the courtroom, not the battlefield . . .

" . . . But instead of following Minnesota's example, other States, led by the renegade Governor of Texas, have taken steps to secede from the Union. They are joined in this despicable action by gangs of gun-toting vigilantes plus certain radical elements of the Religious Right. Should these other States decide to do as Texas has done, they will be dealt with harshly . . .

" . . . My fellow Americans, a Presidency is defined by the crises it inherits. Let me only tell you this: Of the epic struggle we currently face, we cannot lose. If you have doubts — and we all do — know this in your hearts: We will prevail and we will triumph . . . "

" . . . For those of you who have forgotten, let me remind you. As a Nation we have faced terrible challenges before. At times we have been anxious. But we have always managed to pull through. For those of you who have forgotten, let me remind you. The snow of Valley Forge was streaked with red blood. It was the red blood of America's cold and starving fighting force — and yet we are a Nation. Then there was that day at Shiloh, when the Union was surprised to learn that the fight would not be easy — and yet we are a Nation. And that terrible day in December 1941, when our fleet was wrecked and our continent lay exposed — and yet we are a Nation. And again in September 2001, when our innocence was burned to the ground and our fury unleashed — and yet we are a Nation. And again in 2015. And again in 2107. And still we are a Nation. Now comes this day. If you have doubts — and we all do — know this in your hearts: We will prevail and we will triumph. Tomorrow we will still be a Nation.

"Good night and God bless."

The vid panned off President Benjamin's face and onto an American flag, fifty-two white stars on a field of blue, thirteen stripes, seven red, six white. Then the stage went black as God Bless America played quietly in the background.

Noah Benjamin pushed back from behind his large, oak desk, loosened his tie, looked across the Oval Office at a familiar face.

"I think you set exactly the right tone, Mr. President."

The speaker was Alexander Hoagland. His jaw was set. He had been sitting off-camera while the President spoke. The vids were now disengaged and the Oval office quiet.

"You think I did okay?" the President asked as he crossed the room.

"My only criticism is that you may have revealed more about our battle plans to the enemy than necessary."

"Xander, I fear death is upon the land."

"Sir?"

"Must our civilization perish in a hail of fiery atoms?"

President Benjamin sat down hard. His face was ashen, nothing at all like the face he had just shown the public.

"Brinkmanship can be an exceedingly dangerous game to engage in," Hoagland said cautiously. "In the wrong hands, it is doomed to failure."

"Are you suggesting we not answer their attacks?"

"Not at all. The New Republic's threat of war is a brazen attempt by them to frighten our side into acceding to their demands."

"You make this sound like a labor negotiation. This crap could lead to all-out war."

"You don't think I know that? All I'm saying is that you have to be careful how rapidly you ratchet this thing up. It has to be one notch at a time. Not too slow, not too fast. Successful brinkmanship requires you be on both sides of the issue at once. You must permit matters to spin far enough out of control that you begin to lose the ability to avoid taking the dire action you have threatened. This is the only way for your threat to remain credible. At the same time you must be seen as retaining sufficient control over the situation to keep the risk from becoming too large. Otherwise, your threat becomes too costly."

"I got all that, Xander. But this damn thing may very well spin out of control no matter what I do, even with all the safeguards I have put in place."

"Mr. President, sometimes things boil over at the very moment the heat is reduced."

"I gave them three hours. My next step will be to federalize the National Guard. Truth is, I would really rather not take this step. I would give almost anything to avoid sending in paratroopers from the 101st Airborne to retake ten State capitals."

"Still, it may come to that, Mr. President. You may have no choice but to land Marines on the coast of Texas. But here's the thing. If at some point the people in charge over there actually do comply with your demands, you must be able to go into reverse immediately. You must be able to reduce the pressure quickly, thus removing the perceived threat from the picture.

Otherwise, they gain nothing by compliance, and the situation *will* spin rapidly out of control."

"The devil is in the details, old friend. None of us here in Washington is really sure who *is* in control over there. You know these people better than I do, Xander. Is Thadamore Mills running the show over there, or is it Roland Whitmore? I wouldn't be so damned afraid of bungling this monster if I knew for sure who it was I was actually dealing with."

"That's the nub, isn't it? — knowing your opponent. All successful games of strategy depend on it. And I can think of only one man who excels at working out such things. Elijah Montrose. He and I are close friends. If only Elijah were here to help advise us. He's the man who helped school me on Game Theory and strategic bargaining. Right now he's serving a term on the Terraforming Commission. But I haven't spoken to Elijah in weeks. He's off in space somewhere, aboard the *Mars Voyager*, I believe."

"Small world. I happen to know precisely where your friend is."

"How so?"

"Remember the other day, when I told you about our little asteroid problem?"

"How could I forget the Doomsday Scenario?"

"A bit of overreaction, if you ask me. But yes, I think that's what you called it at the time."

"I thought you told me the problem had been solved, that we were no longer in danger?"

"The problem *has* been solved. And the thanks belong to a team of no-name spacejockeys onboard that same *Mars Voyager*. I'd lay bets your friend Elijah Montrose had a front row seat to the proceedings. And someday, when things quiet down, that team of spacejockeys has a Medal of Honor coming their way."

"If you want Elijah's help, I'm sure there's a way for us to get him on the horn."

"The *Voyager* will dock at the Station soon enough. Anyway, I'm not talking strategy and tactics long distance with a man I hardly know. You're already worried I revealed too much to the enemy. Even on a secure channel, there are just too damn many prying eyes. Or ears, as it were. We can't afford for the other side to become privy to our most intimate private conversations."

"Then let's arrange for his transport here when he lands."

"My thoughts exactly. I can dispatch a security team to pick up your man after he disembarks the Space Elevator."

"Makes sense," Xander agreed. "But back to the question of who's in charge over there."

"You mean in the New Republic?"

"I'd rather you didn't call it that just yet. Until we say different, those renegade States are still part of the one and only United States. Now, to the question. Whether the chief dog over there is Thadamore Mills or Roland Whitmore or someone who hasn't even shown his hand yet, one thing is for absolute certain — our opponents are not going to give up easily. Not if you choose to fight them on their own soil. A man defending his home will fight to the death, if you make him. That's what made the first Civil War so long and bloody."

"You would rather we fought them on *our* soil?"

"We may have to do that as well." Xander turned thoughtful. "You know my philosophy on this, Mr. President. Everyone should have his own plot of land. Land you can hold in your hand. Land that can get under your nails and into the creases of your fingers. It is land that integrates a man fully into life. Which is why a rented flat is always disastrous. Rented property is like a disease; a sort of prison."

"I don't disagree. I love my home in the mountains, you know that. Blue Ridge Manor has been in my family for generations. Besides, ranch life is simple. You work all day with your hands. You get dirty. Build fences. Clear brush. I love the outdoors. And I love the land."

"Which is why they will fight to the death if you attack them in their homes. Westerners are even more wedded to the land than you and I are. They are strong believers in the Castle Doctrine. You must not run afoul of that — or we will lose."

"I always knew you were a bit of a philosopher, Alexander. But it seems you're even deeper than I remembered."

"I do not favor the intellectuals of our time, if that's what you mean. I have found many of them to be dim bulbs, even if they should happen to score high on some politically correct IQ test."

"Do I smell the stench of arrogance?"

"Say what you will, but I do not think that people with great degrees or great success are necessarily smart — though some certainly are. I have little interest in credentials. They are frequently a veil for stupidity — or worse. If you must call me anything, Mr. President, do not call me arrogant, call me a skeptic."

"And yet, you don't dislike intellectuals."

"Actually, many of my heroes are intellectuals. Not Thomas Jefferson. That one was a mloron, with no understanding of economics whatsoever. But, yes, certainly James Madison. Alexander Hamilton. Milton Friedman. And that Elijah Montrose I was telling you about."

"Yes, yes, we'll get Montrose here straightaway after their ship docks. Though it occurs to me, landing may become a problem for those people."

"How so?"

"On account of the shelling."

"I hadn't thought of that," Xander admitted. "The Houston Spaceport is closed, isn't it? But then again, there's always Hilo. The big control tower in the Hawaii Free State monitors all space and air traffic over the Pacific."

"Yes, yes, of course. Take my suborb to Hilo and meet your friend. I'll have my Chief of Staff check with Space-Traffic Control, but I'm sure they'll be re-routing inbounds from the Station to Hilo. On your way out West, I may ask you to make a stop in Texas."

"Thadamore Mills?"

President Benjamin nodded. "I think you're the only one from my circle the man trusts. I'm confident he'll tell you the truth about the way things are over there."

Xander suddenly seemed distracted.

The President looked at him, asked. "Something you still want to get off your chest?"

"There is a difference, you know, between a Republican and a conservative; between a Hamiltonian and an Objectivist."

"You'll tell me, I'm sure."

"Above all else, a conservative respects ideas; a Republican respects money. A Hamiltonian respects business; an Objectivist respects the individual."

"So what does that make me?"

"Due respect, Mr. President, but you should have vetoed that bill. None of this would have ever happened if only you had vetoed that bill."

"Is it too late for me to change my mind?"

"Regimes planted by bayonet do not take root."

"Let's just see what tomorrow brings, shall we?"

"Armageddon. That's what tomorrow will bring. Armageddon."

CHAPTER TWENTY-FOUR

▼

Butch Hogan was as surprised as anyone seated in the main space lounge of the solar sailship *Mars Voyager* when President Benjamin signed off after his speech.

Could it be? he asked himself. *Is there any possible way I heard that right?*

Butch searched for confirmation in the faces of those seated around him. Red Parsons. Kaleena Flanagan. Elijah Montrose. Everyone was silent, stunned by the news.

Red Parsons was the first to break the silence. "Bloody hell! Where in the world will we land?"

Kaleena locked worried eyes with Butch. "What does he mean?" she asked.

"Normally, the putdown spot is on the north side of Houston. Same place you boarded the Space Elevator, when you first left for Mars."

"That's exactly what I mean," Red said. "If the President isn't spraying us all with bullshit, right about now the U.S. Navy is shelling the Houston area from out in the Gulf. No way is the Space Elevator going to unload passengers anywhere near that kind of trouble."

Elijah Montrose frowned. "I seriously doubt whether President Benjamin is going to go on national vid and — to use your words — spray us all with bullshit, and certainly not about a matter as weighty as this one. That kind of bluff would be far too easy for an enemy to call. Remember, young man, a threat is impotent unless you mean to carry it out. Anyway, I believe you have asked the wrong question."

Red was incensed. "Frigging hell, old man. The only one around here who is impotent is you, you old fart. What bloody question *should* I be asking?"

"Where we land shouldn't be our primary concern. We won't have any say in the matter anyway. No, the more pressing issue is whether or not they will even *let* us land. With a shooting war already in progress, no one may even let us set down until they are absolutely certain of our loyalties. There are a hundred and eighty-two passengers onboard this boat, plus I don't know how many crew. Some of them may be armed. Some of them may be sympathizers to the cause."

"Which cause?" Butch asked. "I own a gun. So does my father. In fact, we own several guns between us. People out our way believe in a body's right to own and carry a gun."

"Me, I'm opposed to guns," Kaleena said. "You know that. After the stadium massacre, my father's legislation was a good thing, the right thing to do."

"Frigging hell! Your father is the one behind this crap?" Red asked, exasperated. "It's like I always said — You know one Irish, you know 'em all. The whole lot of 'em are tree-huggers, if you ask me. But you, Butch, you're the one I can't understand. You're sleeping with the bloody enemy! How could you?"

Butch started for his friend's throat. There was unexpected fire in his eyes. The two men started to grapple clumsily.

Elijah stood, hands on hips, like a referee. "Fine, knock each other's brains out. No wonder we're at war down there, if two friends can't even get along up here. Kaleena has a right to her opinion, even if it happens to be wrong. And she and Butch have a right to their happiness, even if their politics mix like oil and water. And you, Red, you have a lot of nerve to stand there and criticize your closest friend. The two of you are on the same side in this bloody war! So why don't you both just dummy up and knock off this nonsense!"

Butch pushed Red away and straightened his clothes. Red pushed back, still angry. "You done?"

"Yeah, I'm done," Butch said. "You?"

Red nodded. "Maybe I was out of line with that crack. I just feel we need to stand firm on this whole gun rights thing. I feel that strongly."

"I know you do, Red . . . And I happen to agree with you."

"I just don't want to see our country ripped apart at the seams over this crap."

"And you think I do?"

"No, of course not. Look, I'm sorry."

"Apology accepted. Now can we please get back to the question of a landing site?"

A new voice joined the discussion now. It was Woody Dunlop's voice. He and Gulliver Travels had just moments ago joined the other four in the space lounge.

"Don't forget," Woody said. "Aside from Houston, there are two alternate putdown spots."

"Two?" Doc asked.

"Yes. Sri Lanka and the Hawaii Free State. Both locations have Space Elevator depots."

"I'd forgotten about Sri Lanka," Elijah admitted. "But it'll be a tough nut for us to crack if we're forced to get home from the middle of the Indiastan Ocean."

"Hawaii's closer, that's for damn sure."

"What do you think, Woody? Will they bring us down in Sri Lanka or Hawaii?" Elijah asked.

"I'll have to ask the Captain, but the Hawaii Free State, almost certainly. With any luck, the local suborbports will be re-opened by then. Most of us should be able to hitch a ride home from Hilo easily enough."

"That's good, because I was hoping to take Kaleena home with me after we land, introduce her to my father, maybe blow off a little steam banging around my old stomping grounds," Butch said.

"Where's home?" Gulliver asked.

"Wyoming. My father has a small ranch there."

"Big Sky Country?"

"No, that's Montana. But the mindset's about the same. Outdoorsmen the world-over believe in guns. They also believe in the Castle Doctrine. There is almost universal agreement on this out West."

"Dare I ask?"

"No, Kaleena, your man's right. I believe in it too," Elijah said.

"I never thought you were the libertarian type," Butch commented.

"Now it's my turn to be insulted. Honestly, Butch, after everything I've tried to explain to you — the Paradox of Choice, the Broken Window Fallacy, Game Theory — what kind of political stripes do you actually think I'm wearing?"

"Would someone please explain this Castle thing to me?" Kaleena demanded.

"May I?" Elijah asked.

Butch shrugged his shoulders, let Elijah talk.

"The Castle Doctrine. It places into law the fundamental right of self-defense. If a person is in a place he has a right to be — in his front yard, on a public highway, working in his office, strolling in a public park — and if he is confronted in any of these places by an armed predator, that person has a right to respond with force in defense of his life."

"But it's much more than that . . . "

"Yes, it is. The Castle Doctrine also protects a law-abiding citizen from any criminal or civil charges which might arise should a citizen have to defend himself against an attacker."

"Castle Doctrine or not, other States may get sucked into this frigging cyclone," Gulliver said. "The President made it sound that way anyway."

Butch spoke. "If the authorities come knocking on my door looking for volunteers, I might get involved. Otherwise, I'm likely to stay out of it. Live and let live and all that."

"I'm with you, Brother," Red said. "Live and let live."

"Don't want to get involved?" Gulliver scoffed. "Not much of a man, if you ask me."

"But then again, no one asked you," Red snapped, his fur up.

"Again with the bickering?" Elijah growled. "Could we please just stay on topic?"

"Excuse me, but I saved this moke's ass, when he nearly got it shot off on that spacewalk. If I had known the man wasn't gonna stand his ground when push came to shove, I might just as well have let him drift off into space."

Elijah shook his head. "Honestly, boys. It's critical we make sense of the situation on the ground before our ship docks at the Space Station. We need a solid strategy, or every last one of us risks being labeled a terrorist before we even have a chance to set foot again on Earth."

"You don't need a strategy, old man — you're one of them!" Gulliver Travels said, still aching for that fight.

"Exactly which *them* am I supposed to be one of?" Elijah said, starting to get angry.

"You work for the Terraforming Commission. That makes you one of them. A bureaucrat. A stooge of the sitting government. They don't want you, old man. If anyone's gonna be locked up, it's gonna be one of these two gun-toting buffoons from Wyoming."

"I'm from Wyoming. Red's from Colorado."

"Seen one drill bit , you seen 'em all."

Red started for Gulliver, but Butch held him back. The President's speech had set everyone on edge.

"Doc's right, we need a strategy," Butch said, still restraining his friend. "What do you propose?"

"Follow me on this, Butch, because Game Theory might be a good place for us to start. It's most useful when trying to analyze situations like the one we presently face. Plus, it's a subject I happen to know a lot about."

Butch objected. "Spare us all the school lesson today, will you, Doc? No one needs any more of your crackpot theories, least of all right now."

"Now I'm a crackpot? I liked you better when I was just an old fossil. Or was it a raisin-crapper?"

"Butch is right," Red exclaimed. "Everyone is sick and tired of your pompous mouth. Frigging hell, old man. We need to be practical here, not twelve flights up some goddamn ivory tower."

"Boys, I assure you: This is no ivory tower we're twelve stories up in. Give me five minutes. Then you two — what did the man say? — you two buffoons can be practical the rest of the way home."

Butch threw up his hands. "Okay, Doc, five minutes. Not a second more."

"Game Theory helps us to understand how people act. It also helps us to understand how people re-act."

"Are you serious? You actually mean to waste our time yapping at us about bloody games?" Gulliver shook his head in irritation.

"Give the old raisin-crapper a break. We promised him five minutes."

"Let the man make fun, if it makes him feel better. But almost all our decisions — whether they be in business, politics, or war — are a function of how we believe an opponent will respond in the second round to what we do to them in the first round. And, knowing that there *will* be a response to our actions in the second round, affects what we will actually *do* to them in the first round. And so on to subsequent rounds. Linkages and feedback. That is the essence of Game Theory."

"Why are we wasting our time talking about games, when we ought to be talking about the festering war down on Earth?"

"We *are* talking about the festering war down on Earth. We are talking about every single war ever fought since the first intelligent beast walked upright on the surface of our fair planet. Most strategic players prefer to wait for an opponent's first move and then respond to it. That strategy is less risky than going first themselves, although some games confer a first-mover advantage. In the most basic game, the game we call Tit-for-Tat, a player echoes what his opponent did to him in the previous round. People, businesses, even entire nations, respond in kind to how they have been treated in the past. If you were treated well by someone in the first round, you're apt to treat them well in subsequent rounds. If you have previously been treated poorly by someone, you will subsequently treat *them* poorly. Long before Game Theory existed as a science, we had a name for this kind of play. We called it the Golden Rule."

"Actually, Doc, the Golden Rule is nicer than Tit-for-Tat. The Golden Rule doesn't include retaliation."

"No, actually the Golden Rule dictates how one ought to play when they are forced to go first — *Do Unto Others As You Would Have Them Do Unto You.* After the first round, it's strictly Tit-for-Tat. *Do Unto Others As They Have Done Unto You.*"

"I thought the Bible asked us to *Turn The Other Cheek?*"

"No, it says — *An Eye For An Eye.* But not all games are that simple. Everybody plays them — teachers, students, corporations, labor unions. Particularly nasty players follow a *Get Them First* strategy, something we've come to call the Brazen Rule. *Do It To Them Before They Do It To You.*"

"Four minutes, Doc . . . "

"Okay, then. Let's move quickly onto something more complex. I call this next game the Unscrupulous Diner's Dilemma."

"We move now from games about people to games about food?"

"Right you are, young man. Imagine it is Saturday night. You and a group of friends are dining out at a fine restaurant. The group orders, but with the proviso that when the bill comes you will divide the check evenly among all the members of your party. Here's the question — What should you order?"

"Now you lost me, Doc."

"What should you order? — the modest chicken entree or the pricey lamb chops? The house wine or the rare Rothschild? If you are extravagant, you could enjoy a superlative dinner at a bargain price."

"But that's not fair," Red said.

"Of course, it isn't fair. If everyone in the group reasons the same way and everyone decides to splurge, the group will end up with a hefty bill to pay and no one will come out even one credit ahead."

"But why should I settle for pasta when everyone else is having grilled pheasant at my expense?"

"Precisely my point. And it is one we shouldn't trivialize. The Unscrupulous Diner's Dilemma typifies a whole class of serious problems we face as a society. Why should I work hard if I can easily collect welfare? Why should I turn down my thermostat in the winter to conserve fuel if my neighbor doesn't? Why not make full use of free medic care, when everyone else does?"

"You might have some libertarian leanings after all. But this Diner's Game of yours has less to do with war than it does to do with cooperation."

"Actually, it's about more than just simple cooperation. It's also about promoting the common good."

"And here all this time I thought you economists didn't give a tinker's damn about the common good."

"Ah, but you are wrong. Like Adam Smith said, the common good is maximized when people are allowed to maximize their private good. But it only works if prices and wages are flexible."

"I don't always follow your thinking, Doc — but I do love to watch your mind at work."

Elijah smiled. "I'll take that as a compliment. Now please allow me to me finish. In the Unscrupulous Diner's Dilemma, the common good is achieved by minimizing the total amount of the dinner bill. Individuals fall into one of two categories — cooperative, if they choose a less expensive meal, or uncooperative, if they splurge at everyone else's expense. Each person can choose to either contribute to the common good, or else shirk and hitch a free ride on the sacrifices of others."

"But wouldn't every last one of them eventually become a free rider?" Butch asked. "I mean, given the tradeoffs, aren't the incentives to defect just too great?"

"The incentives are hard to resist; that much is true. But wants and needs are two different things. Plus, there are other variations on the theme to consider. If the players know they are going to repeat the same game over and over again with the same group of people, the situation changes considerably."

"That makes sense."

"A smart individual has to consider the repercussions of a decision not to cooperate. The diner who goes out with a group just once is more likely to splurge at everyone else's expense, as compared with someone who goes out repeatedly with the same group."

"But group-size also makes a difference, doesn't it? In a large group no one notices what any one single person actually does."

"Ah, the very essence of free-riding. When the actions — good or bad — of any one single player are diluted by the sheer size of the group. For groups beyond a certain minimum size, cooperation becomes a challenge of a much higher order."

"Or, like you said, the longer a player expects the game to go on, the more likely he is to cooperate."

"Which is precisely why Game Theorists believe there should be less free-riding in a small group, especially one that has much at stake and interacts as a unit for a long time."

"Like a squad of Marines," Butch observed, thinking back on his training.

"Or a nuclear family," Kaleena said.

"But a big country? — No way."

"As long as a large enough fraction of the population is cooperating, most people will feel pressure to fall in line and cooperate as well," Elijah said.

"But what happens when cooperation breaks down?"

"Then there is a crisis, like a financial panic. Once the number of panicked sellers exceeds some critical mass, the entire market melts down in an uncontrollable rout."

"Do you think that's where America is headed? — into some kind of uncontrollable rout?"

"To tear down a bull market might take only a matter of a few bad days. To collapse an entire civilization might take only a matter of a few bad months. But to build either one back up again . . . "

Elijah Montrose let the words hang in the air. Then he continued:

"It took a thousand years for civilization to recover from the collapse of the Roman Empire. Just how long do you think it will take to rebuild things a second time should they now happen to fall apart again?"

"What a sunny thought."

"Okay, old man, enough!" Gulliver exclaimed. "Your five minutes are long past due. — And I didn't learn a goddamn thing."

"No surprise there."

"Now who's picking a fight?"

"The man's right, Doc. — What exactly have we learned?" Butch asked.

"Two things. The passengers on this ship are a comparatively small group. The six of us are an even smaller sub-group. If we don't cooperate, none of us is ever going to get home. When that elevator door opens in the Hawaii Free State and we step out onto the tarmac, we may find ourselves having to swear allegiance to a new flag — or perhaps the old one. We'll have no choice but to choose up sides *before* we land, while we're still up here. And to do that, we simply must understand what sort of game is being played out on the surface below our feet. War is a negative-sum game — always and forever. The sum total of everyone's losses will always exceed the sum total of everyone else's gains. Everyone is always worse off afterwards. — And that includes us."

"Well, Doc, I don't even have to think about it," Butch said. "Win, lose, or draw, I'm going home when we land. Game or no game, there is no way I'm going to goose-step my way into throwing away my Second Amendment rights — or any other rights for that matter. The Hogan family owns a ranch. My father and I live there. We don't bother anyone. That's where I'm going to go when we put down — home — and I'm not going to pledge allegiance to any other flag 'cept the one I was born under."

"I'm with you, Bubba," Red said. "But I'm not so sure I want to choose up sides on this one."

"As much as it pains me to say so, I happen to agree with you," Gulliver said. "But which is more important? — preserving the Second Amendment or preserving the Union?"

Woody seemed to share Gulliver's assessment. "I'm on the fence myself."

"Me, too," Kaleena said. "What about you, Doc?"

"My loyalties are divided. I am indeed one of them, as this young man suggested. But that's not all bad. One of my closest friends is a U.S. Senator. You may have heard of him. Alexander Hoagland. Xander is close to the President. He's equally close to Thadamore Mills, Governor of Texas. I'm sure once we get on the ground, Alexander will help me to sort out this mess. I need to see which way the wind is blowing before I choose up sides."

"There is no wind in space, Doc," Butch said. "Whatever flag you are planning on pledging your allegiance to just won't flap in that breeze."

CHAPTER TWENTY-FIVE

▼

In a sense, modern securities markets never closed; they remained open twenty-four hours a day every day everywhere.

But only in a sense. To a great degree, local tradition still trumped technological prowess. Even in an electronic age, an age where computers could talk to one another uninterrupted round the clock, markets still had "hours," those times when most traders were physically at their screens answering customer calls. On the east coast of the United States, formal trading began each day at 9 a.m.

On this particular day, brokers thought the first hour of trading would be the worst. If only it were so. Severe margin calls didn't even set in until noon, when the Circuit Breaker limits had been reached and later breached. Trading was suspended for a while, but the carnage continued overseas.

At times like these, times of panic, questions of "when" are beside the point. Once a thinking person admits that a stock market crash is on its way, he will immediately get out of the market and not try to time the collapse or try to hang on in hopes of wringing out more profit before it happens.

But, of course, rationality and panic do not belong together in the same sentence. Late that afternoon, when the markets were still in free-fall, the Chairman of the Federal Reserve stepped into the President's office.

Spencer Trask had what his admirers called a "silicon chip" mind. Precise and analytical. A high-powered intellect capable of cutting through a maze of difficult problems with dazzling speed. The man had a knack for reducing the complex to the simple, an ability to quickly visualize a solution to a difficult problem, laying it out in simple terms before people's amazed eyes. He and

Alexander Hoagland went way back, back to their Wall Street days. In fact, it was Alexander Hoagland who first suggested the President make Spencer Trask head of the nation's central bank. It was an inspired choice. Now, this morning, Spencer Trask sat across from Noah Benjamin in the Oval Office.

The President looked tired. And well he should. Events on the ground were moving fast. The Illinois National Guard, backed up by units from Indiana and Ohio, had crossed the Missup River into Missouri and had their asses handed to them. The stock and bond markets were in free-fall and interest rates were spiking across the land. More States had joined the rebellion. Thadamore Mills was rumored to be under house arrest and the Reverend Roland Whitmore had just been named Acting President of the New Republic. A provisional government would soon be formed. Now the Chairman of the Federal Reserve was here, in the Oval Office.

"Thank you for coming on such short notice, Spencer."

"Truth is, my very presence here in the White House may send the wrong signal to the markets."

"If it shows the markets anything, it shows that we are taking this thing very seriously."

"If the Fed is seen as bending to political pressure, that may do more harm than good. I don't want people smelling blood in the water."

"If we don't quell the financial panic in its infancy, we are lost — the rebels win. Can you put a stop to this thing or not?" President Benjamin asked. He was trembling, if not with fear then with anger.

"The moral of the story is a simple one, Mr. President."

Spencer Trask was relentlessly pragmatic. By force of habit, he would reduce every decision to the remorseless logic of a mathematical equation — coolly assessing the risk factors, the odds for success or failure.

"I want neither morals from you, Trask, nor stories. Can the central bank put a stop to this rout or not?"

"On the whole, Mr. President, markets work pretty well and should be left alone. Occasionally, though, they are overwhelmed and in need of help. That may be the case here today. But it's far too early in the game to know for sure."

"You expect me to just sit back and do nothing? That will not do, Spencer! Collapse may follow panic if government refuses to step in during times of crisis."

"Sir, the analogy is rather straightforward. Because no great strength is required to hold back the rock before it starts a landslide, does not mean that the landslide, once underway, will not be of immense proportion. *Should the State always intervene?* Of course not. Nor should it always refrain from intervening. In the absolute, both stances are wrong. Thus, the role of lender of last resort is fraught with ambiguity and dilemma."

"By lender of last resort you mean you — the Federal Reserve?"

"Yes, that's precisely what I mean. The role of a central bank is to provide liquidity to the system. In this country, this was known as far back as Alexander Hamilton. If the markets know in advance that help will always be forthcoming, they will tend to break down more often and function less efficiently. Should the markets ever become convinced that the Fed will always step in to save them from folly, self-reliance would be destroyed and all caution thrown to the wind."

"Don't be a mloron, Spencer! We'll worry about next time, next time."

"Due respect, sir. We have to worry about next time, this time, right now. The specific boulder that precipitates a landslide will vary from crisis to crisis. It could be the failure of a bank. Or of an industrial firm stretched too tight. It could be the revelation of a financial swindle. Perhaps a default by someone seeking to escape his distress by dishonest means. It could be the widespread adoption of a new innovation with pervasive effects — canals, maglev trains, the automobile, the bubble memory chip. Perhaps a bumper harvest. Or a crop failure. The outbreak of war. Or the cessation of hostilities. Each time is different from the last. And yet, each time is the same."

"Now you're talking in riddles. How can each crisis be different and yet the same?"

"The commonality is a fall in prices. It is the one thing all panics have in common. Whatever was driven up in price by earlier speculation, panic now deflates, be it oil, farmland, tulip bulbs, gold, what have you. At the outset of the panic, these assets alone are seen as being vulnerable and overpriced. It doesn't take long, though, for the panic to spread. Then the rush is on. Prices decline. The value of collateral crumbles. Bankruptcies soar. Loans are called. Households dump securities to raise cash. But one thing is certain — liquidation is never orderly. In fact, it can be quite messy. More often than not, it degenerates into widespread panic as the realization spreads that there is only so much money to go around, though not nearly enough to allow everyone to sell out at the top. As scared people crowd through narrow doors before the doors slam shut, panic begins to feed on itself. *And it will not stop until one of three things happen.*"

"What three things?"

The Chairman of the Federal Reserve looked at the President but found no reason to rush his reply.

"Goddamn it, Trask, I need some straight answers here! I have to go on national vid tonight. I have to tell the nation that everything will be okay. I need to give the People some hope, assure them we're not headed off a cliff."

Spencer Trask stared at President Noah Benjamin with thoughtful eyes. Spencer's wealth allowed him to do as he pleased rather than what was expected. But he never just wanted to be the richest man in the graveyard; he wanted to make a difference. *Otherwise, what would be the point?*

"Three things, Mr. President. The panic will not end until one of three things happen. Either, prices fall low enough that people are once again tempted to move out of cash and into less liquid assets. Or, trade is cut off either by setting limits on price declines or by outright closure of the markets . . ."

Noah interrupted. "That's what you want me to do? — Shut down the markets? For God's sake, Spencer . . . the Circuit Breaker limit prices have already been violated."

"There is a third option. The lender of last resort can succeed in convincing the markets that money will be made available in sufficient quantity to meet the increased demand for cash. The mere knowledge that speculators can get their hands on enough cash is often sufficient to restore confidence, whether or not the money is actually issued."

"That's what we must do then. After my speech tonight, the Federal Reserve must issue a statement. You will provide all the liquidity the markets require."

"I don't have a problem with that. But I can't keep the money spigots open long or else inflation will take off. In the long run, there must be a political solution to the crisis."

"And there will be. Even as we speak, Alexander Hoagland is on his way to Texas. Texas first, then the Hawaii Free State."

"You sent Xander into the lion's den? Xander is my friend."

"He's my friend too. And it's hardly the lion's den. Don't forget, Hoagland is from Texas. He and Mills are close. Besides, I've given him my suborb plus my security team. They wouldn't dare lay a finger on the man. Alexander is to meet with Thadamore tomorrow, perhaps work out the terms of a truce."

"Are you even sure Mills is still in charge over there? I heard he was under house arrest, that Whitmore had taken over."

That question was answered with silence, a silence that made Spencer Trask wary.

"I don't claim to be a politician, Mr. President. But a truce looks to be a nonstarter."

"I'll thank you to stick to managing the money supply, not trying to make policy."

"I go my own way, as always. If you don't like it, I can always tender my resignation. I'm sure that will do wonders to calm the markets."

"Let's not be too hasty, shall we?"

"For God's sake, man, show some backbone, will you? The only hope for this country is if the Supreme Court rules quickly on Minnesota's legal challenge and declares Flanagan's law unconstitutional."

"The Court wouldn't dare rule against me."

"We wouldn't even be facing a crisis right now if you'd had the stones to do the right thing from the start and veto that godforsaken bill."

Noah Benjamin stared hard at the other man. Spencer Trask was not someone you could argue with. Spencer would listen patiently to an opposing opinion, reflexively pat his shirt pocket where he kept his e-pad and stylus, then pull them both out to make a note. But his reflex action was never anything more than that — an act of politeness on his part. So far as Noah Benjamin knew, Spencer Trask had never once changed his mind about anything.

The President hung his head. "I thought I was doing the right thing."

"Well, you were wrong. Government never does the right thing."

"Never?"

"I would gladly put my faith in private enterprise over politicians and their blundering bureaucracies any day of the week, and twice on Sunday. Private enterprise can move mountains in the time it takes government to staff a commission, pass a bill, hire people, construct a headquarters building, and then, if there is any money left in the budget, deal with the problem."

"You and Xander Hoagland. You're both crazy capitalists."

"You say that like it was a bad thing."

"Isn't it? You hate government and despise bureaucracy. What, then, is the ideal organization in your opinion?"

"The private corporation, of course. And not one of those committee-run abortions that presently rule the land, but one run by an egocentric maniac. I think it was Cornelius Vanderbilt, who said it best."

"Commodore Vanderbilt? The robber baron? He's your hero? The man's more folklore than fact."

"The man was quite real, I assure you. And the Commodore had a distinctive business model he adhered to. First — run the most efficient, lowest-cost organization possible. Second — compete fiercely, cutting prices until the opposition is either broke and can be bought out cheaply, or agrees to pay you to stop competing. Finally — be honest, and live up to your agreements."

"Yeah, honesty and politics — like those two are gonna mix."

"And yet there continues to be honest men in politics. I believe Alexander Hoagland is one of those men. In the world Xander and I came from, we aspired to a higher ideal. In that world, a man's word was his bond. Thus, he would make no threat he could not fulfill."

"Is that what you're accusing me of?"

Before Spencer could answer, Noah's wife Ruth walked into the room. Ruth Benjamin was typical of her day and social class — intelligent, educated, schooled in the classics — and utterly impractical. After so many years together, Noah could no longer stand the woman.

There was contempt in her voice when she spoke. "Darling, it's time for your bath. You need to freshen up before your speech tonight."

"Yes, love, almost done here."

Spencer Trask resisted the overwhelming urge to crack a smile. He knew the back story. Noah Benjamin had more than one downfalling. But his worst was a girl who worked for the American News Network, one Annabel Clark. Very petite and slender, with a superb figure she often put on display. The woman had wonderful legs, which she always managed to put to good use in some alluring way. She knew what she was doing, a real flirt, and she loved being the President's mistress, couldn't wait for them to sneak away for a "naughty weekend."

But there would be no sneaking away this weekend. This weekend, the President had other, more pressing things on his mind.

Noah shooed his wife away, turned to his Chairman of the Federal Reserve:

"One last thing, Spencer."

"Yes, Mr. President?"

"The people at Treasury have urged me to slap on a war tax of some size, to help finance the battle ahead and to help focus the people's minds on the task before us."

Spencer reacted sharply. "The people at Treasury have their heads up their asses."

"Are you sure you want to sugarcoat it like that?"

"No, I mean it. The people at Treasury don't know what they're talking about. Slapping on a war tax would be about the worst move you could make right now."

"What makes you say that?"

"Taxes are a drag on the economy, everybody knows that. The Federal Reserve can't be adding liquidity to the system to calm nerves while the Treasury Department is simultaneously draining it all away with higher taxes. This is something you simply must not do."

"Then maybe we ought to let Treasury set trading prices on all publicly traded stocks and bonds. We can't have banks and brokerage houses failing all over the country on account of declining or insufficient collateral."

"The more you intervene in the markets, the more likely you'll chase away risk capital. Only if people fervently believe they will have no problem selling what they have bought, will they ever be willing to part with their hard-earned cash to purchase those things in the first place. Ultimately, markets are about one thing — trust."

"You don't think I know that? Cut to the chase already, Spencer. My wife wants me to take a bath before I go on the air."

"Since when did you start taking orders from your wife?"

"Since she started telling me to do things I was going to do anyway. Now, please. Finish your explanation so I can make a decision."

"The point I'm trying to make is this. In small groups, where everyone knows everyone else, the group tends to enforce its own rules. Rules like Tit-for-Tat and the Golden Rule keep everyone in line. But in larger groups, especially impersonal groups like the equities markets, social norms have to be enforced differently, by actual law and regulation. As a society, we have, through hard experience, evolved a system of rules and regulations which provide a framework for successful results when two or more strangers come together to trade securities."

"You mean like the Securities Commission?"

"The Securities Commission, the Treasury Department, my agency, the Banking Commission, the entire financial regulatory bureaucracy. Oversight and surveillance. To keep things fair and honest."

"Trust only goes so far."

"Trust is the essence of a free and functioning market. In fact, our markets are so well regulated, most people simply take it for granted that the markets will open on time each business day without fail, that the companies they invest in will be honest, that their broker will not lie to them, that their trades will be dealt with in a defined and fair manner, and that they can commit their hard-earned money, all without fear of being misled or swindled."

"And yet, people still do get swindled."

"A trustable market does not mean people will never overpay for a stock. Nor does it mean people won't make mistakes or let their emotions get the better of them. The market performs different functions for different people at different times. In fact, at any moment, three types of game are being played simultaneously. Games of Chance. Games of Skill. Games of Strategy. The same market, the same stock, the same day, even the same trade — these identical events hold different meaning for different players."

"You are talking above my head, Spencer, and I don't much care for it."

"We certainly can't have that in a President, now can we? So let me boil it down for you. Three games, three players. First and foremost are the investors. They gather information, look at the fundamental competitive position of a given company, purchase the stock and step aside to allow management to build share-value over time. Like the marriage between a man and a woman, this is the ultimate game of trust. For investors, truth plays out over time, often taking years or even decades. They play a Game of Strategy."

Spencer continued. "Speculators play a different game, a Game of Skill. They know they're playing a fast game, but they consider themselves better and more skilled at it than their competitors. They believe they understand the other fellow's psychology, sometimes better than the fellow himself. Not only that, they believe that understanding the other fellow's psychology makes all the difference to their success. And, even though the underlying mathematics resemble a set of musical chairs, the speculator is confident there will always be an empty chair leftover for him. For these sorts of people, truth plays out over weeks or months rarely years.

"Finally, there are the gamblers. They play a Game of Chance. They look at the market through the eyes of a lottery ticket. In the short run, stock prices cannot be predicted. That is a fact, backed up by empirical study. These people prefer a random walk down Wall Street over a stroll up Main Street. They pull the lever on the world's great equity slot machine. They are optimistic and believe the mathematics works in their favor. For gamblers, truth plays out in minutes and seconds and hours, rarely days."

"Is there a point to all this?"

"The point is this, Mr. President. If you go around arbitrarily setting prices in the marketplace, all three players will get confused, all three games will be thrown off."

"Well, if we can't calm the markets by fixing prices, how the hell do we calm these players?"

"Humans are excitable animals, there's no getting around that. When people anticipate a monetary reward, they begin to salivate, just as a lion does over a kill. The circuits that switch on in the brain when money is involved are the very same ones that go wild when they anticipate a delicious meal or a bout of incredible sex or, in the case of a blue-devil addict, the sight of that little blue pill."

"Are you accusing me of something?"

"Don't be paranoid. — I'm not accusing you of anything. I'm just trying to explain how the chances for a financial high are like any other high. That goes double for depression or any other low. The brain can perform the strangest of feats. It will seize on even the slimmest evidence of pattern to arrive at a conclusion. After a couple repetitions of some event — good or bad — certain brain circuits begin to fire in anticipation of another such repetition. In this way, we become habituated to an event. For instance, after two calls from the police that our daughter has been arrested for shoplifting, we might expect the next call to turn out the same way. Or, we might become

· convinced that if a stock has beaten profit forecasts two quarters in a row, it will do so again a third time."

"And if it doesn't?"

"Then the shit hits the fan. Neurons in the emotion-processing regions of the brain begin to fire like crazy, generating a sense of anxiety and dread. The result is that when a nice, reliable stock misses its earnings target — by even a little — investors abandon ship in a hurry. As a rule, the longer a stock has held up well, the worse a beating it will eventually take."

"I hate it when that happens."

"We all do."

"Why is that?"

"Because the longer a pattern has endured, the more alarmed the brain becomes when it is disturbed. A string of setbacks ramps up activity in the regions of the brain that process emotional memories, swamping pure reason. That's also why, after collapsing, markets tend to linger near lows."

"Spencer, much as I hate to admit it, I hold you in awe. You are downright intimidating. A complex mixture of reason and logic."

"The field of neuro-economics is well established, a required course of study for any successful money manager. Surely you've heard of it?"

"A President can't know everything. That is why he must surround himself with good people. Xander was right to recommend you as Fed Chief."

"Not everyone is as logical as I am. Hormones and emotion rule most of us. That is why the same brain system that responds to sensory rewards also perks up at the prospect of monetary ones. The reward circuit runs on the neurochemical dopamine. We get a dopamine surge whenever we anticipate a nice, healthy return on an investment. But dopamine neurons get extra juiced when a long shot comes in. And it is the addictive, feel-good nature of dopamine that makes us willing to take those long-shot financial risks in the first place."

"Okay, okay, okay. So we don't close the markets, we don't freeze prices, we don't slap on a war tax, we don't upset the players. None of that for now. But we do agree to provide liquidity, all the liquidity the markets require."

The Chairman of the Federal Reserve nodded his assent.

"Now, if you'll excuse me, Spencer. I'm going to take that bath. Then I'm going to take a nap. Then I'm going on the air."

"Remember. Don't promise more than you can deliver. — And make no threat you are unwilling to fulfill."

"What would be the fun in that? Isn't that what brinkmanship is all about? — playing the game to the very edge?"

CHAPTER TWENTY-SIX

▼

The two men huddled quietly in the shadows of a warm Kentucky night. One of the two was Major Branislav Karpinski. A small scar still marred his face where the wildfire had badly burned his skin. With repeated applications of Acceleron, it was healing fast.

The second man was Lieutenant Derrick Barnes, Pappy's oldest son. Derrick had grown up with guns and explosives, served two years in the U.S. Coast Guard. He knew his boats and rescue protocols but had no formal Omega training. Pappy had left it to his X.O. to add some meat to his son's bare bones military education. But this didn't sit well with the Major. To Karpinski's way of thinking, this assignment was a bit like babysitting.

"Do you think this contraption will actually work?" Lieutenant Barnes asked. He was doing what they had practiced, what Major Karpinski had taught him to do: wire the firing circuit, battery to blasting cap to explosive.

"You never used one of these before? Your daddy and I used to deploy these dried-seed timers all the time during the Siege of Johannesburg. A few beans, a little water, a suitable delay, then — Blammo! — goodbye enemy target."

"Why not just use a conventional e-timer to set off a charge? Why all this hocus-pocus with dried beans and water?"

"Electronic timers are more precise, no argument there," Branislav said as he worked. "But they're easily sniffed out by bots, and there isn't a bot alive that's programmed to give a frigging hoot about dried beans."

Branislav spread the materials he needed out on a piece of canvas before them on the ground. The light from his headband illuminated the work area.

On the canvas were several things — A cup of dried peas (though beans or other dehydrated seeds would have worked equally well). A wide-mouth glass jar with a non-metal lid. A pair of one-and-a-half inch threaded bolts. A thin metal plate that was neither painted, rusty, nor otherwise coated. A hand drill. A bolt driver. A tin snip. All these, plus the customary battery, blasting cap, and block of Enhanced C4.

Earlier in the day, in preparation for this moment, they had experimented to see just how quickly a given volume of dried peas would rise when hydrated. The idea was to estimate how much of a delay the dried-seed timer would actually allow them. To run the test, they placed a cup of dried peas from the same batch they were now using in the glass jar and covered the seeds with water. Then they set their chron to measure how much time elapsed until the seeds rose a given height. A fifty percent increase over the course of sixty minutes was about par for the course.

Tin snip in hand, Branislav now cut a circular disc from the thin, bare-metal plate. The disc was just large enough to fit loosely inside the glass jar.

Next, he took the hand drill, drilled two holes in the jar's lid, about two inches apart. The diameter of the holes had to be small, small enough that the bolts would thread tightly into them. If the jar originally came without a lid — or with one made of metal — a piece of wood or plastic could be substituted as a cover instead.

Branislav handed the lid to Derrick Barnes, who turned the bolts through the pair of holes he had drilled. To make this device work, both bolts had to extend precisely the same distance below the container cover, about one inch.

Next, Branislav poured the cup of dried peas into the wide-mouthed glass jar. The quantity was based on the previously measured rise-time and intended delay. Three-quarters full gave them about a one-hour delay. Finally, he placed the metal disc he cut inside the jar on top of the dried peas.

To make the timer operational, Branislav instructed Derrick to add just enough water to completely cover the peas. Then he placed the lid on top of the jar. To the bolts, Derrick attached connecting wire from the firing circuit he had assembled earlier. Expansion of the wet seeds would raise the metal disc until it made contact with the bolts and closed the circuit.

Then they walked calmly away. By the time the explosive went off and the power plant's cooling tower collapsed, they would be far away, inside the D.C. dome, and Branislav would be scouting out a sniper's nest for his next target.

•
•

Branislav Karpinski settled into his lair. Just like that day outside the stadium, he checked the wind, verified distance to target, did a final survey of his surroundings. As Branislav got comfortable, he consciously slowed his heartbeat. He had left Derrick Barnes behind hours ago. This was no place for a tenderfoot, certainly not one as jumpy as that zibb. How he could be Pappy's boy was anybody's guess.

Karpinski drank in the silence. Like all accomplished shooters, he preferred to work alone. It had to be that way. Sniping was not a team sport. There were no hoorays or congratulatory raps to the shoulder afterward for a job well done.

No, sniping was more like masturbation. You know, gripping your favorite tool under cover of darkness in the privacy of your lair. Always alone, your hand soon to be filled to overflowing with hot self-gratification.

Yet, sniping was more than just simple masturbation; it took skill. Camouflage, distance, wind speed, muzzle velocity, lighting — these were some of the variables. A sniper could have everything right and still miss.

Breathing, concentration, practice, eyesight — these were other factors that entered the equation.

Training was important. But it wasn't everything. The average guy could practice making corner shots in hover hockey until he was blue in the face and still blow the big game if his adrenaline was pumping hard enough.

Today's snipe was of a different level of difficulty from those he took that day at the stadium. On that day, he was shooting fish in a barrel with a conventional sniper's rifle. Today, he had in his hand an S25 rifled bullet launcher, a weapon that dispatched smart bullets.

With a conventional rifle, no matter how powerful, everything was practice. That, plus concentration and equipment. Only a handful of weapons could actually do the job, especially at great distance. The M35 sniper rifle was a good choice. It was not the fanciest of rifles, but loaded with the right shell, the M35 had a maximum effective range approaching 2000 meters. Plus, it had almost no recoil.

Shooting a conventional sniper's rifle was a science with elements of art. The science was an equation with two variables — equipment and ballistics. *How consistent was the powder load? The bullet's shape and throw-weight? The accuracy of the barrel?* These were scientific matters.

Plus, there were other considerations. *How well did a given bullet perform in flight? How well did it retain its initial energy? How did its flight path compare with its sight path? How much was it affected by atmospheric conditions? — wind, rain, humidity? What did the bullet do upon impact?* Answer all these questions properly and a man had mastered the science of shooting the long gun.

But science was not art. The art of shooting such a weapon was totally different. It was purely human. *What happened to a man when he clutched a rifle in his trembling hand? Did his adrenaline surge throw off his aim? Or did he remain calm, then let go a round at the precise right instant necessary to cause the bullet to impact a tiny spot exactly where it was intended to go?*

While the art remained pretty much unchanged, the science of firing a smart gun was totally different from that of a conventional weapon. A smart bullet was self-propelled. Plus, it had what was called "target memory." Once the gun was aimed and the bullet acquired its target, the bullet "remembered" and tracked its target even if the target moved a short distance, up to as much as several meters. As a consequence, initial aim was all-important, atmospheric conditions less so. More concentration here, less calculation.

But even when a man was very good at what he did — as Branislav was — there was always room for improvement. The mastery of these skills began early, with the military. It was the starting point for an Omega, indeed for all men in Special Forces. Without such training, he would just be an ordinary soldier, nothing special at all.

Many skills were involved at this level — proficiency with guns, with explosives, with combat at close quarters. But an Omega sniper was chosen from a field of many only after extensive psych testing and evaluation. There were a number of attributes the trainers looked for in a sniper; there were two they didn't ever want to see. Branislav suffered from one, perhaps both.

The first was what they called the "Tower Syndrome." The details of the actual incident have been lost to history, but the syndrome referred to a massacre of a dozen or more students by a sniper holed up in the bell tower of a large university more than a century ago. The sniper never meant to kill so many people. But sometimes, when a sniper starts to shoot, he is unable to stop. The chemical rush can feel so good, there can be such an overwhelming sense of power, the man cannot turn it off, even when no further legitimate targets remain. It is like a fire burning out of control, or passion at that moment just before ejaculation. It cannot be stopped. The shooter will keep on firing so long as anyone is still in sight and moving.

Army trainers know all about this very real compulsion. They watched for it in the men they trained, the men under their command. They knew that every sniper they trained ran a genuine risk of being overcome by this urge. It was the usual reason for washing a man out of the unit.

The second syndrome was just as lethal as the first, only in a completely opposite way. It was referred to by trainers as the "Olympic Games Syndrome," on account of where it was first observed. In that instance, athlete hostages ended up dead because of it.

The only way to understand this second syndrome is to try and get inside the head of a sniper and analyze how he works. A military or attack-team sniper doesn't just set up shop in some high-rise building and start shooting.

No, this kind of man spends most of his time watching. Getting to know his targets. Observing their routines.

But it is here, in the observing, where the danger arises. When a sniper stares down through the cylinder of that high-powered scope of his, he can see the faces of the people he is stalking. It doesn't matter whether they are hostages or terrorists, he can see them as clearly as if he were in the same room with them. He sees their features, the expressions on their faces. He sees them when they smile, when they sneeze, when they eat a sandwich, pop a zit, get drowsy, snap awake, go to the bathroom.

But the reverse is not true. The people being surveilled have no idea they're being watched. They have no idea the sniper can see them. They have no idea where he is, or that he is even there. They certainly don't realize how easily he can punch a hole through them with a bullet.

The threat runs only in one direction. It is not reciprocal. The terrorists represent no threat to the sniper, none whatsoever. They are far away. They cannot kill him. They cannot even harm him.

Now comes the difficulty. As the sniper spends hour after hour observing his targets through his spotting scope, waiting for the "Go!" order, he may begin to bond with them. He gets to know the people he is watching. He may begin to see them as human beings, rather than as bad guys or terrorists. Thus, he becomes intimate with them.

Then, when the order comes to shoot these human beings, he may not be able to do it. He may not be able to bring himself to kill people he has come to know, people who are of no threat to him. It is a real-live risk, and it is known in the trade as the "Olympic Games Syndrome."

The ideal sniper must not suffer from either compulsion. He can no more allow his pent-up adrenaline to take over, thus driving him to kill everything in sight, than he can afford to bond with his target and subsequently refuse to pull the trigger at the required moment.

The problem for trainers is that the psychological niche where such a man can be found is actually quite narrow. Not many men can set aside both behavioral impulses and succeed at their craft.

Still, there were a few who could. The ideal sniper was a man who could kill when it was required but remain immune to the impulse to continue killing once the threat was neutralized. He was that rare individual whose beliefs were so brilliantly centered, he didn't suffer months of anguish from the taking of a human life when ordered to. The ideal sniper was a decent, thoughtful, intelligent, unshakable man.

If only such a man had his hand on the trigger today.

CHAPTER TWENTY-SEVEN

▼

Laura Hoagland loved her husband. The two had been college sweethearts, marrying shortly after graduation. She had given Xander a fine son, though they lost their boy ten years ago to a senseless war.

Even in his Wall Street days, Alexander Hoagland had lived a high-profile existence. Once Xander was elected to the U.S. Senate, there was no turning back. As a couple, the two lived a very public life, every move scrutinized by one powerful faction or another — the press, labor groups, Enviros, school teachers, you name it.

Plus, Xander found it hard not to speak his mind. He was a sensible man, but more than once in his early days, Xander was taken to task by the media because of something he said. In one of his more memorable gaffs from that first senate race, Xander was overheard to say: *Enviros and liberal morons. They both try to mask a hatred for wealth and progress beneath a loud love for endangered species and pseudo-science.* That's when Laura knew she had her work cut out for her.

Laura Hoagland was not typical of a Senator's wife. She lacked the kind of glamour some found mysterious. But she also lacked the kind of mystery others found glamorous.

Laura tried to protect her husband any way she could. The task was to separate the gold from the gold-diggers. There were those who were attracted to his power and wanted to serve him. Fine. There were those who were looking for a free ride and wanted to use him. Not so fine. There were those who would shield him at any cost. Good, keep them close. There were others who would throw him under the wheels of a train to save their own skin. By all means, lose those types fast.

In her role as protector, Laura made a lot of smart judgments. But she made plenty of dumb mistakes too. Thought some gold was actually gold-digger; some gold-diggers, actually gold. Laura made her calls the best she could. But she always did it alone, for with their son dead, there was no one else for her to turn to.

Now, as the two of them strode off the President's suborb, into the waiting limo, and up to Governor Thadamore Mills' official residence, shielding her husband was foremost on Laura's mind.

Alexander Hoagland and Thadamore Mills were friends, about as close as two powerful politicians could be expected to be. It helped that their spheres of influence were nearly congruent, both important leaders from the same important State.

The two men shook hands warmly, sat down across from one another on the long couch. Xander dismissed his security team to go get some rest, ordered them to place the security bots in hibernate mode. He knew his wife would be worried, so he wanted to put her mind at ease.

"Wife of mine," he said. "There is nothing to fear here. We are among friends. Relax. Let down your guard. Please."

"Yes, Laura, please. You know your way around. Bathroom's upstairs, kitchen down the hall. My people will make you a sandwich, if you are hungry."

Laura nodded her thanks, started up the stairs. The tension melted out of her eyes. *There was nothing to fear here. She could relax.*

Thadamore Mills was the first to speak once she left earshot. "You've come a long distance, old friend. And under trying circumstances. Can I offer you something cold to drink?"

"A cold beer might taste good about now."

"Syn or nat?"

"Syn beer should be outlawed."

Thadamore pressed a contact on a flat device next to the couch, spoke into the receiver. "Two natural beers, Henry. Soon as you can." Then he returned his attention to his guest:

"So, Xander, what brings you winging in here aboard the President's suborb?"

"At least you still refer to the man as President."

"He's got his country, we've got ours."

"You have to put a stop to this craziness, Thadamore."

"Honestly, Xander, I don't think I can. I'm not even sure that I would if I could. Anyway, it's grown beyond just you and me. Whitmore's in control now, not me. He's backed up by serious men, men like General Pappy Barnes, plus thousands of armed militiamen. Montana and both of the Dakotas have said they're coming in on the side of the New Republic."

"That practically splits the nation in two, border to border, from Canada to the Gulf of Mexico."

"That's really only the half of it, Xander. My staff at the NGA tells me that California looks to bind to Mexico, at least the portions south of Monterrey — the agricultural areas, plus L.A. and the surrounding counties. Florida may seek asylum with Mexico as well, though perhaps not the Panhandle. Same goes for our fifty-second State, Caribe Cay. That includes all our possessions in the Caribbean, everything from Grand Cayman clear over to the Virgin Islands. Oregon and Washington are petitioning to join Canada as a single province, along with those parts of California that don't seek to be annexed to Mexico. If all this actually comes to pass, Canada and Mexico will share a common border for the first time in their history. This will further isolate Alaska, which is already talking of becoming a Free State, much as Hawaii did years ago."

"We must put a stop to this. Surely you can see that?"

"And just which one of us do you suggest should head up that charge? — The Second Amendment means something to these people, something serious," Thadamore said as his butler Henry arrived with their beers.

Xander gratefully accepted his, thanked the man, then went on.

"The thing is, Thad — with Whitmore in charge, this so-called New Republic of yours is lurching in the direction of a gun-slinging Christian theocracy. That scares me."

"It scares me too. But which is scarier? — a gun-slinging Christian theocracy or a paranoid police state that suspends the Bill of Rights to maintain law and order?" Thadamore Mills calmly sipped the head off his beer.

"Are you saying that's where the rest of the nation is headed? — in the direction of a paranoid police state?"

"Isn't it?"

"The immature are always finding new truths; the cynical are always discovering new false Gods to believe in. Nothing ever changes."

Xander said it, then fell silent to contemplate his beer.

Mills did the same. "I can't let you go back, you know. Not back to Washington anyway."

Alexander Hoagland was stunned. "Are Laura and I to be held prisoner then? By God, Thad, you and I have known each other for years, since our college days. I thought we were friends, Kemo Sabe?"

"We *are* friends. That's why I'm letting you go. Otherwise, you would be detained."

Laura wandered back into the room, holding a plate of food. She had overheard the last several lines of exchange. "Xander? I thought you said we had nothing to fear here?"

Xander looked over at Thadamore, who had a hard time meeting his friend's gaze.

Now Laura got angry with the Governor. "How dare you? In case you have forgotten, Governor, my husband is a United States Senator. He got you elected, for God's sake. Which one of your number would dare detain him? This man — your friend — deserves to be treated with some respect."

"Your husband is a senator from a State that has withdrawn from the Union. And I'm a Governor that, for all practical purposes, is under house arrest. Holding Xander wasn't my idea, Laura."

"Who then?"

"Pappy Barnes. He thought Xander might make a valuable bargaining chip that could be put into play later on."

Laura objected. "Pappy Barnes has no axe to grind with my husband."

"You and Xander can choose to remain here in Texas, if you wish. Texas is your home, after all. It is the place where you both were born and still live. Or, like I said, you are both free to leave. Only I can't let you fly east. You need to go west, to the Hawaii Free State perhaps. Or someplace in Asia. They'd have my hide if I gave you clearance to fly back to D.C., and certainly not onboard Benjamin's suborb."

"The Hawaii Free State was our original destination all along. The President has ordered me there."

"Anything you want to share?"

"It's the *Mars Voyager*. With the Houston Spaceport closed, the passengers will be putting down at Hilo. I have to meet one of those passengers."

"Must be somebody pretty important, for the President to have sent you all that way alone. Anyone I know?"

"An economist by the name of Elijah Montrose, Dr. Elijah Montrose."

Thadamore thought a moment. "Jewish fellow? From Philadelphia? Sits on the Terraforming Commission?"

"Your memory is as sharp as ever, Thad. But Elijah's not the only VIP onboard that ship. There is also Senator Flanagan's daughter. Plus the heroes from the EMD incident."

"He still hasn't told the public about that one, has he? What's the man waiting for? The public has a right to know. That asteroid could have been the end of us all."

"A very close call indeed. Those two spacejockeys deserve to be given the Medal of Honor. They're genuine American heroes. But I'm not sure that's ever going to happen. The President has his plate rather full right now, wouldn't you say?"

Thadamore was just about to offer Alexander another beer, when a knock came at the door. It was the Governor's chief-of-staff.

"Sir. There's a bulletin from the American News Network."

"What bulletin?"

"It's an unconfirmed report, so far."

Thadamore put down his beer. "Unconfirmed report of what?"

"An unconfirmed report of an assassination inside the D.C. Dome. The victim was shot from a great distance by an exceptional sniper."

"An exceptional sniper?" Thadamore Mills got abruptly to his feet. "This smells an awful lot like the work of Bran Flake again."

"Bran Flake?"

"Branislav Karpinski."

Thadamore's chief-of-staff nodded his agreement. "Given all that's happened, Karpinski is as likely a guess as any. We'll know more at the top of the hour."

"Who the hell is Branislav Karpinski?" Xander was now on his feet as well. Laura was staring hard at her husband.

"Branislav Karpinski. The Carp. You probably know him better by his media name — the Stadium Sniper."

"Are you saying this Karpinski fellow is responsible for the stadium massacre?"

Thadamore Mills nodded.

"You knew who this man was, and you didn't turn him in? Good God, Thadamore — why the hell not?"

"I only just recently found out the truth myself. And honestly, Xander, who the hell should I have turned the bastard in to?"

"Oh, I don't know. The Bureau? Maybe Secret Service? Perhaps Homeland Security. This Karpinski bastard is a wanted man. You're harboring a fugitive." Xander settled back into his chair.

"Harboring? Don't be ridiculous. I know the man's name, that's the extent of it. If I get in Whitmore's way I'm a dead man for sure."

"You saying Whitmore knows about this Karpinski affair as well?"

"Pappy Barnes, Roland Whitmore, all the higher-ups in Puritan City, they're all in on it. And I'm now odd man out. Branislav Karpinski is Pappy Barnes' Number Two man. They would never surrender him, much less let me live if I tried to turn the man in. People in the know tell me he may already have put out a contract on my life."

"Now who's living in a paranoid police state?"

"I wouldn't kid about such a thing."

Fuming with anger, Xander turned to Thadamore's chief-of-staff. "Did News Central report who this sniper assassinated?"

"Yes, it just came across."

"Who, goddamn it? Who was killed?"

"Senator Patrick Flanagan."

Total silence from all corners.

Laura was the first to speak. "I think we should leave, Xander."

"Wife of mine . . . "

"No, Xander, Laura's right. You two must leave right away. Before someone in Puritan City changes their mind and places you two under house arrest just as they have me."

Xander got to his feet, looked at his wife. She was trying to protect him as always. He looked at Thadamore with dead serious eyes.

"If you truly believe your life is in danger, Thad, you should leave with us. No one need know — I have the President's suborb."

"I can't be seen as a coward. Besides, reason may eventually yet prevail."

"Nothing ever changes. You know that, Thad. Every revolution is the same. Greater freedom can lead to greater disorder. And greater disorder can lead right back to a loss of freedom. This is the paradox all free men must reckon with."

"I have made my bed."

"Then good night to you, old friend. — And thanks for the beer."

•

•

After the Fed released its statement that it would provide "all the liquidity the markets require," relative calm returned to trading. For the next two days the markets trended downward, but on low volume. It seemed the worst was past. A mountain of margin calls had gone out over the weekend. But, with a few notable exceptions, they were met without trouble. — Then came Thursday.

The news of Flanagan's assassination by a sniper's bullet made bigger headlines than the President's week-ago speech trying to calm the rattled nerves of an anxious nation.

This time around, there was no stopping it. The market plunged from the opening bell and kept on plunging continuously throughout the day. After two hours of trading, volume was 10 times the level of a normal day. The tape ran four hours late, this in an era when prices were posted with electronic rapidity, at the speed of light.

Friday morning the President shuttered the exchanges and declared a bank holiday until the following week. Saturday, Spencer Trask, Chairman of the Federal Reserve, convened a meeting of the country's leading banks and industrialists to form a buying pool with a 100 billion-unit line of credit from the Fed. The idea behind the buying pool was two-fold: as a show of confidence and as a way to stabilize stock prices when the markets re-opened Monday morning.

Monday, the markets rallied sharply. The Fed flooded the Street with money and the emergency buying pool used its stash to grab everything that came up for sale.

By Wednesday, most thought the crisis had passed. Volume dried up and volatility lessened. The country breathed a collective sigh of relief, even those living in the New Republic. No major banks had failed, and even though the market averages had declined some 45 % since the rout began, certain market sectors were already starting to recover.

But it was a bear market rally. When Alaska, with its immense oil riches, declared its intention to become a Free State like Hawaii, all confidence evaporated. That night the President slapped on a punitive war tax to finance the effort.

This was economic folly, and Spencer Trask told him so. Taxes are a drag on the economy, and always will be. UniBank failed the next morning, and the emergency buying pool folded along with it. Now there was nothing to stop the market's fall.

CHAPTER TWENTY-EIGHT

▼

What can be said of planet Earth?

Five days out, it is a dot of white and blue.

Three days out, it is a ball of blue, with patches of brown and green that spin slowly past once every twenty-four hours.

One day out, details come into focus. Familiar shapes and landmasses, white caps hugging the poles, verdant green in the equatorial latitudes, rivers of brown, lakes of blue, white clouds floating overhead.

Only in the final hours of approach do the structures of man become apparent — the giant gleaming domes over certain important cities, the electrical illumination of metro areas at night, the cultivated fields that dominate the middle latitudes, the lights of the orbiting ore smelters used to service the asteroid trade.

A ship the size of the *S.S. Mars Voyager* wasn't built to land on solid ground. The rigors of a hot, atmospheric reentry followed by a planetary landing were simply beyond the capabilities of its modest frame.

To get the *Voyager's* contingent of passengers down to the surface took several steps: first, braking for docking orbit, then linking up with the orbiting Space Station. Only later, after a suitable interval, would the passengers be transferred to the Space Elevator. It would ferry them the last leg of the journey, from orbit to surface.

The Space Elevator was one of those amazing marvels of human engineering. Thick cables hung from a pair of large satellites hovering in geosync orbit. Each cable was attached to a massive counterweight. The satellites took turns raising and lowering loads, so as not to disturb their relative positions in the sky. The mathematics were daunting, but the name of the game was the preservation of angular momentum.

Even with its solar sails furled, an inbound sailship from Mars still traveled at enormous speed. The pull of the sun, coupled with the even greater pull of the nearer Earth, imparted to it tremendous velocity. Aerobraking was the only way to cut that great speed sufficiently to drop the enormous ship into docking orbit. It is truly as uncomfortable as it sounds. Like a six-hour-long roller coaster ride.

A large spaceship moving at thousands of kloms per minute packs untold joules of kinetic energy. To shed all those calories means converting them into heat. Heat comes from friction. A low-angle plunge into the upper atmosphere to increase drag. Once the Kevlar and asbestos bags deploy, stand back — there's about to be quite a lightshow.

It takes nine orbits, six hours of continuous braking, and a couple hard bounces off the outer reaches of the upper atmosphere to slow the ship down enough to dock with the Space Station. This is followed by a short trip in the ship's dinghy to transport the passengers in small groups to the Station proper.

It had been twelve hours, now, since that transfer of passengers took place.

•

•

Invariably, the Station's central tube was the first stop for every visitor after docking, whether they were coming up from Earth or down from the Moon or Mars. The tube was in the zero-g section of the Station and the fun lasted as long as the stomach stayed quiet.

Like every other tourist, Butch and Kaleena swam up to the glass just for the view, which was spectacular. The news about her father hadn't reached them yet, so she was calm and self-assured.

They found that if they worked at it, they could float forward and position their faces close enough to the glass that the superstructure of the Space Station seemed to disappear. Then it was just him and her, the glass and the indigo blackness of space.

It was a view unsuitable for words, a memory that would remain forever etched into their brains. For other people, people who never left the ground, it is sometimes difficult to get used to the idea that in orbit there is no up or down.

But when you look out the glass from that far up, you see the Earth, all round and peaceful, only thirty-odd thousand kloms away. The whole thing seems so close, a man could easily brush it with his hand. You know instinctively that the Earth is pulling you down toward it. But in orbit, when actively swimming in the Station's central tube, there is absolutely no feeling of weight, none whatsoever. And unless a person is strapped in, he will float.

They took turns looking, the two of them. The view changed constantly. After a few minutes they came upon a zone of gray. It was sandwiched between the blackness of night and the bright blue of day. At the center of that gray zone was a narrow pink slice, the atmospheric dawn as seen from above.

Daylight is for the oceans — first the Indiastan, then the Pacific, which is very large, then later the Atlantic. Remove the Atlantic Ocean and South America would fit snugly up against Africa, just like the geologists said they once used to, in the days before continental drift busted them apart.

Atolls appear, along with coral reefs and turquoise lagoons. Then clouds and more open water. Then the pink slice of sunset. Then night.

Kaleena touched his hand for the first time since they arrived, and they both laughed.

"I'm beginning to like this zero-g stuff," she said. "Thanks for the meds." Butch had handed her a Tranquil patch even before the *Mars Voyager* positioned itself for docking a couple hours ago.

"Floating's okay for some things," he said. "But when it comes time to eat or sleep or go to the bathroom, it feels a whole lot better to have a bit of weight tugging on your hindside. Your dinner stays quieter and you feel immeasurably better down below."

Butch knew the drill; he had worked in space. Once a man is weightless, if he tries to throw a switch without first anchoring himself, the switch will throw him. On the other hand, once a man is firmly anchored, it's no great strain to push around a multi-ton mass with little more than his fingertips. You can also fly around without wings, perform countless back-flips, or simply float carefree, resting in midair.

But for many, there is also the problem of motion sickness. The sudden change from high-g acceleration to micro-g space-gravity takes an inevitable toll on even the most experienced of stomachs. As soon as one of us landlubbing earthworms plunges into weightlessness, five million years of arboreal evolution go straight out the window. We become like a drunken chimp that has lost its balance in a big, old tree.

As soon as Butch heard the hydraulic arms extending the umbilical out from the side of the ship, he began to fish in his pocket for a Tranquil. He slapped it on Kaleena's upper arm before she could protest.

Some travelers preferred Sea-Bands, of course. A slender, elastic cloth band worn on each wrist, three "fingers" down from the first wrist-crease, about where a person would take their pulse. Located on one side of the narrow band was a hard plastic button or sometimes a stud that the wearer positioned on his skin between the two wrist tendons. The button worked by exerting pressure on the Nei-Kuan acupressure point. Newer versions had tiny electrodes imbedded in the cloth instead of a button. They extruded from the cloth a thousandth of a millimeter and put pressure on the identical tendon. To be effective, a band had to be worn round-the-clock on each wrist.

But Butch didn't go in for such witch-doctor remedies. *Feed me a pill for what ails me. But don't make me wear some sort of device.* That was his thinking anyway.

Kaleena did a slow somersault, floated back from the window. "I don't need to wear this ugly patch everywhere on the Station, do I?"

"Color clash with the blouse?"

"Get serious, will you?"

"I guess space makes me a little whimsical. But no, you don't have to wear that unsightly patch everywhere. The Station is like an enormous Ferris wheel, all girders and spokes. But unlike a Ferris wheel at an amusement park, here a giant tube runs up through the wheel's center. That's the tube we're in now. It's hard to tell from this angle, but the tube is about forty meters in diameter. It sticks out of the center of the Ferris wheel about half a klom on each side. Plus, if you haven't already noticed, the tube is much shinier than the rest of the Station."

"Yeah, I noticed that on the way in. Why is that?"

"The central tube is sheathed along its entire length by a thick metal skin of Glare, and the skin is peppered with what, from a distance, look like dimples. The dimples come in various shapes and sizes. They are used for docking ships like our own, and for cargo haulers and the like. The Ferris wheel is the Station's living quarters. Centrifugal force pinch-hits for gravity, though not as much as earth-normal-gravity. The wheel spins on the axle that is this tube, though the tube itself is motionless. The spin is slow and leisurely. It imparts about one-third-g to its outer circumference. Enough to keep a man's lunch quiet anyway."

"I do like the part about keeping lunch quiet. But why the tube and the wheel? — one spinning, the other fixed?"

"They could've spun the whole Station, but that makes docking even a small ship alongside her a nightmare. You can't berth a big ship like the *Voyager* against a spinning top. So instead they built a spinning part for creature comfort and a stationary part — the tube — for docking and storage. The spokes and the wheel are closed-in and pressurized. The rest is a skeleton of metal girders. Since it doesn't have to withstand much in the way of blastoff stresses, the Station itself is rather flimsy, at least compared with a larger ship of the line like the one we just got off."

"Flimsy or not, you have to admit the thing is rather pretty."

"What could be finer? A man's favorite woman, plus a great network of shiny struts set against a black sky. Titanium alloy — light, strong, and won't corrode. Plus, thousands of square meters of Glare — that's glass-reinforced-aluminum to you and me."

"I like the part about man's favorite woman. But how do we get from the stationary tube to the spinning wheel? Jumping the gap would seem like a monumental engineering problem."

"Oh, not really. Where the two meet is really nothing but a giant airlock. You stand at a certain spot inside the tube, run your keycard through the reader and wait. The computer checks your authorization, calculates your weight and I don't know what else, then you enter what amounts to a big pneumatic tube, and whoosh, you're in. If you think about tying a string to a rock and spinning it 'round your head, you'll quickly realize that the velocity of the rock out at the end of the string is much higher than it is down by your hand. It's the same way with the Ferris wheel — the center, where the tube runs through the wheel, where we are now, hardly moves at all. So the airlock exchange really isn't that tricky."

Kaleena seemed satisfied with that explanation and grew quiet. They floated a while longer, then returned to the main part of the Station, where the others were engaged in various pursuits to pass the time until they could board the Space Elevator for the surface. The wait could sometimes be lengthy, as much as several days.

CHAPTER TWENTY-NINE

▼

Passing the time wasn't a problem for Butch and Kaleena. They ordered lunch and enjoyed the view out the big picture windows. Here they were, in this giant Christmas-tree ornament, thirty thousand kloms above the surface, watching the world go by. All the colors of Earth were there — blue, white, brown and green. Plus the stars. Uncountable millions of them. No, make that billions. Faraway planets, distant stars, countless nebulae.

By contrast, their meal was regrettably bland. Space-grown soy was incalculably cheaper than real meat or green vegetables brought up from the surface.

But no matter how well prepared, with what sauces or side-dishes, soy was still soy, and recycled water remained this odorless, tasteless compound of hydrogen and oxygen, not that rich-tasting stuff that bubbled up from wells sunk deep into underground aquifers down on Earth.

Butch picked unhappily at the meal on his plate. *Oh, what a space-traveler wouldn't give for a home-cooked meal, real meat, and a glass of fresh water !*

The only thing not bland about Station life was the characters you met onboard. After lunch, when they were cleaning their trays, Kaleena knocked her drinking glass over and onto the floor. Moments later, a black janitor · showed up, electrostatic mop in hand.

"Here, Missy, let me help you with that," the man said, running his mop over the wet spot. "Low grav will mess a body up if you're not careful."

"I feel like such a fool," Kaleena apologized.

"I seen worse," the black man said, reaching out his hand to the two of them. "Name's Lexus. Lexus Johnson. Been around these parts two days shy of forever."

"Glad to make your acquaintance, Lexus," Butch said. "If you're such an old hand, maybe you wouldn't mind showing us around."

"Do I look like a bloody tour guide to you?" he barked, mop still in hand.

"Well, no, not exactly. I only thought that if a man had been stuck up here two days short of forever, he might know a little something about the place. You know, like the back stairways, the freight elevators, where the bodies are hidden, that sort of thing."

Lexus sized Butch up, decided he was okay. "I like the way you put that, son. Here, follow me. We'll start with the Station's lifts and ladders."

"Certainly there's got to be something more interesting than that," Butch said, briefly wondering if the man could be trusted. "No hidden bodies?"

Lexus flashed a toothy grin. "Station-elevators don't behave like they do in a skyscraper earth-side. If they did, passengers would get a jolt every time they stepped aboard. It would be a wild, even dangerous ride each and every time."

Butch was skeptical. "I don't follow."

"Me neither," Kaleena said.

Lexus explained. "Has to do with the Coriolis pseudoforce, which you experience every time you move vertically inside the Station."

Butch's forehead crinkled in doubt. "You don't talk like any janitor I ever met."

"Oh, yeah? How's an AfriAm janitor supposed to talk? Like some jive-ass-parakeet from south 'a the Mason-Dixon?" Lexus sounded irritated.

"What I meant was: you sound educated."

"Graduated M.I.T."

That seemed to confuse Butch, so Lexus explained:

"Sweeping up's not my only job around here. I am responsible for a great many things. All hydraulics, plus enviro, waste processing, and airlock maintenance. Takes an M.I.T. graduate in engineering just to keep things running smoothly this far off the ground."

"Which is why you're such an expert on this pseudoforce thing?"

"The forces are real enough — they're just generated under contrived situations, like the spinning of the Station. Earth-side, when an elevator begins to descend, it accelerates downward, which briefly reduces your weight. When the elevator stops its descent, it accelerates upward, thus *increasing* your weight. Anyone who has ridden an earth-elevator is familiar with these effects, even if they are quite mild. But here, onboard the Station, things are quite different, especially near the axis. Here, the elevator's rate of acceleration can easily exceed the local centrifugal force."

"Could you try that again in English?"

"Let's see if the black janitor from the south side of Chica can dumb it down for the white-folk, shall we? If a space-elevator worked like an earth-elevator, a ride down to the basement might go something like this — As soon as the car began its descent, you would instantly feel nasty in your gut, as if the car had been turned upside down. You would fall against the ceiling lamps. Then, on account of the Station's spin, the elevator car would seem to tumble crazily until it was tilted nearly on its side. You would fall against the anti-spinward wall and slide along it to the floor."

Lexus continued. "Gradually, as the elevator descended, your weight would increase and the tilt would lessen. Finally, the car would right itself and come to a halt. The doors would open and out you would stagger, though not before barfing, I should imagine. And this would happen every single time you rode that friggin' elevator down."

Kaleena's face darkened. "Talk about needing your Tranquil patch. No one's gonna ride a crazy elevator like that."

Lexus moved his electrostatic mop along. "Well, it's either that or a stairway. And let me tell you, Bright Eyes, stairways have their own special problems."

"So what's the remedy?"

"Two remedies, actually. Slow the elevator down. Or, if you must keep it running fast, secure everything in it, passengers and cargo alike. Either way, it's a pain in the ass. In order to keep an elevator ride from feeling like a tilt-a-whirl, you have to triple the transit time by making it accelerate continuously from a very low start speed."

"Slow elevators in a tall building can make for a very long day," Butch said.

"The only other option takes even longer, strapping everyone and everything down before setting it in motion."

"I'm not sure I like your Space Station after all," Kaleena said. "How can a simple staircase be worse than a careening elevator?"

"Here's the thing. Back on Earth, stairs that lean are standard fare in a funhouse. But here on the Station, *all* the stairs seem to lean one direction or the other, especially when you're trying to climb them."

Butch shook his head. "Surprised more people don't blow their cork."

"You think I carry this high-tech mop around just to clean up coffee spills?"

Butch laughed.

Lexus continued. "When you climb to port, the stairs all seem to lean right. When you climb to starboard, the stairs all seem to lean left. This lean makes the stairs appreciably harder to climb, especially if you're unprepared. When you climb to spinward, the stairs will seem to lean forward. When you climb to anti-spinward, the stairs will seem to lean backward . . . "

"I thought we agreed you would stick to plain English. Spin? Anti-spin? What the hell? A body needs to be a physicist just to climb a set of stairs in this place."

Lexus found that funny. "Oh, yes, the Station's just one big, crazy funhouse in the sky. Where else but up here would it take a mechanical engineer to push a mop? Because of the spin-effects the apparent slope of every set of stairs is altered. The safety implications ought to be obvious."

"I guess people slip and fall all the time."

"It's a nightmare for our insurance carrier. Therefore, a piece of advice. Until they call you to queue up for the Space Elevator, always keep a firm grip on the railings whenever you move about inside the Station. Climb any stairs you should happen to encounter slowly and deliberately. Should they ever seem to suddenly be leaning out too far, stop long enough to gather yourself. Then resume climbing, only slower. Oh, and one more thing — don't even think of running the stairs like people frequently do back home. Stairs are our biggest source of serious accidents. The pseudogravity onboard the Station is only about one-third-g. That just doesn't make for enough friction between your feet and the floor to hold most people down."

"Now you've really gone and taken all the fun out of it," Butch quipped.

"Fun nothing. Back in the day, at the time when the first multi-floor Station was built, no standards had been established yet regarding staircase steepness or orientation. As a result, no two staircases in that original Station behaved alike. Since every staircase behaved differently, even old-timers on that first Station had to be extra careful when climbing stairs they seldom used. But, after a few accidents — one serious — all that changed. The lawyers got involved. Now, every staircase is anti-spinward up. That way, if someone falls — and many people still do — they fall *against* the stairs, not away from them. The other sorts of stairs — spinward up — tended to get out of people's way when they fell, causing them to fall further and faster."

Butch scratched his head. "Frankly, I don't see why people put up with it. After all the time I've spent in space, I'm glad to finally be going home, where down is actually down and up is actually up. I've spent enough hours floating upside down hanging from a tether to last me a lifetime."

"What kind of work you do?"

"EMD Enterprises. It's a division of Transcomet Industries."

"Should have figured you for a spacejockey. Just in from Mars, are you? Asteroid trade?"

Butch nodded. "And you? You push a mop here year-round?"

"My history's a bit more complicated. Wife divorced me, moved in with a younger man. Daughter met with misfortune, ran away from home, settled in Hedon City. Now she lives under an alias — Muffy something or other — sells her body on the streets. Yeah, I push a mop here year-round. Is that so bad?"

"No, not at all."

"And you? Is there any place in space you haven't been?"

"The Moon."

"I should think not. Everybody knows the Moon's off-limits to civilians."

"Yeah, why is that?"

"Friggin' politicians."

"Careful now. This girl comes from a political family."

"Then, Missy, please accept my apologies in advance. Politicians and lawyers — two of the biggest wasters of a private college education on the planet."

"Spoken like a true M.I.T. graduate."

"No, I mean it. Ever since that first proto-nation drew that first line in the soil of that first populated savanna, countries have been steadily — even greedily — extending their boundaries. It began with a circle of stones around the campfire, then a zone from the campfire to the coast, then from the coast out to a three-mile line in the ocean."

Kaleena interrupted. "Mile?"

"Yes, Bright Eyes, in those days they still used miles. Three miles would be about five kloms. After the dawn of the space age, the three miles changed to two hundred and the direction began to shift from out to up. That's when the nations of the world began to fret about how lines would be drawn in space."

"You're talking about the Moon Treaty." Butch's turn to interrupt.

Lexus nodded. "Yes, the Moon Treaty. The treaty on which all subsequent treaties would be based. It was supposed to ensure that there would *be* no lines in space. Here's where you got to love your politicians and their lawyers — maybe your diplomats as well. The treaty guaranteed all sorts of things: That outer space would forever remain de-militarized. That no country would declare an Earth orbital zone as their own. That land claims would never be made on the Moon, Mars, or any other place humanity's rockets might one day reach. That . . . "

"Hah!" Now Butch really had to laugh. "Had those people no sense? What was going through their fuzzy heads? No lines in space? Forever de-militarized? Just what kind of pill were those people popping anyway?"

"You can't blame an idealist for being a mloron. Truth is, as soon as someone figured out how to turn an even buck in space, people started drawing lines everywhere, beginning first with geosync orbit, then later with the Moon."

"Don't I know it. Transcomet has laid claim to just about everything out here."

"You're talking about the mining operations."

"Not just that. Mining, nuclear waste handling, medical refuse, tourism, the whole shooting match."

"That includes me," Lexus said. "I work for the company too. The Space Station is one of their most profitable operations."

"So how come the Moon's still off-limits now?"

"Surely you know the story. After the Fornax Drive came off patent, everyone — and I mean everyone — rushed to the Moon to recycle the spent nuclear fuels the previous generation had dumped there without giving it a second thought. Before long, the radioactive sludge was spewn everywhere. The entire surface of the Moon was contaminated. The cleanup will take years."

"More politicians and lawyers?"

Lexus smiled a toothy smile. "Well, enough about me. Let's get back to the two of you. You folks still have the better part of a day to kill before you have to shove off. Have you tried one of the zero-g rooms? All the newlyweds rave about them."

"Oh, we're not married." Kaleena reddened.

"Since when do two people have to be married to have sex?"

Kaleena reddened further. "No, what I mean is, we're just good friends."

"Like that has stopped two people from having sex before."

Butch looked at Kaleena, but didn't know what to say.

Now it was Lexus's turn to get red. "If I've spoken out of turn, I truly apologize. The two of you seemed so happy together, I naturally assumed you were a couple. Forget I ever brought it up. — Now, if you don't mind, tour's over. I have other spills to clean up after."

Lexus took his electrostatic mop and walked away, whistling. He left Butch and Kaleena to ponder how best to spend their remaining hours onboard the Station.

CHAPTER THIRTY

▼

The Station's central tube ran for nearly one full klom from end to end. It wasn't very wide — barely forty meters — but wide enough to house several banks of zero-g rooms, the kinds with beds, for having sex.

They didn't get to it right away. After Lexus broached the subject, they retired to an onboard lounge to have a drink. It was a blue-colored drink, some sort of space hooch neither one of them had ever heard of.

At first, Kaleena wanted to talk about anything but. Then, out of the blue, she grabbed his hand and said, "Let's."

"Let's what?"

"You know. Try one of those rooms."

"You serious?"

"Do I look like I'm kidding?"

"I like the way you think, woman."

"I want you inside me," she panted. "Make love to me. Now."

For a moment, Butch thought it was the space hooch talking. But Kaleena undid the top two buttons of her blouse right there in the space lounge. He supposed she was hoping to seal the deal before the moment passed and she changed her mind. The crests of her firm breasts greeted his ravenous eyes.

"Do you want this body?" she purred.

"God, yes." Butch swallowed hard. "Yes, I do."

Butch was unaccustomed to Kaleena being so direct. It put him off his game. He leaned across and gave her a tentative kiss.

There was no hesitation in Kaleena's response. She kissed him back hard, her red-hot tongue searching feverishly for his.

"We need a room." It was everything Butch could do not to lose control.

The two moved quickly to the registration desk, picked up a keycard and a couple Tranquil patches, then rushed to the zero-g room. They threw open the door and literally flew in.

Now that Kaleena's passion had been ignited, things moved rapidly. She braced herself against the door and pressed her body forward against his. Her nipples were hard, like polished stones. They etched out an unmistakable message of love on his heaving chest.

Kaleena reached down, below his belt, and touched his trousers. The burning heat of his lust was hard, hard against her leg. At its touch, her heart began to race.

Her breath came in gulps, now. Butch found himself swamped by a tremor of hot craving.

Locked now in tight embrace, they drifted across the room in zero-g. Like autumn leaves, they settled to the floor in slow motion, a jumble of arms and legs. Weightlessness cushioned their impact.

"This'll never work!" He panted breathlessly, hands caressing her bosom. "There's no gravity! Curse that damn janitor! As soon as I move on top of you and begin to thrust, my every motion will only serve to push you farther away."

"What can we do?" she asked, begging him to hurry.

"Check the bed. It must be equipped with sleeping tethers."

"Ooh, that sounds downright pagan! I can't remember the last time a man tied me to a bedpost and had his way with me."

Kaleena gleefully tore off her clothes, stripped bare, and launched herself towards the waiting bed. Butch followed, in hot pursuit, launching himself along the same trajectory.

They landed laughing, a spaghetti bowl of arms and legs. "Okay, bub, tie me up, I'm all yours." She lay back, legs up, knees apart.

From where Butch sat, it was a splendid view. Nothing beat a girl where the cuffs and links matched. Or, as some said, the carpet and drapes. Either way, her nakedness drove him wild.

For her part, Kaleena took a glance around his nether regions and seemed properly impressed. "Mighty fine kickstand, if you get my meaning."

Butch fished around and found a set of elastic tethers attached to each side of the bed. At night they could be used to prevent a sleeping occupant from floating out of bed. Now, though, he found that by strapping one tether across Kaleena's waist, well below her breasts, he could fix it so she wouldn't float away yet would still have full range of motion with her legs. He was finally beginning to appreciate the value of Lexus's advice.

They began to go at it enthusiastically. But, no sooner had they begun than they discovered something new: There were certain wonderful things a lover could do for his mate when unburdened by the evil forces of "up" and "down."

The coupling didn't last long. Something about the setting or the ultra-low-gravity made them crest rapidly, almost too rapidly for their own good. Without ever meaning to, they both came almost immediately.

Butch rolled off her, slid a tether across his chest and put a hand on her belly. "Tighten those muscles down there."

"You saying I'm flabby?"

"No, not at all. You have a body that just won't quit. What I'm worried about is leakage."

"You can't be serious."

"Everything floats in zero-g, little lady. Don't ever forget that. Orange juice, barf, sperm, you name it. It all floats. If you don't want to be combing that stuff out of your hair two days from Sunday, I suggest you tighten those love-muscles of yours real soon."

"Oh, shut up and hand me that blanket. We'll keep those floatie things under wraps, if you get my drift."

Shortly, Kaleena closed her eyes and fell asleep. A satisfied smile was painted across her moistened lips. Butch stared at her a moment, then dozed off himself.

．
．

Butch woke three-quarters of an hour later with an enormous hard-on. At first he was surprised, then he remembered where he was.

Kaleena noticed it right off. "Still in need I see."

"Ask a man and he'll say he's always in need. But this place has a lot to do with it."

"Space makes you horny?"

"In a manner of speaking. Us spacejockeys have a word for it — extreme morning wood. In zero-g, excess fluids collect in a man's penis while he sleeps, and he wakes up this way almost every day."

"From the size of things, looks more like morning lumber to me."

"I'll take that as a compliment. But if you think my wooden puppet friend swells with fluids in zero-g, giving me a hard-on, what do you think happens to that cute little button of yours? Your member swells up just like mine does, and with pretty much the same result."

"No wonder I'm so damn horny."

"That itch of yours is gonna need to be scratched over and over again as long as we're up here."

"Is that the voice of experience?"

"Naw. Just stories around the campfire."

"Well if the sex is so great, why go home? Why not live in zero-g all the time?"

"Weightlessness has its downsides. Loss of bone mass. Constipation. Upset stomach. Plus, zero-g can be dangerous, especially long-term exposure."

"I'll have to put that in my report to my father. What makes it so dangerous?"

"For some reason, prolonged exposure to micro-g harms our immune system. The theory is that our lymphocytes are seriously damaged by weightlessness. Without those white-blood cells to help fight disease, it doesn't take long before the body's immune system is left seriously impaired. Apparently, at the cellular level, certain signaling systems do not function properly in zero gravity. It's just one more reason why a woman must be absolutely sure not to get pregnant while in space. That, plus the fact that fetuses won't develop properly and babies born without gravity haven't the strength to live in a gravity field."

"I thought you worked the high steel. How does a drill bit like you come to know so much about biology?"

"All of us spacejockeys learn to take precautions."

"But your little wooden puppet friend looks so lonely, like he doesn't have a friend in the world."

"I admit, the little fellow may need some handholding, maybe a kiss on the forehead for good luck."

"Oh, I just love it when you talk dirty. You simply must have your way with me again."

"If you insist."

"I surely do."

•

•

Butch woke the second time, crawled out from beneath the sleeping tether, and fairly glided across the room to a small aft alcove. There were windows back there, fairly large ones, where a person could look out into space, plus handholds so a person could maintain their orientation.

The windows were darkly tinted now, to protect a looker's eyes from the unfiltered sun, but also to keep voyeurs from getting a glimpse of people having sex in the zero-g rooms. It was a favorite pastime for visitors and staff alike in the lounges of the main part of the Station. And the tinting was a good thing too, for the windows were large, considering the small size of the room and the modest dimensions of the central tube.

Butch steadied himself on the handhold, took a look around. Above him was the main part of the Station, all spokes and girders. He could see it through the glass, but just barely. One thing stood out clearly, though — a trans-comet barreling its way through the ether toward its eventual rendezvous with the planet Venus. Wrapped as it was in its giant plastic liner, the trans-comet was all shiny, far out of proportion to its size. As always and forever, Man was fiddling with his environment, molding and reshaping it more to his liking, just as he had been doing since that first day he climbed down out of the African savanna and stood on two legs.

Kaleena woke, saw him by the window. She propped herself up on one elbow, said her head hurt and that she was hungry.

Butch signaled for her to come join him, and she launched herself out of bed and in his direction. On the way over, she tangled herself up on his trousers still hanging in mid-air. By the time Kaleena arrived, she was hurtling across the room in an out-of-control spin. She crashed into him then ricocheted into the wall.

"Damn. That hurt."

Kaleena rubbed her head, shoved his trousers angrily away. "Didn't your mother ever tell you to hang up your clothes before bedding a girl?"

Butch laughed at her antics. "Good morning to you too."

Kaleena was still spinning, and Butch grabbed onto her arms to steady her. He knew the score. What catches most people off guard in zero-g is the amount of rotational velocity they can acquire when they push off a wall or stationary object like a bed. A person picks up a terrific amount of unintentional spin. Plus, you can't just put anything down, not in a room where there is no gravity, not like you can on Earth. There is always some inertia remaining when you move about. Whatever you put down — be it a book or an empty milk glass — will always float off, causing trouble later on. An hour afterward, you get bopped in the head — or your friend does — by the book you set down earlier. Air currents, mainly, but also ship movements, cause objects to move off slowly from where you left them. That includes clothing you ripped off in the heat of passion.

"Don't laugh at me. I have a bad enough headache already."

"That's the fluids in your body trying to redistribute themselves. It happens to everyone in zero-g. Clogged sinuses. Stuffy nose. It can make you feel like you have a real bad head-cold until you get used to it. Plus, you may find yourself needing to go pee a lot."

"Yeah, now that you mention it. That's what first woke me up."

"The pee'll get you every time. That's just the body dumping what it considers to be excess fluid. You'll be peeing constantly until your body establishes a new equilibrium. But get ready — you're just gonna love that zero-g toilet."

Butch pointed to a small alcove adjoining their bedroom. "It's really nothing but an inverted vacuum cleaner, with straps to hold you down. Me? — I find the whole damn thing quite disturbing."

"Maybe a little mood music would help. Though I can't for the life of me find a radio pod or a vid in this place."

"Sorry, but there's no electronics in the central tube."

"Not anywhere?"

"Nope. Not in the zero-g rooms anyway."

"Why not?"

"It's the same old problem of containing free liquids. Remember what I told you about those floatie things after we had sex?"

"Okay, nothing to drink, nothing to eat, can't take a pee. I still have a headache, and I'm still hungry. Can we please go back to the grav part of the Station already?"

"Yeah, I think we've both had enough zero-g for one day."

"That's why there's a two-hour limit on the room, isn't it? The hotel manager mentioned it when we checked in, but I couldn't understand why."

"Yeah, most people just want to get it on so they can tell the folks back home that they did so. But when they're done doing the deed, they want to get back to grav as soon as they possibly can."

"It was fun though, wasn't it?"

"Where I come from, getting it on is always fun. But there's one other thing you ought to know about zero-g."

"What's that?"

"You're gonna need help getting dressed. A body can't just sit down on the edge of the bed and slip on his shoes. So let me help you, okay?"

"You helped me take 'em off, so it's only fair you help me put them back on again."

Together, they floated back to where their clothes hung, still in mid-air. Then, with each other's help, the two of them dressed and made their way up to the Space Bar. It was not in the zero-g tube, but out in one of the spokes comprising the Ferris wheel portion of the Station. The trip included a ride in one of those infamous elevators Lexus warned them about. Fortunately, the ride was short, so no harm, no foul.

Butch sat across from her, now, in the tiny thousand-klom-high pub. He glanced rapidly around the place, and immediately his heart sank. Talk about your fish out of water. The bars Butch was used to, the kind he normally trawled back home or on Mars, were jungles — hot, sweaty, and filled with evil, pungent smells. Plus, they were filled with animals, strange animals, some of them dangerous — merc marines, DUMPSTERS, chemical dregs, people like that. These sorts of bars, the sort he was used to, were in neighborhoods where the police traveled in pairs, if they came out at all.

But this bar was different. This bar was clean, almost antiseptic. No rotten smells. No shady characters. Good lighting. Comfortable chairs. *God, what an awful place!*

If Butch felt anything at all, it was that he did not belong. He couldn't help it. Men are creatures of habit. They like to be left alone. If forced, they can, for a short while, be sociable. Dim lights, flowing alcohol, pretty waitresses — these are the lubricants that may bring out the social creature. Otherwise, men like Butch want their favorite chair, their favorite vid, their favorite woman, doing it their favorite way.

Butch tried to screw up his courage. He looked across the table at this beautiful woman. Kaleena's eyes were unlike any he had ever seen. As he sat there, he felt it happen — the line between love and lust suddenly blurred.

Her hands were on the table, now, reaching for his. "Let's eat something then fly back to the zero-g room to have another go at it. I think we may still have a half hour left on our room rental."

There was a small loaf of hot bread on the table and she hungrily broke off a piece. Her headache was already starting to go away.

"I thought you'd had enough of zero-g?"

"Can't a girl change her mind?"

"Honestly, had I known the Space Station would make you so horny, I would have brought you here ages ago." Butch squeezed out some butter from the tube and spread it on a slice of his own.

The pub was slowly filling with travelers, when the waiter finally made his way to their table. He had an impertinent, unpleasant air about him.

"I'll be with you in a minute," he said.

"What's wrong with right now?" Butch snapped impatiently.

"There's only one pub on this tub, Bub — and this is it. You don't like the service? Feel free to step off any time."

Butch felt a flash of anger, instinctively tightened the muscles in his jaw. "Feel free to step off? That's how you want to talk to me?"

"It's okay, Butch. Let it go," Kaleena pleaded.

"Yeah, Butch, let it go," the waiter parroted, staying just out of Butch's reach.

"But you said you were hungry." By then Butch had decided he wanted to be anyplace but here.

"We'll order in room service," she said.

"Yeah, you do that," the waiter scoffed as he walked haughtily away.

"Now who's stepping off?" Butch shouted after him, fists clenched. But the waiter shrugged his shoulders and headed back to the kitchen.

"Let it go, Butch. I'd much rather have another taste of you than eat in this dump."

She grabbed what was left of the loaf of bread and stuffed it in her handbag. Butch pocketed the tube of butter.

"If it's another taste you want, it's another taste you'll get."

.

.

It was unhurried lovemaking at its best.

Rather than take another zero-g room, they went straightaway to the hotel located upstairs from the pub. The room wasn't much — space was at a premium onboard the Station. But it did have a bed. One of those plump, oversized affairs with a brass headboard and a nightstand on either side. The floor was covered in a thick blue pseudo-carpet. The windows, which looked out on the verdant Earth below, were dressed only in auto-shades. The room lights were low.

She came to him at the window. He was watching North America go by. The sun had set and the coasts were aglow with light. So were the shores of the Great Lakes, as well as all the major rivers and their tributaries. Mankind loved his water. It made transport cheap and commerce possible. Every civilization, before or since, has set up shop along the shores of some lake or river.

Now came the less populated northern latitudes. Newfoundland, Greenland, Iceland. Such a strange little island, that one. A world stripped to its essential. Geography reduced to geometry. No forests. No visible vegetation. Black seas. Elemental landscape.

She pointed out Ireland, her family's homeland, on the western fringes of the approaching continent. Then more lights to the east.

Kaleena wrapped her arms around his waist, pressed her head into the small of his back. The muscles of his abdomen rippled beneath his shirt. The tension in his chest brought forth memories of their first time together. She quivered, now, at the thought of the two of them joined again at the hips.

He turned in the circle of her arms to face her. He kissed her on the forehead. She sighed warmly in response.

He worked his lips down to her cheek, then to her neck.

Now Kaleena took control, her hungry mouth devouring his lips and tongue.

Neither of them wanted to rush. It would be over soon enough in any event.

They undressed each other slowly, deliciously, button by button, clasp by clasp. Their clothes fell into two neat little piles on the floor. Panties and underwear remained unshorn.

Still standing, they kissed, tongue on lingering tongue. He pressed her to him, hands on her bottom. She moaned softly, feeling his manhood stiffen against her leg.

They moved to the bed without saying a word. He peeled off his underwear and tossed them to the floor. She did the same.

Kaleena lay back full-length on the sheets, inviting him in. He moved onto her, setting her hips in motion. They had no reason to rush.

For several long minutes he worked on her, patiently, even diligently. A moan escaped her lips. Then another. "Oh, Butch. Butch."

With each stroke, her ecstasy rose. One notch at a time, until Kaleena was in full bloom.

Then, all of a sudden, she put her hands on his chest. She wanted to be on top. It was better that way, she said. Easier for him to caress her breasts. Easier for her to move. Easier for her to come.

Now her breath came faster. His too.

And then it was over. In a warm explosion of energy, it was over.

Satiated at last, Kaleena rolled off him and they lay apart. Gradually, their heart rates returned to normal, and Kaleena slid blissfully to sleep, a contented smile on her lips.

At that singular moment in time, life seemed awfully sweet.

CHAPTER THIRTY-ONE

▼

Kaleena woke before he did, finished eating the loaf of bread she had stuffed into her handbag.

She squeezed out some butter from the tube Butch had palmed, washed it all down with a glass of water from the dispenser. Sixty-four ounces of re-processed water per day came with the price of a room.

She turned on the vid, muted the sound, dialed up the room service e-menu, clicked on the items she wanted. Passenger services would dispatch a bot within minutes to make the delivery.

Then she flipped rapidly through the channels. At one point a picture of her father flashed on the screen. She stopped channel surfing to see what it was all about. A newsline was running across the bottom of the screen.

" . . . dead at fifty-eight by an assassin's bullet. Ironic, considering how the Senator was the man behind the latest gun-control bill . . . "

The remote flew from Kaleena's hand. She spit out a mouthful of water. Most of it splashed onto Butch's still inert body.

"What the . . . ?" He jerked groggily awake.

Kaleena was sputtering, down on the floor, searching for the remote. She quickly found it, turned the sound back on.

" . . . This is Annabel Clark reporting from the American News Network. Sources inside the sheriff's department inform us that Senator Flanagan's killer has not yet been apprehended. They also tell us a city-wide manhunt is underway. Authorities have placed the entire D.C. Dome on lockdown . . . "

"What the . . . ?" Butch was beginning to make sense of it all.

"This can't be happening," she sobbed. "First my brother, now my father? Will this nightmare never end?"

Kaleena broke down crying. The time for love was now behind them. What they would soon have to face would be much more difficult.

●

●

An hour later, the passengers of the *S.S. Mars Voyager* were all gathered near the gate waiting to clear Security before boarding the Space Elevator for final descent to the surface.

It hadn't been an easy hour. When Kaleena couldn't stop crying, when she seemed to be hyperventilating and unable to catch her breath, Butch spoke to Lexus, who tracked down the Station doctor. He quickly administered a sedative. The drug wasn't strong enough to put Kaleena to sleep, but it did calm her almost immediately.

One hundred and eighty-two passengers. That's how many people were nervously waiting to board the Space Elevator. Without exception, every last person in that waiting room was anxious to be home. *And who could blame them?* To a person, they had all been gone a long time, many longer than a year, a few as long as five.

And so much had happened in their absence — the slaughter at the stadium, the passage of the controversial Gun Control bill, the splintering of the Republic, the collapse of the financial markets, now the assassination of a U.S. Senator by a sniper's bullet.

That last one had hit Kaleena especially hard. The news of her father's death had come to them across the airwaves little more than an hour ago. It was almost too much for one young woman to bear.

Kaleena sat now, quietly sobbing. She had sequestered herself in Vestibule #5. It was located in the Space Station's outer ring, not far from the hotel they had just exited. From the vestibule she had a splendid view of Earth, as well as the Moon and ribbon of stars beyond. It was a beautiful place to be anytime day or night, a place that made most people extremely happy.

But Kaleena was not happy. In fact she was quite depressed. At least the tears had moderated. But that was only because the sedative had kicked in. Now she sat at the window glassy-eyed, drifting slowly off to sleep.

Kaleena Flanagan wasn't the only one aboard the Space Station, who was in a foul mood. Elijah Montrose had spoken with Alexander Hoagland within the hour, learned of the failure of the buying pool. Now Elijah was despondent and philosophic. He was in the adjoining alcove staring out the viewport at the still-docked *Mars Voyager*, when Butch came over to talk to him.

"She okay?" Doc asked of Kaleena. He could see her through the glass. She was red-eyed and visibly upset.

"Would you be?" Butch asked.

"No, I guess not."

"What about you, Doc? You don't look much better to me than she does."

"The buying pool failed."

"What exactly does that mean?"

"I've been in contact with a close friend of mine at the Federal Reserve. The buying pool failed."

Still a blank look.

"You don't know much about investing, do you, Butch?"

"Never had the money, if that's what you mean. Nor the smarts."

"The buying pool was a last-ditch effort to stabilize the markets."

"And it failed?"

"Miserably."

"What does that have to do with us up here? I'm more concerned with what we are going to do once we all get back down on the ground than with how the stock market closed. Kaleena wants to return the capital. She needs to make funeral arrangements for her father."

"Not gonna happen. None of us are going east. — At least not right away."

"I go where I please, you know that."

"A wonderful sentiment. But times have changed."

"How so?"

"I can't speak for the rest of the passengers, but our little group will be met on the ground in Hilo by Alexander Hoagland and wife."

"Alexander Hoagland? As in *Senator* Alexander Hoagland?"

Elijah nodded. "Xander, to his friends."

"Senator Hoagland is something of a hero to us Westerners. Do you think he'll be able to help Kaleena get back to Washington?" Butch asked, thinking that before long he should return to her in Vestibule #5.

"I assure you: Alexander Hoagland won't be in Hilo to meet Kaleena Flanagan."

"Who then? — You?"

Again, Elijah nodded.

"I'm impressed. To warrant the personal attention of a genuine U.S. Senator, you must rank pretty high up in the government pecking order."

"Truth is, Xander and I are good friends. We go way back. Though I imagine he'll be there in Hilo as much to look after you as he will be to rescue me."

"Since when did any of us need rescuing? What the hell is going on here, Doc?"

"I think things on the ground are far worse than we have been led to believe."

"But why should a United States Senator from the lake district of Texas give two hoots about an old country boy like me from Wyoming?"

"Ah, a hero. — And modest too."

"Wars make heroes, Doc — not asteroids."

"In every human pursuit, there are two extremes of predictability. At one extreme is the absolute predictability of physical law. If, A, you slam the door, and, B, your thumb is in the door when you slam it, then, C, it will hurt. The results are reproducible by anyone who runs the experiment . . . And there are no known exceptions."

Butch scratched his head. "Where are you going with this?"

"At the other extreme of the experience-spectrum are truly random events. If, A, you roll snake eyes in a fair game of dice, and, B, your second roll is boxcars, then, C, it's anybody's guess what your third roll will be. No fixed mechanism exists that will definitively link the first and second rolls to the third."

"And this is news? We live in a world filled with dumb luck. Dumb luck and brick walls."

"Two extremes, Butch — absolute predictability, total uncertainty. Between the two extremes is that thing we call the stock market. Never entirely predictable, not like that pain in the thumb. But not quite random either. The stock market lies somewhere between slammed doors and rolled dice. Its long-term trend is invariably up. But, in the short run, it is inexorably random."

"Except now?"

"Normally, the market is stabilized by the interplay between short-term traders and long-term investors. What makes the market susceptible to mega-events like the one now in progress is a sudden pullback by long-term investors. That is what is happening now. The trouble begins when long-term investors start to think and act like short-term traders. They change their stripes when something happens that makes them fear the future. — A war. An oil embargo. A giant corporate failure. A new tax. — We've got all of the above on our hands now, and then some."

"That's why the long face? Because you're losing your shirt in the stock market?"

"Not me, you drill bit — the whole country. Haven't you been paying attention to a single word I have said? *The buying pool collapsed.* UniBank failed.

Punitive taxes have been slapped on by a dumb-ass President chasing votes. Inflation is rising. Resource supplies are stretched thin. We are in trouble."

"And yet Senator Hoagland is taking time out from his busy schedule to wing his way from the capital all the way across the country to the Hawaii Free State just to meet us?"

"His own freedom has been threatened."

"By whom?"

"He didn't say. But from what I could gather, it was one of the higher-ups inside the leadership of the New Republic. He said he'd been to see Thadamore Mills. Mills is the Governor of Texas. That might be who threatened him."

"I don't know," Butch said. "A U.S. Senator attracts an awful lot of attention. The man travels with a security detail. Those kind of people carry pulse blasters and are backed up by free-roving robots. That kind of ensemble attracts attention. And that kind of attention makes a man like me nervous. Maybe we ought to split up, go our separate ways once we reach Hilo. If things are really as bad as you say they are, staying together may be hazardous to our health."

"Actually, *not* staying together is the one thing that makes me nervous. Though I have to agree with you about not wanting to attract too much of the wrong kind of attention."

"But didn't you already say Senator Hoagland was under some sort of cloud? Which makes the two of you high-value targets. Being around either of you two is just plain dangerous for us ordinary folk. I really don't want Kaleena and yours truly becoming collateral damage on account of you and your buddy Hoagland. Hell, they've already killed Kaleena's old man — and he *was* a Senator. Who the hell knows what they might do to his daughter?"

"So what is your plan?"

"She'll be safe with me."

"At your father's ranch?"

"Yeah, why not? The Hogan's have a five-hundred-acre spread in eastern Wyoming. I always go there between duty assignments. Anyway, my father is expecting me."

"But don't you think you have to choose up sides in the coming battle?"

"Listen, Doc. I'm one-hundred-percent in favor of the Second Amendment. But I feel just as strongly about preserving the Union."

Elijah was about to answer, when an announcement crackled over the public comm:

"Attention in the terminal! Attention in the terminal! The Space Elevator is now ready for boarding. All passengers who have been cleared by Security, please make your way to Vestibule #2. Have out your biometric card and green boarding pass."

There was an audible pause, then it started again. "I repeat: All passengers . . ."

"I guess that means it's time to go," Doc said, getting to his feet. A steady stream of passengers was already in the corridors, heading down towards Vestibule #2. They had to board one of several small shuttle ships that would ferry them across the short gap from the Space Station to the Space Elevator.

"I'll go collect Kaleena, meet you shortly in the gate area with the others."

And then Butch was gone.

•

•

Any descent from orbit can be unnerving. Though, truth be told, the most harrowing return of all was like in the old days, a red-hot drop from orbit, slowed to a jerky stop by parachute.

By comparison, this descent was actually quite pleasant. Ballast was supplied by ingots processed at the orbiting smelter.

The Skyhook cables that hung from the satellite made it more like a rapid elevator ride than the high-g fall it otherwise would be.

A "steady" line hung from beneath the Elevator, like the tail on a kite. Without it, the Space Elevator would swing like a pendulum from orbit, sickening everyone onboard. Plus, the tail was a good way to dispel the static charge that built up on the cable as the Elevator descended. Motion through a magnetic field generates electricity.

The island they were lowered down to was the Big Island of Hawaii. It was a topographic mapmaker's nightmare. Tortured rivers, cavernous ravines, lava-belching volcanoes, hidden lakes, sulfur hotsprings, intractable jungles. But all this was inland. Along the coast were kloms of picturesque beaches, as well as two large cities and a myriad of smaller ones.

When viewed from across the horizon, the landing zone resembled a giant metallic ice-cream cone jammed point-down into a large hill. It was in fact an inverted tower two hundred meters tall, hollow, with a gaping maw of a hole up top. The Elevator was lowered into it, still dangling from the Skyhook at the end of a cable that extended all the way to that satellite in geosync orbit, and a bit beyond.

If, on the way down, that dangling ship acquired even the slightest hint of a back and forth rocking motion, it was quickly damped down as the "steady" line beneath it was secured and the Elevator slipped ever deeper into the narrower and narrower recesses of the giant inverted cone. It grew progressively darker down there as well, as more and more sunlight was squeezed out by the encroaching walls of the metal cone.

The "steady" line continued to be reeled in, and finally the Elevator came to rest on a large concrete platform at the bottom of the cone. The end was always the same. After such a long journey, a boisterous cheer would go up from the passengers: *They were home!*

Only the trip wasn't over, not by a long measure. There was still paperwork to attend to, plus the purely mechanical issues of safely stowing the passenger compartment. It had to be physically separated from the descending cable. The cable itself had to be grounded, this to cope with the static electricity that inevitably built up on the line.

In time, the Skyhook cable was detached from the passenger compartment. The uncoupling was a slow process. The kinetic energy of descent — now stored in an orbiting counterweight — would later be transferred to an ascending payload, which could then be hauled up to orbit. It was an amazingly modern and efficient system, using simple physics the Greeks had devised nearly three thousand years earlier. Whatever energy was lost to friction in the raising and lowering was reacquired by solar cells, both orbiting and ground-based. No need for fossil fuels here, or for volatile chemical brews.

Now came the final wait. One more pass through Security, plus a stop at Immigration, including a physical examination of all belongings. Each returnee then had to spend fifteen minutes with the Psychiatric Computer answering questions with hidden meanings. Where space-travelers were concerned, the authorities could never be too careful. More people cracked up on the way home from space than from any other location.

Finally it was over. The passengers were eager to be out of the Elevator and on their way. Some had been gone from Earth a very long time. Even those who had been gone only a short while had nearly forgotten the way the Home Planet smelled. Earth had smells, wonderful smells: baking bread, fresh-mown lawns, electric air, nectar everywhere. After so long away, the return was a delicious change.

The air inside a sailship was dry, bone-dry, dry as a desert. Mars, too, was dry. Not a breath of humidity to be had anywhere. And no smells, not even one. Flowering plants were nonexistent and the air thin and cold. Always cold.

But Hawaii was different. Everything they missed, everything they longed for, was here: Humidity. Aromatic scents. Natural light. Warm air. Very warm. The entire island was green and buzzing with high-energy life. Hot. Humid. Tropical.

Boy, was it good to be home!

CHAPTER THIRTY-TWO

▼

The refugee camp on the shores of Kentucky Lake was overflowing with newcomers.

Distraught people, people stricken with fear and trepidation, people who were wet and cold. They were all streaming into the refugee camp from war-torn areas throughout the region — Tennessee, Illinois, Missouri. Maybe a hundred thousand at last count. The equivalent of a medium-sized city.

The Kentucky National Guard had done their best under impossible circumstances. This was a heavily wooded area, thick with mosquitoes and biting flies. The Guard had set up tents in a big field — maybe ten thousand in all — but even that number wasn't enough to house every last one of them. It was a humanitarian disaster in the making.

Elixir Coventry was a good-hearted person, warm and caring. She had journeyed a great distance to help, all the way from her home in eastern Tennessee. Kentucky Lake was a highly popular recreation area, a narrow manmade lake lodged behind Kentucky Dam in the southwestern corner of the State. After the initial skirmishes of the war, when sizeable numbers of people were first displaced, the Wiccan Nurse's Association put out a call for volunteers. Elixir quickly answered the call, along with several other wiccans from her clan.

Elixir had done volunteer work like this before, mostly in big cities like Chica or Hedon City, once in Chat'nooga, which wasn't far from where she lived in the Tennessee mountains.

Modern health care was often a contradiction in terms. There was perhaps no place in the world worse than Chica or Hedon City to fall ill. Even an injury that was survivable most other places was often a death sentence in a big-city medical center.

Wealthy hospital patients, those with private health coverage or ready cash or a government identicard, were attended by actual nurses and doctors, not just mech staff. Oh, private hospitals had their share of robots too, but not like in a municipal hospital, where live doctors and nurses were a rarity. A bot staff was completely impersonal and detached despite their "compassionate" programming.

So, when the call for help went out, Elixir was only too glad to lend a helping hand. The wiccans were not there at Kentucky Lake alone, of course. There were others, many others, each there at the Lake to try and help people put their fractured lives back together again — health care professionals, first providers, police, Boy Scouts, god-fearing Christians of every stripe.

Elixir moved among the injured in the big tent. Some were in pain, a few reached out to her for assistance. Many had chemical burns and their situation was hopeless.

This was a troubling part of Elixir's duty, for the same painkillers that numbed a patient's nerve endings, also numbed their senses. Many of the injured knew they were alive. But they didn't know who they were or where, and they had no sense of what lay ahead.

Dealing with depressed patients was a challenge for Elixir. She generally had a positive outlook on life. Plus, she wasn't a psychologist and she didn't know the latest techniques to combat depression.

But the woman could follow instructions, and she was compassionate. Elixir helped change dressings, dispense medications, talk to patients, dump bedpans.

Between doing rounds in the medic tent, Elixir assisted in the mess hall, dishing up meals from the large vats that arrived in an unending stream from the kitchen, or else cleaning tables. Most of the injured weren't injured at all, just hungry, thirsty, dirty, and tired. Many were depressed. They needed help, not all of it medical.

On the third day, the shift supervisor stopped her in the mess hall, asked her to come to his office right away. Licks removed her apron and dutifully followed the man across the compound, not knowing what to expect. It crossed her mind that no one had ever asked for her nurse's license, so maybe the shift supervisor was tidying up loose paperwork.

The supervisor's office was a makeshift affair, in a hastily-built, plywood and canvas-walled hut situated across from the main medic tent. There was an air conditioning unit in one wall and brown file cabinets occupying every inch of open floor space. There was an air of order to the disorder. Elixir took a chair and sat down.

The shift supervisor had a red file folder in his hand. On the outside was written "Wiccan Nurse's Association." Beneath it was written the Wiccan Rede — *An it harm none, do what ye will.* Inside the folder was a list with four names on it. They were in alphabetical order. These were the names of the four nurses who had dropped everything to be of assistance here at the Kentucky Lake Refugee Camp.

"I really don't want your kind around here." The man was gruff when he spoke. She didn't even know the man's name.

"My *kind?* Just exactly what kind am I?"

The man shook the red file folder at her. "You know exactly what kind you are — a godless she-devil, a shameless witch. I want Christians ministering to the sick and hungry, not unrepentant heathens."

"Begging your pardon, boss. But I don't minister to anyone . . . about anything . . . ever. All I do here is try and lend a hand — ladle food, hand out pills, change bandages, stuff like that. How can anyone possibly find any of those things offensive?"

"Your hands are not clean."

"That's ridiculous. I scrub in before each shift, just like everyone else." Elixir turned her hands palm up, so he could see.

"You never heard of a metaphor? Your hands are soiled, and they are soiled because you are a devil worshipper."

"Wiccans are hedonists, not Satanists."

The man growled. "I have a full dossier on you people. It's right here on my e-pad. You people engage in unclean practices. You say strange things. And just look at the way you dress. Yellow tennis shoes; no bra; funny hairdo. You should be ashamed of yourself."

"This is about my boobs?"

"I want you and the other three from your clan out of here. I want the four of you out of here this very instant . . . And don't any of you ever dare to come back."

Elixir grinned, gave a wicked laugh, waved her arms and cackled a few unintelligible words.

"What did you say?" he demanded angrily.

"Just a spell." She laughed hideously, arms still in motion.

"What? . . . What kind of spell?"

"The kind that leaves your zibb thin and shriveled and diseased and useless."

"My . . . what?"

"Your zibb, you knucklehead. Your penis, your cock, your . . . "

"You put a spell on my . . . ?"

"Yeah," Elixir cackled. "You'll never be able to get that worthless piece of meat hard again. You'll never be able to please a woman again, not for as long as you live. Every time you try to get it up, it'll just hang there, worthless."

Then, enjoying herself immensely, Elixir strutted out of the man's office. She didn't want him to see the tears welling up in her eyes.

Elixir retired to the visicast room to have a good cry. It was a public area, and people came and went. She stared down at her tennis shoes. They didn't seem so bright and yellow today.

She watched the vidcast with the sound muted. A news loop was playing. The story was about the widening war. Scenes of destruction. Collapsed bridges and roadways. A power plant engulfed in flames.

Soon two other wiccans from her clan joined her in the vid room. They, too, had just been sent packing.

Elixir spoke. "Since when did the value of a person's helping hand get measured by the quality of her faith?"

"Honestly, Elixir," the first girl said. "It's not as if you've never been the target of prejudice before. Religious intolerance is a Wicca's companion every day. It has practically been a bedrock belief common to every successful civilization on the planet since the dawn of time."

The second girl agreed. "Yeah, Licks, xenophobia has always been alive and well, lurking in the shadows of American life, waiting to spring forward and show its ugly face."

"But I only wanted to help. So many of these people have lost everything . . . I mean, everything."

Elixir sat quietly, staring off into space. Suddenly, something on the screen of the vid caught her attention. The letters filled the screen.

NEWS ALERT ! NEWS ALERT !

"Turn that up," Licks said. "Quick. Turn it up."

" . . . This news bulletin is brought to you by Annabel Clark of A.N.N., the American News Network . . . "

The network logo appeared briefly on the screen as the commentator continued. Her voice was cracking, as if she had just been crying.

"First reports are coming in of a nuclear exchange between the United States of America and renegade forces from the New Republic . . . "

"Oh, my God!" Elixir exclaimed, as pictures of destruction filled the screen.

" . . . The American News Network has satellite confirmation of nuclear-tipped missiles being launched from Avenger silos in Holden, Missouri, and from the East Coast Missile System in the mountains of Virginia."

Vid of missile launchers flashed across the screen. The missiles were slender, with stubby red tips. Annabel Clark continued:

" . . . Space Command has been crippled, and the central business district of Houston, Texas, has been obliterated. The epicenter has a blast radius of approximately two kloms. There are maybe as many as six hundred thousand dead or injured. The military is calling this a surgical strike. The President calls it a measured response to previous attacks. Others call it an abomination."

Her voice cracked again. Now a dark mushroom cloud filled the screen.

" . . . A similar tragedy has befallen Philadelphia. The Liberty Bell and surrounding neighborhoods have been obliterated. First blood has now been drawn on both sides of this widening war . . . "

The mushroom cloud thickened and intensified.

" . . . The question this reporter must ask — the question that is surely foremost, now, on everyone's mind — is this: Must civilization perish in a hail of fiery atoms? Is this what the Founders would have wanted for America? I wonder . . . "

The vidcams moved off the mushroom cloud and panned across the surrounding city, where a raging firestorm had taken hold.

" . . . This is Annabel Clark reporting for the American News Network . . . "

Detailed pictures of Houston before and after the calamity flashed up on the screen. The Liberty Bell morphed into a mushroom cloud. Then the news loop repeated.

Elixir Coventry looked at her friends. She had seen and heard enough. The way she saw it, she now had really no choice.

Elixir Coventry was about to set an entirely new course for the future.

CHAPTER THIRTY-THREE

▼

The night air hung wet and low over Pearl Harbor. It was heavy air, the kind that can make a man stumble and sweat. The six travelers, lately of Mars, had disembarked the Space Elevator in Hilo. They were only a few of the many inbound passengers that had been traveling home onboard the sailship *Mars Voyager*.

An hour later the six had dwindled to three, and the three had linked up with Senator Hoagland and his wife Laura. By then, Red Parsons, Woody Dunlop, and Gulliver Travels had gone off together, each looking for a bimbooker or a dose of mech-love in town. Red had promised to catch up with Butch at his father's house in Wyoming in a week's time. Elijah, Butch, and Kaleena went with Alexander and Laura Hoagland, boarded a private airchop for Honolulu.

The five were walking, now, from the airchop pad across the tarmac to a line of restaurants beside the road just outside the gate. They had their eyes on a seafood place two doors down.

The space-travelers hadn't eaten any "real" food for months. Off-planet, sim foods were the rule. Now, just the thought of a mouth-watering lobster tail dipped in melted butter or the crack of a steamed crab leg was enough to make them forget all their cares and walk swiftly, despite the heat and humidity.

"Thanks for meeting us when we landed," Elijah Montrose said, feeling heavy under the pull of a full one-g. "And thanks for ditching your security team, especially the bots."

"The President thought meeting you might be a good idea," Xander

Hoagland replied. "But I was happy to do it in any case. You and I have been friends a long time."

"The President, eh?"

"He sent me to pick you up in his personal suborb. But because of the tensions and the way the country has been fractured, I had no choice but to leave Benjamin's bird behind at the airfield in Hilo. Some Air Force types will have to fly it back to D.C. without me and Laura onboard."

"You in trouble?"

"Maybe a little. That's why I wasn't so keen on dismissing my security detail. Laura hated the idea. But I understood what you were trying to say about not wanting to attract too much attention."

"Where are your bodyguards now?"

"I sent them all back to D.C., along with Benjamin's suborb. At your suggestion, I hired a local security firm to protect us while I'm on the Island." Hoagland motioned to a pair of shadows a few steps behind.

"It's never going to end, is it?" Elijah asked as they walked. He didn't know yet about the destruction of Philadelphia, where he and his family once lived.

"Not before the two sides annihilate each other, I should imagine," Hoagland observed darkly.

"Xander!" Laura exclaimed. "Do you have to be morbid?"

"Not morbid, Laura — realistic. This far on, avoiding all-out war will take a miracle."

"I think your husband's right," Elijah Montrose said. "The problem in this game is that everyone has miscalculated the odds, from the President on down to the local dogcatcher."

By now the five had arrived at the seafood restaurant. It was one of those unforgettable places with a big, red, plastic lobster over the front door and a giant fish tank in the lobby, the sort with live fish swimming around inside. A rack filled with colorful travel brochures advertising local sights sat along one wall; benches for waiting patrons along the other. There was wood paneling throughout the waiting area, and the walls and shelves were decorated with old-fashioned life-preservers, mounted game fish, and wood figurines of grizzled sailors dressed in seaworthy raingear, rain caps pulled low over their faces, corncob pipes extruding from their cracked lips. Alexander Hoagland let his wife take the pole position at the hostess stand to line up a suitable table.

"What did you mean when you said everyone in this game has miscalculated?" Xander asked nervously, as they waited for a table. Crowds made him uneasy, especially now that he had dismissed his regular bodyguards.

"Senator, the miscalculations run the gamut. Bluffs that have been hastily made — and just as hastily called. Threats of ridiculous proportion that should never have been made — and absolutely never carried out. Brinkmanship that was amateurish at best — and plainly went too far. As a nation we are now stumbling blindly towards a free-for-all. I tell you, Xander . . . "

Laura took her husband's hand. "They have a table for us now."

"Wife of mine, that's the first good news I've had all day. All this pontificating can make a man hungry."

The five of them sat down, quickly ordered. Xander motioned his hired muscle to another table. Drinks and salads arrived in no time at all.

Elijah placed his napkin in his lap, raised his glass, offered a toast. "From one peace-loving man to another. May cooler heads yet prevail."

"Hear! Hear!"

"Amen."

"Mazel tov." Clicking glasses all around.

Butch laughed. "Any other words of wisdom, Doc?"

"Actually, I do. Several, in fact." Elijah was serious.

"Wanna share?"

"Let's talk first about tonight's dinner bill. Anyone who knows me, knows my feelings with regard to the Unscrupulous Diner's Dilemma. Just so there won't be any questions later on, tonight everyone pays their own way. We won't be splitting the bill evenly. Agreed?"

"What is that man talking about?" Laura asked, baffled. She knew that Elijah and her husband were friends, but she simply did not care for intellectuals.

"Honestly, Doc. The reason we won't be splitting tonight's dinner bill is because I want you all to be my guests," Xander said, gesturing expansively. "Forget the prices — tonight's dinner is on me, folks."

"Is that your own pocket you're reaching into to pay for this? Or are the taxpayers the ones actually picking up the tab?"

"Okay, you got me." Xander looked at his wife over the top of his glass. "The President gave me carte blanche on this one. So tonight you will be dining at the public trough. By all means, if it makes you happy, order yourselves a second entree and a big dessert. I know how much you like cheesecake, Doc."

"Actually, I don't mind if I do." Elijah put aside his napkin, cleared his throat to speak. "And that might give me just enough time to talk to everyone seated at this table about another Dilemma we all should be concerned about — the Unscrupulous Hunter's Dilemma."

"Can't you see we're eating here?" Butch complained, crunching on his bread. A warm loaf showed up with the salads.

"Last story, I promise. The Unscrupulous Hunter's Dilemma. A group of five hunters set out on the trail to kill big game in order to feed their families. The question before these men is this: Do the five cooperate and hunt together, or does one hunter leave the group to set off on his own?"

Senator Hoagland quickly answered. "If that one hunter is especially skilled, he might do better on his own."

"Spoken like the true Wolf of Wall Street that you once were," Elijah remarked.

"I beg your pardon. I'll have you know, since his younger days, my Xander has learned to get along and play nice with others," Laura said, drink in hand.

"Damn! Have I really? Say it isn't so, wife of mine. I must be getting old."

"Not too old to eat I hope, because here comes our food."

The main courses arrived on a big tray, and they all began to eat with enthusiasm. For a long minute no one said a thing as everyone's favorite dish went down fast. The space-travelers, especially, savored every bite. Then Elijah broke the spell:

"The tracking and killing of a large animal — and the retrieval of its meat before scavengers can devour it — calls for cooperation. If our five hunters hunt as a cooperative unit, their odds of success improve markedly."

"But the hunters have to split what they kill five ways. A hunter on his own gets to keep everything he kills," Butch said between bites. He was busy cracking open the shells on his crab legs and picking out the meat with a tiny fork. *So primitive, yet so satisfying!* he thought.

Hoagland smiled. "Ah, a man after my own heart. What did you say your name was?"

"Butch Hogan, sir. From Wyoming. Nice to make your acquaintance."

"Pleasure's all mine, son," Xander replied. "Hogan's an Amerind name, isn't it?"

"Navajo dwelling. Somewhere, way back, I suspect we had one or two Amerinds jammed in our family tree. That's what my daddy says anyway."

"I have great respect for the Native American. They were cooperative hunters of the first order."

"That is after all the topic, isn't it?" Elijah said, trying to steer the conversation. "As I was saying, a large animal is more than one family can eat before the meat spoils. And to waste meat is to waste a valuable resource, not to mention a valuable chance to collect IOUs."

"IOUs?"

"The IOUs one can collect by sharing."

"I don't follow."

"Let me explain," Elijah said. "Collecting IOUs is a classic survival strategy. You give someone food when his cupboard is bare and yours is overflowing. He reciprocates sometime down the road when *your* cupboard is bare. In this set of transactions you both profit, because food is more valuable when a man is hungry than when he is full. Hunter-gatherers the world over act in accordance with this same logic."

"Sometimes you actually make sense to me," Butch said, searching for something to wipe his hands with. Cracking open crab legs was messy business.

"There is an old Eskimo saying — The best place for an Inuit to store his extra blubber is in another Inuit's stomach." Elijah was halfway through a plate of surf and turf, and loving it.

"You're making that up."

Elijah laughed. "Actually, I'm not. But the point I'm trying to make is this: When the odds are long, men tend to cooperate."

"Maybe. But when the odds are *very* long, a man tends to go it alone." Butch dipped his fingertips in the cup of lemon juice provided by the restaurant. Crab leg-eaters the world over agreed, lemon juice was the best way to clean one's fingers.

"Man's got a point, Eli," Xander said. "The longer the odds, the more a man will tend to want to go it alone. Team-think only works when you're going to win anyway. God put the firewood here, but every man must gather and light it himself."

Elijah frowned. "But what if the sole hunter has a bad month? Should we allow his family to starve?"

Butch wiped his wet hands on a paper napkin. "Back to worrying about the common good, Doc? I thought we were past all that."

Now it was Alexander Hoagland's turn to frown. "This may sound harsh, but the hunters are unlikely to share their kill unless the solitary hunter has something valuable to trade in return."

"Like what?" Laura asked, finishing her sensible meal of grilled white fish.

"Who can say, wife of mine? Exceptional tool-making skills. Good organizational skills. Maybe a tasty strawberry patch. I don't know. But one thing is for certain — There Ain't No Such Thing as a Free Lunch . . . That is true now and forever."

Butch suddenly understood. "There is a free-rider problem here, isn't there? Just like with the Unscrupulous Diner's Dilemma."

By now Butch had cleaned his plate. So had several of the others. Elijah was studying the dessert menu.

"Don't tell me we have another budding economist on our hands?"

Senator Hoagland feigned a groan then looked from Elijah Montrose to Butch Hogan. "And to think I was just beginning to like you."

"I'm no economist, Senator. But the Doc here has been teaching me a few things these past weeks. The lessons helped us pass the time on the long ride home."

"It was an exciting ride home, though, wasn't it?"

"It had its moments."

"But weren't you the brave soul who climbed out on that burning wing and put out the fire?"

"In a matter of speaking."

"Yes, yes, so the boy's a hero," Elijah said, eyeing a slice of cheesecake at the next table. "But what Butch said about free-riding is exactly correct. The larger the group, the more likely it is to attract free-riding."

"Which brings us full circle back to our current problem — what to do next?" Butch struck a serious face. "Doc already knows my thinking on this. So I might as well tell the rest of you. The way I see it, if we stay together as a large group, we are bound to attract attention. Especially if we are traveling in the company of someone as important as a United States Senator. Dismissing the Senator's bots was obviously of some help, but it really doesn't change a thing. I think the smartest thing we can do is to split up. Red, Woody, and Gulliver have already gone their separate ways."

Elijah shook his head. "And, as I've already told Butch, I couldn't disagree more. There is strength in numbers. When we leave here, the smartest thing for us to do would be to go someplace safe."

"Is any place truly safe in the middle of a war?"

"The mountains are safe. The hills of Tennessee are safe. Certainly my home in Philadelphia is safe."

Alexander Hoagland looked at his wife Laura, then turned to Elijah: "You don't know?"

"Know what?"

"Good God, Elijah, don't tell me you don't know."

"Don't know what?"

"This won't be easy to hear, old friend. Maybe you should put down your fork, swallow your food, forget about dessert."

"What the hell are you talking about, Xander? Out with it already!"

"Philadelphia has been bombed."

"What do you mean, bombed?" Elijah looked around the table.

"Destroyed by a nuclear weapon. A good portion of it anyway. More than a day ago."

"Are you telling me my family is dead?" Elijah asked, his voice cracking.

"That is perhaps the case." His voice was flat.

"The Liberty Bell gone? The Franklin Library? Independence Hall? My family? All gone? . . . Who the hell would do such a thing?"

"The New Republic, that's who. It was retaliation for our attack on Houston. We took out most of the downtown, you know?"

Tears filled Elijah's eyes. "That's what you meant, isn't it? When you said we faced mutual annihilation."

Elijah Montrose started to cry. His head sagged forward into his hands. The table grew desperately quiet.

"I'm sorry, Elijah. I thought you knew. Good God, man, why did I have to be the one to break the news?" Xander started to shake. He felt horrible. "Now can you understand why I think it's so important for me to get back to Washington? I simply have to get the President to back off his present course of action before it's too late."

Elijah pushed back from the table, got to his feet, staggered away. Alexander Hoagland followed him with his eyes. Elijah was headed for the bathrooms and the restaurant lobby.

"I must get back to Washington, too," Kaleena said. "To bury my father."

"Well then the three of you ought to go back to D.C. together," Butch said, bristling with anger over Elijah's loss and how he learned of it. "You go, Senator. Take your wife and my girlfriend with you."

A moment later, Elijah suddenly came back to the table. He seemed resolute. There was something glossy in his hand, one of the travel brochures from the rack in the lobby.

"You really want to be safe?" he asked. "You really want to avoid attracting attention? I say we disappear. And what better place to disappear to than Hedon City? No one tracks a body's comings and goings from that godforsaken place. And no one's going to come looking for us there either. Plus, we should have access to untapped comm lines. From there we ought to be able to call or go anywhere we please."

Elijah wiped the tears from his eyes. But Butch was sure his friend was edging slowly into shock.

"Of all the horrible places to hide out!" Laura exclaimed. "Hedon City is a sewer, no place for my Xander."

"Actually, wife of mine, Elijah may be on to something. With all that has happened I think maybe we do need a safe place to hide out, if only for a while. Then maybe we can sneak into D.C. unnoticed."

"My father has an apartment in Hedon City."

"That's right!" Hoagland exclaimed. "I'd almost forgotten about his love-nest."

"Love-nest? What are you talking about?"

"Your father's place in Hedon City."

"And how would you know about my father's place in Hedon City? — He rarely talked about it, even to me. — And why the hell would you call it a love-nest? It was a place he would stay when he went to see my brother in the City."

"Your father and I were longtime political rivals. There was an occasion when I had him surveilled."

Kaleena was floored. "Surveilled? For what? You had no right."

"Yes, Xander, what did you have Senator Flanagan surveilled for?"

Xander turned to his wife, who had asked that question. "I had every right, wife of mine, every right. Kaleena's father was not nearly as pious a man as his public image suggested. At the time and place in question, our good Senator was shacked up with his male lover, a black-skinned she-male with a fondness for cocaine. More importantly, he was under investigation by the Justice Department for influence peddling. That is classified, by the way, and not for public consumption. And, in case either of you doubt my word, my people have the whole thing on vid. Plus, the man may have been involved in his own son's murder. So, yes, I had every right."

"What are you trying to say? — That my father was on the take? That my father may have had my brother killed? How dare you!"

Kaleena moved to slap the Senator across the face, but Butch caught her hand just short of its objective.

"Striking me in the face won't change the truth, young lady."

"No, but it might make me feel better."

"Your father was in Hedon City the night your brother was murdered. That's an indisputable fact. Your father had substantial money balances he couldn't account for. That is also an indisputable fact. The whole sordid affair is under investigation; at least it was before hostilities broke out. I don't know where things stand now."

Kaleena fell silent, retracted her hand from Butch's grip. "I apologize. My brother was troubled, that much is true. And Father didn't approve of his drug use. That is also true. As for the rest of it, I don't know."

"Well, it's settled then," Elijah exclaimed. By now he had begun to rationalize what may have happened to his family and what he must do to again move forward.

"It is imperative I try to find a way to get in touch with my family. If not from here, then from the mainland. According to this brochure I found in the lobby, there's a high-speed catamaran that makes a daily run from Pearl to Vancouver. We should all be on that catamaran when it pulls out of the harbor tomorrow morning. Then, those of us who want to, can continue trying to make our way east. There are bound to be roadblocks and delays along the way; but once we get to Hedon City, we ought to be able to figure out our next move from there."

"I'm with you, at least as far as the coast," Butch said.

"I may be able to do you one better than a secure comm line from Hedon City," Xander said. "One of my many perks as a Senator is a government-issue sat-comm. I always have it with me. By all means, feel free to use it to try and call home. But here's the thing, Eli. Don't get your hopes up. Even if Barbara and the kids are perfectly fine, the comm lines may be jammed. Let's face it: an atomic blast with its electromagnetic pulse likely fried all the comm links. There may be no way of actually getting through to them even if they are okay. You may have no choice but to physically walk through that front door of yours in Philly before you actually know for sure whether or not your wife and children are safe."

"I appreciate that."

"Now that I've had a moment to think about it, I have to admit I like Doc's plan," Butch said. "I really do. If we get off the catamaran in Vancouver, we can ride the maglev VIA Line east to Calgary, then hop a coal-burner south into Yellowstone. From there it's no great shakes to the Hogan Ranch outside Casper. No matter where we decide to go after that, I first need to make a stop at home. I need to see my father and I need to pick up a few things."

"Guns, you mean." Kaleena's face revealed her disapproval.

Butch was quick to reply. "Yes, guns. They're still legal where I come from. Now, more than ever, we have to protect ourselves. Believe me when I tell you, Kaleena — you'll be happier later if we take steps to arm ourselves now. The world has suddenly become a much more dangerous place."

"Don't I know it," Doc said, still visibly shaken.

Senator Hoagland nodded his agreement. "The boy is right. We need to . arm ourselves, and sooner rather than later."

"You'll get no argument from me," Elijah said. He took the sat-comm Alexander had offered him and began to move someplace quiet to make a call. "Excuse me — I need to find out what has become of my family."

Butch's heart went out to his friend. He thought to go with him when he made that call, but Elijah was already out the door.

CHAPTER THIRTY-FOUR

▼

So many of the big decisions we make in life, we make when we are young, at an age before we even know we are making them.

It is also at this age when we solidify our feelings about what is right and what is wrong, when we decide how we ought to act in a given situation.

Elixir Coventry knew what she must do. After being expelled from the Kentucky Lake Refugee Camp for being a wiccan, she knew what she must do — return home, gather her things, and head west.

Elixir couldn't explain her anger, not really. It came from deep inside, from a place she rarely visited. The shift supervisor at the Camp made her feel small. He made her feel ashamed, ashamed of who she was, ashamed of what she stood for and what she believed in. *What gave him the right?*

Elixir had her mind made up even before she hit the parking lot that day. The long drive home wouldn't be long enough to change it. After the way she had been treated by that man at the refugee camp, Elixir found herself wanting to choose up sides, wanting to join the war effort, but on the opposite side.

Several things went through her mind that day as she drove. If she wished to join the fight, she would need a gun. Licks owned two, in fact — a high-powered rifle and a sturdy handgun. Both were projectile weapons. Neither was registered. Nor did she have any intention of surrendering either weapon to the authorities, no matter what the new Gun Control law said. Civil disobedience was a right, if not an obligation, had been since the birth of the Republic. If her kind was no longer welcome in the land of her birth, so be it, she would join the other side.

But getting west would not be an easy task. All flights were grounded. Surface transportation was slow and unreliable, if it ran at all. She would have to cross the Missup River someplace, but as to where, well that was still an open question. Below Sane Lou, transit was strictly impossible. All the bridges on the Lower Missup had either been destroyed in the fighting or were tightly controlled. Her only safe route west was to first head north, maybe Chica, perhaps Hedon City.

When Elixir got home, she pulled out her maps then logged onto a nav site. She found it was no great distance from her home east of Nashville cross-country to Hedon City, barely half a day's drive, north on the auto-road across the narrow part of Kentucky, then up the length of Indiana, around Indianapolis, to Hedon City at the foot of Lake Michigan.

Plus, it was an easy drive. Elixir packed what she thought she would need for the trip, placed the house computer on standby, and programmed the gcar's nav system with her destination. The sensors that lined the automatic-road made long-distance driving relatively painless. The sensors kept the vehicles centered on the pavement and at a safe distance from one another. It was the perfect blend of impossibly high gcar-insurance premiums, cutting-edge laser technology, and super-accurate gps tracking. Not all roads were like this, of course. Short hauls were still driven the old-fashioned way — two hands on the wheel and one foot on the accelerator, occasionally the brake pedal.

•

•

From a distance, nearly every city in the hemisphere is beautiful. Oh, there are exceptions — Denver, with its perennial blanket of green smog; San Fran, with its never-ending shroud of impenetrable fog; Houston, even before the blast, with its choking ring of ugly oil platforms.

But other cities are truly beautiful at a distance — the sparkling, crisp skyline of Chica, the gleaming domes of both Washington, D.C., and Minnepaul, the dazzling bays of Tampa and Boston. Even Hedon City looks attractive from a dozen kloms away. It's only when you get in close that the grit really begins to show.

Traffic slowed to a crawl as Elixir reached the outskirts of Hedon City. The city wasn't really part of Indiana, nor of any other State. It was actually a jurisdiction managed as a municipal corporation by the three bordering States — Illinois, Indiana, and Michigan. It had its own laws and its own militia, its own taxes, its own courts, and its own budget. While it was pretty much anything goes within the city's outer gates, the carrying capacity of the roads leading into the city weren't always up to the size of the crowds. At those times congestion could be a problem.

The traffic inched slowly forward, now. At extremely low speeds the auto-road features kicked off and a person had to drive his gcar the old-fashioned way, which was tiresome and hard on the knees. Elixir was quickly running short on patience.

What could be the holdup? she wondered, drumming her fingers against the steering wheel. The gcars were three-deep as far as the eye could see.

Had to be the war, she thought. Everyone wanted to get away from their work-a-day lives, as far away as possible. They wanted to escape the war, if even for a while, be entertained by some bims, pop a few pills, get drunk, see a pornovideo. *What better place to escape to than Hedon City?*

Elixir glanced at her chron. She was going to be late. She had told her friend 7 p.m.; it was nearly that time now.

Several wiccans made their home in Hedon City, where they moonlighted as bimbookers in the red light district. Elixir didn't go in for such things. But she wasn't critical either. Everybody had to make a living.

Elixir spoke out loud. Her dashboard comm was hands-free and voice activated. She spoke her friend's name; the machine connected. She could hear it ring several times then switch to RECORD mode. *She must be out, working the streets.*

Elixir left a message, said she would be late, was caught in some insanely bad traffic at the edge of town.

Up ahead were flashing lights, a police checkpoint. *Probably looking for people driving under the influence, or without a license*, Licks thought. Underage drivers were a menace, as always. Young men, especially, looking for a good time in Hedon City. She reached for her snack bar, sitting next to her on the seat, and began to munch.

Now she was closer. She could see what was happening. There were security bots. The police were making the occupants of each gcar get out, empty their pockets, open their trunks. *They're looking for contraband*, Elixir thought. *Drugs, probably. Maybe tobac.*

She inched forward. Every once in a while, it seemed, the police would confiscate something from a driver. They made a few arrests, commandeered a couple gcars, but most they sent on their way.

Now it was her turn.

"Stop the gcar, Missy. And please step out." The policeman had a lightstick in his hand, a force gun at his belt. The light shone in her face. A bot stood at the ready behind him, watching, waiting. They could be very patient.

Elixir did what she was told.

"Driver's license, please."

She reached in her purse.

He took the biometric identicard, ran it through his scanner. "You're a long ways from home, Missy."

"Oh, not so far."

"What brings you all the way from Tennessee?"

"A girl needs a reason to cross the border from one state to the next?"

"An outsider is always going to draw suspicions, Missy."

"I'm not an outsider. I'm an American, same as you. Just a single girl out for a drive."

"Well then you won't mind answering a few questions."

"Anything to help the good people of Indiana."

"Now that's the spirit. Are you transporting any controlled substances?"

Licks didn't answer. She sensed trouble.

"Ma'am?"

"No, officer. No controlled substances."

"Open the trunk please."

Now Licks had it figured. The police were looking for firearms. Under the new law, guns were now illegal in the United States. These goons were about to confiscate hers. If she didn't cooperate, there was always the bots.

"Open the trunk, Missy."

"You have a search warrant?"

"Don't need one, Missy. Anyone who refuses to open their trunk during a police stop is assumed to be engaged in criminal activity. No warrant required. That's the law. Now open the trunk."

"Guilty until proven innocent. Is that the way it is now? And here I thought this was America."

"I don't write the laws, ma'am. I just enforce them."

"Good little soldier, aren't you?"

"I'm done asking you nicely, ma'am."

"I know. You're just doing your job."

Elixir handed the officer her key fob. The bot opened the trunk, immediately found her rifle. She had made no attempt to hide it.

"Okay, Missy, you're under arrest."

"Under arrest? For what? I've broken no law. Confiscate my gun, sure. But why hold me? What possible reason do you have for that?"

"I can give you several reasons. Transporting a lethal weapon. Refusing to surrender a lethal weapon to an officer of the law when asked. Claiming to possess no controlled substances, when you actually do. You've broken plenty of laws, Missy — and they're all felonies. You're coming with us. And we're impounding your gcar."

"Don't I get a call? Isn't that my right?"

"You've seen one too many crime vids up there with the hillbillies in the backwoods of Tennessee."

"But where are you taking me?"

"Joliet Civilian POW Camp."

CHAPTER THIRTY-FIVE

▼

Wyoming was a vista of rolling hills and mountain views, wild horses and tamed wheat. The Hogan Ranch was comparatively small, just five hundred acres, barely a dot on the map. But it was home, and it was the sort of place every outdoorsman adored — wild game, soaring mountains, towering pines. The Ranch was bordered on three sides by the Medicine Bow National Forest and lay nestled in the shadows of the Laramie Mountains, south of Casper.

The ten-thousand-klom trip to the Hogan Ranch from the Hawaii Free State had not been an easy one. Sixteen hours on a high-speed catamaran from Pearl Harbor to Vancouver. Then another eight onboard the maglev into Calgary, where they stayed the night. Then south by coal-burner into the United States, getting off at a stop north of Jackson Hole. That's where Butch's father Bridger picked them up. Now they were all in the *Sundance*, Bridger Hogan's mini-bus, riding home with him to the Ranch. The vehicle was a bit of a throwback, but it fit the man down to the last detail. To anyone paying attention, it should have been abundantly clear that Bridger Hogan was a colorful man, of the old school.

As they drove east out of the Tetons, with Bridger at the wheel of his big RV-type bus, everyone enjoyed the scenery. Everyone except Elijah Montrose.

The mountain air was cool and crisp. But Elijah Montrose probably didn't notice that either. Nor the occasional mule deer they saw running in the distance. Or that rare, majestic hawk riding the air currents overhead.

No, Elijah's mind was elsewhere. His face was drawn, his lips tight. In fact, the man was quite depressed. Despite repeated attempts in the past twenty-four hours, he had failed to raise anyone at his home in Philadelphia. There was nothing on the line but intermittent static.

Yet, for everyone else in that big van, it was a pleasurable ride, a distinct change from a month and a half in a spaceship, and who knows how long before that on Mars.

"Beautiful country," Xander Hoagland said as they sped along in the *Sundance.* "Except for the snow on the mountains, it kind of reminds me of home."

"Where's home?"

"Texas."

Bridger took his eyes off the wheel, stared at Alexander Hoagland. "We met before?"

"Not that I can recall."

"Your face seems familiar."

"Dad, I already told you who this man is — Alexander Hoagland. United States Senator from Texas. Now, would you please slow down? You're way over the speed limit, and you don't even have your sensors turned on!"

"Thought you looked familiar." Then to his son — "Don't tell me how to drive, boy." Then back to Xander — "I don't much care for government-types. But at least you're a Westerner, not one of those snail-darting liberals."

"What exactly does that mean?" Kaleena asked. Bridger Hogan was a little rougher around the edges than she was used to.

Bridger Hogan was quick to answer. "Sappy Enviros and mlorons. They all try to hide a hatred for wealth and progress with a loud love for junk science and endangered polka-dot butterflies."

"Excuse my father. No one ever accused the man of being opinionated."

"Don't you dare start making excuses for me, boy! Otherwise, you may find yourself hoofing the last two hundred kloms home on your own two feet, while the rest of us ride home in the comfort of this-here vehicle." He pronounced it "vee-hick-ull."

"Sure, Pops, whatever you say."

"No, Butch, your father is right. That bit about liberal morons and sappy Enviros is an opinion I hold myself."

"At least I see now where Butch got that mouth of his from," Elijah grumbled.

Bridger turned Elijah an evil eye. "Bit of a Korinthenkacker, aren't you?"

"The apple doesn't fall far from the tree, does it?" Elijah snapped back.

"What the hell you know about apples anyway?"

"I'm no raisin-crapper, if that's what you mean."

"We'll just have to see about that, now won't we?"

"Dad, give the man a break, will you? Elijah may have just lost his family."

Bridger was about to reply, when Xander Hoagland spoke up. He was feeling a bit vulnerable without his security team. "Mister Hogan, can . . . "

"Call me Bridger."

"Okay, Bridger. Can you tell us what's been happening in the world? We have been pretty much out of touch, now, for nearly two days, ever since Butch called you from Hawaii."

"A lot has been happening. There's trouble everywhere. More nuclear exchanges. It's become like a game of tit-for-tat. Plus purges on the ground."

"More nukes?" Elijah sighed. "Where this time?"

"Denver here in the west, Atlanta in the east. Both took hits in the business district. Thank God the attacks were at night, not during the day, when more people would have been at work. More strikes are threatened."

"We had no idea. There must be thousands dead."

"Sorry, but I haven't been keeping count," Bridger growled.

Hoagland was shaken by the news. "You said there were purges. We had no idea about those either."

"Due respect, Senator. For a big-wig government-type, there's a whole lot you don't know."

"So enlighten me. With the net down, all our e-devices are inoperable."

"With that crazy Reverend in charge, the State militias in the West have been moving against people, non-Christians mainly: Jews, Injuns, and the like. It's not all that much better out East, only the targets have been different — Blacks and Muslims, a lot of which are both."

"Not Injuns, Dad — Amerinds. And the Blacks don't like to be called Blacks any more; they prefer AfriAms."

"My subscription to the Politically Correct News must have run out. Or maybe my secretary just blame forgot to leave that particular memo on my desk."

"Well that's just wonderful," Elijah said. "Here I am, a Jew stuck in the Wild West with Tonto and the Lone Ranger."

"If I were you, I'd keep quiet about that Jewish stuff while I was out here," Bridger replied.

"You're not going to turn me in to the authorities, are you?"

"Not a chance." Bridger was earnest. "The only God I ever knew sits atop that old Grand Teton back there. Actually, I think the rabbis got it mostly right. But me and God don't talk, and I take no official stand on the subject, Kemo Sabe."

Xander Hoagland laughed. "Some say Kemo Sabe means *faithful friend*. Others, that it means *trusty scout*."

"You a fan of the Lone Ranger?"

"Legends will always have their place in American lore. The man was a

Texas Ranger, you know, a lawman from days past. You would be surprised how many Americans still believe in what the Lone Ranger had to say and what he stood for."

"Yeah, like what?"

"The Lone Ranger had a creed. *I believe that to have a friend, a man must be a friend.* Things like that."

"I thought Kemo Sabe was Apache for horse's rear end," Butch quipped.

"Some humorist poking fun, no doubt."

"Actually, I saw it in a collection of irreverent cartoons. Good stuff, from a long time ago."

"That may be. But back in the day, the Lone Ranger's creed was serious stuff. *I believe that God put the firewood here, but that every man must gather and light it himself.* That was another one of his sayings. *I believe that sooner or later we must all settle with the world and make payment for what we have taken.* Or here's another one: *I believe all things change except the truth. The truth alone lives on forever.*"

"Amen, Brother."

By now the scenery had changed. The highlands had given way to grazing country. It wasn't far, now, to the Hogan Ranch.

Butch could sense his father's unease. Visitors were few and far between at the Ranch, and his father was not always a congenial host.

"We won't stay long, Dad — just long enough to pick up a few things. Then we'll be on our way."

"I'm afraid that just will not do. You will stay long enough to eat and get some rest — and that is an order."

Laura spoke up for the first time. "Your father is right, Butch. We all need to get some sleep and have something decent to eat. Thank you, sir, for your hospitality. We accept."

Bridger started down the long road into the Ranch. "Travel 'round these parts has become a mite precarious. That's why I came all the way out to the rail depot to pick up you good folks. Butch told me about your plans. I know some of you's want to go east. But I don't know if you can, at least not safely. The militias are stopping travelers everywhere, but especially at the U.S. border, which for right now, is at the Big Muddy. They're stripping people of their arms and anything else they figure might make a difference in the war effort. People are being incarcerated, sent to civilian POW camps. It ain't a pretty sight, I assure you."

•

•

Steak and potatoes were the drug of choice around the Hogan Ranch. That, plus a keg of cold beer. And not that fake stuff like they tried to peddle out East, but the real stuff, brewed from barley, flavored with hops and sporting a foamy head. Bridger had a large, outdoor grill that stood on a concrete patio behind the house. While they talked and guzzled beer, he shuttled back and forth between his icebox, the grill, and an enormous redwood picnic table set for ten.

First came the steaks. Bridger tossed a dozen thick t-bones on the charcoal, along with a like number of Idaho baking potatoes wrapped in foil. At one end of the grill was a giant tub of water. It was filled with ears of freshly-picked sweet corn. Bridger salted the water as it came to a boil, put a fork through the foil into the potatoes, turned the sizzling t-bones with his tongs.

"How you like your meat?" Bridger asked each in succession as he worked the coals and dispensed more beer.

Butch smiled. He had quietly let it be known that in the end it didn't matter how anyone answered, because every t-bone was going to be cooked the same way, the way Bridger liked to eat them, medium-rare.

The six sat outside at the redwood picnic table to eat. Bridger set out tubs of real butter and sour cream, salt and pepper shakers, corn piks, napkins, and utensils. He gave each of his guests a thick, cast-iron plate. On it was stacked a juicy t-bone, a steaming-hot ear of corn, and a baked potato. They all began to eat enthusiastically.

The setting was near-perfect. A range of snow-capped mountains etched the horizon. Horses grazed in a pasture nearby. Was it any wonder if a calm soon settled over everyone, including Elijah?

Kaleena was surprised by how she felt. A subtle change was going on inside her head. After much delay she was finally beginning to grasp what Butch had been trying to tell her. It was weeks ago, and they were still aboard the *Mars Voyager*, winging their way home. He had tried to explain to her how his upbringing had been different from hers, how she had grown up in a concrete jungle, while he had never known confinement. It was true. The two of them *were* different. But now, with her father dead and her old world shattered, Kaleena was trying to visualize a new way of life. It was slow in coming, but she was gradually beginning to feel at home.

Kaleena took stock of the people seated at the table eating. Bridger Hogan was one of a kind. Named for an early pioneer — or so he said. Named his son for an infamous outlaw of the same time period. That bit of information was followed by a tiny chuckle, as if it were a longstanding family joke.

Bridger had obviously been married at some point in his life. But it was unclear to Kaleena what had become of his wife. Butch hardly ventured near the subject, and his father was equally close-mouthed. *Did she leave Bridger for another man? Slam the door and move out?* If Kaleena was serious about joining this family, she someday might have to broach that delicate question.

Elijah was less of a mystery to her. Onboard the *Voyager*, he talked incessantly about his wife and kids, how smart and inquisitive they were, how much he missed them all. She felt she knew his family, even though she had seen only digi-pix.

But all that was before he received news of the bombing. Now Elijah sulked, occasionally broke into tears. He hadn't been able to reach Barbara, and that worried him profusely. Elijah had begun talking about God at odd times, and that's when she remembered he was Jewish. The word itself held no real meaning for her. Judaism was a foreign belief, and now that there were widespread purges, perhaps even a dangerous one.

Alexander Hoagland was more complex. The Senator loved his wife, he truly did. But he couldn't talk to her, not the way he could talk to a man. Laura was not a deep thinker, and never pretended to be. She liked to talk about people not policy. She knew her husband was smart. But she also knew that she was not. Nor was she an intellectual, and she didn't understand people who were. Laura thought intellectuals were ambitious for themselves, when most of them — like Elijah — were simply ambitious for ideas. Sometimes the ideas were good; sometimes not so good. Christianity, for one. Laura didn't understand the Christian conservatives, many of whom supported her husband. It came with the territory. Texas was a hotbed of this kind of person. Deep down, Laura thought Christian conservatives were somewhat eccentric folk. They likely disciplined themselves with a whip in private, behind closed doors. From what Kaleena could tell, it crushed Alexander Hoagland's spirit to think that these sorts of people were now in charge of the New Republic, that these sorts of people were busy applying their medieval bias to their fellow citizens, using the thunder of modern weapons to enforce by pain the most ancient of ideas . . .

"Anybody for seconds?"

Bridger's question snapped Kaleena back to the present. Now, as bellies swelled and laughter filled the air, their present troubles seemed more distant.

"That was great!" Elijah said, smiling for perhaps the first time. "We never ate like that in space. Not once."

Bridger was still gnawing on an enormous bone. "No matter how they stir the stew, it's still stew. Sim food will never quite measure up to off-the-hoof standards."

"Breaking bread is what a man does with his friends," Elijah said. "Show me a fellow who will not break bread with another man and I will show you a fellow who cannot be trusted."

"That a Jewish saying?"

"Oh, the rabbis would like to claim it, I'm sure. But that particular ethic goes way back to before the dawn of civilization. It is the very essence of the Unscrupulous Hunter's Dilemma."

Bridger had a moment of confusion, but Xander stopped him before he could answer. "You raise that t-bone here on the Ranch?" he asked.

"I didn't butcher that steer myself, if that's what you mean."

"But you do like to hunt?"

"Sure. Me and the boy used to go hunting in these woods all the time. I don't do it so much anymore, not since Butch grew up and struck out on his own."

"I hunted myself, as a boy," Hoagland said. "Still do once in a while." The Senator smacked his lips as he nibbled the last few kernels off his ear of corn.

"If everyone around here is a bloody hunter, why are people getting so cooked up about this Gun Registration thing my father was pushing? I don't see how gun registration can possibly change any of that?" Kaleena said.

"The issue isn't just registration, Kaleena. It's confiscation. Two very different things," Butch explained.

"I might have been able to live with the damn thing, if they'd left it at just registration," Bridger said.

"Not me, Dad."

"Not me either," Xander said. "The problem with gun registration has as much to do with a loss of liberty as it does with a loss of privacy. I had this very discussion with your father."

"Was that before or after you hired someone to spy on him?"

"No, Xander is right," Elijah said. "The more tech-savvy a society becomes, the more often issues of privacy lurch to the foreground. Technology has always been engaged in a tug-of-war between privacy on the one hand and convenience on the other. And it's likely to remain that way for the foreseeable future. At some level, personal privacy rests on a bargain of sorts between Man and his machines."

"That sounds downright ominous."

"And ominous it is," Elijah rejoined. "In the early days of telephone and video, people feared Big Brother. In the early days of genetic tinkering, people feared mindless drones or super-human overseers. Early science-fiction writers like George Orwell painted a bleak future where communications technology was put to malevolent use as surveillance technology."

"But it *has* been put to malevolent use!" Kaleena exclaimed, shooting

Alexander Hoagland an evil eye. "By this very man, sitting right here next to me. He surveilled my very own father."

"The Senator must have had a good reason, little lady. Who the hell is your father anyway?" Bridger asked. The beer was beginning to speak.

"I thought Butch told you. My father is — or rather was — Senator Patrick Flanagan of Connecticut."

"Oh, that one. Bloody hell, I'm surrounded by royalty. A Senator, a Senator's wife, now a Senator's daughter? No wonder you're so ridiculously soft on guns, little lady. That father of yours is famous for only one thing — wrecking the Constitution. Which means he doesn't have many fans 'round these parts. Even less than that Hebrew fellow over there."

"Well you needn't make an effort to like him now. My father's dead. Cut down by a sniper's bullet."

Understanding suddenly dawned, and the color ran from Bridger's face. "I've gone and done it again, haven't I? — Made a jerk of myself. That's why your mother left me, Butch. 'Cause I couldn't keep my damn mouth shut or keep my opinions to myself . . . Please accept my apologies, little lady. No daughter ever wants to lose her father, no matter how poor his reputation."

Kaleena didn't answer. After a space of a few seconds, Elijah moved to fill the uncomfortable void:

"Even if we grant that Senator Hoagland overstepped his portfolio when he had your father followed, you have to admit that people's attitudes toward intrusive technology have changed over the years, certainly since the days of George Orwell."

"What was that? — like two hundred years ago?"

"Twentieth century," Elijah said.

"A long time ago."

"Long or not, the principle's the same," Elijah said. "Nowadays people are happy — ecstatic even — when the authorities keep public spaces under constant surveillance. Almost everyone you talk to agrees it is a fair trade. By giving up a measure of protective anonymity, people gain service and safety in return. Most seem to think the bargain a good one."

Hoagland objected. "But is the majority always right? Go far enough back and a majority thought the world was flat. Even in recent times a solid majority thought Darwin was wrong, that evolution was an elaborate hoax."

"You're a big one to talk, Senator. Can't you see that there is a world of difference between the physical surveillance of a public space and other, more direct invasions of our privacy, like in our homes?" Kaleena was still worked up. "Reading people's email, tapping their comm, filming them in bed with their lover. Please tell me you see the difference."

"I'm an Objectivist — of course I see the difference. Surveillance of a public place is without cause and without warrant. By its very nature, it assumes a man is guilty before he has even committed a crime. On the other hand, surveillance of a specific individual requires just cause plus a legal warrant. We had both on your father, by the way. The difference is philosophical, even if the law fails to make a distinction."

"Well it should!" she snapped.

"That one's really got a buzz saw up her ass, doesn't she?" Bridger said, downing another beer.

"Honestly, Dad!"

"So shoot me — I'm opinionated."

"Here's the thing," Elijah interjected. "Just about every thoroughfare in every city of any consequence is wired for 24-hour monitoring. In most places, that includes motion sensors, closed-circuit vid, and certain more-advanced technologies."

"Yeah, and up in the control rooms across the land, police goons scan everything that moves. Plus, a few that don't."

"Bridger is right," Hoagland said. "The problem with surveillance of public spaces is that it is a contagious habit of mind. It brings out the secret policeman lurking inside all of us. There is a relentless focus, nowadays, on crimes not yet committed, on dots not yet connected, on evidence not yet incriminating, on persons not yet identified."

"And yet, more cities are getting wired all the time," Elijah said. "In most cases by popular demand. Whatever qualms people may once have had about personal privacy, such fears are now giving way to more serious concerns about crime. Every statistic supports this. Every statistic we have demonstrates that vidcams reduce crime. We are now living in a Panopticon."

"I don't know what that means."

"A Panopticon. The ideal prison. A building designed so that every part of the interior is visible from a single vantage point, perhaps a watchtower at its center. Such an arrangement allows an inspector to observe every single prisoner without any of the prisoners knowing when or even if they are being watched. Such a prison inspires a fear of invisible omniscience, a power that is both visible and unverifiable. That's what we live in today, a benevolent prison of our own making."

"Do we really have time for all this intellectual mumbo-jumbo?" Laura complained.

Xander raised his palm, as if to object. "Doc, that sounds even more paranoid and ominous than before. — And just as wrong. Vidcams don't reduce crime; they only relocate it. Surveillance has virtually no impact whatsoever on the overall level of crime — only on where it takes place.

People don't give a damn where the muggers go, just so long as they leave their neighborhood."

"There's no crime out here in the boonies," Bridger said. "Everyone figures everyone else has a gun, so the bad guys stay away."

"Guns do reduce certain types of crime," Elijah said. "Home invasion, mainly. But the subject here is vidcams, not guns. Safety isn't the only reason to embrace surveillance. There is also the matter of convenience."

"You said something about that earlier, Doc. Something about a tug-of-war. I still don't understand what you were getting at it," Butch said.

"Consider the medical identi-chip. It can save your life. Or cost you your identity. All your records are kept in a central database. When you hit that emergency room complaining of chest pains and shortness of breath, the doctors can bring up your entire med history in an instant, perhaps save your life. That's the convenience part."

Elijah continued. "But that same information can be stolen by an ingenious thief. Or used against you by a greedy blackmailer, even a nefarious prankster. That's the invasion-of-privacy part."

"Please! How does a — what did you say? — nefarious prankster — fit into all this?"

"Consider the hacker who thinks it might be a hoot to make a million people think you have a highly contagious disease. Or the angry spouse who hires a hacker to delete a fatal drug allergy from your datafile just before you go in for delicate surgery. And then there are your ordinary lugheads, the sort who have legitimate access to your med records but commit a typographical error. Maybe they list your blood type as O when it is actually A. That kind of mistake could get a man killed."

"Did anyone ever tell you that you're paranoid?"

"You did, a few minutes ago. And it's true — I am. And with good reason. But that doesn't make me wrong. Let's take this business one step further. Let's say you want to turn on your kitchen oven from your desk downtown at work. This isn't hard to do. In fact, this is easily done a hundred thousand times a day over comm lines from every office in the country."

"Remote cooking?" Bridger was aghast. "Who the hell lives like that? I want my meat cooked up-close and personal. I want to hear that luscious fat sizzling on the coals."

"Dad, not everyone thinks like you. Lots of folks don't have the time. They can't live without that sort of convenience. This way dinner's sure to be ready when they finally get home after a hard day's work. Plus, the kids get fed a hot meal, where they otherwise might not."

"My very point," Elijah said. "Convenience trumps privacy. There's your tug-of-war. Any bad guy who lays a tap on these busy people's comm knows *precisely* when they're going to get home. The bad guys can rob these busy people blind and be out of the house before the turkey's even half-done cooking."

"Now you've gone at least a city-block beyond simple paranoia."

"Have I? With each added layer of personalization, each added layer of convenience, comes more identification and less privacy. — And yet no one is complaining."

"What's to complain about? Cooking a turkey is a voluntary act, even if it's done remotely from the office. Forget George Orwell — there's no Big Brotherism here."

"And tapping someone else's line to rob them blind is against the law," Elijah said. "It has nothing whatsoever to do with vidcams watching innocent people on an empty street corner. It's the other kind of surveillance that is so insidious, so robbing of our liberty — The infrared cams that line romantic walks in the park. The vidcams that issue taxicab drivers speeding nicks without human intervention and then automatically pass that damning information on to the hapless driver's insurance company. The smart cams that can recognize a person's face by matching vid images to a file of digitized photos. The micro-identicards that are permanently implanted beneath a subject's skin even before the age of consent. None of these are voluntary acts."

"I thought you were in favor of fighting crime, Doc?"

"I am. But when you hand government the powers of an all-seeing God, then staff such a bureaucracy with mere mortals, can we actually expect these louts to be both competent and merciful? I think not. Then the First Amendment gets tossed out along with the Second."

Xander Hoagland nodded his head. "We're not too far apart, you and me. I guess I'm afraid of many of the same things."

"Now you see why I'm paranoid? The world has become a very scary place indeed."

"Well you've got nothing to be afraid of out here," Bridger said. He pushed back from the table and got shakily to his feet. "But I'm getting tired, so if you're all done eating, I'm going to need you to pass me your plates so I can get started on the clean-up."

"Here let me help you," Laura offered, seeing Bridger sway back and forth on his feet.

"Me too," Kaleena said, picking up her plate. "We'll all help."

Xander yawned, stretched his arms. "You're a good cook, Bridger Hogan. What say we all hit the hay early tonight? I'd like to see us leave first thing in the morning for the rail station."

CHAPTER THIRTY-SIX

▼

Elixir Coventry was a civilian prisoner of war, someone who had broken the law in defiance of the federal government, a government that was at once schizophrenic and slowly losing control of a continent and its 800 million people.

Elixir was now one of many hundreds held in the Joliet Detention Center, all held without rights, all held without benefit of counsel or hope of reprieve.

The Civilian POW Camp was housed in the former Joliet Penitentiary, a federal lockup that was normally home to the most dangerous of American criminals. It was a desolate place, this prison, a cement jungle of rusted rebar, broken concrete, and leaky sewer pipes. Water dripped everywhere. And wherever it dripped, it was chased by cockroaches and rats into the cold, dark recesses of the prison.

Elixir found incarceration nearly intolerable. Her usual life was one of open spaces, bright lights, and fresh air. Now she found herself marooned in the dampest, murkiest, most ultimately confining, closed space ever conceived by the sick mind of man. She couldn't breathe, for there was no air. She couldn't see, for there was no light. She couldn't pleasure herself or have sex, not in a place like this, for there was no privacy, though she yearned for it constantly, day and night.

But in this horrible place, there was no emote wall to sit beside, no Autoclit to wash her cares away, certainly no Comfy Chair that understood her needs. Her only release was after breakfast each morning when, for two hours, the prisoners were expected to be in the exercise yard. Otherwise, they were confined to their cells 'round the clock.

On the fifth day, Elixir Coventry was relocated. Her new cellmate was a recent arrival. The woman was an outspoken, politically active college professor from Ripon, Wisconsin. The college was a hotbed of small "r" Republican thinking. The woman's libertarian leanings landed her behind bars three days ago. To demonstrate her disdain for the new Gun Law, the woman brought a fully-charged force gun into her classroom that day, then dared the campus police to arrest her. They did. Not an hour later, she was on her way to Joliet.

Elixir was sitting on her bunk, head in hands, when her new cellmate was dumped in beside her by a pair of beefy guards. The woman was a petite redhead, perhaps thirty-five years of age. She was a lot tougher than her diminutive size suggested.

The redhead brushed herself off, growled at her captors, looked at Elixir sitting sullenly on her bunk. "You got a name, roomie?"

Elixir looked up through teary eyes. "My friends call me Licks."

"Very onomatopoeic."

"Excuse me?"

"Onomatopoeia. When a word mimics a sound. Buzz. Piss. That kind of thing. I'm guessing your name has something to do with what you do."

Elixir dried her eyes, brushed back her hair. It was no longer done up in tight, corn-row-style braids. The prison guards had made her undo her braids, in case she was hiding a sharp-edged instrument of some kind.

"So tell me, Licks — How does one become your friend?"

Elixir straightened up, rose to her feet. Her yellow tennis shoes were not so yellow anymore. Now they were spattered with blood from the Kentucky Lake Refugee Camp as well as mud from the prison yard.

"I've told you my name — what's yours?"

"Morgan DuPont. Morge to my friends."

"Morgan DuPont, the author?"

"You've heard of me?"

"If you're the Morgan DuPont I'm thinking of, you write a column for an online rag I read."

"The *American Rights Journal*?"

Elixir nodded.

"Yeah, that's me. My mouth has gotten me into plenty of trouble ever since I was a little girl. It's what got my ass thrown in this dump. So tell me, roomie: What was your crime?"

"I was found with weapons in my gcar," Elixir replied.

"You threaten someone?" Morgan asked, inspecting her bunk. The mattress was thin and stained. The springs were shot.

"Not at all. It was a roadside stop."

"If you weren't threatening anyone, then why in blazes did they pull you over?"

"The police were pulling everyone over."

"What were you doing with weapons in your gcar anyway?"

Elixir was suddenly suspicious of this newcomer's motives. "Why all the questions, Morge? You a paid informant? Looking to hurt me?"

"Not at all, roomie. I'm a prisoner, same as you. The mightiest weapon I wield is the pen I sometimes hold in my hand. If you learned nothing else from reading my column, you should have learned that much. The word will always be more powerful than the sword — and it always has been."

"Call me paranoid. But when the Second Amendment falls, can the First be far behind?"

"My thinking exactly," Morgan said, inspecting the toilet. "We're supposed to pee in this thing? Who are they kidding?"

Elixir laughed, but not with joy.

"People in government always try to help those who are powerful at the expense of those who might wish to become so."

"Your next editorial?"

"My last one."

"Sorry, but I must have missed that one. It's been a while since I've been home. But my philosophy, like yours, is quite simple."

"Do tell."

Elixir nodded. "Every mind is unique, as individual as a set of fingerprints. From there it follows that the *product* of every mind — what we call its thoughts — will also be unique. Thus, it is the inherent right of each and every one of us to possess his own unique philosophy. No legitimate government has the right to impose a pre-ordained philosophy upon its citizens, no matter whether it is in the form of a state-run religion, an approved moral code, a certain way of making a living, whatever. Our inalienable rights were enumerated by the Founders: Life. Liberty. The Pursuit of Happiness."

Morgan liked what she heard. "Well put! Maybe that pen ought to be in your hand, not mine. I like the way you think, Madame Onomatopoeia. You and me — we're going to get along just fine!"

Elixir was about to answer, when her thoughts were interrupted by a sudden cavalcade of sound from down the corridor of the cellblock. It began with a series of truncated shouts, then a couple loud pops, like a vehicle backfiring.

Elixir was familiar with weapons; she knew those sounds — *those were the sounds of gunfire!*

Morgan was instantly on alert. "What do you think is going on?"

"I'm not sure. But it sounds to me as if some sort of jailbreak is underway."

"We're getting out of here?"

"You sound disappointed."

"I only just got here. Just met my roomie. Never even had a chance to try out the loo."

"Loo. Now there's a word you don't hear very often anymore."

"You know where that word comes from, don't you?"

"Loo? Haven't got a clue."

"It's actually bastardized French."

As Morgan spoke, they could hear more gunfire in the distance. They pulled back into the shadows, afraid of trouble. Morgan continued to speak, but this time in whispers:

"The original saying was *gardez l'eau*, literally 'save yourselves from the water.' At night, when the servants in the higher stories of the building threw their dirty water from the upstairs windows, they would yell a warning to those down in the street below: *gardez l'eau*."

"Dirty water? What dirty water?"

"You know, piss water and the like. So, *l'eau* — bastardized by the English to loo — came to mean piss, and then later on, the place where you go to take a piss."

Now could be heard angry shouts and clanging metal doors.

"No wonder they threw you in the clink, Morge. Making up ridiculous stories like that."

"No, it's true. I recently interviewed a high-level corporate type at Transcomet who talked like that. Knew all these weird word histories. The man was a total pain in the ass, if you ask me. Said he got that one from the President of the United States himself. That's probably why I remembered it."

Now came an explosion. It was close by. Concrete dust poured through the corridor, along with the acrid smell of sulfur.

Then came the sounds of running feet. The men wore heavy army boots and toted automatic weapons. There didn't seem to be any bots though.

Morgan and Elixir stepped back, away from the locked cell door, away from the swirls of dust.

Then everything changed. The electronic locks on the cell doors released and the doors rolled back automatically.

Morgan looked at Elixir with questioning eyes.

A scruffy, military face popped into the cell. "What're you girls waiting for? Time to get the hell out of here."

"Prison break?"

"You got it, sweet cheeks," the man said as he hurried along the cellblock.

Elixir started after him. Morgan DuPont followed closely behind.

"Who the hell are you?" Licks asked, as they ran. "And where in blazes are you taking us?"

There were people everywhere now. Total confusion. Complete pandemonium.

"Name's Derrick Barnes, lady. We're breaking you out."

"It's not that we don't appreciate the effort, Mister Barnes. But why help break us out? What are we to you?"

"It's Lieutenant Barnes to you, ma'am, not Mister. Anyway, I got my orders. The math is simple, lady. The Major figures any civilian POWs good enough to be locked up by the good ole U.S. of A. must be natural allies to our cause. Besides, we were in the neighborhood and there are loads of weapons stored here that we can use in the upcoming fight."

"Oh, yeah, and just what cause might that be?"

"The New Republic, of course. Now look, lady, I'm not here to argue. You and your girlfriend got three choices. Stay here and die. Come with us and join the rebellion. Or just walk off into the woods and disappear. Me, I don't give a frigging frog what you do. Your call."

"We're coming with you," Morgan and Elixir quickly decided.

"Hang on tight then. The gtrucks are parked just outside the gate. Follow the others. Next stop — Puritan City, Texas."

•

•

The five settled into their seats on the coal-burner — Butch Hogan, Kaleena Flanagan, Xander Hoagland and his wife Laura, Elijah Montrose. Their car was the middle car among five passenger cars. There were maybe a hundred people onboard in all. The train was headed east, out of Wyoming.

Bridger stood on the platform outside, waved goodbye to his son as the big, iron machine stoked its fire and began to raise a head of steam. This was no high-speed maglev like they rode across southern Canada, but rather a much slower coal-burner of the old sort.

Butch looked out the window at his father and waved back. The old man seemed sad to see them go. Butch had tried this morning to shore up his father's spirits. He told his father he might have visitors. Butch's friend Red

Parsons, whom Bridger had once met, had intimated he might follow Butch and the others to the Hogan Ranch in a few days' time. Butch suggested his father feed the man, then send him on home. Red lived south of the Ranch in Colorado. That seemed to make Bridger happy.

The railcar trembled slightly, now, as the big train lumbered out of the station. The tempo of the chug-a-lug from the giant steam engine hastened. The train moved more quickly, the clickety-clack of cars against rails becoming regular as rain.

Kaleena stared out the window of the train at the passing landscape. There were sparse grasslands in the foreground, rolling hills in the distance. She thought about Bridger Hogan, about what life must be like for him alone on the Ranch.

"Your father is a trip," she said to Butch. He was sitting across the aisle from her, consumed by his own thoughts. The others were one or two rows further along.

Butch was startled. "My father, a trip? . . . A trip off a tall cliff maybe."

"Cut the man some slack, will you? I like the old guy."

"I like the old guy, too. He is my father."

"It's more than that. — The man's downright likeable."

"We are talking about Bridger Hogan, aren't we?"

"Forget you. Where does this train go anyway?"

Butch pulled a map out of the seat pocket in front of him. He traced out the route with his finger. "North out of Wyoming, past Mount Rushmore, east across South Dakota, then into Minnepaul."

"Wyoming and South Dakota are New Republic states. What about Minnesota? Have they finally folded and joined the New Republic as well?"

"As far as I know, their court case is still pending. But Senator Hoagland probably knows better than I. If you want to know for sure, you can always scoot down the aisle and ask the man."

Kaleena shook her head. "Nah, just making conversation." She still seemed lost in another world.

"You want to tell me what's really on your mind?"

"If we do actually make it to Minnepaul without any trouble, how do you rate our chances of making it all the way back to the Dome?"

"Honestly, Kaleena, I think getting back to D.C. is a long shot. I think our odds improve, though, if we do like Doc said and go via Hedon City. The big question is whether or not the Minnesota border is still open. The man at the ticket counter said there had been trouble up and down the line, bandits and such. We'll just have to see."

"It would mean a lot to me if we could make it."

"Even after learning the truth about your father?"

"He's still my father, and I still feel as if I have an obligation, even if he didn't turn out to be everything I wished him to be."

Butch nodded that he understood, and for the next half-hour they dozed on the edge of sleep. Then something outside drew his attention.

There was an imperceptible change of sound emanating from the tracks beneath the car. *The train was beginning to slow!*

Kaleena felt it too. She glanced outside. "Are we already coming to the first stop?"

"No, I don't think so." Butch looked at the landscape, then at the map. "There may be a mountain pass ahead. Or an older bridge. Maybe a herd of buffalo. In the West, trains have been known to slow for such things."

The train slowed further, and suddenly Butch was on edge. He got up from his seat, pulled his luggage down from the overhead rack.

From down the aisle, Alexander Hoagland watched Butch unlock his cases. He realized instantly what Butch was up to. He, too, started to gather his things. He slipped the sat-comm out of his pocket and into his luggage beneath some dirty underwear.

The train slowed further.

Butch opened his bag, reached inside. "If the train comes to a complete stop, I want you to get off, no questions asked."

"What do you mean, get off?" Kaleena asked, with wild eyes. "What's going on?"

"Yes, what in the world is going on?" Elijah asked, seeing the worried look on Butch's face. Other passengers were beginning to get agitated.

Xander, already on his feet, signaled his wife to get up as well. The thought passed through his mind — *Maybe his decision to dismiss his security detail hadn't been such a wise idea after all.*

Butch holstered his pistol, threw his rifle over his shoulder. "Pay attention now, and don't anyone argue. If they slow this train down and it does actually come to a complete stop, I want all of you to get off and follow me. I think, for us, the war is about to get up-close and personal."

CHAPTER THIRTY-SEVEN

▼

"Do you really think Puritan City is the right place for a couple of bobcats like the two of us?"

Morgan DuPont stared through the musty darkness at Elixir Coventry as she spoke. The two women were huddled in the back of one of the big gtrucks with twenty other escapees who had also decided to come along. After the prison break from the Joliet Detention Center, many of the detainees had simply walked off into the woods. But nearly a hundred inmates were quickly loaded onto troop-carrying gtrucks provided by rebel forces of the New Republic. These forces were under the command of Major Branislav Karpinski and his junior officer, Lieutenant Derrick Barnes.

The gtrucks were all of similar design. Green, canvas side flaps draped over a plasticized, wooden framework; narrow wooden benches bolted to a slat floor inside. Not a very comfortable way to ride. But now the escapees were in a convoy of such gtrucks bumping across southern Illinois into Missouri.

Elixir held tight to the narrow bench. She had been playing with her hair, trying to get it back into braids, a practical impossibility without a mirror, a light, and two free hands.

"Now you're calling us a couple of bobcats? That hardly seems fair."

"No, I'm serious, Licks. I've heard things about Puritan City, not all of them charitable." Morgan's teeth were rattling, and with each imperfection in the road, the rattling got worse.

Elixir spoke in a soothing tone. "I think we'll be okay once we reach our destination. It's a long trip, though. And it may well be a dangerous one."

"I thought the dangerous part would be escaping from that hellhole."

"Well there is that. But do you really think the bad guys are going to give us a free pass, let us go free without a chase?"

"I guess that would be asking too much."

The gtruck hit a bump in the road and an older woman on the bench next to Morgan rolled to the floor. Another prisoner pointed at the fallen woman and laughed out loud. But Licks reached out to the fallen woman and together she and Morgan helped the older woman back into her seat.

"What makes you so sure we'll be okay in Puritan City?" Morgan asked as she hunkered back down on the bench. "You know someone there?"

"As a matter of fact, I do. The Reverend Roland Whitmore."

"You know the man personally?" Morgan was surprised.

"As personal as it gets."

"As in a sexual act of an oral nature? Is that where the onomatopoeia kicks in?"

Licks nodded, tried to keep herself glued to the bouncing seat. The wind rattled the gtruck's canvas walls.

"Are you for real?" Morgan asked.

"I'm as real as they come, Morge. As real as they come."

"But a religious man?"

"Believe me. The man is not that pious. Anyway, even a religious man needs to get himself off once in a while."

"I don't understand you, Licks. You've explained your philosophy. I understand it, even agree with most of it. Might decide to become a wiccan myself. But why get on your knees for a man — any man — even an important man?"

"You never had oral sex with a man?"

"Did the Good Reverend reciprocate? Did he oral you back? . . . No? . . . Then why submit to the selfish bastard's will?"

"Yeah," one of the rowdier girls barked. "Why submit?"

"I may be the one on my knees. But when a girl has a man in her mouth, who's really the one in charge? — the fellator or the fellatee?"

The rowdy girl snickered. "What the rut is a fellatee?"

Morgan chuckled. "Fellator or not, Licks, you're doing what the man wants. You're making the bastard happy. You're on your knees making the bastard happy. What is the man doing for you? — Nothing. Not a goddamn thing."

"You hate men? — Or just blowjobs?"

"The truth is, I can take it either way."

"Face it, Morge. Just because I'm on my knees in front of a man doesn't make him my master. Nor does it make me his servant. To the contrary.

When a man is in my mouth, I become the master and he the servant. Trust me when I say, we have nothing to fear in Puritan City."

•

•

Soldiers surrounded the stopped train. They were heavily armed but not very well organized. Up to this point they had been curiously respectful, so far making only muted threats. Two squads of uniformed men moved briskly through the train, emptying it car by car. They collected identicards, compared them against a database on one soldier's e-pad. Then, as the soldiers cleared each car, the passengers were put out on the siding with their luggage. So far no shots had been fired.

Now the squad entered their car. Butch immediately recognized the soldier in charge, George Rushmore. George and he were neighbors, went to high school together, dated the same girls.

"What the hell, George?"

George Rushmore was your typical farmboy-type. Flaxen hair, wide smile, broad shoulders, freckles. He saw that Butch was armed and broke stride.

"We don't want no trouble, Butch."

George warily eyed the rifle slung over Butch's shoulder, the pistol in his hand. He knew Butch could shoot. They had competed often at the county fair as boys. Butch usually won.

"What in blazes are you doing, George? You got a lot of nerve pulling over our train. What gives you the right?"

"You know this man?" Xander Hoagland asked.

"Me and George are friends. Went to grade school together, since we were, like, ten years old."

"Well then, tell your boyhood friend to get his men the hell off this train, so we can be on our way."

"Listen, old man, you best stay out of this," George said. "We have our orders. My men and I are commandeering this train for the war effort, whether you like it or not."

"Come on, George, what do you want with a passenger train?"

"We need to move troops, Butch. And to do that we need this train of yours. As fast as we can check identicards and get everyone off this heap, we're going to load my men onto it. Then we're going to run the border, get my men deep inside enemy territory, as far behind enemy lines as we can."

"A sort of Trojan horse?"

"We like to think of it more like a smart bomb. But here's the thing,

Butch. All the passengers onboard this train are civilians; we know that. We're not looking for trouble. And we're certainly not looking to hurt anyone. All we want is to get you and your friends off this train. *Tout de suite.*"

"Still practicing your French, I see." Butch and Xander exchanged whimsical looks.

"It means 'right away'," George said, as if they didn't understand.

"Sonny, I knew what *tout de suite* meant when the poop was still dripping out the side of your diapers," Alexander Hoagland grumbled. "And no amount of fancy talk is going to impress us. Now, are you going to get off my train and let us pass or what?"

"Since when did it become your train, mister?" George studied the Senator's identicard, turned it over several times in his hand.

George began to get red in the face, so Butch moved to cool him off. "We don't want any trouble either, George. Truth is, we were just about to get off this barge, when you came aboard."

"Well then go in peace, brother."

"But where exactly are we to go? There are six of us traveling together, George. We're all on foot. No food, no water, no transportation. Everyone you tossed overboard is in the same boat."

"At least I'm not going to confiscate your guns, not like they would back east."

"That's supposed to make me feel better?"

"Okay, Butch, this is what I can do for you. Give me and my men an hour's head start. Once we're well away from here, I'll alert the local authorities to your situation. I'm sure they'll send buses to pick you up, take you to the nearest town."

Kaleena stepped forward. "Why can't we just go east with you, at least across the frontier into Minnesota?"

"I really can't allow that, ma'am. There's bound to be shooting somewhere down the line. Like I said: you are all civilians. I have my orders: Get the passengers off the train, load on the troops. If you want to go east, you'll have to go south first. Make your way down to Puritan City. See one of Reverend Whitmore's people. Maybe they'll issue you traveling papers. Be prepared to pay, though. I'm told papers like that don't come cheap."

Alexander Hoagland pushed forward now, in front of Kaleena. "Young man, I don't care whether or not you are a friend of Butch's — I must be allowed to remain on this train. I shouldn't have to take orders from the likes of you, nor pay an outrageous bribe to a bunch of hooligans so I can travel in my own country."

George looked again at Hoagland's identicard. "Who the hell you think you're fooling with this? Anyone can see this card's a fake."

"Let's not press the issue, shall we? I assure you, the card is quite real. Run it through your machine, if you don't believe me."

Hoagland didn't dare say he was a wanted man in Puritan City. Or that Pappy Barnes — the man from whom these soldiers no doubt took their orders — would have loved to have him as a prize, a bargaining chip to be used somewhere down the line against the other side.

"Just who the hell do you think you are, old man? Who is this toadstool anyway, Butch?"

Now it was Laura's turn to step forward. "Young man, when you address my husband, you will do it with the deference his office demands. This man is a United States Senator, and worthy of your utmost respect."

"No need to protect me, Laura."

"You need a woman to fight your battles, old man?"

"No more than you need civilians to fight yours."

"What did you say your name was?"

"Alexander Hoagland."

"Stole his identity, did you?"

"That's Senator to you, boy. Or just plain Sir."

"Just how dumb do you think I am? Alexander Hoagland is a hero 'round these parts. You don't look anything like the man. I've seen vid. Hoagland believes in the Second Amendment. Why would such a man want to go east, where guns have been outlawed?"

"Because I took an oath."

"What oath?"

"An oath to uphold the Constitution, an oath to uphold the laws of this great land."

"Even if the laws are wrong?"

"Yes, even if the laws are wrong. We don't get to pick and choose the laws we obey."

"But, Senator, if you truly are who you say you are, how can you deny your heritage? Are you not first and foremost a Texan?"

"Does being a Texan somehow make me less of an American?"

"Of course not. But citizens of the present owe no allegiance to citizens of the past."

Xander turned to Butch. "What did you say this character's name was?"

"George. George Rushmore."

"Listen, George Rushmore. That line about citizens of the present owing no allegiance to citizens of the past is vintage Thomas Jefferson. — And it is complete malarkey, like just about everything else that came out of that man's mouth. Jefferson was a fool. Only Alexander Hamilton — of all the Founding Fathers — had a sound philosophy."

George was becoming flustered. "There are Natural Laws and there are manmade laws. As a United States Senator, surely you must know the difference. A man has a solemn obligation to obey the Natural Laws. But a man is under no such obligation to obey the laws made by other men. Civil disobedience is the only proper remedy for a manmade law gone bad."

"Ah, listen to the dime-store philosopher. Son, let's be clear. Civil disobedience and civil war are two very different things. Laura and I are going east with you, whether you like it or not. Inform your troops who we are. Tell them that we will be traveling under your protection. Do that now and be quick about it. Do we understand one another, son?"

Before George could argue, Xander turned to speak to Butch and the others. "Laura and I are going east with these men. We have to. You folks do not. Kaleena, surely you must know by now that your father has already been buried. Make no mistake about it. The man was too important. He had too many admirers. Plus, too many days have passed since your father was assassinated for them to have just left him on ice in a morgue somewhere. Take my word for it. It simply no longer makes sense for you to return to Washington. I strongly recommend you go with Butch. The two of you should return to the Hogan Ranch. I'm sure you'll both be safe there. I hardly think the same thing can be said of Puritan City. No matter what your friend George here says, I would avoid that bowl of pea soup at all costs."

"What about me?" Elijah suddenly spoke up. "Do you really think the New Republic is any place for a Jew? I simply must be allowed to return home to find out what has become of my family."

"Then come east with Laura and me. The three of us can travel together. I'm sure George here won't mind. Who knows? — our very presence onboard this train might actually help get his men across the frontier. Then Butch and Kaleena can return to the Hogan Ranch on their own, without any of us oldsters slowing them down."

"You can't just tell people what to do," Butch objected. "You're not the boss of me — or of anyone else."

"Bossing you around was the last thing I had on my mind. I just thought . . ."

"If George says it's okay, then by all means go with him. But don't presume to know what is best for me and Kaleena."

"I only thought . . . "

"Kaleena and I will go back to the Ranch. — But not because you told us to; because we have to. If Puritan City is half as dangerous as you make it out to be, we may need to arrive at the front gates armed with our own cavalry."

"You mean to drag your father and that beer keg of his on wheels into this?" George asked. "I don't think either of them are up to the challenge."

"Is that any way to talk about the *Sundance?*"

"Just be extra cautious down there," George said. "In Puritan City, all is not what it seems."

"And yet you are willing to fight and perhaps die for these people?"

"Ideals are perfect — people are not."

Xander still wasn't satisfied. "Let's be clear, shall we? I want it on the record how much I am opposed to you two going to Puritan City."

"Duly noted."

"Can we get going then?" Kaleena asked.

"*Tout de suite*, as they say."

CHAPTER THIRTY-EIGHT

▼

"Are you certain you know what you're doing, son?"

Bridger Hogan was tired. He hung over the steering wheel of his big rig, eyes on the road. Butch sat across from him in the front, Kaleena on the sofa behind. They were in Bridger's RV-bus traveling south through Kansas on their way towards Puritan City in north-central Texas. To avoid the chaos and utter destruction in the Denver metro area, they had been forced to come east out of Cheyenne, Wyoming, then turn south at North Platte. This was flat, dry country, the same for five hundred kloms in every direction. Every once in a while a prairie dog would peek out of its hole, then, when it saw the big rig coming, dive just as fast back down inside it.

"Certain? Come on, Dad. When was the last time you were certain about anything?"

"I was pretty certain at breakfast this morning."

"About what?"

"That I was going to talk you out of this craziness. That at the very least, you were going to go in there with reinforcements."

"You mean Red?"

"Yeah. I told you I heard from the boy not long after you and the others left for Minnepaul on the train."

"You mean before we got hijacked?"

"Yeah. Red says he's now back in Pueblo with his folks, along with two other fellows."

"Did he mention the other fellows' names?"

"Woody and Gullible."

Butch laughed. "Gulliver, Dad. Woody Dunlop and Gulliver Travels."

"Yeah, that sounds about right. So I ask you again, son. Are you certain you know what you're doing?"

"Dad, I'd be a liar if I said I was certain."

"Then why do it at all?"

"You know why. Kaleena wants to go home. We need traveling papers to get across the border into the United States."

Bridger looked at Kaleena in the rear-view mirror. "You must have stolen my boy's heart, to get him to do something this damn dangerous."

"Due respect, sir. What your son does every single day up there in space is far more dangerous than what he is contemplating doing down here. Certainly you must know that."

"I try not to think about it. But here's the thing, little lady. If simpleminded folk like George Rushmore are getting involved, this war may truly be getting out of hand."

"George is a good man, Dad. Anyway, he was just following orders."

"Just following orders? Like the people who cooked Denver with a nuclear bomb? Why the hell did the bastards have to do that?"

"I don't have an answer for you on that one, Dad. Not really."

"Your mother and I loved that town," Bridger said, choking on the words. "We got married there, you know?"

Bridger gripped the wheel of the *Sundance* tighter. Normally, he could simply flip on the auto-pilot for long drives. But not today. The transmission lines that powered everything under the sun, including the auto-road, had been knocked out by the blast.

"I know, Dad, I know." Butch looked over his shoulder at Kaleena in the back seat. She was deeply touched by the emotion on display here.

"She's gone. Left me, she did."

"You look tired, Dad. Why don't you let me drive?"

"You're my responsibility, Butch. How am I supposed to explain it to your mother if something happens to the two of you while you're both down in Texas?"

"Since when did you start worrying about Mom worrying about me?"

"Your mother walked out on us. — That's on me. — But that doesn't mean she doesn't still love you. How do you think your mother is going to feel when she finds out I let you walk straight into the lion's den?"

"That's why we need to have a solid plan, Dad — so you can come break us out if things go south."

"That's the first sensible thing you've said since the Rushmore boy tossed you off that damn train. And I've got some ideas how to do exactly that.

But before we venture any further south, we first need to make a stop at the E-Mart in Liberal."

"What do you have in mind?"

"Well, for starters, we'll need to pick up a tech-shirt for your girlfriend. I know you've got one or two in your kit, but I doubt either of them are small enough to fit her."

"What's a tech-shirt?"

"It's one of those fancy-schmancy shirts like all the delivery and law-enforcement people wear. You know the kind, little lady — a shirt with a built-in comm and personal gps locator sewn in. Cheap ones run about 20 credits apiece. They have a range of perhaps a dozen kloms."

"So you can track us?"

"That's the idea."

"Well then you're also gonna need a good receiver and a zero-point finder as well."

"Yeah, I already got that figured. Plus, we'll also need some supplies — food, ammo, that kind of thing. Plus some sheet metal to armor the wheels."

"If things go off the rails, you'll charge the gates. Is that the idea?"

"Now you're talking my language. I'll monitor your transmissions from the tech-shirt. If the two of you get into trouble, just say the word and I'll fire up the beast and come haul your bacon out of the fire."

•

•

Forty-eight hours later, Butch and Kaleena were standing outside the main gate of Puritan City arguing with a pair of uniformed guards.

It was a dark day and the smell of death still hung in the air, like a sick pall across the land. It was the stench of corpses and other debris brought up by the winds from Houston, a city whose downtown was now little more than a nuclear wasteland. Puritan City had been spared from the blast. But the people behind that tall gate had seen the mushroom cloud blossom along the horizon.

Initially, the prevailing winds had drawn the radiation and fallout east, towards Louisiana, not northwest towards them. Only later did a low-pressure area bring the ill-effects west.

Butch and Kaleena were still there, at the main gate, arguing with the guards, when a convoy of troop-carrying gtrucks rolled up. The gtrucks slowed, ground to a halt. There was a beep of the horn, then a young, rough-looking soldier jumped out of the lead gtruck, shouted "Hello" to one of the guards. The two moved out of earshot to talk. The second guard remained with Butch and Kaleena, continuing to block their entrance to the compound. Behind this second guard stood a tall security fence, barbed wire on top, electrified wire running throughout. In the distance could be seen the steely minarets of the Puritan City tabernacle.

The man that jumped out of the gtruck wore lieutenant's stripes. He spoke excitedly to the guard. "Of all the silly things, Eames. My father's got you babysitting the fence?"

"Derrick, thank God you made it back okay. Everyone was beginning to worry. You know how your father is. The man wants constant updates. But with the comm down and no news from the front, there's been nothing to report. It makes your father crazy."

"The old man's impatient, everyone knows that." Lieutenant Derrick Barnes scratched his stubble. He was a few days past clean-shaven. "Anyway, it's a long haul from Illinois. These gtrucks he sent us across the border with breakdown constantly. Plus, they're ridiculously slow and guzzle fuel like there's no tomorrow."

"You come down through Oklahoma?" the guard asked, shifting his weapon to the opposite shoulder. The man had corporal stripes on his arm, a Velcro strip with his name above the pocket. It read "Corporal Eames."

"Nah, down through Miserable into Arkansas, then into Texas at Texarkana. Took us forever through the hill country."

"Any trouble?" Eames asked.

"Federalies chased us for a while. But we let loose a few volleys in their direction and they quickly gave up the chase. I guess a bunch of moldy old jailbirds was hardly worth the effort."

"I tend to agree."

"Yeah, but at least you know what we were actually hauling. The greased pig's in gtruck Number Five, under heavy guard. Anything happen while I was gone?"

"Actually, quite a bit."

"Yeah, like what?"

"Thadamore Mills was assassinated."

"That can't be good."

"Terrible news, if you ask me."

"So, tell me . . . "

"Sssh, those two newbies are coming," Corporal Eames said.

Butch and Kaleena approached. The other guard trailed behind, gesturing angrily. The whole situation made Butch nervous, though he did his best not to show it. His only comfort lay in knowing that his father was parked over the next hill, ready to intervene if things went off the rail. Butch whispered, now, into the collar of his tech-shirt: *Stay tuned, Dad. Things are about to get dicey.*

"Who the hell are you?" Eames demanded. The other man remained quiet, let Eames do his job.

"Name's Butch Hogan. I hail from Wyoming. Near Laramie. This here is Kaleena Flanagan. She's with me. We'd both like to join up. Only, your man here won't let us onto the grounds."

"You know your way around a gun?" the corporal asked.

"I grew up with a Winchester rifle under my pillow. So did the girl."

"That's good enough for me. Why don't you both climb in the back of the first gtruck and ride on up the Grand Hill with us?" He pointed in the direction of the minarets.

"Much obliged."

Corporal Eames escorted the two of them to the back of the first gtruck in line.

"Make room for these two," he said as he opened the back flap. The canopy was a canvas affair that kept out the wind but not much else. Eames pulled a lever on the side of the vehicle and two mechanical steps lowered from the frame.

A hand reached out of the back of the gtruck and helped Kaleena up the two steps. Butch followed her in. The lighting inside was poor and the air dusty and filled with flies.

The voice at the other end of the hand spoke. "Hi, I'm Elixir Coventry. This is my friend Morgan DuPont. You've never heard of me, but you may have heard of my friend. Morgan's a writer. What's your name?"

"Butch Hogan. And this is Kaleena Flanagan. We'd like to contribute to the war effort."

"Hogan? Like the Amerind house of worship?"

"Frankly, I don't think worship has got anything to do with it, but, yeah, somewhere back in the old family tree there must be a pint or two of Amerind blood flowing through our veins."

As introductions were made, Corporal Eames pulled the canvas flap shut then retracted the mechanical steps. He and the other man got into the cab. The motor on the big gtruck roared to life. The entire chassis shook as the driver tried to slam it into gear.

Kaleena and Butch peered into the darkness. Practically the entire complement of passengers were dressed in prison garb and seated on wooden benches that were themselves bolted to the floor. They quickly found a place to sit and squeezed in between two others.

"Prison bus?"

"More like prison break. These soldiers came along out of the middle of nowhere and set us free."

"That's a curious thing to do," Butch said.

Morgan DuPont turned to Kaleena. "Said your name was Flanagan? — Like the Senator?"

"Actually, the Senator was my father."

"And now he's gone."

"Yes, now he's gone."

"A terrible loss, to be sure."

"You knew my father?" Kaleena turned hopeful. Other gtrucks in the convoy revved their motors and began to jerk forward as well.

"I knew the man. But only by reputation. He was the subject of an op-ed piece I did a while back."

"That's right. She said you were a writer."

"And a good one too," Elixir said. "Me, I actually met the man."

"Really?" Kaleena was even more hopeful.

"We weren't exactly friends, if that's what you think. But on one occasion we were rather friendly."

"Geez, not him too?" Morgan glowered at her former cellmate.

"Nah, I definitely wasn't his type. He batted for the other team."

"What exactly does that mean?" Kaleena's face reddened, her spirit deflated. She knew the truth, now, about her father's proclivity for other males.

"Listen, you're his daughter and I don't want to speak ill of the dead. So please forget I said anything."

"If you've got something to say, why don't you just come right out and say it?" Kaleena barked angrily.

"If I've upset you, I sincerely apologize. When I said your father played for the other team, what I meant was he was a religious man. Me, I'm a wiccan, born and bred. Your father was a card-carrying Catholic. I wasn't exactly his type."

"Card-carrying sounds a bit pejorative to me. For a moment there I thought your comment might be of a sexual nature."

"Well, now that you mention it . . . "

"Why, you little witch . . . "

"Settle down, girls. This is neither the time nor the place for a cat fight."

Kaleena had that look in her eye, as if she might throttle Elixir with her bare hands. But then the big gtruck lurched forward, throwing them all off-balance and toward the rear by the sudden motion. The other gtrucks immediately fell in line and began to follow the lead gtruck up the Grand Hill.

Once the ride became smoother, Butch lumbered to his feet and moved toward the back. He threw open the canvas flap and hung onto the metal frame. The line of gtrucks slowly rumbled up the hill.

Butch was surprised by what he saw. Puritan City was a veritable fortress, an armed citadel preparing for a siege, not at all what he imagined. He had hoped, once they got inside the gates, to find his way to an administrative office where they might get the traveling papers they had come for.

The road threaded them past countless rows of Army-style wall tents, a canvas city that stretched off to the horizon and housed thousands of volunteer soldiers immersed in the initial stages of their training. Then came long lines of artillery pieces, plus modern howitzers, laser cannons, and armored vehicles. In the distance, a rag-tag air force, including drones in great numbers and bombers in lesser numbers. Now came a long series of one-story metal buildings, many with camouflaged roofs, all with smallish windows and a distinctly low-rent profile.

The convoy of gtrucks rumbled to a halt in front of the closest line of metal buildings. There, they were immediately swarmed by a phalanx of soldiers bearing mean-looking weapons. A few armed bots were mixed in.

Corporal Eames and the other man exited the cab of the first gtruck and made their way to the fence of the closest barracks. A minute later they were joined outside by an older man. This older man was clearly in charge of the training camp, if not the entire operation.

Butch jumped down from his perch at the back of the gtruck, edged towards the three men already deep in conversation. He studied the features of the man in charge. It was a familiar face. Butch drew close enough to hear what was being said.

"What you got here, Derrick?"

The speaker was the man in charge, a military man with short, crisp hair. He was good-looking, muscular, and beginning to gray at the temples. He wore the stars of a major general. His name patch read "Pappy Barnes," a name Butch instantly recognized.

The younger man — the man he called Derrick — saluted, answered his father. "New recruits, sir."

"The people from the prison?"

"The ones that wanted to tag along anyway."

Pappy Barnes stared past his son at the waiting line of gtrucks. There was a questioning look on his face.

"What you want is in gtruck Number Five," Derrick said. "Major Karpinski is looking over the merchandise even as we speak."

"Not without me, he isn't," Pappy said, striding rapidly in that direction. "Any of these newbies know how to handle a sidearm?"

"I do," Butch said, running to catch up.

"Me, too," Licks said, briskly approaching. Butch glanced at the sharp-looking wiccan with surprise. He couldn't help but thinking how women and guns were an attractive if lethal combination. This one had her hair up in something approaching braids and wore a distressed pair of brown tennis shoes.

Pappy broke stride, sized the two of them up. He addressed Elixir first.

"What were you incarcerated for, young lady?" he asked as they walked. By this time Morgan and Kaleena had caught up with them as well.

"Police checkpoint south of Hedon City. The goons found weapons in the back of my gcar."

"Why Hedon City?"

"Why not?"

Pappy frowned at the answer, turned to Butch. "And you? Why were you arrested?"

Derrick cut Butch off, before he could answer. "Actually, Dad, we picked this guy up outside the Main Gate. He and his girlfriend wanted to volunteer."

"It's General Barnes to you, soldier. And what were they doing at the Main Gate — spying on our operation? Honestly, Lieutenant, I'm surprised at you. Didn't it ever occur to you this fella might be an operative, working for the other side?" By now they had reached gtruck Number Five and Branislav Karpinski.

Butch's face reddened. "Due respect, General. I'm no spy. In fact, I used to be in your command."

"Former Jarhead?"

Butch nodded.

"What unit?"

"Eight-Oh-Sixty-Third. Logistics."

"Sorry, I can't place the face. Where you hail from, boy?"

"Wyoming."

"Wild country. Good people."

"We were headed east by rail. Our train got hijacked. But then you probably know all about that operation, don't you?"

"The Trojan horse?"

"Your people did the hijacking. Called it a smart bomb. They put us off the train, out on the siding. We had a devil of a time getting back to civilization. Then me and the girl made our way down here."

"This woman?" Pappy glanced sideways at Elixir.

"Nah, that one." Butch pointed to Kaleena. "The gun-slinging blonde — she, I just met. The other one's with me." — Butch pointed to Kaleena again. — "She's Senator Flanagan's daughter."

Lieutenant Barnes looked at his father, who looked at Branislav. Karpinski had just stepped out of the back of gtruck Number Five and quickly closed the canvas flap behind him.

"You hear that, Carp? This woman claims to be Senator Flanagan's daughter," Pappy said, a quizzical look on his face.

"Is that right?" Karpinski said.

"She here for retribution?" Derrick asked.

Butch looked at Kaleena, then at the other three men. "Retribution? Retribution for what?"

"For her father's assassination," Branislav said. It was a smug reply.

When Kaleena saw the man's smirk, the tears came in an instant. "You were responsible for that?"

"Your father was a traitor to his country. We had no choice. The man had to die."

"Now that I think about it, yes, maybe I do want some retribution."

Kaleena launched herself like a wildcat at Branislav's throat. He was caught off balance and she knocked him to the ground, started pummeling him with her fists. Elixir made a move to help her, but Morge held the second woman back.

Pappy Barnes laughed. It was uncharacteristic for him to do so. But he couldn't help himself. "I guess she wants a piece of you, Bran Flake."

About then, two other soldiers came over and started to pull Kaleena off him, kicking and screaming. Branislav got to his feet, smacked her hard in the face, drawing blood.

She screamed and recoiled in pain. But he hit her again, just for the sheer pleasure of it. Then he calmly brushed himself off. Branislav was angry, but not at Kaleena, at Pappy Barnes for calling him a name. He gave the general an evil eye, drew his sidearm.

Karpinski's scar deepened, like his face was again on fire. "Bran Flake? That's how you dare address me? — Bran Flake? — I've killed for less!" His gun arm was extended, as if he meant to empty a round into his commanding officer.

Pappy laughed again. "Lock her up. Lock 'em all up! And holster that weapon, soldier, before I have you locked up as well!"

Elixir elbowed her way forward. "Tell your men to back off, you overgrown ape! And tell every last one of them to holster their weapons! You're not going to lock a single one of us up! I want to be taken to the Reverend Roland Whitmore, and I want to be taken to him this very instant!"

Now it was Derrick's turn to be amused. "The Reverend's a busy man, chickie-baby. Anyway, why would a man of his station care to see a woman like you? I broke your bony ass out of prison, remember?"

Now Licks got in his face. "Be Daddy's good little errand boy now, Derrick-child, and go run and tell your precious Reverend Whitmore that Elixir Coventry is standing here waiting for him. I guarantee you the man will drop everything — and I mean everything — for a chance to be at my side."

"You one of his whores?"

"Tell him, you bastard! Tell him Elixir Coventry is here. Tell him she is waiting — but not for long."

Derrick was about to raise an angry hand to her, when his father signaled him to go. "Call him."

"Are you serious?"

"Do it."

Lieutenant Barnes stepped out of earshot, walkie-talkie in hand. He was gone about two minutes. When he returned, his tone was different.

"The Reverend Whitmore will see you now," he said.

"Didn't I tell you the boss-man would want to see me?" Elixir flashed the younger Barnes her best stick-it-up-your-ass smile and continued to assert herself. "Now, Derrick-boy, I want an armed escort for me and my three friends. — And I want it right away."

"You want a lot, lady," Derrick said.

Elixir stood her ground. "You people have a lot to answer for."

"Like what?" Pappy snapped to attention.

"Let's begin with dragging ten gtruckloads of confused prisoners a thousand kloms cross-country under false pretenses."

"I don't know what you were told, but . . . "

"Screw that! You people have asserted a false claim from the get-go."

"What's dug a burr so deep under your skin, lady?"

"Only this. You people claim to be fighting to preserve the Right to Bear Arms. I have no problem with that. But then you go and use that right as cover for wrecking the country and making a power grab. This is nothing but naked aggression, from start to finish."

"The Right to Bear Arms is a fundamental right," Pappy said.

"Save it for someone who cares. You have abused that right."

"Abused? How?"

"Well, for starters. In the name of protecting the Second Amendment, you have gone and assassinated a public official — this girl's father — just because he happened not to agree with you. Where's the honor in that, General?"

"Those orders came from the top. The very top."

"Whitmore?"

Pappy Barnes nodded.

"I never took you for the kind of man to take orders from a schmuck."

"I take orders from no man." Pappy Barnes was defiant.

"Well you'll damn well take orders from me." Elixir Coventry was just as defiant.

Pappy took a sudden liking to her. "Now if you were to frame that sentiment in the form of a request, I just might consider it."

Licks considered the man's offer and dialed it down a notch. "Sir. If you please. Would you mind taking me and my friends to see the Reverend Roland Whitmore?"

"It would be my pleasure, ma'am. I'll have my son and X.O. escort you. Duty requires that I remain here."

CHAPTER THIRTY-NINE

▼

Puritan City was no longer pretty.

Oh, the beautiful buildings were still there, the steel minarets of the tabernacle, the glittering spires of the cathedral, the golden domes of the assembly hall rotunda.

But, what began as a fashionable cross between the Vatican and an ivy-league college campus was now mostly rutted paths, thick rivers of mud, and uncollected bags of trash. Everything that had once been attractive and charming about the place — the endless rows of flowers, the manicured, well-kept lawns, the trimmed bushes and clipped topiaries — were now all flattened or gone to ruin by the chariots of war. Now there were gtrucks running every which way, troops marching on the parade grounds, free-roving bots, anti-missile batteries holding audience at every corner.

Elixir Coventry was disturbed by what she saw. She and the other three were riding up the glorious, Puritan City Grand Hill in a wide-bodied Helix piloted by Lieutenant Derrick Barnes. Major Branislav Karpinski sat behind them in the second seat. The armored vehicle was snaking its way up the gravel road, now, from the training field on the edge of the citadel, across the Commons, and on into the city center. Elixir was looking out the side window of the Helix, watching the buildings go by, when she spoke.

"I had no idea," she said, under her breath.

Lieutenant Barnes looked at her from behind the wheel of the Helix. "No idea about what, Missy?"

"That things were so bad."

"Why do you say that?"

"The bots, for one. In the old days, Roland would never have stood for it."

"Perhaps a concession that had to be made to the realities of war."

"And the bags of trash? . . . Another concession to reality?"

"I guess I hadn't really noticed. Weren't they always here?"

"You mean to tell me you never knew what Puritan City looked like before?"

"Before what?"

"Before the war."

Lieutenant Barnes thought a moment, slowed the Helix to a crawl, turned off the motor. "Now that you mention it, the City is beginning to look a bit ragged around the edges. I guess it's only when a body has been gone a while that you begin to notice the differences."

"I suppose if I were out busy assassinating innocent people I might not notice the differences either."

Derrick opened the door, growled, and clambered out. "We're here," he said. "Everyone out."

It was fortuitous, but the lieutenant had parked the vehicle in the exact spot where, only months before, Elixir had stood admiring the majesty of the place. Nothing to admire now.

They waited a minute, then Reverend Whitmore made his presence known. He was flanked by four bodyguards dressed in white uniforms, along with a pair of blushing virgins freshly plucked from the Reverend's Sect of the Most Sacred.

"Well, if it isn't my favorite wiccan from the Sixty-Mile-High Club," he said jauntily, extending his hand.

"This is the Neanderthal you got on your knees for?" Morgan asked, under her breath.

"Now that you mention it, the man is a bit of a throwback, isn't he?" Elixir replied, just as quietly. "Funny, but it didn't seem so at the time."

The Reverend approached with open arms. "Come, come, Licks, you and I shall meet privately. We shall embrace and talk of old times."

"Not today, Roland. Today I am here on official business."

"Shame. I haven't had a satisfying one in an awful long time, and you do it better than most. Maybe one of these other two fine ladies that just arrived will have to get on their knees for me instead."

Derrick Barnes snickered, as he knew Roland Whitmore's ways.

"What the hell is this man talking about?" Butch asked, looking in horror at the woman in braids.

"Yes, what exactly is this man talking about?" Kaleena trembled, touching her face where Branislav had struck her. She happened to be one of those other two fine ladies Whitmore was referring to.

Morgan answered for him. "This man, who calls himself a Reverend, is a bit less than that, aren't you, Rev?"

"Which one of these two is the Senator's daughter?"

Derrick pointed to Kaleena.

"I should have known. Have that one brought around to my room. She'll do in a pinch."

Whitmore turned on his heels and started for his private sanctum. Major Karpinski and Lieutenant Barnes swung into action, grabbed Kaleena by the arms.

"Let her go!" Butch exclaimed, moving to insert himself between his woman and the two other men.

But the four white-uniformed bodyguards jumped in, pinned his arms to his sides and pulled him off.

Whitmore was stern. "Lock him up. Put him with the others. I think there's an open cell in the Blue corridor. Then you boys can have a go at the wiccan and the other woman. I want this one, the Senator's daughter, brought around to my room. Later, I'll want the package from gtruck Number Five brought around as well. Please see to it right away, Branislav. I am not a patient man."

Butch struggled against the two men restraining him. "I hope you're getting this, 'cause we're in big trouble here. — Big trouble."

"Right you are, smart guy," one of the guards said. "You're in trouble deep."

"I'm not kidding now, Pops. We're in actual, real trouble here."

"Quit jabbering or you're going to wind up chewing on the meaty portion of a knuckle sandwich."

"If you can hear me, you had better hurry."

"I warned you."

Then the guard smacked Butch on the side of the head with the butt of his gun. Butch groaned and crumbled to the ground like a sack of potatoes.

After that, everything was still.

•

•

When Butch came around, he was in more than a little pain. His head was exploding. Blood filled his eyes. He saw the gray outlines of a body hovering over him. He thought it was the guard, who had hit him.

"You bastard! What the hell did you have to go and do that for?" he said groggily to the shadow.

"Excuse me? What exactly is it you think I did to you?"

Butch wiped the blood from his eyes, tried to focus on the speaker. He was confused by the voice. "Hoagland?"

"In the flesh."

"What the hell are you doing here?" Butch looked around. "Exactly where the hell are we anyway?"

"I think we're beneath the City somewhere, in a sort of catacombs, maybe a sub-basement."

Butch sat up. Near the ceiling was a small casement window that looked outside, like in an ordinary house basement. In the corner of the room, a sink and toilet.

"Together again, I see. For the first time, for the last time."

"Damn it, kid. Didn't I ask you not to come down here? Didn't I tell you to stay holed up at your father's Ranch?"

"And didn't I tell you not to be handing out orders? Besides, Kaleena and I had no choice. I told you that. We needed traveling papers. To get east."

"They're holding me for ransom. What's your excuse, Butch?"

"The bastard took Kaleena."

"Which bastard?"

"The main bastard. Roland Whitmore. They took the other two, as well."

"What other two?"

"Two women from some prison — Elixir Something-or-Other and Morgan Something."

"Elixir Coventry?"

"That might have been her name. Why, do you know her?"

"Unfortunately, her reputation precedes her. You say both these women were in prison before coming here?"

"I don't have the whole story. But Derrick Barnes — that's the General's son — plus another fellow — Branislav Something — a tough guy with a scar on his face — broke a couple hundred people out of a penitentiary somewhere in northern Illinois — don't ask me why — then convoyed them all down here by gtruck."

"There's more than one bastard in this play. The other bastard's name is Branislav Karpinski."

"Ah, yes, Bran Flake."

Hoagland chuckled. "That your name for him?"

"Nah. Though I sure wish I'd been the one who thought it up. Those honors belong to my old commander: Pappy Barnes. He's the one who first called that Karpinski fellow a Bran Flake. The bloke didn't much care for it, I can tell you that much."

"Well, the whole lot of us were in that same convoy, not just those prisoners from Illinois."

"Who else is here with you?"

"Me, Laura, and Elijah."

"What the hell? I thought you were all onboard that train headed east across the border into Minnesota?"

"We were. For a while anyway. The train got underway shortly after you got off."

"Then how the hell did you wind up here?"

"Your buddy George Rushmore."

"George? That can't be right."

Xander Hoagland paced the small, basement-level cell. "It wasn't actually George's fault. In fact, it may have been mine. There was a bit of a mutiny onboard that train. Someone higher up the food chain had a look at our identicards, decided I might be worth something to somebody and that I ought to be held for ransom, maybe used as a bargaining chip. I was afraid of that."

"But all three of you? You, plus Laura and Elijah? Hasn't Doc been through enough already?"

"The bastards probably figured three hostages were worth more in trade to them than just one. Anyway, here we all are."

"What happened to George?" Butch asked, trying to peer out the small, ceiling-height window. It was nearly impossible; the angle was all wrong.

"I think he may have been shot."

"By one of his own men?"

"That was my impression. But you have to remember: things suddenly got pretty hectic inside that train. They confiscated my sat-com, shoved the three of us in an airchop and, an hour later, we were dumped in gtruck Number Five as part of that convoy down from the prison."

"That's a rather roundabout way of getting you here. Why transfer the three of you to a gtruck when you were already safely onboard an airchop?"

"Beats me. Probably more difficult for someone to track us on the ground than it would be in the air."

Butch got up, walked over to the toilet-washbasin combination in the corner of the cell. He looked at his head in the mirror, carefully washed his face. Dried blood gathered in the sink. He took a stack of paper towels, made them wet like a compress, and pressed the wad against the hematoma on the side of his head.

"You okay?" Xander asked.

"Been better."

"Any suggestions how we're going to get out of this mess?"

Butch's eyes lit up. "Think big, gas-guzzling, RV-type bus."

"Bridger is coming for us?"

"Sssh! The walls may be tapped."

Butch looked around nervously, flushed the toilet. He signaled Hoagland to come closer, ran water from the faucet. He spoke quietly:

"Yes, if the message got through, my father should be on his way. I don't know exactly how long I was out after that guy hit me, but I'm expecting him and the *Sundance* any time now."

Xander Hoagland shook his head. "It's gonna take a whole lot more than one mountain man and an oversized RV to get us the hell out of here. This place is a fortress, complete with palace guards, drawbridge, and dragon. They'll never let your father just waltz on in here, sweet as you please, and take us all home."

"Don't be so sure of that. You met my father. The man can talk himself into just about any place, anywhere, anytime, no questions asked."

"I could believe that about him. But just how in the world is your father supposed to find you? There must be a hundred different buildings in Puritan City, not counting the tents. Plus, we're underground and behind bars to boot."

Butch flushed the toilet again. "Tech-shirt." He tugged on his shirt collar. "Built-in comm and locator. Kaleena and I are each wearing one."

"Smart thinking. Very smart thinking."

"Consider it the Hogan Brain Trust at work."

Xander Hoagland was just about to respond, when suddenly there were shouts on the grounds outside their window. Though only shadows, they could see commotion outside on the lawn through the tiny ceiling window.

"That must be the Hogan Welcome Wagon."

Then Butch thought he heard his name being shouted in the corridor outside their room. He turned off the water still running in the sink.

"Did you hear that?" Butch asked.

"Yes, I did," Hoagland replied, edging towards the door.

"There it is again."

"Whoever it is, she is calling you by name! Answer her, for God's sake!"

CHAPTER FORTY

▼

Kaleena looked at her hand. It was shaking like a leaf. She was certain she would be ill.

Kaleena had never fired a gun before. She was aghast at the results. She had no idea how horrible it would be — or how satisfying.

The disgusting man had yelled, "On your knees, woman!" and unzipped his pants. The gun was just sitting there, on the table, where the guard had left it per Whitmore's instructions. The smug bastard had threatened to use it on her if she didn't do as she was told.

Kaleena looked again at her hand. It was still shaking violently. In fact, her entire arm was shaking, all the way up to the shoulder.

The weapon in her quivering hand was a projectile weapon, the sort that fired bullets, not one of those newer force guns, the sort that fired a bolt of lethal energy. She had grabbed the gun off the table, aimed it in the general direction of where Whitmore stood, and pulled the trigger five, maybe six times.

The first two shots were definitely wild. With those first two, she was certain she missed the man outright.

But, with the next two she was equally certain she hit him square, in the chest maybe, perhaps the abdomen.

At the impact, Whitmore staggered backward, clutching at his gut, a surprised look on his face. Blood ran red between his fingers.

She fired two more times, maybe three. One hit his arm, the other his leg. He screamed and rolled to the floor.

Now Kaleena stood over the man triumphant. Her hands were quivering.

Blood was still streaming from the holes she had made in his body. It oozed across the floor in her direction. She began to have the dry heaves. All that adrenaline surging through her system.

By God, what had she done?

Kaleena looked at the gun in her hand. She had just committed evil, the very evil her father had always railed against so strenuously.

And yet, that evil gun — that unholy horrible evil gun — had saved her from an even more unholy, horrible indignity.

So, where was the greater evil? — in the killing of a man or in the refusing to protect oneself from harm?

Isn't that what the Second Amendment was all about? Not just that malarkey about a well-regulated militia, but the Castle Doctrine itself, the very proposition Butch, Elijah, and the rest had tried to defend so eloquently?

It was all becoming clear to her now. *Every man had an unfettered right to protect himself in every location where he could be lawfully present.*

Kaleena gathered herself. Her hand was still shaking. But she gathered herself. She stood over the Reverend Roland Whitmore and, with some satisfaction, watched as he took his last breaths and finally expired. Then she staggered toward the door.

Kaleena knew the direction the guards had come when they first brought her in. She followed that same route out.

Her only thought, now, was of escape. That, plus finding Butch. Any thoughts she may once have harbored about returning to Washington had now all but dissipated. Her father had been wrong about guns, dead wrong. But so too were the leaders of the New Republic, the leaders here in Puritan City. Those people in the stadium — those people who had been massacred at the outset of this nightmare — those people had an absolute right to be where they were as well. Those people at the stadium should never have been targeted, not by anyone, certainly not by a defender of the Second Amendment.

Events helped Kaleena make up her mind. If Butch was still willing, she was now ready to make a life with the man. That offer of starting life over with him at the Hogan Ranch was beginning to sound awfully good right about now.

Kaleena moved along the interior hallway toward the outermost corridor. She listened carefully to every sound, afraid of accidentally stumbling onto an unsuspecting sentry. But in this hall there were none.

She stayed close to the wall, thinking to avoid being seen by any surveillance vidcams that might be monitoring the corridors.

But, of course, avoiding them was impossible. There were vidcams everywhere, in the ceiling, along the walls, in the floor tiles, everywhere.

Kaleena knew she had to hurry. Then she remembered something one of the guards had said earlier, before leaving her in the clutches of Roland Whitmore.

The guard had motioned down an adjacent hallway, where Butch and the others were being held. He said something about it being the "Blue" corridor. This corridor, the one she was presently staring down, was painted blue. *This had to be the one*, she thought.

Kaleena turned down the Blue hallway.

"Butch!" she yelled out. "Butch!"

There was no answer.

Kaleena started pounding on cell doors. "Butch! Butch!" She still had the gun in her hand.

At the second door she came to, Elijah answered from the other side. "That you, Kaleena?"

"Is Butch in there with you?"

"No. But Laura is. Get us the hell out of here!"

"I first need to find Butch. Then I'll come back for the two of you."

"Damn it, Kaleena, don't leave us here!"

"Butch! Butch!"

Kaleena moved further down the corridor and Elijah's frantic voice faded in the distance.

"Butch! Butch!"

Other prisoners answered her shouts. Finally, at the last door, she heard the voice she had been searching for.

"Kaleena, is that you?" The voice came from the other side of the closed door.

"Yes, are you okay?"

"How the hell did you get free?"

"I shot Whitmore."

"You did what?"

Kaleena started crying. Butch could hear it through the closed door. "I . . . shot . . . the bastard . . . Whitmore."

"Do you still have the gun?"

"Yes," between sobs.

"Does it still have bullets?"

"I don't know . . . How do I tell?"

"Is there a padlock or something on the outside of this door?" Butch asked.

"I don't know."

"Look at it, damnit!"

"Don't yell at me! I just shot a man! Can't you understand that?"

"We don't have time for this, woman! Look at the friggin' door! See if there is a padlock. I mean it, Kaleena — Look at the frigging door this very instant!"

"Not if you're going to yell at me."

Inside the room, Butch threw up his arms in despair. "Xander, you talk to her."

Now a new voice came to the door. "Kaleena, this is Senator Hoagland. Please. Examine the door lock."

"Senator? Is that really you?"

"Kaleena, please. Do like Butch asked. Look closely at the door lock."

"Okay, already. It's one of those electronic deadbolts, like in a bank vault."

"Tell her to shoot it."

"Did you hear what Butch said?" Xander asked.

Butch pushed the other man aside. "Kaleena, stand back, take careful aim. Then pull the trigger. Blast the bloody mechanism into the next world."

"That only works in vids, you know that," Xander scolded.

"It's our only chance." Butch was insistent. "Do it, Kaleena. Take careful aim. Cover your eyes. Fire. Do it twice. Do it now."

Suddenly Branislav Karpinski appeared in the corridor toting a force gun. "Put the weapon down, bitch! Put it down or I'll put you down, just like I did your fag father."

"What's going on out there?" Butch yelled from inside. "Kaleena, shoot off the damn door lock. Do it, now."

"I mean it, bitch!" Branislav said, loud enough now, for Butch to hear. "Put down your weapon this very instant, or things will go very badly for you."

Kaleena shook her head. Her face still smarted from where he had hit her earlier. "You can't hurt me any worse than I've already been hurt."

"That's not true. I know how to inflict great pain. I can cut you and leave you hurting forever. Now put down your gun."

Branislav was menacing. What was left of his scar looked downright evil. He drew closer, yelled through the still-closed door.

"Butch, tell your little turnip out here to drop her weapon or else I perforate that pretty little chest of hers with a blast from my force gun. Perhaps blow off a kneecap. Tell her, and I mean now!"

"Kaleena, do what the man says. It'll be okay."

"It'll never be okay again, Butch."

Branislav was closer to her now, barely three meters separated the two.

Kaleena swung her gun in his direction and began to fire. She had no idea how many bullets were left in the gun, but it was in fact a fifteen-round clip. Thus far, she had expended only six shells taking down Roland Whitmore.

Branislav reacted with lightning speed. He crossed the distance between them in an instant, knocked the gun from her hand. Then he doubled up his fist and punched her in the stomach as hard as he could. The force was so great, her feet left the floor.

Kaleena crashed against the wall of the narrow corridor, unable to breath. Phlegm filled her mouth. He hit her again, this time in the lower back. Branislav was at his best, enjoying himself.

Then, for some inexplicable reason, he stopped pummeling her with his fists. Something down the hall moved at the edge of his peripheral vision and he turned away from her to face the new danger. It was an armed security bot. The bot had been dispatched by the computer to investigate the unauthorized activity in the corridor.

Branislav drew his force gun, instinctively fired at the bot, hitting it square. The bot staggered backward, a jumble of bolts and wire.

But, in that instance, Kaleena saw her opportunity. Her gun was on the floor. She grabbed for it and again began to fire.

This time, the woman was relentless. Bullet after bullet flew out of the barrel. The fourth bullet hit home. At the moment of impact, Karpinski still had his back to her, still facing the robot. The bullet penetrated his flesh, plowed through his spinal cord, exploded out the other side.

Karpinski dropped to the floor like a rock — but she kept right on firing until the clip was empty. Even then she pulled back on the trigger several more times.

On the other side of the door, Butch couldn't believe his ears. He stared at Alexander Hoagland as the sounds of gunfire echoed down the hallway. "By God, I think she killed the bastard."

"We have to hurry, Butch. There will be others. And we're both still locked up in here."

"Kaleena? You okay?"

No answer from the corridor.

Kaleena dropped her weapon, yanked the force gun from the dead man's hand. She aimed it at the door lock of their cell and without giving warning blew the door clean off its hinges.

In a frenzy now, Kaleena didn't wait for the occupants of the cell to open the door from the inside, but began moving down the corridor, blowing open door after door. In each case there was a bolt of bright energy and a cloud of blue haze as the metal vaporized. She stepped over the crippled bot and continued on. At Laura and Elijah's door, she blasted the door, kicked it off its hinges. Then she calmly stuck her head inside the cell.

"I think we have to go now," she said.

The hallway quickly filled with people, some Kaleena knew, others she did not. Elixir was there, as well as Morgan DuPont. Also, Butch, Xander, Laura, and Elijah. Butch liberated the force gun from Kaleena's trembling hand, retrieved a second weapon off Branislav's body and handed it to Alexander Hoagland. "Let's get the hell out of here."

Suddenly there were soldiers at the exit door. With all the excitement, Butch had forgotten about the earlier commotion outside on the lawn. He and Xander had seen the activity through the tiny casement window before Kaleena arrived in the corridor outside their cell. Now it looked as if an entire army were streaming into the building through just that one open door.

As soon as Butch saw the men crowd into the corridor, he figured an alarm had been sounded. The arriving men were here either to kill them or else block their escape.

"We're cornered," Butch said quietly to Xander. "Not enough firepower to fight our way out of this one."

Xander looked at the younger man. "Kemo Sabe, we surrender, we go back to lockup."

"If it was just me, Tonto, I might stand and fight. But not with all these good people depending on our success. I really don't know if I could live with the guilt if someone wound up dead on my account."

"Listen, soldier. God put the firewood here. But every man must gather and light it himself."

"What the hell does that mean?" Butch asked.

"One of us had better start doing some real fast talking. Before the bastards start shooting."

Butch nodded. He was about to say something, when one of the approaching soldiers broke rank and spoke:

"You Butch Hogan?"

"Who's asking?"

"This him?" The soldier turned to the man standing behind him. It was Butch's father.

"Yeah, that's my son."

"Lower your blaster, young Hogan," the soldier ordered. "We're here to take the lot of you home."

Now, with the outside door propped open, Butch could hear the sharp reports of small arm's fire. That, plus the high-pitched whine of multiple airchops putting down on the lawn nearby. The soldiers began handing out lightweight body armor to the nearly two dozen people now gathered in the hallway.

"Okay, people, we're moving out!" the soldier yelled. "Keep your heads low, move fast, and get onboard those airchops, six to a bird. Now move!"

"Dad?"

"I'll explain it to you onboard," Bridger said, helping people cinch their body armor in place as they streamed out the door.

As the small group of escapees chased across the open field, the soldiers ran interference.

But bullets were flying, and not everyone made it out to the airchops unhurt. Butch saw Morgan DuPont take one in the thigh and tumble to the ground. As she lay writhing on the tarmac, she was hit a second time. Two soldiers from their group stopped to pick her up and carry her to one of the waiting airchops.

As fast as the airchops could be loaded, they took to the air. The warbirds rose like rockets from the compound, gunfire chasing them into the sky.

The airchops banked and raced north. Below them could be seen row upon row of green canvas tents. Then they were out over the main fence and gone.

Butch turned to his father, with questioning eyes. They sat next to one another on a narrow bench along the inside wall of the airchop. The roar of whirling blades filled their ears, then sudden acceleration as the master turbines kicked in.

Bridger observed his son's face, chuckled to himself.

"Dad?"

"When word filtered back to Laramie what the bastards did to George Rushmore, and when I told the Rancher's Council what happened to you and the girl, heads were turned. A lot of people, who had been sitting on the fence, climbed right down off it. Plus, it was all over the vid that Senator Hoagland was being held for ransom by the leadership of the New Republic. Those people are not the boss of us, no matter what the rumor mills say. Most of us ranchers are dead set against the Second Amendment being repealed. But practically none of us are in favor of armed insurrection, much less revolution or making war on our neighbors. So we got to jawing on the radio and before I knew it, George's father got the ranchers organized. A bunch of 'em took some bulldozers and crashed the Puritan City gates. A bunch more commandeered a squadron of airchops from the airfield at Casper and flew them on down here. A bunch of newbies engaged in training right here on the grounds of this toilet stepped up and grabbed some laser cannons from the armory to help us. They boxed in the other troops. Your friends from space helped too. Parsons showed up behind the wheel of a brand new Helix. Woody and that Gullible fellow helped us by piloting an airchop down here."

"Red's part of this crew?"

"Yep. Said he wouldn't miss it for the world. And a lot of other friends chipped in too. Any other questions?"

Butch let that all sink in. The airchops skirted the foothills of the Rockies as they shot like an arrow north into Wyoming. Inside one of them, a medic was working on Morgan DuPont with poor results.

"You mentioned something about the leadership of the New Republic. Whitmore is dead. So are many of the others. Do you know what became of Pappy Barnes during the assault?"

"I couldn't say. We were busy trying to rescue you, not capture him. The man probably got away."

"That could be a problem later on."

"But not our problem."

"And the *Sundance*? What became of her in all this?"

For a second, Bridger was at a loss for words.

"Please don't tell me you left your pride and joy behind somewhere? That would be a loss the likes of which the Hogans might never recover."

Bridger again had himself a good laugh. "I love you, son. But not enough to give up my vee-hick-ull."

"What then?"

"I safely stowed my honey before the assault."

"Where?"

"An old lady-friend of mine that doesn't live too far from here is keeping an eye on her for me. In a few days' time, when things quiet down, me and one of my drinking buddies will make a trip back down here and retrieve the darn thing. Maybe Old Man Rushmore, George's father."

"What old lady-friend?"

"You've been gone a long time, Butch. Your mother has been gone even longer. Nights get awfully cold up in Wyoming. Don't forget: I'm on the Ranch all alone. A man's gotta do what a man's gotta do."

"Spare me the ugly details. So long as you get your vee-hick-ull back."

"You making fun of me?"

"Wouldn't think of it."

"I dare say — you better not. Or you might find yourself having to sprout a set of wings and fly yourself the rest of the way home from here."

"We're headed back to the Ranch now?"

"Where else? Can you think of a better place to be at the end of a long day than at home?"

"No, sir, I cannot."

CHAPTER FORTY-ONE

▼

"Thomas Jefferson was a fool."

Elijah Montrose struggled to get comfortable on the couch. It was a great big old thing, centered squarely in front of the fireplace in the middle of the Hogan Ranch great room. Next to him on the couch was Elixir Coventry. In the last two days, since the escape, she seemed to have taken a liking to the man, and was now cuddled up next to him on the big couch watching the flames dance in the fireplace. He was less sure about his own feelings.

"What's that you're saying?" Butch asked as he passed through the great room with a plate stacked high with food. He handed Red another beer, thinking his friend from Pueblo might have had enough already. Their other two buddies, Woody Dunlop and Gulliver Travels, had already been called back to work and left early this morning for Transcomet headquarters.

"Doc's saying that Thomas Jefferson was a fool." Elixir found Elijah's intellectualism a pleasant change after all the Neanderthals she had met in her life.

"The man did say a few smart things, though. *I like the dreams of the future better than the history of the past.* That was one of Jefferson's better ones."

"You okay, Doc?" Butch asked, sitting down next to Kaleena at the nearby table. She was still nursing a sore rib and sporting a nasty shiner, both courtesy of the beating she had suffered at Karpinski's hand.

"No, I'm not okay. Would you be?"

"No, I suppose not."

"The thing is: After the bombing, I really have nothing to go home to now."

"Didn't I say you could go home with me?" Elixir said. Her long blond hair, so long in disarray, was once again done up in tight little braids. She seemed to have made up her mind about Elijah, but he was hesitant to return her affections.

"I know, I know. It's sweet of you to offer."

"Yes, very sweet," Red chimed in. He was matching Butch's father beer for beer. They had become fast friends in the two days since the raid.

"What about Barbara and the kids?" Butch wasn't so sure if he approved of this wiccan. Her priorities were at issue. The first thing she asked for after reaching the Ranch was a new pair of tennis shoes. *What kind of girl does that sort of thing?* It seemed her old ones — some bright yellow ones — had been lost in the confusion.

Elijah's voice cracked. "My . . . family . . . Barbara . . . the kids . . . they're all dead."

"You know that now, for sure?" Butch looked at Alexander Hoagland from across the room. "Where was I when you got word?"

"Actually, we haven't gotten confirmation yet. Nothing definitive anyway."

"But then how do you know for sure?"

"Honestly, Butch, I'm as sure as I'm ever going to be." Tears filled Elijah's eyes. Licks reached over and gently wiped them away.

"Can it be any other way?" Elijah asked. "You've seen the pictures. Cinders and blackened soot. That's all that's left of my city. Cinders and soot. No one could survive a holocaust like that."

"But not everyone is accounted for yet."

"Butch is right," Red said. "Give it some more time."

"But what am I supposed to do?" Elijah asked. "Where am I supposed to go?"

Xander Hoagland stepped forward. He put his hand on Elijah's shoulder, tried to console him. "Listen, old friend. Thomas Jefferson said something else that was pretty smart — *So we have gone on, and so we shall go on, though puzzled and prospering beyond parallel in the history of man.*"

"That's supposed to make me feel better?"

"No, but this will," Bridger said, delivering a tray piled high with food.

Elijah started to get to his feet. So did Elixir.

"No, no, no, stay seated," Bridger insisted, grabbing another beer for himself. "Stay seated. Eat right here. I'll bring some food for your lady friend. I got a fire going in the fireplace. Best room in the house, if you ask me."

Elijah couldn't agree more. This *was* the best room in the house, by far. There was a big picture window in the facing wall. It looked out over the prairie, with snowcapped mountains in the distance. The room itself was finished with rough-hewn oak and pine logs. The fireplace, framed with blocks of granite. Now, with the fire roaring, the air had a faint smell of pine. The whole scene was quite idyllic. Elijah began to eat. The food tasted good.

The man reflected as he ate. Life moved slower out here in Wyoming, certainly slower than what he was used to back East. It was hard to believe, but it had barely been three days since they first boarded that fateful train for Minnepaul. Now they were back here again at the Hogan Ranch. The strange thing was, in this remote place, nothing much had changed. Oh, yes, a war had come and gone and still nothing had changed. The towering trees; still the same. The soaring eagles; no change. Eager fish still prowled the rivers. Cougars still ran antelope to ground. The odd coyote still stalked his prey. Pristine air still filled their lungs. Yes, the larger world had changed, irrevocably and forever — as had Elijah himself — but not the Hogan Ranch.

"Actually, I'm quite optimistic about the future," Xander said. He sat down across from Elijah with his own giant plate of food. Bridger had since brought Elixir a plateful of her favorites, and she attacked it hungrily, a big cloth napkin spread open in her lap.

"You're a better man than I am," Elijah said between bites. The meal included a huge slab of prime rib and a baked potato, plus a side of sour cream and butter.

"No, seriously. A couple good things have happened."

"Like what?"

"Foreign aid, for one. America still has a few friends left out there in the world. Now that a provisional ceasefire has been negotiated, aid is beginning to pour in from around the globe. Plus, the U.S. Supreme Court has just declared the Gun Control Law unconstitutional."

"About goddamn time!" Bridger exclaimed. "What happened? — Justices get their robes wedged up between their butt cheeks?" He was in the second hour of hitting the beer pretty hard.

"Come on, Dad. Tell us what you really think."

"Yeah, Bridger, tell us what you really think," Red echoed.

"Mister Hogan, surely you, of all people, should know enough about life to appreciate that the wheels of justice don't always turn swiftly," Xander said.

"So what does the Court ruling really mean?" Elijah asked, mouth full. "Isn't it a day late and more than a couple dollars short?"

"A day late for sure. But still there's cause for optimism."

"Brave talk for a man who only a day and a half ago was still being held for ransom by a rogue government out of control."

"I know I'm being a bit of an idealist here, but hear me out. The principal reason for the sudden breakup of the Union has just been adjudicated. It has been summarily kicked to the curb by the highest Court in the land. This is truly an historic moment."

"Is it?" Elijah wasn't convinced. "Once violence begins to flow, there's often no stopping it. Time after time, it has been the same. Violence continues to gather strength of its own accord. Then the country stumbles from one act of retribution to the next."

"We can only hope that cooler heads will prevail."

"You think that is a real possibility? Even after the two sides managed to wipe out half-a-dozen major cities between them?"

"With Roland Whitmore dead and Pappy Barnes on the run, there is room for negotiation."

"And we have Kaleena to thank for at least some of that."

"Yes, we do. And I'll have you know, discussions are already under way, at the highest levels, to make that ceasefire permanent."

"That is great news. But please tell me you're not just blowing hot air up our asses to make us all feel good."

Xander chuckled. "Believe me, son. I may be a politician, but I can't hold my breath long enough to accumulate that much hot air. What I'm telling you is what the President has told me. Terms of a truce between the United States and the New Republic are being hammered out even as we speak."

"What terms?" Bridger asked drunkenly. The beer was beginning to take its toll.

Senator Hoagland explained. "In order to be readmitted to the Union, each State that seceded will have to vote on a state-by-state basis to make their secession null and void."

Elijah's head spun. "That could take months, maybe years. Besides, some of the States won't be coming back — not ever."

"You're right. Alaska may not return. And who really knows about Southern California? They may be better off as part of Mexico."

"Wouldn't we all?" Red said. "They make the best margaritas down there in Cabo."

"Is that all you think about, Red — getting drunk?"

"It's either beers or bims. Until Transcomet starts hiring again, there's not much else for me to do 'cept go home. Woody and Gulliver got called back right away. But I may have to cool my heels here awhile and wait."

"That's all very interesting, Red. But could we all please just be serious a moment here?" Elijah implored. "What does the peace treaty have to say about reparations? A great many of us have suffered terrible losses."

"People on both sides suffered horrendous losses, Doc."

"Some more than others," Elijah retorted. "War is a negative-sum game. Always has been. Always will be. The South was still poor a hundred years after the First Civil War."

"But that was because of the previous two hundred years of slavery, not because of the war. Besides, the GNP of the New Republic rivals that of the United States itself. I see no basis for reparations — by either party. And I doubt whether the truce-makers will either."

"The very reason a permanent ceasefire may be hard to arrange."

"The taxpayers are gonna take it in the rear end no matter what the brass decides," Bridger grumbled.

Laura Hoagland took umbrage with that statement. "How dare you!"

"Money don't grow on trees, honey. You want to pay reparations? Money's got to come from somewhere."

"Don't honey me, you goofy, unshaven cowboy! My Xander does the best he can. We've been through a terrible ordeal, same as you."

"Calm down, Laura," Hoagland instructed. "And please don't start calling people names."

"Yeah, no fair calling names," Red said as he staggered off to use the head.

"You don't think the man's a goofy, unshaven cowboy?"

"Laura, the man saved our life. Show Mister Hogan a little respect, will you?"

"Goofy or not, Bridger is right," Elijah said. "There is no such thing as a free lunch. The money has to come from somewhere."

"Broken Window Fallacy, Doc?"

"What the . . . ?"

"I'll explain it to you later on, Dad. After we're finished eating."

"Another frigging theory that's over my head?" Bridger carped drunkenly.

"I didn't say that."

"Heh, Mister Know-It-All Economist, aside from spouting numbskull theories no one else understands, you got any useful skills?" Bridger asked.

"Dad, I think you've had enough . . . "

"Hell's Bells. You all want to talk free lunch? I can't afford to feed the lot of you for weeks on end. Money's tight around here, what with the war and all. Plus, I used up an entire year's allotment of fuel running down to Texas and back to save your collective asses. I need my peace and quiet. So why doesn't that egghead over there, and that witch-woman of his, grab a knobby broomstick and fly on the hell out of here?"

"Now, now, that really won't be necessary," Xander Hoagland said, finishing his meal. "I, personally, have enjoyed your warm hospitality, Mister Hogan. Not to mention the daring rescue you managed to orchestrate. And I'll personally see to it that you are reimbursed for your fuel and all your other expenses. You, Sir, are a true American hero."

Bridger Hogan nodded his head in approval and tipped his glass in the Senator's direction.

"But now, with the promise of truce in the air, I truly must be getting back to Washington. Democracy is a messy business. They're going to need a few brave souls willing to carry a dustpan and broom then roll up their sleeves to get the job done."

"I sense that that's not your only agenda," Elijah observed keenly.

Alexander Hoagland screwed up his brow into a frown. He was reluctant to answer. Truth be told, there were more than a few pressing matters he had to attend to. The question had been on his mind for several days now. *Should he expose Flanagan's financial dealings with Transcomet Industries — or should he let the matter die, now that the bum was dead and buried?* Flanagan's dealings had caused incalculable damage to the country and were at least partially responsible for setting in motion these disastrous events to begin with. Then the larger question: *Should he bring down Keith Roberts, perhaps even Noah Benjamin, over the asteroid incident, or should he let the whole matter drop?* Perhaps the country had already suffered enough pain without being made to suffer even more.

"Laura and I will be leaving by suborb out of Laramie tomorrow, day after at the latest."

"Mind if I hitch a ride?" Elijah asked.

"Feel free. There's plenty of room."

"Heh, I thought you were coming home with me?" Elixir carped.

"The President has asked for me specifically," Elijah explained.

"That's wonderful news," Kaleena bubbled.

"Yes, that is wonderful news," Elixir agreed. "But what about that ride on my broomstick? . . . Or was it your broomstick we were going to ride on? Didn't you tell me you wanted to see how us wicked wiccans lived?"

Elijah brushed aside the suggestion. "The President has asked me to join his White House staff, head up his Council of Economic Advisors, draft legislation and Executive Orders to help stabilize the dollar, work with my old friend Spencer Trask to rebuild the financial system."

"The President will wait — I won't."

"Sounds like the girl has made up your mind for you," Bridger said. "Women can do that, you know."

Elijah reflected. It was too soon for him to start up with someone new. *Then again, how much could it hurt to keep an open mind?*

"What about you, Kaleena?" Elijah asked, changing the subject again. "What are your plans?"

"Kaleena and I are staying here," Butch said, before she could answer.

"You've decided for the both of us then?" Kaleena asked red-faced.

"I only assumed my wife would want to live with her husband in the same house."

"And who says I'm going to marry you?"

"I thought we had a deal? Back on the ship. Promises were made, remember?"

"Oh, that bit about your shopping days being over? I told you back then, the merchandise can't be returned once the packaging's been opened."

"You did tell me that. You also said there was no warranty."

"That's right. What you see is what you get."

"A righteous man deserves one mortal life, sweet and long, complete with carnal love, irresponsible youth, disconcerting adulthood, and healthy old age. Say you'll spend it with me."

"I think I've heard about enough," Bridger interrupted, a full beer-buzz on.

"Me too," Red said, rejoining the group. "I can't believe you're permanently taking yourself off the market, old buddy."

"In case you two love-birds have forgotten — this is my house." Bridger interjected. "You two want to live together, you'll have to get a place of your own."

"I've banked two years of space-pay, Pops. Should be enough to buy us a little something."

"And don't forget, I have a bit of an inheritance coming once my father's estate is settled."

"Old Man Rushmore has 400 acres for sale across the road," Bridger said.

"That on account of George's injuries?"

"The Old Man needs to raise a big slug of cash to cover the boy's medical bills. What happened to George on that train pretty much messed him up for life."

"I really don't feel right taking advantage of another man's misfortune."

"Son, that property's gonna be sold with or without you. You might actually be doing the Rushmore family a favor if you bought it off them. No advantage would be taken. They'd rather sell it to a local anyway. Besides, Old Man Rushmore owns plenty of ground, thousands of acres in all. It's not like you'd be putting them out on the street or anything."

"Well, it's settled then. Kaleena and I are finally home."

"Hear! Hear!"

Made in the USA
Lexington, KY
23 January 2010